ROYAL
GAMES

ALSO BY SARIAH WILSON

The Ugly Stepsister Strikes Back

The Royals of Monterra Series

Royal Date

Royal Chase

ROYAL
GAMES

SARIAH WILSON

Montlake
Romance

Published by Montlake Romance, Seattle

www.apub.com

Amazon, the Amazon logo, and Montlake Romance are trademarks of Amazon.com, Inc., or its affiliates.

ISBN-13: 9781503950788
ISBN-10: 1503950786

Cover design by Damonza

Printed in the United States of America

For Justin Baldoni, who plays my second-favorite Rafael
(and who I kept picturing while writing this story),
and for William Shatner, just because Captain James
Tiberius Kirk is the coolest.

Chapter 1

"Genesis, you should probably sit down."

I dropped my overnight bag on the wooden floor. I had been traveling for the last nine hours, and I'd had two layovers and a long ride home from the airport in a very gross taxi. All I wanted to do was go upstairs to take a shower and a nap before my shift at the diner started. I had that horrible airplane smell in my clothes, and my poor hair had gone all tangled and frizzy.

"Nothing good ever happens after someone says that," I told Aunt Sylvia. She fidgeted in her chair, with her hands cradled in her lap. Her fingers were slightly bent and pointing up, trembling. My heart started to beat too fast as worry set in. "Is it your MS? Have you had another flare-up?"

"Oh, no, I'm doing fine. It's something else." I couldn't remember her ever sounding quite so anxious. Not when she told me my mother had died, not when she said the bank was planning to foreclose on the farm, not when she told me she'd been diagnosed with secondary progressive multiple sclerosis. She usually reminded me of the old maple trees outside of our farmhouse—despite everything she'd gone through, she was steady, strong, and unbending.

She wasn't making eye contact with me. I hadn't known her to ever do that. It was freaking me out.

"Please tell me. You're really scaring me."

"I don't want you to be angry, but I rented out the guesthouse."

Relief set in as I sat in the armchair across from her. "That's a good thing." We so needed the money. The taxes were overdue, we still needed to catch up on the mortgage, and we had some serious repairs to do on the house. We were already living tiny paycheck to tiny paycheck. We had sold off everything we could sell other than the land itself, and I was determined to do whatever I had to do to keep the farm with our family. There might have been a time when I would have just believed that we'd make it somehow, some way, but that was before.

"How much did you get?" I asked.

I had spent the summer and fall cleaning and painting the guesthouse to get it ready to rent. All that work felt worthwhile when Sylvia named a sum that was nearly double what we had hoped for.

"But that's fantastic. Why did you think I would be mad?"

"Because there's one thing that you're not going to like."

I relaxed back into the chair. My aunt wasn't usually overdramatic, but I supposed she was entitled to go there every once in a while. "What's that?"

"Who I rented it to." She swallowed several times in a row, still nervous.

Unless she had rented the place to my high school bully, Brooke Cooper, everything would be fine. And there's no way that had happened since the Coopers lived in the biggest house in Frog Hollow.

I mean, the only other person she could have rented it to who would make me upset would be . . .

I sat straight up, my fingers digging into the armrests.

"You didn't. Please tell me you didn't."

She finally faced me, looking and sounding determined. "We needed the money, and I think all of this was just a big misunderstanding. He's so nice and charming, and if you would just sit down and talk with him . . ."

Her words trailed behind me as I stalked through the living room, into the kitchen, and out the back door. There was snow on the ground, but the sun was bright and beaming overhead, making my coat feel unnecessary. Typical Iowa weather.

Three days. I had only been gone three days to be on some stupid morning talk show, again being forced to relive the most humiliating experience of my life. If I had my way, I would never do another appearance or interview for as long as I lived. Unfortunately, they were willing to pay, and I couldn't say no to the money.

This all started because Aunt Sylvia had insisted that I audition for a televised reality dating show called *Marry Me*. I'd been worried that I would be found, but she reminded me that the people I was afraid of didn't believe in electricity or interacting with our "wicked" society in any way. Which meant no televisions. She assured me that there was no way I'd be discovered. No one would come after me.

And it had been eleven years. Surely they'd given up.

But I'd discovered there was another way to get hurt. After miraculously being chosen for the show, I had fallen hard for the male lead, the "suitor," and he had been revealed to be a real-life prince. That had sent me into panic mode because if I really ended up with a prince, there was no way I could hide indefinitely. A life with him would be way too public.

Not that it mattered, because as a final twist, the show revealed that the prince had an identical twin.

A twin who had made me fall in love with him, while deceiving me the entire time.

If there was one thing I couldn't tolerate, it was a lying man. I'd already had my fill of lying men for this lifetime.

I arrived at the small porch outside of the guesthouse and raised my arm, banging on the wooden door with all my might.

The door jerked open, and there he stood.

Rafe.

Or, more accurately, His Royal Highness Prince Rafael of Monterra. Third in line to the throne, son of King Dominic and Queen Aria.

The man who had broken my heart.

I took a step back as my mouth went dry and my pulse exploded.

I had thought I was prepared for this moment. After the show ended, he had sent so many bouquets of flowers I was pretty sure he had deflowered the entire state. He had bombarded me with texts, phone calls, and emails.

Basically, he had tried in every way imaginable to apologize to me, but I didn't want to hear it. I hardened my heart against him. I would never, ever let myself be hurt like that ever again. I kept as busy as I possibly could so I wouldn't think about him and about what we'd shared.

I had even managed to convince myself that I was over him. That he held no more sway over me.

I was so totally and completely wrong. Because I was swaying, big-time.

I had known this moment would come. I knew he wouldn't stay away forever. He was one of the most determined, stubborn people I'd ever met.

But despite all my preparation, I clearly hadn't done enough. Because I was dumbstruck just from looking at him.

He was my physical opposite. Where I was pale, with red hair and green eyes, he had black hair, light brown eyes, and olive skin. I was ordinary, and he was ridiculously and painfully handsome. I enjoyed playing sports, like soccer, but he and his brothers were dedicated working-out types, and it showed in his athletic build. He had at least four inches on me, and while I used to love looking up at him and how feminine it made me feel, now it bothered me. He was too much. Too masculine, too beautiful, and too Rafe.

I hated that I still had a physical response to him. That my arms wanted to throw themselves around his neck, and that my lips were begging to kiss him. That I loved just standing near him because it made me feel better. Like I'd been trying to catch my breath for the past six months and could finally breathe again because he was here. It was both stupid and annoying.

Realizing that I had been staring and not saying anything for an embarrassing length of time, I straightened my shoulders. My gaze settled on his silver-rimmed glasses. "No contacts?" I asked sarcastically. I needed to be angry with him. It was the only way I would get through this.

His twin, Dante, didn't wear glasses. And since Rafe had been pretending to be Dante, he'd worn contacts on the show.

"No more contacts," he said. His voice. I had forgotten about his voice. How deep and smooth and yummy it was, with just the slightest hint of an Italian accent.

My knees started to shake, and I rebuked them. *We're angry*, I reminded them. *We are definitely not attracted to him.*

"No more deceptions," he said.

He took a step forward and my whole world slid sideways. I took another step away from him and he stopped.

"What . . . why . . . why are you here? What are you doing?" I hoped he didn't notice my wobbly voice.

He studied me, and I resisted the urge to squirm under his gaze. It made me too uncomfortable. I had really thought I was much stronger than this. More capable of carrying a grudge.

Finally, he spoke. "I came to apologize. I need to explain why I did what I did."

I crossed my arms, telling myself that the shivers I felt came from the snow surrounding me and had nothing at all to do with him. I didn't want to hear his excuses, but if I didn't let him rationalize his behavior, he'd never leave. "Fine. Explain."

"Not like this. Not while you're angry."

I let out a dark little laugh. "Well, then you're never going to be able to explain yourself." Unfortunately, as I stood there, I was discovering that time had smoothed over some of the rougher edges, taking away most of my anger. But I couldn't let him know that. If I did, he would so easily shatter all the defenses I had built up. I hoped I had more conviction in my voice than I felt because I couldn't let him destroy my heart again. I wasn't sure I could take it.

He shrugged. "I'm willing to wait."

"For how long?" I asked, frantic.

He didn't say anything and again just stared at me.

I covered my eyes with my hands and sighed. This was not happening. This just . . . could not be happening. This had to be some kind of waking nightmare. I pinched myself and then opened my eyes. Nope. Still there. "I don't want you to be here. You have to go."

"I can't leave. I signed a one-year lease with your aunt. Who is just as wonderful as you said she was, by the way."

A shudder of anxiety tore through me when he reminded me of all that I had shared, things I'd never told another person. I hated that he knew what he did.

"One year?" I repeated the words back to him. He nodded. One whole year? Maybe they kept track of time differently in Monterra and it wouldn't be as long as an actual year. Because there was no way I could do this for twelve months. And knowing him the way that I did, he really would stay the entire year. Rafe always kept his word.

Christmas was only a couple of weeks away. He would leave then, wouldn't he? He had to go back to his family's palace to celebrate with all of his brothers and sisters. Then I remembered that he'd mentioned something about his oldest brother getting married at Christmas. He would definitely have to go home then.

Maybe it wouldn't be so bad. I would just keep living my life, staying busy, and he could do whatever he planned to do and leave me alone. I would just have to call on my inner Spock and remain calm and logical. I'd make sure he kept his distance.

"I don't know what you think you're going to accomplish, but let me tell you now that staying here for an entire year is going to be a waste of your time. I can't forgive what you did." I turned to go.

"Genesis, *per cortesia* . . ." Italian. He had to slip into Italian. It always made my insides go all aflutter. He reached out to take hold of my arm, and my nerve endings exploded like a thousand glitter bombs where he touched me. I jerked away from him before I did something really idiotic. Like tell him all was forgiven and we should start discussing names for our kids.

"Don't," I warned him, my erratic heartbeat pounding wildly in my stomach. "Don't touch me. Just leave me alone."

In that moment I didn't know if I was more upset with him or with myself.

I started back toward the house, but I saw my aunt in the kitchen window, watching us with a worried expression. I couldn't deal with her questions or further matchmaking attempts. Forget the shower and the nap. I would go to work now. I could use the extra hours after missing the last few days.

Stomping through the snow-crusted side yard, I headed for my blue Ford farm truck. My purse was still inside the farmhouse, but my keys were in my pocket. It was an old habit of mine because I had a tube of pepper spray attached to the key ring and having it made me feel safer.

Hearing Rafe's footsteps crunching the hardened snow behind me, I hurried my pace and reached the safety of my truck. I loved Old Bess, especially because she had been my mother's truck, but she was a temperamental thing. I said a small prayer to the vehicular gods before I slid the keys into the ignition. "Please start. Please, please start."

No such luck. Just a clicking noise. My heart thudded louder as Rafe came closer. "Come on girl, I promise to get you the premium stuff next time. You've got to get me out of here."

He was nearly to the truck, and I tried one more time, turning the key as hard as I could. Still nothing. The engine refused to turn over.

"Really, universe? Is this how we're going to play this?" I asked in frustration before laying my forehead against the steering wheel and taking deep breaths.

He tapped against my window. So much for my dramatic exit. "Can't one thing in my life work the way it's supposed to?" I muttered as I manually rolled the window down. I probably shouldn't have been surprised. Everything else in my life was currently falling apart around me. Why not Old Bess too?

"It sounds like the battery is not working properly," he said. "That happens a lot in Monterra. Starting an engine in cold weather puts strain on the battery. When is the last time you replaced it?"

How could he just stand there, all gorgeous and serene, like nothing had just happened between us? Like he hadn't just shattered my entire reality?

"I don't know." I gripped the steering wheel tightly, staring straight ahead. Had he always smelled this good and I had just forgotten? Like summer, the ocean, soap, and sexy man all rolled into one.

"I'll go get my car and give you a jump start."

"No!" I yelped. I waited a beat, willing myself to calm down. "I don't have time for that. I have to get to work, and then there's a town meeting where I have to report on how the church bazaar planning is going, and help the kids with the talent show rehearsal, and then I have homework, and I need to do my dailies in *World of Warcraft* and . . ."

He stood silent, and I glanced up at him. To my surprise, he was angry. "I thought you were going to start telling people no."

I remembered that conversation very clearly. Months ago he'd told me I was doing too many things, and that was before I'd started deliberately trying to put myself in an early grave by being busy every minute of every day. He thought people in my town took advantage of my desire to help.

"I . . . I can't."

"Why?" he demanded.

"I just can't." Partly because I had chosen this path to keep him off of my mind, but also because I honestly couldn't explain why, when someone asked me for help, I never said no.

In fact, the only person I ever managed to say no to was Rafe. I was about to tell him as much, but I decided against provoking him when I saw that Aunt Sylvia had moved into the living room and was now watching us from the front window. We were like her own personal reality show. I let out another deep sigh. We needed his money. He had apparently charmed her into liking him and giving him a lease. I just had to wait him out. I could be polite and distant until he went away.

"I worry about you taking on too much," he said in such a gentle way that my heart nearly broke all over again. He reached up to push an escaping tendril of hair away from my face. I felt the tips of his fingers burning up my skin and had to move my head away.

"You don't get to worry about me anymore," I said, my seconds-old resolve to stay nice forgotten.

He looked thoughtful. I glared at him while a smile played at the ends of his lips. "Let me drive you into town. I know where the diner is. What time will your shift be over? I can pick you up."

Logically, I understood that he was being nice. That this was a courteous and chivalrous gesture, and that if any other person on the planet had made it, I would have accepted. But it was Rafe. The still tender and overly emotional part of me did not want to be trapped in a car alone with him.

"No, thank you. I'll call Whitney for a ride." It wouldn't be the first time she'd had to pick me up on her way in, and given my truck's desire to make my life as difficult as possible, most likely not the last time either. I scooted across the seat and let myself out on the passenger side to keep some distance between us. I headed back to the farmhouse.

"Whitney. Your best friend, Whitney?" he asked behind me.

I wished he didn't remember everything and that he wasn't so smug about knowing so much about me.

"You don't need to call her. I can drive you. It's no problem."

"I don't want your help. I don't need it. And I don't need you." I didn't know why I'd felt the need to tack on the last sentence or for whose benefit it had been. I let myself in the front door and slammed it behind me with a satisfying sound. Thankfully, Aunt Sylvia had made herself scarce. I was in no mood for an interrogation. I called Whitney, and she didn't hear anything in my voice that made her concerned or ask questions. She said she'd be by soon. I was going to get my shower after all.

I picked up my overnight bag from where I had dropped it earlier. Straightening up, I saw Rafe through the window. He had opened the hood and was fiddling around inside Old Bess's engine. Weird emotions flared up inside me. I did not need this stress.

What I needed was for him to leave.

But how was I going to make him go away?

Chapter 2

Whitney honked at me, but I was still brushing my hair. Where only minutes earlier I had felt beyond exhausted, I now looked suspiciously sparkly. My cheeks were bright pink, my hair behaving, my skin clear. Like my whole body was saying, "Yay! Rafe is back!"

Glaring at my reflection, I threw my hair into a ponytail and headed downstairs. I called out my goodbye to Aunt Sylvia. She shouted back that she'd see me at the town meeting later on.

When I got outside, I stopped short when I saw my very married and very pregnant best friend flirting with Rafe. Not to mention that my shepherd collie, Laddie (short for Sir Galahad), was sitting at Rafe's feet, looking up at him adoringly. I couldn't be too upset about it, though, because Laddie loved everyone. If we ever got robbed, that dog would take the thieves on a personally guided tour of the house.

Whitney, on the other hand, was a different story. She knew better. I walked up to hear her ask how he knew so much about cars. "I've always loved mechanical things," he said. "The mechanic at our boarding school spent a lot of time teaching me about cars. I almost never get to use that knowledge."

"Such a shame," she cooed.

I cleared my throat. She jumped. "Ready?" I asked pointedly.

"Yes." She seemed very flustered. "So nice to meet you, Rafe."

"The pleasure was all mine," he said, and Whitney nearly knocked into me while she twirled the end of her hair. I half expected her to start giggling, so before she could, I elbowed her. She got herself back under control, and we headed down the driveway. When we got into her minivan, I asked, "Why were you standing out there talking to him?"

"I was going to come inside and get you, but I got distracted by tall, dark, and yummy over there." She started up her car and waved one last time before putting the minivan in reverse. I didn't look to see if he waved back.

"You're married. And about to give birth," I reminded her.

"Married and pregnant, not dead. And not unable to appreciate that he is even more gorgeous in real life than he is on television. How do you not spontaneously combust from lust? And why didn't you tell me he was here?"

I grimaced and crossed my arms across my chest. "To avoid the conversation we're about to have."

She pulled out onto the town's main road. "You mean the one where I tell you that you are a much better woman than I am if you're planning to resist all that? What is that saying from your *Star Trek* show? Resistance is feudal?"

"It's 'resistance is futile.' And he's very resistible. Are you saying you can't resist him?"

"Don't give me that. You know I'd never cheat on Christopher in a million years. But you should totally make out with Rafe. You're letting good lips go to waste. Personally, I think you should lower your shields and prepare to be boarded."

If she had been anyone else, I wouldn't have talked with her about him. But Whitney was special. After my aunt took me in, I was too scared to leave the house. At my request, she even homeschooled me for a couple of years. I justified it by saying I had a lot to catch up on, but fear was the main motivation. When I finally felt confident enough to go to school, I made the mistake of choosing freshman year in high school as my introduction into normal society.

As I walked into the main hallway of the high school, tentative and afraid, Tommy Davis had offered to show me around. He was the first regular boy to ever speak to me. He was a junior and seemed so nice and sweet. At the time, I didn't know that he was Brooke Cooper's boyfriend, and as such, I was apparently forbidden to speak to him. She cornered me to let me know the many rules that I had just broken, and I could only stand there with tears in my eyes as she detailed exactly how she was going to ruin my life.

Whitney had watched this all happen and jumped into the fray. She told Brooke off, threatening to tell her dad just what exactly Brooke and Tommy got up to after the football games. After Brooke and her cheerleading posse sulked away, Whitney turned to me and said, "Girls like that make me sick. Don't worry about Brooke. You and I are going to be best friends."

And we were. Whitney might sometimes be tough and prickly on the outside, but inside she was all gooey with love, devotion, and loyalty. Like a marshmallow. She would deny it, but it was true.

It was one of the reasons why I had been immediately drawn to Lemon Beauchamp, a fellow contestant on *Marry Me*. At least, I thought she had been a contestant. She had reminded me of Whitney, all Southern sass and strength, but sweet, compassionate, and motherly underneath. She had been a good friend to me, supportive and helpful even when she thought we were falling in love with the same man.

But Lemon had lied to me too. About who she really was and why she was on the show. She had even been engaged to someone else. All things she kept from me.

After everything fell apart, she had showered me with phone calls that I wouldn't take. The pain was still too raw and powerful, and I blamed her unjustly. It was an annoying tendency of mine to sometimes take things out on the people who deserved them least. It wasn't Lemon's scheme that caused it all to fall apart. That was on Dante and Rafe.

Eventually the calls and unheard voicemails stopped. I wasn't even angry with her anymore, but so much time had passed that I felt embarrassed about calling her, so I just did nothing. I wouldn't have known what to say. Whitney had told me that she'd seen an article about Dante and Lemon being engaged, so I guess she must have forgiven him for what he and his brother did. I managed to stay away from all the online and televised coverage of the Monterran royals. I didn't want the constant reminder because it felt like somebody was performing unanesthetized open-heart surgery on me every time I thought about Rafe.

Which Whitney knew, because she was the one person in whom I had confided all of my heartbreak. She knew how badly he had hurt me and how I wanted to move on. She had also watched the show. Repeatedly. She saw what I had been through. I knew she was on my side, but she had a soft spot for Rafe and told me more than once that she secretly hoped we would reunite.

And that was before she had even met him.

It had surprised me that my often cynical friend was a romantic deep down.

"You can't be nice to him," I told her. "If we're nice to him, he'll never leave. I need him to go away."

"I'll do what I can," Whitney replied. "You know everyone in town has your back. We'll close ranks. But just know that my heart's not really in it. You belong together. It's fate. And I want to come visit you in your castle."

We pulled up to the diner, and she turned the engine off. "Not that any of it matters. I know you. You won't stay angry with him, and I'll get to plan my vacation to Monterra."

She got out, leaving me alone in the minivan. She was right about one thing, at least. I didn't like being angry. It made me not feel like myself. Despite my hardships, I always wanted to see the bright side. Aunt Sylvia told her friends I was her little eternal optimist. She used to joke that everyone should forget about the glass half-empty or glass half-full debate because I'd see an empty glass and say it was filled with invisible magical water.

I always wanted to see the good. In my life, and in other people. It wasn't that I was blind or unable to see things for what they were, but that I chose to live a certain way.

Or rather, I used to choose to live a certain way. What I had gone through with Rafe had changed me fundamentally. For months, my optimism had disappeared. I had been depressed and surly and not fun to be around. I had only just started being me again, wanting to see the bright side, wanting to be happy.

Right up to the moment when I found him in my guesthouse.

Sighing, I went inside to put on my apron and get ready for my shift.

All of the regulars were there, and I drifted from table to table, taking orders, pouring coffee, and making mindless small talk. I approached Max and his friends, who sat in "their" booth as they had every day for decades. "Hey there, sweetie," he said, holding out his coffee cup. He always smelled of Old Spice. "What do you call a Cyclone fan with two brain cells?"

"What?"

"Pregnant."

His table erupted into loud laughter, and I joined in. Frog Hollow was about an hour's drive from Iowa City, and in a state where football was a religion, these men were diehard University of Iowa Hawkeye fans. Which made the Iowa State Cyclones their mortal enemies. If any of their children or grandchildren went to ISU, they would probably get disowned. "You better not let Whitney hear you making any pregnancy jokes," I warned them after the laughter died down.

"We won't. I don't have a death wish." Max took a sip of his coffee. "How's that aunt of yours? Still the prettiest girl in town?"

I had long suspected that Max had a major crush on Aunt Sylvia. "Maybe you should come over for dinner soon and check for yourself."

He gave me a smile and a wink as I went back to the counter. Whitney stood behind it, cutting two pieces of chocolate pie. "Nicole took pity on us and ordered us some pie."

Nicole sat on the barstool across from us. "I need people to eat with me so that I don't actually sit here and eat the entire pie. Which I totally could."

"I'm guessing the date didn't go so well?" I asked sympathetically.

She nodded and shoved in another bite. She was a very pretty high school teacher about our age who had moved here two years ago. She and Whitney even looked a little alike, with dirty blonde hair and brown eyes. People often mistook them for sisters. But unfortunately Frog Hollow had far more single women than single and available men, so Nicole had resorted to online dating. "I moved here to end up with some nice strapping farm boy, and instead I get stuck with the lying losers who aren't even a little bit interested in a relationship."

I sighed. The dating thing obviously wasn't happening for me either. Marriage seemed far off, but I did want someone who was all mine. Someone who would love and adore me.

Family and friends weren't quite the same. I'd almost had that kind of relationship once, and I wanted it again.

Just not with Prince Lying.

"Wow," Nicole said to me. "I've never seen you sad around pie before. What's going on?"

"You mean the whole town doesn't know already?" I grumbled as I dragged my fork across the top layer of my slice. "That would be a first."

She looked at Whitney, who was only too happy to explain. "Her prince is here and staying in their guesthouse."

"What?" Nicole shrieked, and everyone in the diner turned to stare at us. "Are you serious?"

"Keep your voice down," I hissed at her. They'd all find out soon enough, and I would be subject to their pitying glances. Everyone had finally started treating me normally again, and I didn't want to go back to how things had been after the show ended.

"I have a question for you," Whitney said to me.

"Just one? I have like forty-three!" Nicole said in a stage whisper.

"Hey, Whit, how are your kids doing?" I asked while wiping down the counter. I didn't want to hear her question. Or Nicole's forty-three.

"Abundant and devious, like always."

"You're pregnant with your fourth, right?" Nicole jumped in, smiling at me as she did so. I appreciated the solidarity, but it wouldn't work. Whitney was never deterred for long.

"Yes, number four. And yes, I've only been married for five years. Which is why I'm never having sex with my husband ever again."

"Liar," Nicole said with a laugh. "You wouldn't last a week. I've seen the two of you together."

"Shh," Whitney said with a nod in my direction. "Don't forget we've got virgin ears over here."

"I am going to school to become a veterinarian," I reminded her. "Regardless of my personal experience or lack thereof, I am aware of how all different kinds of babies are made."

The bells that rang whenever the front door opened made their characteristic jingle, and in walked Rafe. A collective silence fell over the diner. We almost never had strangers here, and especially not ones who looked like he did.

We made eye contact, and my heart fell into my feet. He nodded at me and then headed over to an empty booth.

In my section.

"Who is that?" Mrs. Mathison asked her friend. She must have had her hearing aid turned down again and didn't realize how loud her voice was.

Nicole gasped. "Blasphemy! How can she not know who he is?"

Rafe opened a laptop on the table and began to type, either deliberately ignoring or completely unaware of the stares.

"Are we going to talk about the prince in the room?" Nicole whispered.

"Whitney, I can't wait on him," I told her in a low voice. "Please."

"You do know that I'm eight months pregnant, right?" She gestured at her large belly.

"Yes. I'm sorry. I'm being selfish," I said, feeling chastened. I would just have to be a big girl and get this over with. I took a deep breath, trying to calm my jittery nerves. I desperately wanted a Three Musketeers bar.

She put her hand out to stop me from leaving. "I'm totally screwing with you. I've got this."

Whit walked over with what I called her "don't mess with me, I'm a mom" face. She dropped a menu on the table. "What do you want?"

If he was surprised by her change in demeanor from earlier, he didn't show it. "I'll take whatever you think is good. Thank you." He handed the menu back to her without reading it. She glared at him and came back behind the counter. She told the kitchen to make him a turkey club.

"His voice is like music," Nicole sighed. "And he's just how I like my chocolate. Dark and rich." She sighed again until she caught my expression. "Um, I mean, he's your prince. I get that."

"He's not *my* prince," I said. "I don't own him."

"So does that mean you're done with him?"

"Nicole!" I protested.

"I know, I know. We hate him and I can't ever date him. But if anything ever happens to you, I'm jumping over your open grave to get at him."

"Oh!" Mrs. Mathison called out. "That's the nice young man who sent us all those flowers."

At that, Rafe turned to me, the question in his eyes evident. I looked down, hoping my cheeks weren't turning red because he had found out. When he was sending me all those apology flowers, I obviously couldn't accept them. I didn't want them. I could have sent them back, but I decided he deserved to pay somehow. So instead I told the delivery guy to bring them to the widows in our town. I figured they would get more use out of them than I would.

"I'm afraid I'm going to get second-degree burns on my corneas just from looking at him," Nicole said.

The counter had never been cleaner, but I needed to keep my hands busy. "Then stop looking at him."

"I should. He's a total Jules Verne, anyway."

That made me stop. "A nineteenth-century science-fiction writer?"

"No, Miss Literal," she said with a smile. "He's a good twenty thousand leagues out of my league."

Whitney brought Rafe a pop without responding to his thanks and rejoined us. "So what is his plan while he's here? Is he just going to wander around town like some free-range douchebag?"

I could tell she was trying to bring the snark for my benefit, but her heart wasn't really in it. "I honestly don't know what he thinks he's going to accomplish while he's here."

The bell rang again, and Max's daughter Amanda walked in, still in her scrubs. She was a single mom, a nurse, and the owner of the town's only bed and breakfast. She stopped by my house all the time to check on Aunt Sylvia, and she was one of the nicest people I'd ever met. I saw two massive men behind her. With a start I realized that one of them was Marco, the bodyguard Rafe had had with him on the show. When I first met Marco, I thought he was just a member of the crew's security. It wasn't until later I'd found out that he was part of the twins' personal detail.

Amanda kissed her dad on the top of the head and came over to join us.

"Who are they?" Nicole said, practically pouncing on her as she sat down at the bar. Amanda placed an order for chicken fingers and fries to go. It was the only thing her autistic son would eat. I put it in with the kitchen and stayed close so that I could hear what she said. Why was she with Rafe's bodyguards?

"Marco and Gianni. They're here with Prince Rafael. They're staying at the B&B."

I knew Amanda didn't get a lot of business at her B&B, so while part of me was glad that she was making money, I wondered why they weren't staying closer. I knew Marco in particular wouldn't like being that many miles away from Rafe every night.

"Are they single?" Nicole asked.

"I don't know," Amanda said. "All I do know is that they eat like we're going to run out of food soon."

That must have made her happy. Amanda had always loved to cook. Her uncle ran the diner, and I remembered her working in the kitchen with him when she was in high school.

"I've been experimenting with Monterran dishes, and they're nice enough to say they like them and eat every single bite."

"How long are they staying?" I asked, trying to be as casual as possible. I didn't want to be irritated that Amanda was another person who could have called or texted to let me know what was going on but didn't. I knew she had other things to worry about.

"They paid for a year in advance."

My shoulders sagged in. Now I couldn't wish for Rafe to go away because Amanda needed the money as much as we did. Her son's father had left them after they got the diagnosis, and she really struggled. I knew the commute alone killed her. She probably should have moved to Iowa City to be closer to her job, but all of her family was here in Frog Hollow, and her family was her support system. One of her nieces had even learned something called applied behavioral analysis so that she could work with Amanda's son on a daily basis.

The kitchen finished Rafe's order, and Whitney retrieved it, bringing it over to him and putting it down so hard the plate rattled. Rafe thanked her anyway.

"This is why I try to stay on your good side," I said to her when she came back.

"Ha. Joke's on you. Ask Christopher. All of my sides are bad."

I knew that wasn't true and impulsively hugged my friend. She didn't like hugging people, but she tolerated it for me for a few seconds. Then she took his check over to the table and stood there with her arms folded.

When he looked up she said, "Just so there's no confusion, we're all on her side."

He glanced at the other patrons, and I could see a hint of a smile. "I'm on her side, too. I know I don't deserve her."

Every woman in the room sighed as my stomach started back-flipping all over the place. I asked my lungs to function normally and ignored all of the stares that had moved from Rafe to me as people put two and two together.

The kitchen finished up Amanda's order, and I handed it to her. Then Max called me over, and for the next few minutes I was so busy that I forgot Rafe was even there.

Yes, that was a lie, but I needed the lies to get me through this.

He did finally finish his meal and took some bills out of his wallet, leaving them on the table. He didn't say anything as he left the diner. When he drove off in his black SUV, I saw Marco and Gianni get into an identical SUV to follow him.

Whitney came over and showed me a twenty-dollar bill. "He left this to pay for his check, and he left this"—she held up a hundred-dollar bill—"as my tip. He gave me *one hundred dollars* even though I was terrible to him. This makes it really hard to be mean to him." She sounded guilty, and I felt bad because she had done it for me.

She collapsed on a barstool. "You know your plan to have the town be against Rafe? I think that's going to be an uphill battle."

I had the sneaking suspicion that she might be right.

Chapter 3

We helped close down the diner, and then I carpooled with Whitney to the town meeting. Whenever there was a meeting, almost everyone came and all the businesses shut down. There were so few forms of entertainment in our town that this constituted a night out.

They held the meetings in the church. Snow had started to fall, and Whitney and I said hello to everyone as we entered. I pasted a bright smile on my face as I watched people whispering to one another and looking at me. The word had definitely spread.

After the show there had been this long period of time where everyone tiptoed around me and acted strangely. Like they didn't know what to say or how to behave. It was Max and his constant ISU jokes that got everyone back on track. But now with Rafe here . . .

Whitney found her mother and her children. Her mom babysat the kids while Whitney worked.

"My favorite little monsters!" I said as Meredith, Beau, and Gracie all started talking to me at once. They were four, three, and two, and I was devoted to them. As they climbed all over us and fought each other,

I was struck with an intense and unfamiliar longing to have a baby of my own.

My biological clock shifting into hyperdrive was so random and unexpected that I wasn't sure what to blame it on. I mean, I always assumed that someday I would find the right man and we would fill up the farmhouse with little ones. But that was always far in the future.

I worried that my baby-making parts were acting up in response to Rafe's flawless genes. "You're so lucky to be their mom," I said.

Whitney seemed confused at my out-of-the-blue statement. "You know I love them, but nobody told me being a parent would be like that summer after high school when I did an internship for that advertising firm in the city. Most of the time I don't know what I'm doing, I have to do all the crap work, and I'm not getting paid."

Gracie had settled into my lap. I never told anyone, but she was my favorite. "You know you'd quit tomorrow and stay home with them if you could."

"Yes, because they are adorable and precious and I love them more than my own life. But parenting is hard."

I smoothed down Gracie's bright blonde hair. "Everything worth having is."

"Yep. Including your prince." Whitney was far too smug.

"I wondered how long it would take for you to bring him up again. I had under five minutes in the pool. So I win."

"If I'd known there was money on the line, I would have waited longer—and I'm not letting you change the subject again. Why won't you let him explain?"

Gracie reached for my cell phone, and I let her play with it. Having occupied her, I turned to reply to her mother. "In case you were wondering where your nose is, I found it in my business."

Whit frowned and started to respond, but then Rafe walked in with my aunt, drawing our attention. He was helping her walk down the aisle. Amanda usually picked Aunt Sylvia up for town meetings. I wondered what had changed.

Despite the snow outside, he wasn't wearing a coat. Just a totally impractical cream cashmere sweater, and the light color of his sweater contrasted starkly with his black hair, tan skin, strong jawline . . . I shook my head, trying to clear it. Not able to help myself, I wondered how cold it got in his homeland. I'd only been to Monterra once, during this past summer. It was such a charming country, with little chalets that looked like gingerbread houses, and green as far as the eye could see. The surrounding mountains were so tall that they still had pockets of snow at each apex.

"All that chivalry is giving me goosebumps," Whitney whispered, interrupting my memories. "I can't imagine what it's doing to you."

It was making happiness and other unwelcome feelings rise up like a balloon inside me. I had to look away as I felt him seating Aunt Sylvia next to me. "Thank you for bringing me," she said as she eased into the pew, leaning her cane against the pew in front of us.

I couldn't help it. I looked.

"I am always happy to be of service," he said, before raising his gaze to meet mine. "Good evening, Genesis," he said.

"Um, hey." Why did he make my skin flush like this?

Gracie peered up at him. "I'm two." She held up three fingers.

He crouched down to be eye level with her. "I'm twenty-three. That's too many fingers." Gracie just smiled and then stared at him through her lashes. Even she wasn't immune.

Did he seriously have to be adorable right now? I was trying to be strong. I reminded myself that he had younger sisters. He was good with kids because he grew up around them, not because of some natural and overwhelming charisma.

Meredith spoke up. "That's almost the same as Jen-sis! She's old too!" I loved how all the kids pronounced my name—"Jen-sis" instead of Genesis.

Slanders to my age aside, I'd forgotten that Rafe and Dante had a birthday in October. It was weird to think that at one point I had hoped that we would celebrate it together.

Rafe smiled at the kids. He didn't smile the same way his twin did. When Dante smiled, he did it with his whole body. There was never a question whether or not he was happy. Rafe's smiles were slower and harder to come by. You had to earn his smiles, and you had to be paying attention to catch them before they were gone. Dante gave his smile away to everyone, but Rafe's meant something. It made me feel even stupider for not figuring out their deception earlier.

Although, when we were together, he used to smile at me all the time.

Meredith wiggled with delight at having captured his attention. "Gwandma says you're a pwince."

Whitney and her mother tried to shush Meredith at the same time. They had correctly guessed that I was dying inside and wanted him to go away. This close proximity was affecting my ability to properly inhale and exhale.

"Your grandma is right," Rafe told her.

This seemed to embolden Meredith, and she ignored the adults trying to quiet her. "Do you have a castle?"

"I do."

"And a pwincess?"

"Someday." His gaze was intense, burning, and directed at me. Stupid smoldering eyes.

My baby-making parts swung back into full force, letting me know they thought I was an idiot.

"I could mawwy you. Or Jen-sis! She doesn't have a husband. She could mawwy you."

All the blood drained from my face. Whitney's mom picked Meredith up and carried her to the back of the room, effectively ending the conversation. Meredith protested the whole way, apparently wanting to stay and finalize suitable marriages for both of us.

"What do you think, Genesis?" he asked. He was teasing me. I could hear it in his voice, see it in the way his eyes gleamed and how he tilted his head to one side.

But I couldn't think. Couldn't move, couldn't respond. I wanted to shrug off his flirting the way I'd seen Lemon do a thousand times with Dante, but I couldn't.

When I caught my breath, I finally managed, "I could never marry you. I can't be Princess Genesis. Think of how stupid that would sound."

"I'll abdicate. You don't have to be a princess if you don't want to be."

"You would do that?" I forgot that I was mad. Forgot that he had hurt me. Forgot his lie. Forgot that we were sitting in a roomful of people who would gossip about this interaction for at least the next year. "Are you being serious right now?"

He must have been encouraged by my lack of animosity, because he reached out to put his hand on top of mine. Warmth flooded my hand, sending sparkling tingles up my arm and tiny shivers down my back. "Have I done anything to indicate that I'm not? I'd do anything you ask."

Fortunately, before I could shove Gracie off of my lap like a sack of potatoes and launch myself at him, Brooke Cooper called the room to order, banging a gavel on a wooden podium. He stood up and walked toward the back of the room, leaving me.

"I'd marry him tomorrow," I heard Nicole murmur behind me, squashing any hopes I had that our interaction hadn't been the most entertaining thing to happen in this town since Myrtle Williams got drunk and ran over her cheating husband's collection of stuffed moose heads with their riding lawn mower.

"You and me both," Whitney whispered back.

"Calm down," I told them. "He didn't ask me to marry him. He was joking." They exchanged amused glances, but they did stop talking.

I'm mad, I had to remind myself. *I'm hurt. He lied to me. He humiliated me on national television. He doesn't have the right to make me feel the things he makes me feel.*

But it wasn't doing me a lick of good.

No, instead I watched him out of the corner of my eye. He leaned against a large wooden pillar with his arms crossed over his chest. He was the only person I'd ever met who managed to look both devastatingly elegant and completely relaxed at the same time. He had always been clean-shaven on the show, but now he had a five-o'clock shadow, which served to make him even hotter and more masculine than before, if such a thing were possible. Something about him tugged at my heart.

I might be in trouble.

Brooke's imperious tone managed to drown out my thoughts as she directed the town council's secretary to run through the minutes from the last town meeting. I focused on the kids and helping to keep them quiet. Brooke didn't like being interrupted.

They discussed the upcoming holiday talent showcase for the town's children. Nicole, who headed up the high school's drama club, had taken it over from me this year, and I had offered to help her. She stood up to announce that rehearsals would start tomorrow night.

"Report on the church bazaar?" Brooke called out. She knew I was in charge, but she scanned the room as if she couldn't remember which one of us peons was running it. I handed Gracie back to Whitney. I took my notebook out of my purse and flipped to the right page. I waited for her to call on me, but she didn't.

So I stood up and cleared my throat, feeling every eye in the room on me. Correction: feeling every eye looking at me and then looking at Rafe and then looking at me again. Like they were watching a tennis match. I didn't know what they thought was going to happen other than me telling them about the current plans and how things were coming along.

Although I couldn't see him, I could feel him staring at me. Like he had gained heat vision as a super power and was pointing it directly at me. Suddenly sweaty and more than a little nervous, I tucked the end of my ponytail into the rubber band, getting it off of my neck.

I wasn't going to think about Rafe. I was focused solely on my report. Our church had been built in the mid-nineteenth century and currently was in dire need of a new roof. Somehow we had to raise thirty thousand dollars.

We had planned to have a ticketed dinner, a bake sale, and a silent auction, and Nicole had recently added a bachelor auction. I had put her in charge of it, hoping she wouldn't wreak too much havoc.

"Do you have any other ideas about how to make the event more profitable?" one of the council members asked.

I opened my mouth, but Whitney suddenly popped up alongside me. "What about a kissing booth?"

It was quite possibly the stupidest thing Whitney had ever said. Because I knew why she'd said it and what her plan was. She was going to get Rafe to volunteer for it and get us to work together.

I had to put a stop to that.

"What is this, eighth grade? And who is going to staff it? Genesis the Giraffe?" Brooke asked, lapsing out of her mayoral role and back into the high school mean girl she'd been. There were a couple of laughs, and I could feel my face turning bright red. In addition to teasing me about my height all through school, my inexperience with men was another insecure spot of mine that she poked at relentlessly.

"Why not?" Rafe's voice stopped the tittering and Brooke's preening at her own cleverness. Her face fell as he said, "I happen to know that Genesis is an excellent kisser."

"That is so, so romantic," Nicole immediately whispered. The room was so quiet I was sure everyone else had heard her.

Unwanted images and feelings flooded into me as I remembered exactly what it had felt like to have his lips against mine, how he had pressed me against him and wrapped his arms around me. How wanted he'd made me feel. How much I'd loved it every time we touched.

Then I remembered that everyone in here had seen us kiss. Repeatedly. My cheeks actually hurt from the flaming humiliation. I wanted to die. I prayed for a personal sinkhole to form under the floorboards and suck me into it.

Instead I just sank into my chair and felt thankful to Brooke for the very first time in my life as she banged her gavel and moved on to another issue.

When I could talk again, I leaned over and asked Whitney, "What is wrong with you? Where did you even come up with that?"

"I was rewatching that episode last night when Dante went to Lemon's house and her mom talked about making him run a kissing booth and how much money her charity would make. And I thought that was totally true and we should do it given that we have his identical twin."

"Why were you rewatching the show?"

"Um . . . er . . . uh . . ." She made little soft sounds without actually responding to my question. And I knew she wouldn't.

"Fine. Don't answer. But there's no way we're doing a kissing booth."

She shifted Gracie from one side of her lap to the other. "Why not?"

"Because what if Brooke . . ." I trailed off, realizing what I'd nearly said. I might be mad and hurt, but I didn't want to share him with anyone else. Especially not her.

This was the curse of an overactive imagination. I could see him, all suave and sexy, bestowing kisses on the enthusiastic women of Frog Hollow. Could just imagine Brooke waiting for her turn. And as she puckered up, I imagined that I would run over and grab her by the hair to jerk her out of line.

I put my hands on the sides of my still-warm face. I was upset about fictional Brooke and pretend Rafe.

What was wrong with me?

"You're jealous," Whit crowed.

Sometimes I wished she couldn't read me so easily. I shrugged one shoulder, trying to act like I didn't care. "It's not jealousy. I just have all these old, bad feelings about Brooke." Bad feelings and a rabid desire to keep her away from Rafe.

"Jealousy *is* a bad feeling."

I could hear Nicole shifting forward in her seat behind us, trying to catch our conversation.

"It also shows that you still care," Whitney continued. "Which you should, because you belong together. You were so 'love at first awkward.'"

Whitney was right. It really had been love at first awkward. For me, anyway.

Well, not at very first.

My aunt Sylvia had been obsessed with *Marry Me*. I'd watched every season with her because it was her favorite show, and during a recent symptom relapse she'd gotten it into her head that I should audition. I think because she was sick and convinced of her own mortality, she thought the best way to make sure that I was taken care of after she was gone was for me to get married. I couldn't figure out why that was her plan considering how disastrously her own marriage had ended. He had bankrupted us.

But she'd stuck to her totally unreasonable goal. Given my aunt's tough, no-nonsense personality, it would probably surprise most of the town if they ever discovered what a romantic she was, and how much she lived for romantic movies, shows, and books. She was certain that I would find my true love and future husband on *Marry Me*. Which was silly because no one on those shows actually ended up married. But to humor her, I sent in a video of myself. I had zero expectation of getting chosen and had honestly forgotten all about it.

Nobody was more surprised than me when the show called to say that they were considering me. They flew me out to California to audition, which was my first time on a plane. I went through so many different rounds, and at each stage of the interview process I expected to be sent home.

I had met some of the other possible candidates, and I was nothing like any of them. I didn't belong. I didn't wear makeup, and every woman there looked like she'd just stepped out of the pages of a fashion magazine.

Then they chose me. Me. Genesis Kelley from Iowa. I was sure I'd just be filler, one of those girls who would show up in the beginning and get sent home the first night.

And while I expected that outcome, it surprised me to discover that I didn't want to be sent home. I had sought comfort in routine and familiarity, but when I went to California, my life back home suddenly felt stifling. Too predictable. I wanted something more. An exciting once-in-a-lifetime experience I would never forget.

Part of it might have been deliberate. I'd spent so much time hiding, so this was like some kind of delayed adolescent rebellion. I'd put myself out there in the most public way possible, like I was daring John-Paul to do something about it. That false bravado didn't last long.

The show gave us hair and makeup artists for the night, and I spent more time than I'd like to admit getting beautified. The wardrobe stylist pulled a dark green dress for me that was floor length. It had princess cap sleeves and sparkles all over the skirt. I wanted to ask where they'd found a dress so long (I'd never actually been able to find a skirt or a dress that went all the way to the floor), but I didn't get a chance before they zipped me in and stuffed me in a limo.

I waited in a long line behind other limos and watched from a distance as one girl after another climbed out, walked up the driveway of the famous *Marry Me* mansion, and met the suitor.

As I got closer, I realized that he was easily the most handsome man I'd ever seen. He was so exotic looking. My stomach started doing queasy flips.

It was almost my turn. I saw the girl in front of me get out of her limo. She was wearing jeans and a baseball jersey. His whole face lit up when he saw her, and even though I couldn't really see her expression, her body language said that she was just as excited to meet him. I knew then and there that she was the girl who would win. She walked away, and he watched her go all the way up to the house.

What possible chance did I have after that? It was a little like having to go on stage after the headlining act has finished for the night. Nobody was there to see me.

But turning around and going back to the hotel was not an option.

So I took a deep breath, pasted on a smile, and got out of the car.

Chapter 4

I did not trip over my skirt or slip in the ridiculous shoes, and I was pleased to see that he was several inches taller than me, despite the heels. He was even better looking up close.

He reached out his right hand. "Hello, I'm Dante."

"I'm Genesis." I nearly glanced at the camera crew standing to one side. Was I supposed to say my last name? I couldn't remember.

I took his hand and felt . . . nothing. I had hoped there would be more of a chemical thing between us, but nothing happened. Objectively he was handsome, but I wasn't feeling any kind of spark. I hoped my disappointment didn't show on my face.

"Genesis, it is an honor to meet you."

"You too. Thanks for having me."

He raised one eyebrow, and I realized how that might have sounded. A warm flush spread through my cheeks. "I mean, you're not *having* having me. You know, like physically or anything. Not that I was thinking that you were thinking that, I'm not trying to put words in your mouth. Or thoughts in your head. I just realized how it sounded and I . . ." I trailed off, looking at the cameras. I couldn't help it.

I swung my gaze back to him. I sighed. There was no way out of the hole I'd just dug for myself. "Never mind. I talk a lot when I get nervous. And this is definitely nerve-racking."

His eyes twinkled at me, and I could tell he was fighting off a smile. "Don't worry. I understand completely. I hope we'll have a chance to talk later."

Thankful that he'd given me an out, I walked to the house as quickly as I could. Part of me wanted to run into a corner and hide, but just inside the house I found the girl who had gone before me. That was when I met Lemon. I introduced myself and told her that I had seen the chemistry between her and Dante, though she brushed that off. That seemed strange to me. Any other girl probably would have been thrilled to talk about how the man they were here to marry liked them right away.

We socialized, met some of the other girls, and bonded over the insanity of our situation and the fact that so many of the other contestants were out of their minds. Every time I thought we had reached the bottom of their crazy, we discovered their crazy underground garage.

Their consumption of all the available alcohol did not help.

Being in full possession of all my mental faculties was apparently going to be another strike against me. I wasn't in the mood to be judged or to fight my way through the crowd in an attempt to get close to him.

I accepted my fate of being sent home that night, and I decided to explore the estate so that I could give Aunt Sylvia a full report. It seemed so much smaller in person than it appeared on television. None of the crew followed me, apparently deciding, as Dante had, that I wasn't worth investing any time in. I went out the front door, making my way carefully over the cobblestone driveway. I walked toward the north side of the house, and I thought I detected the homey smell of hay and horses.

I missed my horse Marigold so much it hurt. She was a lovely chestnut American Saddlebred who was entirely too vain and lazy to be of much use around the farm. But I had adored her. I had helped deliver her ten years ago with our local vet, Dr. Pavich, and it's what made me decide to become a veterinarian myself. I loved animals and thought I could be very happy spending my life taking care of them.

But when our financial crisis struck, Marigold had to be sold. There was no choice. We couldn't afford to keep her. It had been the second-saddest day of my life.

The scent got stronger, and I could see the barn through the tall fence in front of it. It had to be about eight or nine feet, made out of patterned wrought iron. I tugged at the gate, but it was locked. There was a row of decorative spiky arrowheads all along the top. I knew that I should probably go back to the party. But if there were horses in that barn, I would much rather spend the evening with them than the women back at the mansion.

I checked behind me to make sure that I was still alone, and then I hiked up my skirt. I grabbed the metal bars and started to climb. This did not turn out to be as easy as you might expect in high heels and formal wear. The soles were so slippery. I considered kicking them off but was worried I might hurt my feet.

That decision turned out to be a huge mistake. I got toward the top, grabbing a couple of the arrowheads to pull myself up. I threw my left leg up to go over, and my right foot gave way underneath me. I yelped as my foot slipped and I started to fall.

Some of my skirt caught on one of the arrowheads and abruptly stopped me from falling. I was hanging awkwardly, holding the top of the fence, my legs dangling and my skirt caught on the top of the fence. Both of my shoes slid off my feet and dropped to the ground.

It was so ridiculous I had to laugh. I was trying to figure out how to get down, but I couldn't stop laughing. This was *so* something that I would do. I wasn't particularly accident prone, but I was very good at finding ways to embarrass myself.

I tugged a few times at my skirt, still giggling. It wouldn't come loose. I had to give mad respect to the designer, because this thing was sturdy. I worried about ripping the dress completely. It didn't belong to me. Would the show charge me if I came back with the skirt all shredded? I could possibly fix or explain one hole, but an irreparable tear was a different story.

Then I tried pulling my legs up higher, but I wasn't strong enough. I was so stuck. I laughed again.

"May I be of assistance?"

I looked over my shoulder to see Dante standing there. He had undone his bow tie and the first few buttons on his tuxedo shirt. He seemed both amused and concerned.

"Yes, I could definitely use some help."

He took off his jacket and scaled the fence much more easily than I had. I hoped I wasn't flashing him, but he didn't even look. He easily lifted the dress up, with me still in it, over the spikes. He used just one hand. I couldn't help but be impressed. Finally free, I regained my footing. The iron felt cold and rough against my feet.

"Thank you!" I said. He had possibly just saved me thousands of dollars.

"My pleasure," he said. There was a heat in his eyes that I hadn't noticed earlier. It made my skin tingle with delight.

"Race you down?" I asked. He smiled, and my heart sped up in response to it. He had a breathtaking smile.

"What do I get when I beat you?"

"What makes you think you'll beat me?" I said, trying not to laugh again. Something about him made me feel even happier than normal.

His response was to scale down a few feet and then jump the rest of the way. "That's what makes me think I'll beat you."

"Cheating?" I responded.

"It's not cheating. Just superior climbing skills."

"When you save a damsel in distress, you're not supposed to leave her behind," I teased him.

He put his hands back on the bars, obviously intending to climb back up.

"No!" I called down to him. "I was kidding." I tried not to laugh, seeing the annoyed expression on his face. He seemed to take the jab at his honor very seriously.

I carefully climbed back down, and he stood respectfully off to one side, but still within arm's reach to catch me if I fell. It wasn't necessary, but it was sweet. When I got down I grabbed my heels and held on to the fence while I slipped them back on. I inspected the new hole in my dress. I had a small sewing kit in my suitcase. "Maybe I can stitch it up without them noticing," I murmured.

When I glanced up at Dante, I realized that he was studying me with a serious look in his eyes. There was a sadness there that I hadn't noticed earlier. It made me want to hug him and make everything better. "You were laughing."

"What?" I laughed a lot. That wasn't very descriptive, so I tried to clarify. "When?"

"When I found you. You were laughing." He said this like it confused him and he didn't understand.

I shrugged. "I was laughing because it was funny. You have to admit that what just happened was pretty funny."

A smile played at the edge of his lips. "It was, but I'm too much of a gentleman to say so."

That made me want to laugh again, but I just grinned at him instead.

"Is this situation so terrible that you were trying to escape?" He gestured toward the fence.

"My mom always used to say you can't fight the moonlight. That being outside under a full moon makes you do things like scale fences because you thought you smelled horses. I'll let you in on a little secret."

I leaned forward, and he did the same. I was struck by how distinctive and tempting his cologne was. "Sometimes I like horses better than people."

"Sometimes I do too," he said in a whispery voice that made little thrill bumps pop up all over my exposed flesh. "But there aren't any horses here, which is why the gate was locked."

"Oh." That was disappointing. "I was kind of hoping I'd get to go riding. I haven't done it in a long time."

Then my stomach rumbled so loudly that there was no way for either of us to pretend it hadn't happened. I laughed again, and this time he joined me.

"Hungry?"

"Very. But I'm not willing to face the horde of raving lunatics inside to forage for food."

He reached inside of his tuxedo jacket, which he'd put back on after he climbed down. He brought out something wrapped up in napkins, and opened the wrapping to reveal two large chocolate chip cookies. He offered them to me.

I took one, leaving the other for him. "So, you always walk around with cookies in your pocket just in case?"

"You never know what kind of distress a damsel will be in," he said, winking at me. "It's partly out of habit. I have a younger sister with a sweet tooth, and I always grab extra for her. But I took them because the crew seem determined that no one's going to eat tonight."

The cookie was heavenly. Soft and chewy with just the right number of chocolate chips. I swallowed my bite. "The girls can't get as drunk if there's food to absorb some of that alcohol."

"You're not drunk."

"I had a super strict upbringing," I said, not sure how much I should tell him. "And the guy in charge believed in purity of mind, soul, and especially body. So no alcohol, no sugar, no processed foods, no drugs. I didn't even have cake until I was fifteen and at a birthday party." It was one of my fondest memories, and to this day that was the best slice of cake I'd ever had.

"That sounds like cruel and unusual punishment."

"You don't miss what you've never had." I held the remaining cookie up. "But once you find out how delicious it is . . . well, that's why I'm a dessert junkie now."

"So you've defiled yourself with sugar," he said with a mocking sad face that made me giggle. "'Guy in charge'? Your father?"

"No." Not my father. My almost husband. But that was a can of crazy I wasn't willing to pop open yet.

He picked up on my cue and changed the subject. "I'll have to feed you some Monterran desserts. Those are decadence on a plate."

The idea of him feeding me anything made my stomach spin. "Monterra? Is that the city you're from? What country is that in?" There was a slight European accent to his voice, but I couldn't place it. Not that I'd met a lot of Europeans or anything.

"Someplace you've never heard of," he said. Now I was the one picking up his reluctant cues, but it seemed strange. It was a pretty basic question. Like when you met someone in college for the first time it was always hi, where are you from, what's your major? Not hard.

I filed that bit of information away. Monterra. Maybe there was a computer inside the house and I could look it up.

"You really listen. I feel like I want to tell you things." I probably should have thought before I spoke, but it was honest and I didn't regret it.

"Oh?"

"And not in that way guys do where they only listen to you because they want to, um, take things further. Like it's their reward for putting up with your jabbering." There was a slight ocean breeze, and my skin broke out in tiny bumps. It wasn't cold. I was pretty sure this was all due to him. I rubbed my hands up and down my arms.

He noticed and took off his jacket again. This time he placed it over my shoulders. It was so old-fashioned and thoughtful that the bumps turned into mountains. I thanked him. It was still warm from his body, and it smelled of him. I slid my arms into the sleeves, letting the delicious warmth envelop me.

"And you don't reward them?"

He was either a good guesser or I somehow radiated my virginity. I wasn't embarrassed by it. So many other girls came on this show as virgins, and it got turned into this major plot point. The ones who just told the guy up front made it not a big deal. And it wasn't.

"That purity extended to relationships. I may indulge in sugar, but I'm waiting for the right guy and the right time."

There was a slight moment of surprise, followed by a big self-deprecating grin. "What?" I asked.

"Let's just say that I gave my oldest brother a hard time about something, and he's going to enjoy some payback."

I wondered if I could hijack his jacket and take it back to my room tonight. I could sleep in it, surrounded by the scent of his amazing cologne. I understood the general patheticness of that desire, but I didn't care. "How many brothers and sisters do you have?"

He looked uncomfortable for a moment before he responded. "Three sisters, two brothers, and a brother who died when I was young."

I put my hand on his arm. "I'm so sorry. I lost my mom when I was thirteen."

He put his hand on top of mine, and I tried not to shiver. "Now I'm the one who is sorry."

We stood there for a moment, and I realized that he was watching my lips. Would he kiss me? Did I want him to? I mean, I did not want to be one of those girls who was making out with the eligible bachelor on the first night. I'd never had a very high opinion of those women.

But I suddenly appreciated why they'd done it.

I let out a breath I didn't realize I'd been holding. "Wow. That just got super depressing super fast, didn't it? We should probably head back."

He nodded and tucked my hand into the crook of his elbow. It was so romantic it made me weak-kneed. We walked from the fence to the front of the mansion. I stopped, pulling my hand away from his arm. His nearness intimidated me. I folded my arms and stared up at the huge house, telling myself to calm down.

"What are you doing?"

I tried not to jump. "Taking a mental picture. They took our phones, and I want to remember it when I go home."

"Why would you go home?"

"I'm . . . I'm not like . . . I . . ." There was no way to tell him that I felt out of place and uncomfortable. That like any good redshirt, I expected not to be alive at the end of the episode. There was no way this guy could really be interested in me.

But he came to my rescue again. "This is embarrassing, but I don't know your name."

I wasn't surprised he didn't remember it. "Genesis. Genesis Kelley."

He held out his right hand, and I shook it. When we'd first met and shaken hands, there'd been no spark. I had felt a stronger connection to Lemon when we met for the first time.

But suddenly that spark was there. And it had brought its entire extended family along with it. To be more accurate, a volcano roared to life inside me, sending lava flowing through my veins when we touched.

I wondered if he felt the same. I suspected he might, because he was still holding my hand. "Genesis," he repeated, his voice caressing the syllables in my name the same way his thumb was caressing the back of my hand.

I gulped. He was sending shockwaves of electricity through me. So much so that even my jewelry seemed to have been affected. I heard a clanking sound on the ground and realized that one of my borrowed, heavy, and dangly earrings had leapt to its death. Probably due to the electrical shock.

"My earring," I said. It was the only thing I was capable of saying. I bent down to get it and he followed. I didn't realize what an issue this was until I started to straighten up, only to discover that somehow my upswept hairdo was caught on his cufflink.

"Ouch!" I said, staying crouched down, not able to stand up.

"Just a moment," he said. "Let me . . . if I could just . . . My apologies, but I'm going to ruin your coiffure."

"Coiffure?" I repeated. Who even said that? The word and this situation made me giggle inappropriately. He was going to think I was the worst kind of airhead. "It's fine. I had no idea how I was going to undo it anyway. Better you than me."

He tugged at bobby pins, pulling them from my hair and letting them land on the ground. "You didn't do this yourself?"

"Um, no. I'm not really that kind of girl. I hardly ever even wear makeup. They had all these people dressing us and taking care of our hair and outfits. They're only doing it for tonight. So tomorrow I go back to being just plain old me."

He paused, and I wished that I could see his face when he said, "I would very much like to see plain old you."

That made my heart flutter like a trapped butterfly. I hoped he couldn't see my embarrassed blush from his vantage point. Locks of my hair hit my shoulder and neck as he released them. When his fingers brushed against my scalp, it tingled.

So I did what I always do when I got nervous. I babbled. "I can't believe my hair is caught in your cufflink. This kind of thing never happens in real life. Although, I guess this isn't real life, is it?"

"Not really, no," he agreed.

Just as I started imagining his fingers running through my hair while he kissed me, he finally finished. "There," he said. "All done."

I stood up, and was glad that he wasn't going to touch me again. All of my senses felt totally overloaded.

"You know, now that I think about it, it probably would have been easier for you to have just opened your cufflink." He didn't seem surprised by my suggestion.

Which made me realize that he had already thought of it.

"Easier," he said, nodding. "But not nearly as much fun."

What? What did that even mean?

He took a step toward me, and it required every ounce of willpower I possessed to stand still. "Or . . . maybe I just wanted to see you with that all glorious hair down."

I opened my mouth to respond but didn't know what to say. Men did not flirt with me like this. Ever. And this very beautiful man with the face of a fallen angel said my hair was glorious. I hadn't passed out in a long time, but I realized there was suddenly a very real possibility of it happening. "Dante, I . . ."

He put a hand on my shoulder. "Rafe."

I was almost a hundred percent sure that he'd said his name was Dante. "But I thought that . . ."

This time he put one of his long, tapered fingers against my lips, making my whole body go limp. "Everyone I care about calls me Rafe. Just don't tell the other girls." He moved his hand away.

"Okay. Rafe." I tried it out. I liked it. He took another step toward me so that we were practically touching. He reached out, and I wondered what he thought he was doing. My heart slammed into my ribcage so hard I was pretty sure I'd have bruises. I realized at the last second that he was reaching into his coat pocket.

He'd nearly made me stroke out. "More cookies?" I asked. My voice only quivered slightly.

"No," he said. He held out a small red pin. "Would you take this piece of my heart?"

I knew what that was. It was the First Sight Heart.

"I would love to." I took the pin from his hand, trying not to brush my fingers against his palm and failing miserably, which sent more shockwaves through me.

Somehow I managed to attach the pin to the bodice of my dress. This pin meant that he liked me enough to spare me that evening's elimination. I wouldn't be going home.

It meant he wanted to keep me around.

Chapter 5

Of course, now I knew that I would have been better off if he had sent me home at the beginning.

"The last item is the annual book drive," Brooke called out. "Who headed that up last year?"

"Genesis Kelley." The secretary looked terrified to say my name. Brooke somehow refrained from trying to insult me again.

"So you'll do it again, won't you, Genesis?" one of the council members asked. It was a good thing Brooke hadn't asked, because I might have said no immediately.

"I've got a lot going on," I said hesitantly. I didn't want to say no and leave them in the lurch, but I was really busy. To be fair, though, I did have the most experience with that project.

Rafe cleared his throat, and I turned to see him narrowing his eyes at me. I knew what he wanted. He wanted me to say no.

He wasn't the boss of me. "Yes, I'll do it." It would help with my keep-busy-so-I-don't-think-about-Rafe plan.

That got shot to smithereens seconds later. "I would like to volunteer to help with the book drive," he announced.

Another one of those eerie silences descended over the meeting. So much for putting a stop to us working together.

"And you are?" Brooke asked. She knew darn well who he was. I'd overheard her talking about him and me after I got back from the show. You can guess the tenor of that particular conversation.

But she flirted with every breathing man under the age of thirty, and she probably thought pretending not to know who he was made her more desirable. Or something.

"Rafael." He paused. "Rafe. Rafe Fiorelli." It took him a second to add on his extended family's last name. He didn't actually have a last name. Just a bunch of first ones and a royal title.

"Fine, put Rafe Fiorelli down on the book drive list."

Little pockets of anger bubbled up inside me. He had done that just so he could spend time with me. I didn't need his help. I could do the book drive all by myself.

And go to school. And take care of Aunt Sylvia. And help Dr. Pavich. And work at the diner. And help with the talent show. And run the church bazaar. And do my homework. And take care of the farm. And play my games.

Yep, no problem at all.

The longest town meeting in the history of the entire world finally finished, which meant I could say my goodbyes and hitch a ride home with Amanda. Getting far, far away from Rafe.

Which flooded me with relief right up until I remembered that he would be going to the same place I was going.

Whitney stood up, putting Gracie down. She whined to be picked up, but Whitney explained that she couldn't carry her because of the doctor's orders. Gracie put her thumb in her mouth. "Good luck with everything. And now I'm going to have to be nice to him because he was sweet to my kids. It's a mom law."

I hugged her goodbye. I felt a hand on my shoulder. Rafe. He turned me around. I blamed my quickened heartbeat on my anger at what he had just done. "Should we talk about the book drive?"

Sneaky jerk. "Not now. I've got to get Aunt Sylvia home."

"I can meet you out front." He took his keys out of his pocket.

"No, Amanda's going to give us a ride home." I technically hadn't asked her yet, and I really hoped she said yes.

He put his keys back. "May I ask you a question? About the flowers?"

That caused a torrent of emotions that I did not want to deal with. Especially not in front of all the prying eyes and straining ears. A heavy pounding started right behind my eyes. I took a deep breath in and slowly let it out before I answered. "I didn't want to keep them. So I sent them to people who could enjoy them."

"Of course you did." If Whitney had said that, she would have sounded sarcastic. Rafe just sounded like he approved. As if he liked my decision and had expected it. I had anticipated that he would be upset.

I offered Aunt Sylvia my arm, and he did the same. She held on to both of us as she got up. "Thank you," she said.

Rafe gave her one of his rare smiles. I tried not to feel wistful about all the times when he used to smile at me. I imagined my heart, and then I mentally constructed a wall of ice around it. I had to keep it guarded and safe, and I had to stop it from feeling so many things when he was around.

There was a commotion in the back, and I turned to see Christopher burst through the crowd, looking for Whitney. Something was really wrong.

"What is it?" Whitney sounded panicked.

His face had gone completely white. "They closed the factory."

The nearby factory made computer printer parts, and half the people in Frog Hollow were employed there.

Whitney was frozen in place, unable to respond. There would be no way for them to survive with Christopher unemployed. Nausea rose up in my throat while my stomach churned. I hoped I wouldn't actually throw up. I was worried about Whitney's family, and I didn't want her to move.

The second part was entirely selfish, but I needed her. Especially now.

"The doors were locked. There's just a sign on the door saying it's been shut down. There's no final paycheck. No more insurance." He sat down hard in one of the folding chairs, staring ahead at nothing.

"But the baby," Whitney whispered. I knew the cost of a normal delivery could run into the tens of thousands, and I couldn't even begin to fathom what kind of bill they'd run up if there were any complications.

I felt Rafe shift next to me. I turned to see an expression on his face that I had seen many times before. It was one that said he was figuring something out. "I'll see you later," he said. "I wanted to talk with the town council. Excuse me."

What was that about? I didn't have long to think about it, though. I found Amanda, who agreed to drive us home. I hugged Whitney and told her I'd call her after she and Christopher had had a chance to talk.

I couldn't bear for Whitney to go through this kind of stress. I hoped it wouldn't affect her health, or the baby's. This was seriously all I needed. Just one more horrible thing to add to the heaping pile of crap that my life had become.

I wanted to see the silver lining. But right now I was surrounded by rain clouds.

My alarm clock went off much too early. Technically it was the same time as every other morning, but I had stayed up way too late. I'd talked to Whitney for a really long time, trying to figure out ways we could make money. Neither one of us wanted to say what this probably meant—that she and Christopher would have to move closer to the city for him to find work. And that it would kill me to lose her.

After we hung up, I had logged on to *World of Warcraft*. My guild was supposed to run a raid, and as main tank I was scheduled to lead it. But they'd gone without me and had already finished up. I'd looked forward to our raid all week. Whenever I played, I was able to become someone else. I was somewhere else. Nobody knew who I was. Nobody knew about Rafe or the show. I was just Eclipse, the death knight. I could turn my brain off and forget about everything around me.

But I had responsibilities, and so I forced myself out of bed. I had to feed the few animals we kept because of their ability to provide food for us. I put my hair in a bun and threw on some sweats. I grabbed my coat on my way through the kitchen. Aunt Sylvia would be up soon and would make us some breakfast. I'd told her repeatedly she didn't need to, but she seemed to enjoy feeling useful.

I yawned and saw my breath in the cold, dark morning. I rubbed my hands together as I headed for the barn. I pulled the door open and closed it behind me. I turned on the lights and reached for the pail.

It wasn't there.

Had it landed on the floor or rolled somewhere? I didn't see it. I went over to check on Clover, our milking cow, and discovered there was no milk left in her teats. And she had a trough full of hay. I turned to see that the pigs had also been fed, and the chickens were all happily squawking and pecking at the ground. A search of their nests showed that all the eggs were gone.

Danny, the teenage son of our nearest neighbors, had helped with the chores in the past when I was gone on trips. But he knew I was back. We had talked at the diner the night before. And he'd been at the town meeting.

But if it wasn't Danny, then who was it?

I tromped back to the kitchen, where the light had been turned on and the delicious scent of breakfast made my stomach rumble. I went in and hung up my coat. The milk bucket was in the kitchen.

Aunt Sylvia stood at the stove. "Back so soon?" From the tone of her voice I knew that she knew what I had just found.

"Rafe," I realized out loud. "Rafe did my chores, didn't he?" How did he even know what to do? I was sure he didn't do a lot of farm chores back in Monterra.

She just hummed to herself, scrambling the eggs. "Such a sweet young man."

I opened the cabinets to get plates and silverware for us. Sweet. He was sweet, all right. And a lying liar. "You need to let it go. That door is shut."

"You know what they say: when life shuts a door . . ." she replied, carrying the eggs over to the table.

"Open a window?"

"No. Open the door again. That's how doors work."

I had no intention of reopening that particular door. I was trying to figure out how to install heavy-duty locks and nail it into the frame. Because that particular ship had sailed, crashed into rocks, and sunk to the bottom of the ocean.

"Will you grab another place setting?" She had her back to me.

Now he was coming to breakfast? "Really?"

But before I could demand more of an explanation, Rafe came in through the kitchen door with Laddie, letting a blast of cold air inside. He had an armful of firewood. "Good morning," he said to us, kicking the door shut behind him like he'd done it a million times before. Aunt Sylvia responded to his greeting, but I just glared at him. He carried the wood into the front room, giving me one of those intense Rafe stares that made my insides go rubbery. I grabbed another plate but refrained from slamming the cabinet door shut. He had his own kitchen. He didn't need to invade ours. I asked Aunt Sylvia to sit down while I brought the rest of breakfast over.

He took off his coat when he returned to the kitchen and put it on the back of the chair. He was still sporting that scruff on his jaw. I wanted to reach over and see what it felt like. Which made me mad at myself.

So now I was officially mad at every person in the room.

We started eating. Ever the gentleman, Rafe made sure to serve Aunt Sylvia first. Laddie trotted over to beg me for scraps. "You're a traitor," I whispered to him. He laid his head on my lap and gave me his sad face. He knew just how to manipulate me. I gave him some of my bacon, and he ran off with it.

I didn't want to be rude to Aunt Sylvia, but I couldn't stay. I couldn't sit this close to Rafe and not react. He seriously smelled good enough to eat.

Or maybe that was the bacon.

"Genesis, do you have something you want to say to Rafe?"

"Yeah. I don't need you to do my chores." I shoved some toast into my mouth, but realized that I had lost my appetite.

Aunt Sylvia coughed into her milk and gave me a look of disappointment. It made me feel overwhelmingly guilty.

But that guilt went away when Rafe replied cheerfully, "You're welcome," choosing to ignore my foul mood and that he was the reason for it. "I wanted to mention that I spoke to the mechanic and he agreed that it was the battery."

"Great. I'll just run out with the money I don't have and replace it." I carried my plate and silverware over to the sink.

"I can just—"

I whirled around. "No, you can't 'just.' I don't need you to take care of me."

He stood up, breakfast forgotten. "I know you don't need me to, but I want to take care of you. And I want you to take care of me. That's how relationships work."

The ice encasing my heart was starting to melt a bit around the edges. *I can be strong.* "In case you hadn't noticed, we aren't in a relationship!"

I could tell he wanted to walk over to me. Which I couldn't let him do because he'd get handsy and I'd give in.

But he didn't, probably because we weren't alone. He gave me one of those slow, sensual smiles that made my breath catch in my throat. "Not yet."

Aunt Sylvia stifled a laugh behind her hand, and I'd had enough. I practically ran upstairs, texting Amanda as I went. She responded right away and said she'd pick me up. It would mean I would get into Iowa City several hours before my classes started, but I had to get out of this house.

College was taking me forever to finish because I refused to take out student loans and only went as I could afford it. It was a priority for both me and Aunt Sylvia, but I should have graduated a couple of years ago. Even after I got my degree, I would still have several years of veterinary school and training ahead.

I thought of everything I had to get done that day. School this morning, shift at the diner, rehearsals for the talent show, maybe arrange another meeting for the committee working with me on the bazaar?

After showering, getting dressed, and making myself somewhat presentable, I threw on my backpack when I heard Amanda honking. I went downstairs and heard Sylvia and Rafe laughing in the kitchen as they cleaned up the breakfast dishes. It made me grumpy that she seemed to be on his side. If she liked him so much, she could marry him.

Stepping out into the cold winter morning, I ran over to Amanda's idling truck and let myself in.

"Thanks for the ride."

I must have said it more gruffly than I intended to because she glanced over at me as she backed out of the driveway and said, "I know it's none of my business, but there's something I want to ask you."

None of her business. Like that ever stopped anyone here from constantly giving their opinions about everything.

"Why are you trying so hard to make yourself mad at him?"

I opened my mouth to respond and couldn't. Amanda had always been someone I admired and respected. I couldn't lie to her. Because if I was being at all honest with myself, it was an effort to stay mad at him. It didn't feel natural at all.

"Since I've known you, you've always been this happy and mellow person. Which you haven't really been since you got back. And especially not since he got here."

She flipped her brights on, given that we were the only ones on the back road this early in the morning.

"I'm not sure what to say," I finally admitted.

She shrugged. "There's probably not much to say. I think it says a lot about Rafe that he has this kind of effect on you."

Amanda reached over and turned on a radio station, leaving me to my thoughts. Had I really changed that much? And why was I working so hard to be angry with Rafe?

I knew why. Because it was the only way to keep myself safe from him. I ran through my list. He knew too much. He'd made me feel too much. He'd betrayed me and humiliated me.

Maybe you should let him explain why, something inside me said. The voice sounded a lot like my aunt.

I told her to be quiet and closed my eyes, trying to get some sleep on the way into the city.

Whitney had asked to take my shift at the diner, and I couldn't say no. According to Rafe, I never said no. But in this instance it was justified, because she needed the money more than I did.

It should have given me time to study, but instead I drifted off. Facedown, on my keyboard.

Which I discovered because the smoke alarm started going off. I awoke with a start, my face throbbing from all the places where the keys had poked it. "Sylvia!" I called out, racing downstairs. I didn't smell any smoke.

She was taking a nap on the couch, oblivious to the sound.

I burst into the kitchen, but there was no smoke there either. The oven wasn't even on. It was then I realized that the alarm wasn't coming from inside the farmhouse.

It was coming from the guesthouse.

That was seriously all I needed. I was pretty sure that we had no insurance on the farm, so if the whole place burned down, we'd have no way to replace anything, and then we really would lose it all.

I knocked on his door, but I didn't think he could hear me over the alarm. So I let myself in and saw the kitchen was full of smoke. Rafe was reaching out for the burning pan on the stove.

"Wait, don't!" I said, but I was too late.

He dropped the pan on the floor as he realized he was burning his fingers. I rushed over, grabbing the pan with a spare dishtowel and putting it in the sink. I hit it with the towel until the flames went out. I opened the window over the sink to let the room ventilate.

Without thinking what I was doing, I took Rafe's hand and put it under the faucet. I turned on cold water and held him in place, letting the water take away the sting. It didn't look too bad. I didn't typically deal with burns because animals didn't have a tendency to burn themselves.

I was about to tell Rafe that when I suddenly became very aware of the physical situation I had put myself in.

He was pressed against my back. He must have bent his head, because I could feel his lips very close to my neck. He was breathing on that sensitive spot right behind my ear. His arm was against my waist as I kept his hand under the water, and he just seemed to radiate this warmth that I wanted to sink into.

This was not good.

Chapter 6

Correction—it was very, very good. So good I didn't want to move. Which was the bad part.

"Trying to cook for yourself?" My voice sounded shaky. That connection between us, the one I'd felt when I met him for the first time, was still there. And so strong. Stronger than I had expected. Like a million ropes tethered us to one another.

"Trying. Not succeeding," he murmured, and he must have moved his head because now I could feel his breath in my hair and it sent sparkly shivers all through me. I was so painfully and achingly aware of him pressed against me. How strong he was, and how amazing this felt. His heart pounded quickly against my back. My own heart was matching him beat for beat.

"Why don't you get Marco or Gianni to help you?"

"They aren't here to cook for me. They're here to protect me," he said, and I could feel the words against my skin.

I accidentally sighed. "The smoke alarm didn't concern them?"

He reached over to the sink with his other hand, which pressed us even closer together. My heart ricocheted around in my chest. He turned the water off.

"That happened a lot while you were gone. I think they got used to it." He was saying the most innocuous things, but every word felt like a physical caress. I should have moved. He should have moved. Neither one of us did.

I had to close my eyes against the emotional and physical onslaught when he put his hands on my upper arms. My palms were damp. Not from the water. He literally made my palms sweat. I gripped the edge of the sink.

His hands moved slowly from the top of my arms down toward my wrists, and then he trailed them over to my waist. I could feel his breath again on the back of my neck. He was going to kiss me there, and then I was going to lose all control and reason and maul him.

I'd had all that I could take. I pulled away and walked across the room, grabbing an extra dishtowel to dry my sweaty palms.

"You could teach me."

I blinked rapidly. "Teach you what?"

He didn't miss how high my voice had become, and he gave me a slight smile. "Cooking. So I don't keep catching things on fire."

I was so glad he was talking about cooking and not about anything else that I stupidly agreed. "Okay. But just know that what you were doing was not cooking. That's called burning."

And he already knew a lot about making things burn. Me, in particular.

He headed toward his bathroom, brushing past me, getting me all riled up again. He reached under the sink and pulled out a tube of ointment.

"I can't believe you want to stay here," I blurted out nervously. "This whole place is smaller than your bathroom in your palace."

He finished putting the ointment on his burn and put the tube back down. "It is small, but there are other benefits to being here."

He was talking about me. Did he have to have such a sexy voice? I leaned against his table and mentally pleaded with my knees to not give way. I was going to properly freak out now.

But then I saw his laptop. He had been playing *World of Warcraft*, and he was in an unfamiliar area.

Which wasn't possible, because I had been everywhere and done everything in that game. "Wait, is that the new expansion?"

"It is," he said, coming closer than I was comfortable with. There were some papers on the table, and he hurriedly shuffled them together and put them into a folder.

"How do you have that? It doesn't even come out for another two months." I couldn't help it. I reached over and pulled up the map to see the names of the new lands. So unfair! I had been dying for this expansion and the new playing class it was going to introduce.

"A perk of being a prince, I guess. Do you want me to get you a copy?"

I did. I really, really, really did.

And I wasn't doing a very good job of hiding my response. Because he suddenly looked way too self-satisfied. He knew how badly I wanted it. He was the only person I'd ever met who truly understood my gaming addiction. It helped that he had one of his own. We had instantly bonded over our mutual obsession while we were on the show. I almost smiled as I remembered the night he had snuck a laptop into my room so that we could play *Mortal Kombat X*. I usually felt like an oddball, because most girls weren't into those kinds of games, but Rafe acted like it was the coolest thing in the entire world. He loved that I got something so important and basic about him. I'd felt the same.

"If not, I understand. I do have the new *Call of Duty*, if you'd like to play that instead."

He turned on his big-screen TV and showed me the paused game. I never got to play console video games anymore—just the ones I could play on my computer. My fingers itched to pick up one of the controllers.

If he suddenly whipped out a plate of candy bars and a chocolate cake, there was a strong possibility I might never leave the guesthouse again.

No wonder he didn't mind staying here.

"I actually have to finish studying, and then I have this rehearsal thing tonight at the school."

"Speaking of which," he said as he walked around the couch and grabbed something off the kitchen counter. It was only when he tossed it to me that I realized it was a set of keys.

My keys.

"I had your truck fixed."

That brought me crashing back to reality. "I asked you not to do that."

"No, you told me not to do that, and I did it anyway because it needed to be done."

While part of me was outraged that he'd done something I'd asked, okay, *told*, him not to do, another part of me was touched and grateful. I didn't know which face to show. I was floundering. If I was nice, he'd think he had a chance still. But If I was mean, I'd be acting like an ungrateful, spoiled brat.

So instead I asked, "What are you doing? What kind of game are you playing?"

"Game? I'm not here to play a game." Then he came and stood right in front of me. He couldn't possibly have missed my sharp intake of breath. He stood so close we could have kissed if either one of us moved forward just an inch. Then I stopped breathing completely while he said, "The only games I play are of the video game variety. But if this were a game, I would win. I don't lose."

The rest of my day consisted of unkind thoughts about arrogant, conceited men who believed they could do whatever they wanted. It was like real life was some video game and Rafe thought he had a god mode cheat. It got worse when I started up my truck. The engine purred, and I realized he had done a lot more than just replacing the battery.

"I'll pay him back," I told myself, as a way to make things okay. He would be very far down the list, though, given that some of the other debtors had the ability to make us homeless.

He only had the ability to make me insane.

While working at the diner, I thought of what Amanda had said about how I was trying to make myself angry at him. Logically, he had done something nice and thoughtful. And I was mad at him for it? I couldn't rationalize that he was implying I was too weak or was unable to do it myself. I was sure that never even entered his mind. He saw something that needed to be done, and he did it. That's how Rafe was.

Part of me expected him to show up at the diner again, but he didn't. Instead, just before my shift was supposed to end, I got a visit from Stuart.

That would be Stuart, the flower delivery guy, with whom I was on a first-name basis thanks to Rafe.

"Stuart! What are you doing here?"

He held a large bouquet of sunflowers. He didn't have to say anything. I knew they were for me. I'd told Rafe once how much I liked sunflowers and how I missed them in the winter. And somewhere in his royal bloodline he had an ancestor who must have been part elephant, because he never forgot anything.

"You know the drill, Genesis." He set the flowers down on the counter. "Enjoy!"

I did know the drill. The drill was he told me I had flowers, and I would tell him to bring them to one of the widows in Frog Hollow. "Wait!" I called after him. But apparently he had forgotten the drill himself, as he was already out the door and climbing back into his delivery truck. Stuck, I took the note out and read it.

Thank you for saving me today and preventing me from burning the house down.

—Rafe

P.S. I had Stuart deliver flowers to all the women on your list, so you can keep these.

Then I had to deal with dueling desires—I wanted to strangle him and kiss him at the same time. He needed to stop sending me flowers, but how could I not be touched that he'd had flowers delivered to all of the widows in our town? He had gone out of his way to make a lot of people happy. That kind of thing probably wouldn't even have occurred to most men. They would have just been mad that I didn't accept their gifts and then punished me by not giving me more.

Not Rafe. He had to go and be twice as thoughtful and considerate.

We technically weren't supposed to use our phones while at work, but this required some feminine backup. I texted Whitney.

FLOWERS!!!!

She immediately responded, but she didn't say what I had expected.

Send me a picture because Christopher hasn't brought me flowers since we got married. I'm pretty sure I've forgotten what they look like.

Where was my female solidarity? I glanced around before I answered.

That's not what you're supposed to say.

My phone buzzed with her quick reply.

Sorry, just overwhelmed—and on top of everything else, I have to take Mere to a birthday party tomorrow morning at 7:00 that's apparently being hosted by the devil.

After apologizing and telling her that we would talk soon, I put my phone back in my pocket. Laura came in to relieve me so that I could head over to the high school. I left the flowers at the diner. I'd let the customers enjoy them.

I didn't want to admit that part of me wanted to take them home and keep them in my room. I knew that if I did that, though, Rafe would know somehow (even if I was sneaky) and then he'd misinterpret my actions to mean something that they didn't.

And I needed to keep the lines between us very clear.

When I got to the school, Nicole picked up on my not-so-great mood. "What happened now?"

"He fixed my car."

"The nerve of that jerk! Want me to lay into him?" Her sarcasm implied that I was overreacting. She didn't have all the details about my past.

I was usually the one doing things for other people. So I probably should have been fine with Rafe doing stuff for me. But I had worked so hard to be independent. To stand on my own two feet after having every moment of my life controlled by someone else. I understood that Rafe wasn't trying to control me. He was just being kind. But something inside me instinctively reacted negatively whenever he did things after I told him not to.

We were standing on the stage where they had just finished putting together the balcony for the *Romeo and Juliet* scenes. Sarabeth was in the process of climbing up the back side of the scenery to get onto the balcony, though the set appeared wobbly.

"Is that safe?" I asked Nicole.

"Technically speaking? Maybe. But it's okay. We've got someone coming to help out with building scenery."

From her evasive tone I knew who she was talking about. "He's a prince. He doesn't know how to build sets."

"You know I can't turn anyone away. We need all the help we can get." She walked off with her clipboard, telling Sarabeth to come down until they could get it properly tested. Sarabeth looked crushed. She was performing a scene with Malcolm Schroeder, and he was the most popular boy in the entire county. She looked at him the way I used to look at Rafe.

And speaking of Prince Fibbing, my entire body knew the second he entered the auditorium. Like I was attuned to his presence and every piece of me stood at attention when he came into a room. All of the teen girls on stage turned to watch him walk down the aisle. He jumped up onto the stage, greeted everyone, and came to stand next to me. "What play are you doing?" he asked. He seemed oblivious to his newly formed fan club.

There were so many things I wanted to say to him. I wanted to let him know he couldn't send me flowers and fix my truck. That it wasn't okay for him to be living in my guesthouse and to basically be infiltrating my life. That he was turning into a stalker. A gorgeous, tasty, brilliant, charming stalker, but a stalker nonetheless.

Mostly, I wanted to ignore him, but Sylvia had raised me better than that. "They're doing scenes from *Romeo and Juliet*, and some other plays. Love stories and fairy tales, that kind of thing. And it's not just scenes from plays. It's a talent show, so there's singing and dancing and other stuff."

He was standing too close. I swear he did that on purpose. "What's wrong with fairy tales?"

So he'd picked up on the disdain in my voice when I'd said those words. "There's nothing realistic about them. If you lose your shoe at midnight, you're just drunk."

For a second I thought he was going to put his arms around me. I must not have been far off because he put his hands in his pockets instead, like he was making himself not touch me. Or maybe I was wildly conjecturing. It had been known to happen. "You didn't used to feel that way."

His voice sounded pained. But he was right. It was unfair that he knew practically everything about me, even my deepest, darkest secret. But the reverse was not true. I hadn't even known who he really was.

Sarabeth had apparently worked up enough nerve to approach us. She stared at Rafe for a moment, and I couldn't blame her for her nervousness or her adoration. Finally she blurted out, "I, uh, know, um, who you are."

"So do I," Rafe responded, his lips rising up slightly at the corners. I could see from her expression that that was not what she had intended to say or how she'd intended to say it. He so dazzled her that she'd stumbled over her words. I had so much empathy for her, because it still happened to me and I was around him all the time.

"Oh. Okay then." She appeared flustered. "Uh, Miss Brady sent me over here to get you." Nicole stood by the balcony set and waved Rafe over.

"Duty calls," he said, giving my shoulder a squeeze. That sensation traveled down to my heart, squeezing it too.

Stop it, I told myself for the billionth time. *He hurt me. He humiliated me.* My traitorous heart still sported the scars from his betrayal and lies.

Nicole put Rafe to work on a different set. I saw him pull out his phone, and if I had to guess, I'd have said he was on YouTube looking up how to hammer in a nail. Because there was no way he had ever done that before in his life. Instead he put on some music, plugging in his earbuds. Then he went to work on that scenery like he had been building things his whole life.

My mouth might have been slightly agape. I had a strong temptation to confront him and ask him how exactly he knew how to build things. But Nicole intercepted me as I walked across the stage. "You don't want to be with him, so let him work. Leave him alone."

"For your information, he's the one not leaving me alone." I ignored the fact that I had been on my way to talk to him.

She ignored it too. "You want him to leave you alone? Then send him a message. Go out with someone else."

I had grown up with the boys in this town. They were either already involved with someone else or I'd known them for so long it would be like going out with a brother.

Then she managed to land on the one exception. "Isn't that Tommy Davis back there?"

Tommy Davis. He was that guy from high school who was always called by his first and last name together, mainly because I never knew him very well and we were basically strangers. He was sitting in the back row of the auditorium, texting on his phone. I remembered that he had a younger brother who was still in high school. He must have driven him and was waiting around for the rehearsals to finish.

My sixteen-year-old self had harbored a massive crush on Tommy Davis, but since he was Brooke's boyfriend, and then her husband, he had always been off-limits. While Whitney was the poster child for a successful young marriage, Brooke and Tommy were the opposite. They'd only been married for six months before they filed for divorce. It was quite the scandal in town, and it had made things awkward for everyone because they'd both stayed in Frog Hollow.

It had never even occurred to me to talk to Tommy because I didn't think he'd be worth the drama. But considering that I was heavily embroiled in my own personal drama, how could a little more hurt?

He would most likely not be interested, but I wouldn't know unless I tried, right? Lifting my chin, I left the stage and marched up the aisle. I wished I had a hairbrush. Or Lemon here to do my makeup. Before I could say anything, he glanced up and smiled widely at me. "Hey, Genesis."

I came to a stop, surprised. I had been carefully constructing a potential line-by-line conversation in my head and he'd disrupted it. "Hi, Tommy. I was just thinking about you yesterday."

At that, he put his phone down. He looked nothing like Rafe, which right now was in the pros column. He had light brown hair, bright blue eyes, and was just a little taller than me. "Oh? What were you thinking?"

His question had a slightly seductive tone to it, which made my stomach lurch sideways. If Rafe had said it, I probably would have melted into a pile of redheaded goo, but Tommy Davis saying it felt a little squicky.

I was probably just reacting to the residual Brooke on him. "About how nice you were to me when I started high school."

He blinked a couple of times, as if trying to remember. I could see the moment when he did. "Oh! Right! I showed you around."

And then his ex-wife had tried to ruin my life, but I left that part out.

I couldn't help but peer over my shoulder, back at the stage. Rafe had stopped what he was doing and was staring directly at us. He had his arms crossed across his chest, and his face had gone from fallen angel to avenging angel. I was a little scared. I knew he'd never hurt me, but right then he might have done some bodily harm to Tommy Davis. I stepped into his line of sight so that the two men couldn't see each other.

Having never asked a guy out before, I didn't know the right way to go about it. Aunt Sylvia enjoyed lecturing about letting a man chase me, but I never had the heart to tell her that men did not do much chasing as far as I was concerned.

Well, excepting whatever nonsense Rafe was up to right now.

I started to clear my throat, but then Tommy Davis spoke up. "Hey, are you doing anything tomorrow night?"

Chapter 7

Tommy Davis surprised me by asking me first. Like he'd been able to read my mind. Or he could understand my awkwardness and took one for the team to spare me further embarrassment.

"Doing?" I repeated.

"Yeah. We should hang out."

Hang out? What did that mean? I didn't speak guy. Was that the word in his native tongue for a date?

I guessed if I wanted this to be a date, I was going to have to lock it down. "Where and when?"

He stood then, and I saw his younger brother coming toward us. He was like an emo version of Tommy. He walked past us without slowing. "I'll come by your house at seven. We'll figure something out. See ya later!"

He went after his brother, and the teenage girl still living inside me was giddy. When I returned to Nicole's side, that teen part of me practically shrieked, "Tommy Davis just asked me out!"

The rest of me wasn't too sure about it. I worried that my behavior was some combination of a teenage dream finally realized and wanting to make Rafe jealous.

Which I should not have wanted to do. Why did I care what Rafe thought? Why would I want to make him jealous? Wanting him to be jealous implied something deeper and more emotional that I didn't want to examine.

"Of course he did," she replied. She was watching Rafe work, and he was currently engrossed in what he was doing. The part of me that wanted him to be jealous was miffed that he was basically ignoring me after I had gone to so much trouble to get his attention.

But when I considered Nicole's words, they didn't make sense. "What do you mean by that?" Had she bribed him to do it or something? Was she so worried about my self-esteem that she had somehow talked Tommy Davis into it?

"His caveman genes couldn't help it."

Now I was even more confused. "Again, what?"

"A dominant alpha has moved to town and wants you, so the only way the other eligible men can respond to the threat to their masculinity is to try to get you first."

The thought of Rafe wanting me did inexplicable things to my ability to breathe. "That makes no sense."

"It's all instinct and genetics. It doesn't have to make sense. But I minored in anthropology, so I totally know what I'm talking about. It's the same thing where the women in the town will either try to mean girl you out of the way or befriend you to get closer to that magnificent specimen of man." She looked startled, as if she realized what she had just said. "But not me. Because I'm totally your friend."

Should I be more concerned that she'd felt the need to tack on that last sentence? I decided not to analyze it. Instead I told Nicole I had to go. I had plans to do some PvP with my guild later on and I wanted to get home.

I did not want to think any more about caveman or cavewoman impulses. I particularly did not want to think about what my personal ones were urging me to do.

I stayed up later than I probably should have and thwarted my master plan of getting up before he did. I got up at my regular time (a time that should be banned from all clocks) and looked out my window before I got dressed. Sure enough, Rafe was out back bringing hay and feed into the barn. Aunt Sylvia would be up soon to make breakfast.

I decided to do the most sensible thing that I could: go back to bed. That would mean forgoing my favorite meal of the day, but it would also mean I could avoid Rafe.

Unfortunately, I was one of those people that when I was up, I was up, no matter how tired I was. I wanted to sleep more, but my internal clock wouldn't allow it. I stayed in bed defiantly, even when the smell of Belgian waffles and bacon wafted upstairs. My stomach gurgled and protested, miserable to be missing out.

I turned over, opened up the top drawer of my desk, and pulled out a Snickers bar from my candy stash. It wouldn't fill me up, but it'd have to do until I could get to school.

It was a Saturday, but I had labs to make up that I'd missed earlier in the week. The hours seemed to fly by faster than an Internet startup, and I was surprised when it was time to go home.

Trying to delay the inevitable, I stopped by the library to get the list for the book drive. Our librarian was extremely ambitious and wanted to create a world-class library on a small-town budget. While I applauded her drive, we didn't have the money to get it done. She sent me out to beg people and companies to donate their old books, and I typically ended up with romances and thrillers. I'd never gotten even a fraction of her massive list completed.

You can imagine my surprise when I walked in to see the floor covered with opened and unopened boxes. "What's all this?"

Bonnie was prancing around the library like some kind of demented sprite. "It's all the books from my wish list! Every single one of them!" She unpacked several books, laying them out on the table and smiling at them like they were the children she'd never had.

"But . . . how?"

"Prince Rafael. He talked to me after the town meeting and got the list. They arrived this morning."

I shouldn't have asked. I should have known. That must have been what he had to talk to the town council about, since Bonnie also served as a councilperson.

I drove away faster than normal, because I was trying to decide what I was going to do to Rafe when I saw him. He couldn't just hijack my entire life. He didn't get to make these kinds of decisions for me. He couldn't wave his money around and do whatever he wanted. There had to be repercussions for his actions.

I went inside, calling out for Aunt Sylvia. She didn't respond, and I remembered that she and some of her friends had planned a shopping trip in Iowa City. She wouldn't spend any money, but she enjoyed it as a social activity. I went into the kitchen, intending to go to the guesthouse and give Rafe a piece of my mind.

A rhythmic sound outside made me stop, and I went to the kitchen window that overlooked the backyard to see what it was.

Rafe was outside chopping wood. At first, I shook my head at the ridiculousness of it. He was actually chopping wood. Back in Monterra he probably had a servant just for wood chopping. And the wood-chopping servant would have some underling to do most of the work. I expected him to get the axe stuck or to aim for a knot that might glance his blade the wrong direction.

But he wasn't doing it wrong. No, he was swinging that axe with strength, precision, and the perfect amount of momentum—and it was obvious he had done it before. I couldn't even make fun of his outfit. He had on the right kind of boots and gloves, as well as dark jeans and a button-down shirt.

Even his stance was right. He stood square to the wood and had his legs spread a little wider than his shoulders. I had seen wood chopped before, but there was something different about watching him do it. The power he wielded, the satisfying thunk as his blade neatly split the pieces, the way he engaged his entire body on that one repetitive and intriguing task.

He must have been doing it awhile, because beads of sweat clung to the ends of his black hair. He stopped, leaving the axe in the stump. My stomach hollowed out and all my anger fled when he took his shirt off, laying it on the snowy ground. He had a white tank top on underneath, and he retrieved the axe to keep chopping. I didn't know whether I should feel quite that much disappointment over a tank top.

I watched as he swung and hit, swung and hit. Over and over again. Like he was a machine with only one program to run. The wood was no match for his strength. The muscles in his arms flexed and rested with each swing. I liked the way they tightened and stretched his skin. I knew he was strong, but I was impressed by how strong he really was. It was so . . . masculine. And thrilling.

He would stop every once in a while to push over the wood that didn't automatically fall into the large pile he had created.

My mouth went completely dry, like somebody had shoved it full of cotton balls, when he lifted up the end of his tank to dry the sweat on his face. I got a good peek at his abdomen, which looked like somebody had airbrushed it on. My skin went hot as I remembered the last time I'd seen him without his shirt on, how he had kissed me and held me, how I had touched him . . .

As if he sensed he was being watched and fantasized about, he chose that moment to look up.

I dropped to the floor like a sack of potatoes. I tried to hold my breath and not make any sound at all. Maybe he hadn't seen me. Maybe I had gotten down fast enough.

There was a knock at the kitchen door. My heartbeat pounded in my ears. *Go away! Please just go away and don't make this worse!*

But not being able to read my mind, and showing that he wasn't averse to doing things that embarrassed me, he called out, "Genesis?"

I stayed put. The door wasn't locked. If he walked in, the jig would definitely be up. Would he come inside? It didn't seem like something he would do. Given my luck, though . . .

As I considered my options, I was starting to edge my way along the floor. Then there was a knock at the window. There stood Rafe, still in his tank top, looking down. He raised one eyebrow at me. I had a flush that I could feel all the way to my toes.

Getting up, I went over to the door to let him in. He came inside with an amused expression on his face, chilly air rushing in behind him. It did little to cool me off. My body swayed toward him, and I forced myself to take a step back. I knew my face had gone so red it probably matched my hair, but I remembered why I had gone searching for him in the first place. It wasn't to admire his many assets. It was to confront him about the library books.

So before he could say or do something that might make me forget my intentions, I said, "No more gifts. Can I make myself any clearer than that?"

Even I flinched at the sound of my voice. There was a flash of hurt in his face that was so brief I nearly missed it. Then he asked, "Which gift are you talking about?"

"All of them. But especially the library books."

It was then that I noticed he had brought his shirt in, because he chose that moment to put it back on. I was glad I didn't have to worry about being distracted by more rippling muscles when I was trying to be mad.

"That wasn't a gift for you. It was a gift for the library. And now you don't have to worry about finishing up the book drive. It's finished." He said this like he couldn't understand what my objection might possibly be.

"That's *so* not the point!"

"What is the point?" His demeanor was calm, but I could tell I had provoked him. "For you to spend hours working on something you don't need to work on? You have too many other things on your plate. I've taken this off."

I couldn't be bought and paid for. A voice whispered, *That's not what he's doing*, but I ignored it. Six months ago I would have thought it was romantic. Now, it was just too much.

"Send them back." Petulant and sulking, party of one. I didn't want to act this way, but it was literally the only thing I had to keep him at bay. He wouldn't leave. He wouldn't stop pursuing me and insinuating himself into my life. He wouldn't stop making gestures and being sweet. I had to put a stop to it, but other than being angry, I didn't know how.

"Don't be ridiculous. I'm not sending them back."

"You should. They must have cost you a fortune."

He sat down at the kitchen table. "It's just money."

Just money. How I could use that "just money" right now! I thought of how much we needed it. But I couldn't be upset over how he chose to spend it, because I knew all I had to do was ask and he would give me whatever I wanted. Happily. Cheerfully.

But it would be like he owned me. Like I had to forgive him for everything that he'd done because he'd thrown around enough money to make my life better. It made our relationship totally unequal. I didn't know how to explain to him how small it made me feel. How inadequate. It was one of the many reasons I needed him to leave me alone and let me get on with my life. I wasn't going to become a princess, and he wasn't going to become an Iowa farmer.

I let out a long sigh while flexing and unflexing my hands. "I can't do this right now. I have to get ready."

"For your date?" His eyes flashed with such force, I felt taken aback.

How did he know? "Not that it's any of your business, but yes, I have a date. So if you'll excuse me, you can see yourself out."

He got up so quickly from the chair that it nearly tipped backward. "Is that what you want? For me to leave?" He was usually so even-keeled with his emotions I didn't know how to react to his raised voice.

"Yes, that's what I want."

As he slammed the kitchen door shut behind him, I had to ask myself whether or not that was actually true.

I got ready for my date. I heard Rafe and Aunt Sylvia having dinner together downstairs, and I didn't join them for two reasons—first, I didn't know if Tommy Davis planned on us going out to eat, and second, I wasn't quite ready to face Rafe yet.

Not knowing his plans or how fancy this date would be, I put on jeans and a nice blouse. I decided not to wear heels or my cowgirl boots as they would make me taller than him. I sort of had a complex about being taller than the guy I was going out with. *They don't make you taller than Rafe*, that voice taunted.

I took a picture of myself and sent it to Whitney to get her opinion.

Thumbs up!

I thanked her and was going to put my phone in my purse when it buzzed again. Another message from Whitney.

Have fun. Not too much fun. You can say no. And no again. And more no.

Tommy Davis was an adult now, not a teenage boy. His reputation in high school shouldn't follow him around his entire life. Shaking my head, I responded.

I got it. You're making me feel like I'm back in Pastor Dave's "health education" class.

She sent me some smiley face emojis, and I heard Tommy's car pull up. Hurrying downstairs, I came to a halt on the bottom step. Rafe stood in the front room, looking out the window. He had his back to me, his broad shoulders blocking any possible view of the yard.

I didn't want any more confrontations. Not between me and him, and not between him and Tommy Davis.

Tommy Davis opted out of any potential fight by blaring his horn. Shock slammed into me. Did he really just honk his horn at me?

"You don't have to respond. You're not one of Pavlov's dogs." Rafe's low voice filled the room.

"They responded to a bell, not a horn."

His regal profile was lit up by a nearby table lamp. I wondered if Tommy could see us through the window. "Regardless, it was disrespectful."

Rafe and his respect and honor and chivalry. I put my hand on the knob to leave when he suddenly reached out for me. He tugged at my wrist, pulling me close against him. My blood heated and raced as he put his hands on the side of my face, like he was afraid I might pull away. But the look in his eyes did the trick. I couldn't have moved even if I wanted to.

Then he kissed me. And there was nothing gentle or tender about it. It was all heat and desire and want. The passion shut down my ability to think, leaving me with only the ability to respond.

And oh boy, did I respond.

Chapter 8

I had to stop this. I couldn't let Rafe just kiss me whenever he wanted. I was in control, right?

One of his hands moved to the back of my head, his fingers kneading my scalp. I fell toward him, my knees giving out. He held me up with his other arm around my waist. I had been fooling myself. I had zero control. That whole I-am-the-boss-of-myself philosophy didn't seem to be working too well. Instead I curled my fingers into his sweater, holding on like I was falling off the side of a mountain.

This. I remembered this. I'd missed it. The blazing wildfire, the overwhelming sensations, how everything else stopped and we were the only two people in the entire world. That kissing him felt like the only thing that mattered and how I wanted it to go on forever.

Just when it got really interesting, he broke off the kiss. My chest was heaving as short little breaths compressed my lungs much too quickly. I leaned against the wall for support.

He seemed totally fine. "Have a good evening."

Then he walked out of the room, like he hadn't just laid the greatest kiss on me since Ryan Gosling and Rachel McAdams in the rain in *The Notebook*.

Dazed, I walked outside. Tommy Davis sat in his truck waiting. He waved and smiled at me, which let me know he hadn't seen the glandular combat I had just engaged in. He did lean over and open the door from the inside, which I supposed was something.

I climbed up, closing the door behind me, and buckled my seatbelt. My lips still tingled, the skin around my mouth sensitive from where Rafe's scruff had rubbed against it. I still hadn't gotten my breathing back to normal. I could smell Rafe's cologne on my skin. I wondered if Tommy Davis could, too. I touched my fingers to my lips, because I couldn't believe that had really just happened.

Tommy Davis was talking, and it sounded really far away. Like I was standing in a tunnel and he was at the opposite end. I closed my eyes, exhaled a deep breath, and forced myself to pay attention. "I'm sorry, what?"

He didn't seem to notice my Rafe-induced temporary insanity. "I said, where to?"

"Where to?" I repeated.

"Yeah. Where did you want to go?"

"Oh." He'd asked me out. I had at least expected him to plan something. Not that I had dated a ton, but I'd gone out on enough dates to know that the person who asked was in charge of that part.

We were extremely limited on options. There wasn't much to do here—going to the diner was about it. All the outdoor choices like the lake or hiking were out of the question given the weather. Iowa City had much more variety, but that was an hour away, and I didn't like to be that far from Aunt Sylvia without letting her know first. Not to mention that it might be expensive. I didn't know what Tommy's financial situation was, but I guessed that if he'd wanted to drive into the city he would have already decided on it.

"I don't have a preference. Whatever is fine with me." I was glad I hadn't dressed up more.

"Want to hang at my place?" I knew he lived in an apartment in the center of town.

"S-sure," I said. I didn't know if that meant something more, but I had to hope it didn't. That he really did just want to hang out. Because I hadn't ever been inducted into that particular club, and I didn't know what all the code words were for various activities.

"Hey, I heard this really cool song today. Want to hear it?"

I nodded, rubbing my arms. I had left without a coat. He didn't seem to notice, and then the sound of metal filled the cab of his car, making me wince. It didn't sound much like music—more like multiple cats being tortured by electric guitars. "Isn't this awesome?" he yelled over the sound.

Trying to smile, I nodded back. I was already miserable, and I blamed Rafe. First, for kissing and confusing me. Then for being a much better date than Tommy. Whenever we'd gone out, he always planned something amazing. Not that we hadn't had our quiet nights in, watching movies or playing video games, but he always thought of me and what I might like. And when he took me out, he took me out. On real actual dates. Like the kind you read about or used to see on old television shows.

But that was during a dating reality show, which made it unfair. Rafe had had unlimited resources and a staff. Tommy Davis didn't. I decided to try to make the best of this and give him a chance, and not think about how Rafe had spoiled me.

Unfortunately, things did not get better from there. Mistaking my fake smile for enthusiasm, Tommy Davis took me into his apartment to show me his "music" collection. He played song after song very loudly, yelling to make himself heard as he explained songs and what he liked about them.

He had a very old couch, a coffee table made out of cinder blocks, and an actual beanbag, along with expensive visual and audio electronics. He had graduated a while ago, and it wasn't like he had just gotten divorced. That was years ago. Maybe he didn't care about how his apartment looked. Some guys didn't. Technically, I was still in college, but apparently I didn't want to date guys who decorated their homes like they lived in a frat house. I didn't care if he was poor. I was poor. But our home didn't look like a flea market had thrown up in it.

He offered me a beer, but I declined. So our date consisted of me sitting on his couch while he played records and drank.

Yes, it was just as thrilling as it sounded.

Things were not going to get better unless I did something about it. "Hey!" I shouted, right as one of his songs ended. Modulating my voice back to normal level, I said, "Maybe we could just talk."

Tommy, who at some point had lost the right to the "Davis" part of his name, stood up and then came to sit next to me on the couch. He put his arm along the back. He had on a smarmy smirk. "I like talking."

He said "talking" like it was in quotes. Code word?

"I don't even know what you do," I responded, as his fingers reached out to play with the ends of my hair. Would it be totally obvious if I scooted back out of his reach?

"I'm sort of in between things right now. I have my alimony checks."

Wait, he lived off of alimony checks from Brooke? Maybe I'd misheard. I wasn't sure I could respect someone who was physically able to support himself and chose not to. "Brooke pays you alimony?"

He moved closer to me. "Yeah. But don't worry about her. She's past tense."

My throat was starting to close up. I hoped he didn't see me trying to move away from him. "As in you two have a past and now it's tense?"

My attempt at humor fell flat. "No," he said. "It means we're not together anymore, so you don't have to worry about her."

I wasn't at all worried about Brooke right then. I was, however, more than a little worried about myself.

"Maybe we could watch a movie?" I suggested, still backing away while he kept advancing.

"Or maybe we could move this into my bedroom," Tommy said. Acid burned at the back of my throat as I hit the arm of the couch. Limbs shaking, I stood up and moved myself to the opposite side of the room. How had I ever thought he was cute? Or imagined that I was attracted to him? Right now he just disgusted me.

I was about to tell him that he needed to drive me home when there was a hard knocking at the door. Tommy answered it, and my entire body sagged in relief when I saw Rafe over his shoulder.

Tommy straightened up, but he was nowhere near as tall or as imposing as Rafe. Maybe Nicole's theory did have some merit. "Can I help you with something?"

Rafe didn't even look at him and pushed into the room, walking toward me. "Hey!" Tommy called after him.

Handing me my purse, Rafe said, "You left this at home. Your phone's been ringing nonstop. Dr. Pavich needs your help at the Montgomery ranch. They have a mare about to give birth, and he's busy with another delivery."

His kisses had so addled my brain that I'd left my purse behind. Along with my phone and my keys. I had come out tonight totally unprotected, and that disturbed me more than I would have cared to admit. I took my purse, checking the contents. My phone had several missed calls and texts from Dr. Pavich.

"I'll let you say good night, and I'll be waiting outside to drive you to the ranch." Normally I might have protested about him driving me, but I was so thankful for his interruption that I didn't care. He could have informed me he was going to throw me over his shoulder and walk all the way to the Montgomery place, and I probably would have been okay with that too.

Rafe showing up reminded me of the time on *Marry Me* when another contestant, Abigail, had crashed one of my dates with Rafe. He had been very nice to her and tried to put her off, while she went on and on about how they belonged together and that all of America was rooting for them. I'd been so impressed by how much of a gentleman he was, though I had wanted to maim Abigail for attempting to sabotage our date.

If Tommy felt the same way right now about Rafe, I didn't care. There was a foal that needed me, and I was glad for the excuse to get away from Tommy.

Rafe let himself out without saying a single word to Tommy. I followed behind him, but Tommy grabbed my shoulder as I walked outside. "Hey, weren't you even going to say good night?"

I was being terribly rude. Rafe walked down the steps and headed for the street. I should have apologized to Tommy for having to leave early, or thanked him for the date. If I did either one of those things, though, I would be lying. I didn't feel sorry or thankful. Just glad I'd be able to get away. "You're right. Good night, Tommy."

But before I could finish my sentence, his cold, wet fish lips were on mine. I immediately reared back, putting distance between us. I came this close to slapping him. The kiss had felt wrong and gross. Like he had been trying to eat my mouth. "I'll call you," he said.

Please don't, was my unspoken reply.

As I went down the stairs, I wiped my mouth off with the back of my hand. It felt wrong to leave any remnants of Tommy's disaster there after the artistry of Rafe's kisses.

Kiss felt like such an inadequate word. Rafe hadn't just kissed me. He had . . . ravished my mouth. Like some kind of invading Viking horde bent on total domination.

And it had been fantastic.

He stood by the passenger door of his SUV. He held it open for me when I approached, and closed it shut after I'd gotten inside. Not because I couldn't do it myself, but because his mother had raised him to be polite.

He got in and started the car, adjusting the heater and showing me where the seat warmer controls were for my seat. "Do you need my coat?" he asked. He was in the process of removing it, but I held a hand up. "I'm fine. Thanks." His SUV had heated up so quickly it wasn't necessary.

I asked him if he needed directions, but he showed me his GPS. He pulled out onto the road, and we sat in silence for a few minutes before he said, "How did your date end? Because it sounded like—"

"Like it wasn't your business?" I could only imagine how the end of that nightmare might have sounded to him. At least he seemed like himself again. Calm, levelheaded. He was back to being my Rafe. Which made me feel the way I used to feel when we were together. Like we were missing pieces of a matched set. And that left me torn between wanting to thank him for rescuing me, admonishing him for interfering, and throwing myself at him with reckless abandon.

"You're right. It's not my business." I saw his jaw clench. "And I need to apologize for my behavior earlier."

My heart skipped so many beats I worried for my health. His kisses were behavior problems now?

"I didn't mean to seem angry. I'm not mad. I'm just frustrated."

Were we thinking of the same thing? I probably should have responded, but I didn't. What could I say? That some part of me was glad he'd gone all Neanderthal? I shouldn't be encouraging him if I didn't see this going anywhere. I wanted to forgive, but I wasn't sure I was capable of forgetting.

"I get it," I finally said. I was frustrated too, but for other reasons.

He glanced at me. "I shouldn't have kissed you either."

That sent a jolt straight through me, putting me into one of those thought-free stupors. My gaze was drawn to his lips. "Oh."

"That was about frustration of a different kind. I won't do that again."

Masterful wordsmith that I was, I said, "Oh" again. I waited for those twin and disparate feelings of gladness and disappointment, but was surprised to discover that I only felt disappointment. I wasn't going to think about what that meant.

"Not unless you ask me to." He was teasing, but because of his seductive tone I was too busy imagining how I could get him to kiss me without seeming like I had given in. Mistletoe? A bet? A dare?

What was wrong with me? He had reduced me to my sixteen-year-old self. And she was more than a little boy crazy and would have put out a hit on me for not wanting to start things back up with him.

She had terrible judgment, though. She was the one excited to go out with Tommy.

I had to redirect my thoughts and feelings to safer territory. "You could have just called Tommy to let me know what was going on. Aunt Sylvia could have tracked down his number."

"I could have," he agreed. But he didn't say anything else.

He left me to wonder what that meant while we pulled into the long driveway of the Montgomery ranch. If this were some romantic comedy, I'd be scheming ways to chase him off, but I was currently too busy and too conflicted. I would have to tolerate the situation until I didn't have to tolerate it anymore.

Because at some point he had to get tired of just waiting around, didn't he?

I directed him to the right barn, and he came to a stop. "I'll get a ride home," I told him as I hopped out. "Thanks for bringing me."

I was met by Zeke, the lead wrangler at the ranch. He was in charge of handling the horses. Dr. Pavich was watching two other mares who were foaling, so he wanted me to keep an eye on Autumn Rain. Adrenaline pulsed through me as we entered the barn. Usually I was just assisting. Tonight I would be on my own.

Dr. Pavich had left me supplies to help with the birth. I wasn't really dressed for it, but I could wash off whatever gross liquids ended up all over me. Autumn Rain was pacing back and forth, clearly in the early stages of labor. I held out my hand to her, talking gently. I let myself into the stall because no one had bothered to bandage up her tail. That could cause an infection for the foal if it came into contact with it.

I shouldn't have been surprised when Rafe walked up and stood outside the stall. He watched as I finished binding the tail. I felt the horse's stomach, and she snorted and shied sideways. I pulled my hand away and continued talking to her softly, letting myself back out of the stall.

In the best-case scenario, she would take care of this all by herself. My job was to watch and wait. Just in case.

"You don't have to stay," I told him.

"I know I don't. I want to. I've never seen a horse being born."

"It might take a while," I warned him. "I mean, she is waxing, but even then . . ."

"Waxing?"

There was no comfortable way to say this, so I just didn't look him in the face. "When mares are close to delivering, they start to wax, or make secretions out of their teats."

Autumn Rain ate some hay and continued her pacing. "Is she okay in that stall?"

"Normally we'd let her foal out in the field, but with it being winter, that wouldn't be safe for either one of them. In here they have security cameras, and they can monitor her and tell when it's time. She and her foal are too valuable to be left alone." I crossed my arms over the stall door, and Rafe did the same.

"What could go wrong?"

"A million things. The foal could be too big. It could be breech. It could have one foot turned back. Get stuck in the birth canal. The sac could rupture. She could hemorrhage." I tried not to think about each and every terrible way this could go wrong, and how Dr. Pavich was relying on me to make it go right. It felt like a lot of responsibility.

Her pacing stopped, and she started switching from getting down on the ground to standing back up. She repeated the process until she got down one last time and, finally, her water sac appeared. Amber-colored liquid started to stream out.

"It's time!" I said, excited and joyful to watch as another living creature came into the world.

She seemed to have a pretty easy labor. It wasn't her first foal, and she reacted better than a newer mom might have. Not much longer after the labor started, the foal was out.

"He's here!" I said, jumping up and down while tugging on Rafe's arm. It might not be a he. I couldn't tell yet. Rafe gave me a huge smile, and I couldn't help but respond. Some piece of me was glad I'd shared this moment with him.

"Now what?" he asked.

"Now he'll break the sac, stand up, nurse, and be fine." We watched as the foal struggled on the ground.

"Come on, come on," I urged. But it was no good. He wasn't breaking the sac.

The foal couldn't breathe. He was going to suffocate.

Chapter 9

"Crap!" I said, rummaging through the kit to find a knife. The adrenaline was back as I pulled the stall door open.

Rafe started to follow me, but I told him to stay put. I didn't need Autumn Rain getting upset. I took the knife and carefully cut open the amnion over the foal's nose, praying I wouldn't slip and accidently nick him. I widened the hole to get his nostrils clear of the sac. Definitely not breathing.

"I need the suction bulb. It's the thing with a bulb on the bottom and a tube at the top." Dr. Pavich probably had a more technical and precise version with him, but I would make do with what I had. Rafe quickly found it and brought it to me. He stayed in the stall with me, too, but I was too busy to worry about him.

After I sucked out the mucus from the foal's nose, I held him upside down to get the fluid out of his lungs. It rushed out, and I put him in my lap. "Come on, baby," I urged. "Breathe!"

I slapped his ribcage, and as I was mentally running through a checklist of what I could do next, the foal took in a big, raspy breath. I laughed with relief and put him down on the ground next to his mother. Rafe and I left the stall. Both mare and foal lay there, exhausted by what they had just been through. The foal started to weakly kick at the sac, trying to get the rest of it off.

"Should you do something else?" Rafe asked as I closed the door.

"More waiting. They need to recuperate like this, because he's still getting blood from the placenta. When she stands up, the cord will break."

Ten minutes passed in silence while we waited. Finally, Autumn Rain began to clean the foal, and I did another internal cheer. The licking not only cleaned him, but stimulated the baby's senses and would help bond them together. There had been a possibility that she might have rejected the foal, but her cleaning him meant that wouldn't happen.

It could take several hours before the foal would stand up and start nursing. I slumped to the ground, all of the energy dissipating from me. Fear, followed by exhilaration and relief, had taken its toll on me physically.

Rafe sat down next to me. "That was . . ."

I was too tired to turn my head. "What?"

"I always knew you were incredible. You are generous, kind, smart, funny, such a hard worker. Everything about you is amazing. But I didn't comprehend how amazing until this very moment."

His words sent a light, bouncy feeling through me, fluttering in my heart and my stomach with glittery sparkles. Without thinking, I reached for his hand. He grasped my hand in return, our fingers intertwined, his warmth seeping into mine.

It was what you would call "a moment." And from the way he was studying my lips, it was about to turn into a whole different kind of moment, and all this euphoria I was feeling told me that was a super idea.

I bit my lower lip in anticipation, and he sucked in a breath sharply, his eyes dark and fierce. My nerves went taut, like my skin had been pulled too tight. He pulled me close, hugging me against him. Some part of my brain thought, *A hug? Really?* But it was so nice to be held after everything I'd just gone through. That physical contact made me relax, and it made me feel better. Even lighter and happier.

He makes me feel safe.

His arms went slack, and I pulled back slightly. He'd said he wouldn't kiss me.

But I wanted him to.

My body was totally intent on sabotaging my brain and my heart. I thought I'd had enough time to get over it, to move past this attraction, but it turned out I was wrong. Before I could do anything to ratchet up my current stupidity, we were interrupted by Dr. Pavich and Chuck Montgomery. I got to my feet quickly, as did Rafe. I brushed the dirt off of my jeans while I told the vet what had happened and what I'd done. Both men looked in on the foal.

"Do you have a name?" I asked, trying to ignore Rafe and the way he'd just made me feel.

"Summer Breeze," Mr. Montgomery said, behaving like a proud father.

"You go on with your boyfriend and get back home," Dr. Pavich said. I started to protest that Rafe wasn't my boyfriend, but he continued. "I'll take over from here and finish up with everything."

"If something goes wrong, you'll text me?"

"I will," he promised. "But I don't think I'll have to. You did a great job."

Leaving behind the supplies, I followed Rafe back to the car. I focused on putting one foot in front of the other. A heaviness settled on top of my chest. A lot had happened today, and I was feeling wiped out. He opened the door for me again, and I got in. When he entered on his side, I suddenly started to cry.

"What's wrong?" he asked, his concern evident.

"This is so dumb. I don't even know why I'm crying," I said, wiping the tears from my cheeks.

"That was a very emotional experience," he offered.

I nodded, not trusting myself to speak.

"Did it make you think about Marigold?" He seemed to have a sixth sense where I was concerned. He knew what I was feeling when I felt it, and why. I used to love that deeper connection we had, but now it made staying upset with him really difficult.

Other than my best friend and Aunt Sylvia, Rafe was the only person who knew about my horse and what it had cost me to lose her.

It had been the first big group date on *Marry Me*. After our first meeting, I had been outside running laps around the backyard, since we weren't allowed to leave the grounds. Rafe had been out there too, and when he saw me, he joined me. We had another fantastic conversation, and I told him all about my farm and how I wanted to be a veterinarian. He told me how he wanted to design software and applications, and again asked me not to tell anyone. It should have been a red flag, but he was too cute and too fun and that was all I could think about.

When we arrived at the horse ranch, I was beside myself with excitement. It had been so long since I had last gone riding. Lemon and I were the only ones who knew what we were doing, and I spent a lot of time helping the professionals keep the girls in a group. The horses could tell that their riders were clueless, and a lot of them just did what they wanted.

I chased after Emily, whose horse had gone pretty far off course toward a small creek. When I reached her and grabbed for the reins, I saw that Emily had her eyes squeezed shut and her fingers knotted in the horse's mane. I spoke gently to both of them and showed Emily how to make the horse do what she wanted. It seemed to help, and when a ranch hand came by to gather her up, she gave me a grateful smile as she followed behind him.

My horse, a little black-and-white Arabian named Dolly, took an interest in the creek and lapped at the water.

Rafe emerged from the trees on top of a blue roan stallion, looking like he'd spent his entire life riding. There was no hesitation or discomfort, and he had total control over his horse. It surprised me because I would have pegged him for a city boy.

"That was kind of you," he said, pulling up alongside me. Dolly sidestepped, intimidated by the bigger horse. I let her go where she wanted, patting her on the neck.

"Purely selfish, actually."

He raised his eyebrow at me, confused.

I let out a laugh. "I wouldn't have been able to sleep tonight if she'd broken her neck because I hadn't helped her."

He smiled back at me, a slow, lazy smile that gave me goosebumps. It reminded me of the sun slowly emerging from behind rain clouds. "May I show you something?"

"Sure." I followed behind him, and the horses trotted along, happy to be out in an open meadow. Dolly strained against the bit, acting like she wanted to break into a gallop. She was probably feeling competitive with the stallion. But because I didn't know how far we were going, we stayed at a trot so that she wouldn't tire out too soon.

I had noticed something earlier while running with Rafe—he didn't feel the need to fill up silence. And in every other date-like situation I'd been in, when things got quiet, I would talk and talk. It tended to make things more awkward, but I couldn't help it. I always thought that I was boring the other person and that we'd never go out again unless I could singlehandedly keep the conversation going.

But I didn't feel that way with Rafe. When I was with him, the silence was comfortable. Like he was just happy to be there with me, and we didn't need to say anything.

We approached a small grove of trees, and after we guided the horses through it, I saw that we were on top of a cliff with a perfect view of the ocean. Rafe got down, loosely tying his horse to a tree to keep him from wandering off.

He came over to help me dismount, and I wavered between letting him and showing him that I was totally capable of getting off of a horse on my own. Deciding it would be silly to waste the opportunity, I threw my leg over and put my hands on his shoulders. He put his hands around my waist, and I noticed for the first time how big his hands were. He lifted and I jumped down. He could have taken total advantage of that situation, but he was respectful. Which I both admired and regretted, just a little.

Walking toward the edge, I shielded my eyes to see more clearly. The sun was directly overhead, and it made the water sparkle and glimmer. A soft breeze blew, making the leaves in the tree behind us rustle. The light blue sky seemed to stretch on for miles. It was the first time since coming to California that I hadn't had to look directly up to see the sky. I took a deep breath in and thought I could just barely make out the briny smell of the sea.

We stood together quietly, enjoying the spectacular view.

"Thank you for this. I love riding and I love this scenery," I said. The scenery also included him, with the wind tousling his black hair, the sunlight kissing his sculpted features like even the sun itself adored him. It was the first time since arriving here that I felt calm and like myself again.

"Why don't you ride anymore?"

A lump formed in my throat, and the tears that welled at the corners of my eyes surprised me. She'd been gone for a couple of years, and I thought I could talk about it without turning into a sprinkler. "I had a horse. Marigold. I helped deliver her on my farm right after I came to live there with my aunt. Her mom died from complications from the birth, and I sort of took her spot. I adored Marigold, and she used to follow me around. I probably spoiled her." I let out a little laugh, not letting the tears leak. "Anyway, things went really bad really quickly financially, and we couldn't keep her. Horses are expensive to feed. She was the last one we sold, and it was one of the hardest things that has ever happened to me. I still think about her and miss her all the time. I hope she's okay."

"I'm sorry."

"Me too," I said, trying not to choke on the words, smiling even though I wanted to cry.

He put his arm around my shoulders, his thumb rubbing against the top of my arm. I leaned into the comfort he offered, grateful for his strength and warmth that somehow made me feel better.

Standing so close, with his side pressed against mine, was more than my little pulse could take. It sent out a frantic Morse code to the rest of my body, which responded by directing my arms to wrap around his waist.

Without warning, he turned me toward him so that we were facing each other.

The wind blew my hair into my face, and he reached up to brush it away before I could, tucking it behind my ear. Then he studied me, taking me in. He was going to kiss me. But he was giving me the chance to stop him or walk away.

I had no intention of going anywhere. I'd wanted him to kiss me ever since he'd rescued me from that fence.

His hand went to the side of my face, and he moved in so unhurriedly. Part of me was impatient, but the other part enjoyed the anticipation, the waiting to see what it would be like when our lips finally touched. Like I was standing at the precipice of something, realizing everything was about to change. I breathed in that expensive and yummy cologne he wore, the one that made me a bit dizzy. My heartbeat thudded low and slow, although I imagined it wouldn't stay that way. My breath caught at his expression, at the fire and promise in his eyes.

Then he kissed me.

To say it was an overwhelming, life-changing kind of experience would have been an understatement. It was more like I finally understood why Sleeping Beauty woke up. It was because she got kissed like this.

He kissed me softly, our lips barely even brushing together. Tentatively, like he was trying it out to see what he thought. His peppermint-flavored breath washed over my face in between his exploration. Little ripples of delight pulsed through me while he tightened his embrace, and I melted under the light caresses of his mouth.

When I let out a sigh of pleasure, something changed in him. The scale tipped from sweet and innocent to *holy caliente*. There was nothing tentative or soft about what he did then, the powerful way he captured my lips. My nerves had turned into a minefield, setting off a series of detonations everywhere he put pressure. Like I had a gallon of Pop Rocks bathed in cola exploding inside me.

His mouth was warm and perfect and delicious and made me totally unbalanced. Like I was on a boat in the middle of a raging storm and couldn't get my balance. Everything spun and roiled out of control.

My pulse beat so hard that it seemed to be everywhere, including inside my ears. It was all I could hear, and the pressure of his amazing kiss was all I could feel.

I realized that in the past I had only ever kissed boys. It was a completely different experience kissing a man.

A man who held me so close it was like we were the same person. A man who was doing funny things to my insides, while making little bumps pop up all over my skin.

Kissing him like this, so intently and blissfully, reminded me of riding at a full, hard gallop. There was that same wonderful feeling of flying and freedom with a hint of something more, just out of reach.

His arms were around me so tightly I could barely breathe, his hands moving and stroking as he deepened the kiss. I had my arms around his neck, and I couldn't concentrate on anything except all the amazing sensations I was experiencing. It was like I had been made to kiss him, to be held by him. Like I had wandered the planet for two decades not knowing exactly why I was here, and in that moment, I was convinced it was to be with him.

My lungs had started to burn from a lack of oxygen, but I didn't care. If it was my time to go, this was exactly how I would choose to spend my last moments on earth.

He had broken it off suddenly, his gaze drawn toward the trees. His chest heaved, his heartbeat strong and fast against my palm. I was breathing so hard I could have blown a house down. As my senses returned to me, I realized that the horses had been neighing, disturbed by something. And just past them I could make out a camera crew.

I knew my cheeks must have been cherry red, but my skin was so flushed that I wasn't sure anyone would be able to tell. I put my hand to my mouth as it fell open. I didn't know if my thundering heartbeat was because of what I had just experienced, or the shock of discovering that they had recorded our first kiss. Rafe's posture had gone rigid, and he stepped in front of me so that the crew couldn't film me.

"We should go," he murmured against my skin, making me sigh again.

We walked back to the horses, hand in hand. I even let him help me get back up in the saddle. Everything was different now. Everything had changed. Surely he couldn't be going around kissing everyone like that.

It was special.

We were special.

And this was real.

As I remembered our first kiss, I was glad that I hadn't known then how things would turn out. How he would lie to me and use me. How an intimate and personal moment had been captured and shown to the whole world, but none of it had been special or real. It hurt me now to think about it, but I hoped that someday I would be able to look back and remember that moment, that perfection and chemistry between us, with a smile instead of sadness.

"I'm okay," I told him, smiling as best I could so he would just take me home. He hesitated, but then he started up the car.

This should be my lesson learned for not staying home and doing homework. And for taking Nicole's advice. Look where it landed me.

He pulled his SUV to the very end of the driveway, halfway between his guesthouse and my kitchen. As the dome light turned on, it was then that I realized we were both covered in horse blood and other birth-related liquids. I didn't want to do it, but I didn't have a choice since it was my fault he had stuff on him. "You should probably come inside so we get can cleaned up."

As I crunched through the snow, I cursed myself for wearing flats that the cold could slip inside. Now my toes were freezing. At the top of the porch, I tried to shake off as much moisture as I could.

"Do you ever dress appropriately for the weather?" Rafe asked, looking at my shoes.

"It changes so often you never know what you're going to need." I didn't deliberately dress inappropriately, I just wore what I wanted. Okay, maybe he was a little bit right. But wasn't it my prerogative to dress the way I wanted to?

He came into the kitchen behind me, and I grabbed some dishtowels to clean up the water from the floor. I tossed them into the dryer.

Originally, our washer and dryer had been in the basement, but when I moved here Aunt Sylvia had put them upstairs because I was too terrified to go down there. It was an old basement, windowless, dark, damp, and musty. It was like entering a tomb.

I stood at the sink, washing what I could from my skin, scrubbing with the industrial-type soap I kept in here for this purpose. I knew he was watching me, because my skin tingled from the attention. "Here, go ahead," I said when I had finished.

While I dried my hands, I tried not to watch him, the way his forearms moved under the water and soap, how his corded muscles flexed in a way that made me a little light-headed. In this brighter light, it was easier to see all the stains on his shirt.

"You should probably let me wash that for you," I said. He didn't have a washing machine at the guesthouse, and if it didn't get cleaned soon, it would probably set.

"Okay," he said. Before I could comprehend what was happening, he took off his coat and then did that sexy thing guys did when they took off their shirts—he grabbed it behind his neck and pulled it forward, handing it to me.

Leaving him very shirtless and me very tempted. My eyes widened as my mouth turned into an O shape.

I think a full minute passed while I devoured him with my eyes before I realized what I was doing. My skin was prickly and hot. He was painfully beautiful, but extremely aggravating. I pressed a hand against my cheek.

"I didn't mean right now," I finally said.

"Didn't you?" he said in a silky tone, and I almost gasped in outrage. "I wouldn't blame you for it. You know you can't fight the moonlight."

My outrage multiplied. That was my mom's saying, not his. And certainly not ours. "It's a crescent moon," I retorted. I barely refrained from sticking out my tongue at him and adding, "So there."

You are not a child, I reminded myself. And he . . . he most definitely was not a child, either.

"Good night," he said with a knowing smile, walking out the back door. He didn't shut it, and he let the screen door slam behind him.

So infuriating. He deserved to freeze on the way back after that little stunt.

And after all I'd put up with tonight, I deserved to watch him go.

Chapter 10

The next day was Sunday, and after he'd finished his morning run, Rafe insisted on driving us to church. Aunt Sylvia accepted on my behalf. Which I was not okay with, but there was nothing I could do.

He was wearing a very expensive suit that made him look like he'd just walked out of a James Bond movie, and he was clean-shaven again. It made me sentimental and wistful, so I forced myself to pay attention to the sermon instead. My immortal soul probably needed it.

Especially since my mortal body was interested in breaking some commandments with Rafe. It was like every molecule in my body wanted to gravitate over to him. Like he was some black hole and I was incapable of resisting.

After church ended, Whitney found me and grabbed me with her free hand. She held Gracie with the other. "You didn't call."

"Call?"

She rolled her eyes so hard I was surprised she didn't see her own brain. "About your date with Tommy Davis. What happened?"

Tommy had become such a minor player in last night's craziness that I had actually forgotten about him. I glanced over at Rafe, who clearly stood within earshot. He had offered Aunt Sylvia his arm and was helping her to his car. I took Gracie from Whitney, perching her on my hip. It made me nervous when she forgot and held the kids this far along in her pregnancy, and I wanted to wait until Prince Misleading was gone. "Remember how much I wanted to go out with Tommy in high school?"

"Definitely."

"That's what happened last night. I went out with Tommy from high school. Or the college version of him. It was unfortunate. And it made me sympathetic toward Brooke, which is the worst."

"Did he kiss you?"

"He did, and it was gross. And it didn't help that I had Rafe's to compare it to."

"What!" she gasped. "What do you mean? Did Rafe kiss you, too?"

"Before the date." Gracie was sucking on her thumb, and she laid her head on my shoulder. It was close to her naptime. My pulse felt a little frantic just thinking about the kiss.

"Obviously. He had to mark his territory. Or he wanted you to be thinking about him the entire night and not Tommy."

"It doesn't matter what his reasons were. And he's not going to do it again."

She looked so crestfallen. "That sucks."

"Not unless I ask him to."

She perked right back up. "Excellent. So now we just have to—"

Pastor Dave interrupted us, asking to speak with me. I put Gracie down, and she toddled off with her mom. He and I discussed the upcoming church bazaar meeting. We were closing in on the date of the bazaar and needed to finalize the details. I asked if I could pass out a sign-up sheet next week to the congregation for some of the food assignments. He agreed to let me do so.

By the time we finished talking, the church had emptied out. My eyebrows knit together as I tried to figure out where Aunt Sylvia had gone. Maybe she was out in the car with Rafe? They wouldn't have left me behind.

I put on my coat and opened the front door. Rafe stood outside, his car running. I didn't see Aunt Sylvia in the front seat. He opened the door for me like he was my own personal chauffeur. But as he closed the door behind me, I realized my aunt wasn't in the backseat either.

"Where is Sylvia?" I asked as soon as he joined me.

He started the car and signaled with his blinker, checking his mirrors before leaving the parking lot. "She got a ride home with Amanda."

I let out a huff of disgust, folding my arms as I leaned back in my seat. Did she really think her matchmaking schemes were going to work? She knew what he'd done. She was the only one who really understood how deep his betrayal had gone.

"Will we have time for a cooking lesson today?"

Ugh. I'd forgotten about that. "I'm going over to Whitney's after I go home and get changed." There was no need to mention that I hadn't actually been invited. She'd understand, and she'd want more details about the thing we were calling a "date" with Tommy.

"How about after that?" He drummed his fingers against the steering wheel while he talked, and I tried really hard not to think about how much I loved it when he ran those same fingers through my hair.

My mind scrambled to find reasons. Truthful ones. I wouldn't lie. "I have homework. *WoW* stuff. Lists to make up for the church bazaar—"

"I get it. You're busy. Maybe tomorrow?"

"School, more homework, the diner, another talent show rehearsal I promised I'd be at."

"Well, at least I'll see you there."

Of course he would. He was everywhere. He was just smashing through all these walls I'd put up, pushing his way in.

Apparently not noticing my scowl, he said, "I hope you enjoy your time with Whitney. Do you plan on giving her *all* the details from last night?" So he had overheard us. But no matter what I said, he would read too much into it. If I said I'd told her all about how he had rescued me and helped me with foaling Summer Breeze, he'd be smug. If I insisted, truthfully, that he hadn't come up, he'd probably think I was lying.

Even though I was not the one in the car whose pants were usually on fire. I was pretty sure he was still keeping stuff from me. I decided to just ask. "How did you find me last night?"

I hadn't had my phone with me. Tommy didn't even know what we were going to do, so it's not like I had told Rafe where we would be. I narrowed my eyes and gritted my teeth together. Had he followed us, taking this stalker thing to a whole new level?

He tugged at the collar of his shirt with one finger. "Marco knew."

Marco? How in the world did Marco know? Did he have Marco follow me? "How?"

"He's been keeping an eye on you." He swallowed a couple of times. He had to have known how angry that would make me, but he'd done it anyway.

I held my breath for several counts, letting it out slowly. "That stops right now," I said as calmly as I possibly could. I didn't feel calm, though. I had spent my entire childhood being watched. I had never had any privacy or time to myself. Ever. Once I'd gotten my freedom, I had no plans of giving it up again. I didn't need his protection. More accurately, his bodyguard's protection.

Sighing, I pressed a hand to my stomach. If I dug my heels in, so would he. I could be nice. You'd catch more flies with honey than with acid, anyway. "I'm not in danger. I don't need to be tracked or watched. Okay?"

So much time passed I thought he might not have heard me. "Okay," he finally said.

"You'll stop? Marco will stop?" I clarified.

"We'll stop." I could hear in his voice that it had cost him to agree. After I had found out about him being a prince, he admitted that he was a little obsessive about security when it came to the people he cared about. He didn't tell me why, and I had just accepted his statement at face value. Even though I was mad at him, I knew he still cared. Why else would he be here? Giving up his worldly, glamorous life to live in a house smaller than his family's jet?

Oddly, gratefulness welled up inside me and tugged at my nicer emotions. His hand was between our seats, and I had to fight the impulse to reach over and hold it again. I loved holding his hand. It was always toasty, soothing and exciting at the same time.

I put my hands under my legs to make them behave. I looked at the snowy, never-ending fields as we drove past. I pictured myself mentally building an igloo wall back up around my heart, brick by frozen brick.

And I saw an image of Rafe dismantling it just as quickly.

But I didn't need to worry about him destroying my defenses when I kept unlocking the gate and inviting him inside.

I somehow managed to make it all the way to my diner shift the next day without thinking about Rafe incessantly, but when I got to work I saw that the sunflowers were still blooming. Mocking me. Of course he would buy an expensive kind that would last forever so I couldn't forget.

It didn't help matters that Nicole stared at them and sighed every five minutes.

Then Whitney arrived, her face all aglow, and she actually hugged me. "What's that for?" I asked.

"For bringing that wonderful man into our lives!"

It was like somebody had transferred a new personality into her. I'd never seen her beam like that before. "Are you talking about Rafe?"

She sat down carefully on one of the barstools. "Yes! He's started a software company here in town, and he's hired all the people who lost their jobs to come work for him."

It did not compute. "What?"

"He even rented out the old pharmacy across the street for his offices." She pointed, and I saw the red brick building that hadn't been open in years. Christopher's parents owned the building, and they'd been losing money on it for a long time.

I put my fingers to my temples. "Wait, wait, wait. This doesn't even make sense. Nobody there knows anything about software. They made printer parts." Most of them hadn't even been to college.

"He's planning to hire some trainers and programmers to come out and teach them everything they need to know. Maybe even enroll them in classes at UI. He's going to pay them while they learn, and the benefits are incredible. It's not going to cost us anything out of pocket to have this baby. Everyone starts at the end of this week."

At that, Nicole's ears perked up. "Programmers? Aren't those usually men? Possibly single men?"

She and Whitney started to discuss the possibility of an entire new dating pool moving into town while I stood there in shock.

I wanted to ask her how. How had he done this? How had it all happened so fast? It didn't seem possible.

But I knew how. An insane amount of money and a staff in Monterra who probably had the whole thing wrapped up and ready to go with a shiny bow before breakfast this morning.

I realized that was what he wanted to talk to the town council about last week. Christopher had announced that the factory had closed at the end of that meeting.

And SuperRafe had come to the rescue.

That was what I got for trying to ignore him. He went and made the whole town fall in love with him.

Jobs with benefits. Renting out unused space. Potentially importing eligible men.

It was diabolical.

"Son of a . . ." I muttered under my breath. I didn't finish the sentence because I actually really liked Queen Aria.

Mr. Olafsson was outside of the old pharmacy—I mean, Rafe's new offices. He had owned a printing shop in town many years ago. Rafe came out to shake hands with him. They chatted for a few minutes, and Mr. Olafsson showed him a big banner that read, "Royal Productions." Rafe went in and came back out with a ladder, hanging the banner on the awning over the main door.

This made no logical sense. And if nothing else, Rafe was logical. How did he expect to start up a software company in Frog Hollow? And have it succeed?

Here I thought he was spending all his time playing video games and figuring out ways to win me over. No, he was masterminding a plan to end all plans.

It was like the more I wanted him to go away, the harder he tugged back on the bridle like some obstinate mule. He was putting down some roots here. I'd be in serious trouble if he bought a house.

But the main problem now was the devastation his leaving would cause this town.

Because he was going to leave. We were not getting back together. That was nonnegotiable.

"Sorry I'm late," I told Nicole, out of breath.

"No worries. Can you go check on the younger kids? I'm going to run lines with the older ones."

"Sure thing . . ." My voice trailed off when I saw Rafe again hard at work constructing a set. He was talking to a couple of the teen boys who were helping out, teaching them how to reinforce corners. Off to one side, a group of high school girls were watching his every movement, their heads swiveling in unison whenever he moved. Like a herd of crazy, starving cats watching a bird fall out of the sky.

"He's all broody like a vampire." Nicole sighed, her eyes widening when she realized she'd said it out loud and I'd heard her.

I couldn't be mad. I didn't own him. *And you know he'd never go after Nicole, so you don't have to be jealous,* an impish voice whispered. "You know that's not a good thing, right?"

"Speak for yourself. In my world, broody vampires are an excellent thing." She called her group over to start practicing, and the teen girls reluctantly tore themselves away. It was then that Rafe spotted me, giving me one of those smiles that made my blood blaze.

I wanted to ask him about his business plans and how they related to me. I wanted to understand why he had done it. But if I let him explain, it might be one less thing for me to be upset about. So instead I asked, "Where did you learn to build things?"

He looked down at the hammer still in his hand. "I worked for Habitat for Humanity in Eastern Europe the summer after Veronique died."

Veronique? Who was Veronique? I nearly asked him. I didn't have to, though. I could have looked it up online. But I wouldn't. What if I looked it up, and Veronique was related to this explanation he kept hinting at, and it changed how I felt?

Would that be such a bad thing?

Stupid voice. Yes! That would be a very bad thing. He had already destroyed my heart once. If I let him do it again, I wasn't sure I would recover. Rafe was dangerous. He was not the reliable, husbandly type. He was the international, hot, supermodel-esque, royal prince type. The kind of guy who probably had to spend a good twenty minutes every morning peeling off all the women who had thrown themselves at him.

I believed in forgiveness, and in theory I wanted to practice it, but I wasn't dumb enough to forget.

"Okay. Cool. I'm supposed to be over there." I pointed to where the elementary and middle school kids were working on props and routines for the talent show. A whisper of a smile played over his lips, and I knew he knew that I was trying to hide from him.

Exasperated, I walked over to the kid I knew and liked the best. Henry. He was eleven years old and reminded me of a young Harry Potter, with dark brown hair that was always sticking out in forty different directions and thick glasses that he could never keep up at the top of his nose. He wore a magician's hat and a cape.

You like that he looks like a young, Americanized Rafe. The voice was back. I told it to shut up and leave for the night. I was busy.

He stood in front of a large cabinet, which was all scraped up on one side. "What'cha up to, squirt?"

Henry pushed his glasses up the bridge of his nose. "Magic. I'm going to make somebody *disappear.*" He said "disappear" in a low, whispery voice. Like he would do real magic. "My grandpa gave me his old disappearing box. Will you help me?"

"Sure. What do you want me to do?"

"Get in the box."

My throat constricted, making it difficult to breathe. Dark circles appeared at the edge of my vision. "I don't know if I . . ."

"Please, Genesis."

I swallowed hard, trying to reopen my airway. If it had been anybody else, I would have refused and walked off. But I'd never been able to say no to Henry. I had been his babysitter since he was two years old. His parents had died in a car crash, and like me, he had been shipped off to Frog Hollow to live with his grandparents.

"Can you keep a secret?' He was adorably serious, which helped my panic abate a little.

I was the world's greatest at keeping secrets. "Yes."

"It's super easy. You step in, I close the box, and the secret is you pull the latch here." He used his magic wand to point it out, hidden in the top right corner. "The back will open, and then I'll open it up to show everyone that you disappeared."

He gave me the same face Laddie did when he wanted bacon. I was powerless to resist. It would be a few seconds. I could do it for a few seconds.

"Okay." I nodded, realizing that my lips had gone numb. "Okay."

I could do this. To help Henry. And maybe to prove to myself that confined spaces weren't as bad as I thought they were.

"Step in!" he directed, waving his arms widely. "Watch closely, everyone, as I make Genesis *disappear!*"

Bracing myself, I stepped into the box. "Don't go out the back until I say abracadabra," he whispered. I nodded, unable to speak. It was tolerable until he shut the door behind me. I clutched my hands together, closing my eyes as my stomach churned. I counted out loud. I'd give him until twenty, and then I was leaving no matter what he said.

I reached up to find the latch, keeping my fingers on it while I counted. My heart beat ridiculously fast as my dinner threatened to make a return visit.

"One, two, three," I counted as Henry went through his prepared speech. Sweat formed at my hairline, spilling down my forehead. It was stuffy. Why was it so stuffy?

"Abracadabra!" he called out loudly. Finally.

I pulled hard on the latch, but nothing happened. I pulled again, pushing at the back of the box. Still nothing.

My tongue swelled up in my mouth, making it so I couldn't breathe. My chest hurt and felt unbearably tight. I would not freak out and terrify Henry and half of the kids in the town. I would not get hysterical and start screaming.

Why had I agreed to this? I kept tugging at the latch, willing it to work. Praying that this time it would make the door spring open. Hot tears spilled down my cheeks, and I banged on the door as gently as I could manage. "I'm stuck, Henry."

There was a sound outside, as if Henry was trying to open the front of the cabinet. "I can't get it open."

The box shook as he tried his best, and I sat down on the floor, curling myself up into a ball. I rocked back and forth, trying to stave off a full-blown panic attack.

"Go get help," I told him in the calmest voice that I could manage. Pretty soon I wouldn't be able to think at all because I was about to suffocate and die.

"Okay," he replied, but suddenly the front of the box was flung open.

And there stood Rafe.

Chapter 11

Light, cold air, and relief flooded in as Rafe reached in to pick me up. I put my arms around his neck, resting my head on his shoulder as he carried me to the back of the auditorium. I should have protested, but I felt too weak.

He sat me down in one of the seats. He knelt in front of me, rubbing my arms up and down. "You're okay. Everything's okay. You're okay." He just kept repeating himself as my tears dried up and my breathing started to return to normal.

Henry approached, his eyes big. "Is Genesis all right?"

Rafe tried to turn his body to talk to Henry, but I realized he couldn't because I was gripping his sleeves too tightly for him to move. I attempted to relax my fingers. They weren't cooperating.

"She's fine," Rafe told him. "Can you do me a favor and go see if Miss Brady has a blanket we can use?"

I got a chance to collect myself before he returned. I even finally managed to let go of Rafe's sleeves. Rafe took the blanket and put it over me. "I'm okay." My voice sounded creaky. Fortunately, the only person who seemed to notice what had happened was Henry.

And Rafe.

"How did you know?"

Rafe cocked his head. "How did I know that when you stepped into a small, confined space things would go bad?" His voice had the slightest trace of sarcasm, which I probably deserved. He had been there the last time I freaked out like that, and he had been the one to comfort me.

That was also when I'd treated him like my own personal confessional and told him way more than I should have.

Henry kept pushing his glasses up, and I leaned in to whisper to Rafe. "I don't want him to be scared."

Nodding, Rafe stood up and went over to Henry, crouching down so they could be eye level. "I should have tested it first," Henry said.

I pulled the edges of the blanket tightly around me, the cocooning pressure making me feel safer, for some reason. I was starting to feel ridiculous. I knew I had totally overreacted. I wished I didn't have such horrible claustrophobia, and that I didn't get totally hysterical and irrational because of it.

"Now you know. Maybe I can help you with it. I bet together we can fix whatever's wrong with it," Rafe said.

Henry visibly brightened. "Okay!"

Rafe looked back at me, over his shoulder. "Although we should probably find you a different assistant. Genesis is going to be very busy that night."

"I didn't think of that. You're right." Henry screwed up his face, like he was concentrating. "I can find somebody else."

Watching Rafe talk to Henry and smooth over the situation, I could feel the ice around my heart starting to fracture. Little fissures were spreading all over the surface.

It didn't matter if he was nice or rescued me or was good with children or saved the town's economy.

What I had to remember and focus on were the lies.

Because the next time I let him in, those fissures would give way and I would fall in and drown.

We didn't talk about what had happened. I didn't want to relive it, and Rafe knew me well enough to back off. My days proceeded as normal—school, work, volunteering. Only he was there. All the time. At meals, driving Aunt Sylvia to doctor's appointments while I was out, clearing our porches and driveway when it snowed, building scenery, sitting at the diner surrounded by people who wanted to talk to him and thank him.

He had pretty much won everybody over.

Except for me.

He was always around, but he didn't try to have any serious conversations with me. That was the whole point of him coming to Iowa, wasn't it? To explain why he had done what he did? Part of me was morbidly curious, but the other part didn't want to think about his reasons or about him.

The second part was failing miserably.

Early Friday morning, there was a knock at my door. Which surprised me, because people didn't typically just show up. They usually called or texted first. Laddie ran to the door, barking gleefully. He kept jumping up toward the knob, like he wanted to open it himself.

And I couldn't have been more shocked to find Lemon and her best friend, Kat, standing on my porch.

I grabbed the knob tightly, my other hand flying to my chest. "Rafe's not here," I told them. What in the world did they want?

Laddie leapt against the screen door, paws up, tail wagging, tongue hanging out of his mouth.

"We know," Kat told me. She had dark hair and brown eyes and a smirk that indicated she'd enjoyed surprising me. She was a bit taller than me, while Lemon was a dainty little thing in ridiculous high-heeled boots. "Our bodyguards talked to his bodyguards and we timed our visit for while he's out running."

It didn't surprise me that his bodyguards could perfectly time him coming and going. Rafe's running routine was common knowledge in our town. His route had become like his own personal mini-parade route, whether or not he realized it. All the women in town lined up at their front windows to watch as he went by.

"I don't understand why you're here."

They exchanged glances, and it seemed like they could read each other's minds.

"I know you're angry with me," Lemon said in her Southern drawl, her bright blonde bob swinging as she talked. "But I need to talk to you. Can we come in?"

"She's not angry with me. Hey, how's it going," Kat said, opening the screen door. She patted Laddie on the head and then went by me, sitting on our couch. "I thought Monterra was cold. It is freezing here!"

"Sure?" I didn't mean for it come out as a question, but Lemon accepted it. I moved back, grabbing Laddie's collar so he wouldn't jump. She sat next to Kat on the sofa, both of them looking around the room.

Before I closed the door, I saw several men in sunglasses and black suits, wearing earpieces and walking through the yard. Gianni was with them. I closed the door slowly, trying to gather my thoughts.

After telling my dog to stay and behave, I sat in the armchair across from the couch, perched on the edge of the seat. Lemon put her expensive purse on the coffee table while Kat put up her feet. I was sitting across from two future princesses. They were engaged to Rafe's twin, Dante, and his oldest brother, Nico. That shouldn't have seemed like a big deal considering a prince was living in my guesthouse, but it felt different somehow.

"You have a lovely home," Lemon said, her back straight, legs crossed at the ankle.

Kat's eyebrows went up. "Yes! A lovely home. Sorry, I'm still working on this gracious etiquette thing."

"Thanks," I said. I watched as Laddie edged across the floor in a doggie army crawl toward the women. He caught me looking at him and stopped.

"Thank you for letting us in," Lemon said. She brushed some hair away from her eyes, taking in a deep breath. She rubbed her hands together in her lap. "I know you don't want to talk to me, and I deserve your anger. But I wanted to apologize for what I did. I thought Rafe was Dante, and when I saw the two of you kissing, well, I kind of lost it."

That was the understatement of the year. She had been like a hissing polecat, throwing things and calling Rafe names.

"I only thought about myself, and I'm so sorry. That's not how you treat a friend."

I knew she was sincere. Since she'd found out about the switch and had gotten engaged to Dante, she had reached out to me repeatedly. I didn't know how she'd gotten my email and my phone number. I'd guessed one of the producers from the show must have given them to her. Or she used the royal private investigator to track me down. I didn't know if they actually had one of those, but it wouldn't have surprised me.

I didn't read her texts, I didn't take her calls, and I didn't open her emails. The only way that I knew how to get through that dark time was to keep away from everything that would remind me of Rafe. When I made those appearances I didn't have a choice, but in my private life, I absolutely did.

Now I felt guilty as I saw the pain on Lemon's face. "I should have talked to you. It was just so awful and you were a reminder of him."

"I totally get that. You should have seen me after I left Nico," Kat interjected, talking about her fiancé. I must have looked confused. "We broke up and I left Monterra and went back to Colorado. I told him

I never wanted to see him again. I was like the living dead. I didn't let Lemon talk about him or his family, either."

Relieved that someone finally understood, I settled back into my chair. "I'm sorry I didn't call you back. At first I was too angry, then too hurt, and then I didn't know what to say."

Lemon moved over to the chair closest to mine, holding out her hand. I grabbed it and she squeezed. "Can you ever forgive me?"

"Of course. If you promise to forgive me too."

"Done." She stood up, pulling me along with her, and we hugged. It felt like a massive weight had been taken off of me. I didn't like that we hadn't spoken in six months. I was glad to have my friend back.

Laddie had taken advantage of my distraction and was lying on the floor in front of Kat. He was on his back, tongue lolling out while she rubbed his belly. It was his favorite thing ever.

Lemon went for her purse. "I brought you a bribe to sweeten the pot." She handed me a beautifully wrapped present with a bow so perfect I was afraid to open it.

"Just tear into it," Kat offered. "She always does that."

So I did. It was a picture frame. When I turned it over, I started to gasp and sputter.

"I think that means she likes it," Kat said with a wink to her best friend.

"You brought me a personalized, autographed picture of William Shatner? Freaking Captain James Tiberius Kirk?" It was one of the things Lemon and I had bonded over while on the show—her obsession with zombies and mine with intergalactic space travel. "Thank you. Thank you! How did you even get this?"

"Royalty has its privileges," Lemon said with a sweet smile.

I put it down on the table next to my chair. Then I moved it so that he was looking directly at me. I was aware that this made me weird. I didn't care. Lemon sat back down on the couch next to Kat.

"Your nerd is showing," Kat teased, and I smiled back.

"Where are my manners?" I said. "Can I get you guys anything to drink?"

"We're good," Kat responded. "Oh! Offering guests drinks. I need to be better about remembering that." When I met her in Monterra during the show, she'd told me a bit about her background. I knew she'd grown up mostly in a trailer park, was homeless for a while, and then ended up in foster care. I could only imagine how difficult her transition would be from regular girl to queen of an entire country after her fiancé became king.

Lemon asked about my aunt, and the conversation took off from there. Lemon showed me her engagement ring and told me how Dante had proposed, including a charming story about how the men in their family knew when they'd found their true loves because of a gypsy. She also filled me in on her former friend and field producer Taylor Hodges, and how Taylor had conspired to keep Lemon in the dark about both brothers being on the show. Kat told me about the details of her upcoming wedding, which was only a couple of weeks away. She was getting married on Christmas, and apparently there had been less planning and strategizing involved with the invasion of Normandy.

A beep sounded from Lemon's phone. She picked it up. "Rafe will be back soon. We have to go."

"You don't want to stay and see him?" I asked, confused.

"If he finds out we're here, he'll be madder than a wet rooster in a tote sack." That made me smile. I'd missed her Lemon-isms.

"Yeah, this is our stealth mission. None of them know we're here," Kat added. Laddie had moved onto her lap and was snoring. She petted him absentmindedly.

"We're supposed to be in Paris getting this one lingerie for her honeymoon," Lemon said as she elbowed Kat. Kat blushed, and I was glad to finally meet someone who had the same issue with blushing that I did.

"And with Iowa obviously being on the way you thought you'd swing by?"

"It was important to me that I apologize," Lemon said. She pulled out a compact, checking her bright red lips before putting it back in her purse. "And I thought with Rafe being here that you might be open to . . ." Her voice trailed off at my expression. "What? What is it?"

"Maybe you should stay until he gets here so that you can take him back with you to Monterra."

Kat and Lemon exchanged serious and heavy glances, again seeming like they could communicate telepathically. "What the frak? You want him to leave?" Kat asked, sounding really confused.

Hadn't she watched the show?

"You haven't forgiven him?" Lemon asked, just as confused.

Obviously Rafe was not making regular reports home on his lack of progress here. "No."

"But hasn't he explained?" Lemon went on.

"No. And I'm not interested in his explanation."

She wasn't going to be deterred. "Out of anyone, I understand where you're coming from. We were both lied to and deceived."

"Dante didn't lie to you. Taylor did. Rafe lied to me. Deliberately and repeatedly."

"But that was only for Dante's benefit!" she protested.

I let out a deep sigh. It was bad enough he was winning over my whole town. I didn't need his future sisters-in-law here fighting his battles. "Whatever's happening with Rafe and me is between the two of us. I understand that you care about him, but he's a big boy and I'm a big girl."

"That means 'stop giving me your opinion.'" Kat smiled. "I always liked you."

I smiled back to let her know the feeling was mutual.

"Besides, with that whole software company thing, I don't think you're getting rid of him anytime soon," Lemon said.

"What software company thing?" Kat interrupted.

Lemon raised an eyebrow at her. "You know how he was planning on starting up a software company in Monterra? He transferred his plans here instead. I told you about this already."

"You did not. When?"

"This morning."

Kat let out a big sigh of disgust. "You know I can't hear anything before noon!"

There was another beep from Lemon's phone. "We really have to get going."

They both stood, and I stood up with them. "I wanted to give you this," Kat said as she pulled something from an inner coat pocket. She handed me an obviously expensive cream envelope. I lifted the flap, and the interior was lined in a red satin. I pulled the card out far enough to see that it was a wedding invitation. "We'd love it if you'd come."

"And after Kat gets back from her honeymoon in the Maldives," Lemon said while Kat blushed again, "the king and queen are hosting an engagement party for me and Dante. You're invited to that, too."

Oh yes. I'd just ring Jeeves and have him pull the jet around front so that I could attend both events.

Some of that must have shown on my face, because Lemon leaned forward. "Don't worry about the travel. You'll stay at the palace, and we'll send the plane for you if you want to come."

In what universe did people say things like "we'll send the plane for you"?

Kat hugged me first. "We're here for you. You are not alone. We Americans have to stick together."

Lemon hugged me next, promising to write and call. I promised to answer as I walked them out.

"I know my opinion isn't worth two plugged nickels, but once I got to know you, I thought you and Rafe would be perfect together. I even tried to set y'all up, but he told me was seriously seeing someone. And that turned out to be you, so I was right."

I appreciated the sentiment, and that they wanted to fix things, but this wasn't their problem to resolve. I walked them all the way to their waiting black SUV.

"Call us anytime," Lemon said once she'd settled in. "We're here for you."

"Just don't call us in the morning," Kat leaned around her to say.

That made me grin. "I won't." I closed their door and watched as the circus of SUVs and bodyguards tried to make their way down the snowy driveway and back onto the main road. Lemon rolled down the window and waved goodbye one last time.

As I waved back, it was odd to think that in some alternate universe we might have been a family. Sisters. I always wanted sisters.

There was a twinge in my heart that felt suspiciously like homesickness.

Chapter 12

That night I had a "family" dinner with Prince Deceiving and Aunt Sylvia. In some ways he was making my life harder by always being around, but in other ways he made it so much easier. I used to feel like a chicken with its head cut off, running around trying to get everything done but never having enough time.

Now with Rafe here we had more money from his rent, we had help with the chores, and he was devoted to taking care of Aunt Sylvia. That was the hardest thing for me to ignore. I absolutely adored my aunt. When I was younger, I had planned to go somewhere far away and exotic for college, wanting to get out of Iowa. She had encouraged me. She wanted me to live my life, make my own choices. But I couldn't leave her. She needed me, and I needed her. So I went to UI to stay close.

But since he'd arrived, there had been some distance between me and my aunt. In part because she supported his attempts to get my attention, and seemed to really enjoy being around him, but also because Rafe was helping out so much that I realized that a lot of the time we used to spend together she was now spending with him.

And I was grateful for it, glad that I finally had enough hours in my day. That I had some time to myself and wasn't constantly burning the candle at both ends.

Not to mention that he took up so much room in my head that I had little time to think about anything else. Like whether or not I was being a good niece.

I listened to their conversation, not participating. Rafe had his first meeting with his new employees, and he talked about his plans to train them in front end and back end development, database development, and networking.

Today they had brainstormed ideas for possible phone applications. Using the needs of people in Iowa as his jumping off point, he had invited his team to come up with ideas. They talked about an app that could diagnose blight on crops and suggest solutions, a climate application specifically for farmers that was divided by region, sprinkler calculators to figure out the best path for each field, and maybe even a social networking app that would connect farmers across different counties.

Nicole would probably sign up for that one.

"We're surrounded by potential market testers," Rafe said. "None of this is new. We're just going to make it better. And we'll have a higher marketing budget and a relatable headquarters."

I glanced at Aunt Sylvia, but she was smiling at him like he was the awesomest person who had ever lived. She didn't know as much about computers and software as I did.

"That's going to take years," I said. "What if your employees don't have an aptitude for it?" I mean, if they did, wouldn't they already be programmers?

"Anybody can program," Rafe said, raising one shoulder in a shrug. "Some will be better than others based on their natural talents. And if they really can't get it, we'll find something else for them to do. At least

I'll be giving them a skill they can use even if . . ." His voice trailed off, and he didn't finish his sentence.

He didn't have to. We all knew what he'd nearly said.

Even if he left.

He started discussing his plans to build a gaming division in Monterra. He wanted to support his brother's vision by turning the kingdom into a center for technology firms. He had always planned on creating different divisions, which was why it was so easy for him to start one up in Frog Hollow when he saw the need. He had wanted a company here in the States, and figured Iowa was as good as any other place.

Once we finished eating, I started clearing the plates. He stood up. "Here, let me help you."

"I've got it," I said, tugging the plate out of his hands.

Aunt Sylvia asked him a question about what kind of games he hoped to create, and while they talked about that I started washing the dinner dishes. Even though I had my back to them, I knew he was looking at me. I turned off the faucet after I filled the left side with water and dishwashing soap. I had always found washing dishes soothing. Right now it was anything but.

Every time he shifted or moved, I knew it. Like I was tuned in to a frequency he emitted and I was the only person who could hear it. Then he laughed, and I grabbed the sink, locking my elbows into place. That laugh. It did something to me. Not something physical. Something emotional. There had been a time when we'd laughed constantly while we were together, and I realized that I missed it. This moodiness was different. Like somebody was walking around with a Rafe suit on, impersonating him.

Of course he's sad. He's in love with you and you can't even stand to be in the same room with him.

In love? I raised a soapy, wet hand to my throat, trying to calm down the emotions that swelled there. He'd never told me he loved me.

He obviously cared about me. And we were so attracted to each other we were like a couple of powerful magnets.

My physics professor had once mentioned that the Chinese were the first people to discover magnetic rocks. They called them "loving stones." They had meant that the magnets loved metal just like a parent loved a child, but I was discovering that there was a whole different level to the loving stone. I wanted to repel him, but instead I kept ending up in his arms.

While I was caught up in my thoughts, I realized that Rafe had been showing Aunt Sylvia pictures on his phone. Of his home, his family. And then there were the ones of us.

"Genesis! Here's the two of you in Mexico! Are you in an elevator?"

The plate I had been drying slipped out of my hand, landing on the ground with a loud crash.

Rafe came over to help me clean it up, but I shooed him away. I didn't like to think about what had happened in Mexico.

It had been my very first time out of the country. And definitely my first time traveling with a man. We'd gone on a private jet, and I'd made sure to keep the window shades up. For some reason I didn't feel so confined as long as I could still see outside.

We talked and laughed and kissed and cuddled together on one of the built-in couches. I told him about growing up on a farm, and he told me what it was like to come from a large family.

Some part of me felt guilty that we liked each other so much and that I was so deliriously happy. I would think about Lemon and the other girls and how they talked about him, how hopeful everyone was. And even though Lemon denied liking Rafe, I mean, Dante (as everyone else called him, including me when we weren't alone; it gave me such a thrill that I was the only one who got to call him Rafe), I got the feeling that it wasn't true—that Lemon liked Dante more than she let on. Which turned out to be right, seeing as how she and the actual Dante were about to get married.

Anyway, after we had landed in Cozumel, a limo whisked us away to a stunning four-star hotel. When we arrived, I saw a large banner and shrieked with glee. "There's a Comic-Con going on here?"

"I thought you would like it," he said, grinning as I bounced up and down on my seat. "You're the only woman I know who would enjoy this as much as I would." The limo pulled up in front of the hotel, behind several other taxis and limos. I had thought we were coming down here to lie on white sand beaches and drink virgin piña coladas. This had never even occurred to me as a possibility, but I would more than just enjoy it. It was one of the best things that had ever happened to me.

"But I don't have a costume!" How could you go to Comic-Con and not dress up?

"Don't you?" he countered with a wink. "Maybe you should check your room first."

Giddy, I leaned forward in my seat, craning my neck toward the window. "How long will this line take?" I asked impatiently. "And what kind of costume is it?"

"You'll have to see." I narrowed my eyes at him. He was being mysterious and seemed awfully pleased with himself.

"What. Costume?" I said. If he put me in some thigh-high outfit with plunging cleavage, there was going to be a discussion.

"Well, since you're a Trekkie . . ." His voice trailed off when I smacked him with my purse. "Ow!" he laughed. "I guess I should be glad you had your phasers on stun."

I was tempted to smack him again, even though I secretly loved it when he talked nerdy to me. "I'm not a Trekkie. I just like *Star Trek*."

"You like every version of it. Television and movies. And books and some fan fiction."

"So do lots of other people."

"Yes. They're called Trekkies. Plus, I'm pretty sure denying your fandom is a violation of the Prime Directive."

I tossed my hair over my shoulder, while he cracked himself up over his joke. "I like to think of myself as a Trekspert."

He took my hand and squeezed, sending a thrill straight into my heart. "I think it's adorable that you're a nerd."

The limo edged forward. "I prefer scientifically-abled. And you're one to talk. That's the techie calling the geek a nerd."

He raised his eyebrows at me, clearly lost. He'd mentioned once that English wasn't his first language. I'd asked him what was, but he changed the subject. He seemed to do that a lot when I asked anything too personal.

"Sorry," I said. "I was trying to do a pot, kettle, and blackness thing and it didn't work. Don't mind me."

It was like I was hopped up on half a bag of Halloween candy. And considering that I was regularly hopped up on candy, I knew exactly what that felt like.

Finally, it was our turn. I couldn't wait for the bellhop to load up our bags. I grabbed my overnight bag that Lemon had helped me pack from the pile. "Do we have to check in?" I asked.

"All taken care of," he said, grabbing my hand. We hurried, leaving our camera crew behind. They hadn't even assembled their equipment yet. They weren't going to be happy that we were racing off, but they'd have to get over it. I wasn't willing to wait.

Despite the fact that most of the people around us were wearing costumes, we were the ones attracting attention. To be more accurate, Rafe was drawing the gaze of every woman in a slutty superhero getup. People at these events did not normally look like he did, unless they were movie stars doing a panel. For the sake of my sanity, I hoped his costume had a mask.

We headed straight for the elevator bay. I took a deep breath. I was usually okay with elevators. And I had Rafe with me, which made it seem not as bad.

The down arrow lit up and dinged, and the doors slid open. We waited for several people to clear out before getting in. We were the only ones who boarded. "Which floor?" I asked.

"The fiftieth floor." He grabbed me, pulling me in for a quick selfie after I pushed the button. That was the picture Aunt Sylvia had seen.

The fiftieth floor was the very top button. "Don't they usually put the best rooms on the top floor?" Not that I had any experience with staying in the best rooms. It was just what I had seen on TV.

"Let's find out." The doors closed again, and the elevator lifted up.

We stood together, hand in hand, watching as each floor lit up.

"There's something I wanted to say to you," Rafe said. I glanced up at him, worried. That sounded ominous.

"What?"

Then he pressed me against the elevator wall with his body, and I sighed as he captured my lips in a searing, knee-buckling kiss. He pulled back to give me a little smile, clearly pleased with himself for catching me off guard. I pressed my lips to his neck, loving the rapid pulse that beat there. "You have such a way with words," I murmured against his warm skin.

"Oh?" he said in a low timbre that made my quiver. "Well, listen to this."

Then he kissed me again, causing a perfect storm of fireworks and lightning and nuclear explosions.

This time when the world stopped, it was because it had actually, literally stopped. I broke off the kiss, pushing slightly against his chest when I realized that the elevator wasn't moving. "We're not moving."

For a second, I thought he might have pushed the emergency stop button, but he looked as bewildered as I felt. I pushed the button for our floor a few times, as if that could fix it.

Definitely stuck. He opened the phone box underneath the keypad. He pulled out the red receiver and began talking in fluent Spanish to whoever was on the other end. I both marveled at the fact that he could speak Spanish and freaked out at the idea of being trapped.

He hung up the phone. "Well?" I asked.

"They're not sure what caused it, but they're hopeful that it won't take long to fix."

I nodded, gulping. Was it my imagination, or were the walls edging toward us? We were going to get squished. Like we were in a garbage compactor on the Death Star. Well, I supposed that was appropriate for a Comic-Con-related death. My arms started to shake, and my lower back suddenly felt drenched and cold from all the sweating.

As I lurched sideways from dizziness, Rafe managed to catch me. "Are you all right?"

"Did I mention that I suffer from claustrophobia?" I could hear the tremor in my voice. I fanned myself with my hands as my heart tried to pound its way out of my ribcage.

He put me down on the floor, leaning me against the closing-in wall. He grabbed the phone and made another call. This time he sounded angry. My head lolled to one side as I tried to catch my breath.

Slamming the phone down, he came and sat next to me. He pulled me into his lap, murmuring soothing words against my head that actually seemed to help. If I closed my eyes, I could concentrate on the feel of his strong chest and arms and let his delicious scent overwhelm my crazy senses. I almost forgot about how we were going to get smooshed between the walls and then plummet to our death.

"Why are you claustrophobic? I took a psych class at M . . . I mean, at college. Isn't it usually because of some childhood trauma?"

I barked out a harsh laugh, folding my arms as chills racked my torso. "It is most definitely because of some childhood trauma."

"Do you want to talk about it? Maybe it would help."

I never talked about it. But there was something about him filling all of my senses that made me put my guard down. I normally didn't tell people because I didn't want to be treated differently. I didn't want them to pity me or think I was weird. But somehow I knew Rafe wouldn't feel that way.

"I've never told anyone else this. I was raised in a cult." That was the first time I had ever said those words out loud. "My mother was a bit of a wild child. She'd left the farm in Iowa to become an actress in Hollywood. All of that caught up with her and she got pregnant. She got married, but my father walked out before I was born and he disappeared. And she was so devastated by getting knocked up at such a young age that she did a total one-eighty and got super religious."

"Which is why you're named Genesis," he encouraged me, pressing feathery soft kisses against my temple, giving me strength.

"Yeah. But apparently it wasn't enough. Nothing was strict enough for her. She wanted a religion she could practice on a daily basis. One that she could devote her whole life to. Obviously it was a little late for her to become a nun, but she kept searching. That's when John-Paul found her."

I hadn't said his name out loud in eleven years, and even now it made me feel a bit like the characters in *Harry Potter*. I almost would have preferred to call him He Who Must Not Be Named. Like saying his name would make him suddenly appear.

"Who is John-Paul?"

Even though I hadn't seen him in years, I could still picture him perfectly. He had seemed almost like a giant when I was a child, with dark brown hair and dark eyes. He had a charming, toothy smile that masked the devil underneath. "He was the cult leader. He was charismatic and a lying thief. My mom and my aunt had a nice inheritance from their parents, and my mom turned her half of it over to him. When I was a year old, we moved from California to his commune in Washington State."

"This was the man who taught 'purity in mind, body, and spirit'?"

I let out a shuddering breath and nodded. "He also believed very strongly in 'spare the rod, spoil the child.' Most of our day was spent either in prayer, church services, or doing chores to support our community."

I forced my eyes shut. I would not cry. I promised myself I would never cry about all of that ever again. "That's what he'd called it. A community. A family. So that no one would wise up one day and leave when they realized that they were all basically slaves to one man's desires. So if you didn't do something perfectly . . ." My voice trailed off.

Rafe's arms tightened around me. "He hit you?"

"No. Nothing like that. He just locked me in a coal bin. One hour for every year of my life."

Chapter 13

He let out a string of angry-sounding words in a language I didn't recognize. Spanish? Italian, maybe? Whatever it was, while it sounded beautiful, I was pretty sure he was swearing.

As if he realized what he was doing, he switched back into English. "And how often did he put you in there?"

"Two or three times," I said, leaning my head against his shoulder, burying my face into his neck. I hadn't thought there was a cure for my condition, but it turned out all I needed was one hot man to hold and distract me.

"Total?"

"No, two or three times each day. He told me I was a very wicked child, that God expected me to be more somber and serious. No matter what I did, it was never enough. I was always being punished."

He swore again, this time in English. His cursing vocabulary was impressive in both range and breadth. "What is his last name? Where is he now?" he demanded.

That made me sit up as terror and panic clawed at my insides. "You can't go looking for him. You can't let him find me. He'll take me back. Promise me. Promise me that you will never go looking for him."

His eyes flashed angrily, and he let out a deep breath. "I give you my word. I won't go looking for him. But if you're so afraid of him, why did you come on a national television show?"

The terror receded, and I shifted myself back into his embrace, letting him cuddle me. "I'm not worried about that. They shun all 'wicked' civilization, and they don't believe in electricity. No computers, no televisions, no movies. They stay on the commune where they grow all their own food, make their own clothes, and build their own homes." John-Paul would go off on recruiting missions sometimes, and while he didn't seem to have an issue traveling in cars, he wouldn't have done something so base as read a newspaper or watch a TV show.

"Where was your mother? Why did she let him do this?"

That was one of the hardest things to deal with. I had loved my mother, but I'd always felt like she never loved me like she loved John-Paul. Like I was a reminder of her sins. "She was one of his wives. I think all the women there were brainwashed. He had conditioned them to put him first and to do whatever he said when he said. Even the wives of other men. She never interfered when I was being punished."

"No wonder you're claustrophobic," he said.

I thought of the hours I'd spent in that giant wooden box. Light would filter in sometimes through cracks in the wood, but never enough so I could see. I would beg and plead not to be put in the box, but my cries always fell on deaf ears. I would scratch the lid until my fingers bled and scream until I was hoarse. And I would push against the lid with all my might. It never did any good.

I tried so hard to behave, to be the way he expected me to be. But it didn't make any difference. Looking back now, I realized the punishments had nothing to do with my actions and were just a part of his brainwashing process, intended to make me totally dependent on him and terrified of him at the same time. I would do whatever John-Paul said just to avoid being put back in the box.

"How did you get out of the cult?"

"My mother got sick. I think it was probably cancer. But they didn't believe in doctors and planned to heal her with chanting. I was twelve. And John-Paul told my dying mother that the only way to purify me and remove my sins was for me to become one of his wives and take her place. He gave me a new name to signify my change in status. Mary-Pauline. He arranged for the ceremony and had the whole community prepare. To make sure I didn't run off, he put me in the box for three days, having my mother bring me food and water. The day before the wedding, he stopped by to tell me that I should be grateful to him because after we were married, he wouldn't put me in the box anymore." I pulled in a shaky breath. "That if I continued to misbehave, he'd administer my punishment in his bed."

More swearing from Rafe. "What kind of man wants to marry a child?"

"A manipulative, lying, disgusting megalomaniac like John-Paul. He told me he'd never let me leave him. And that if I somehow managed it, he would always find me. He told me that I belonged to him." A shudder ran through me as I perfectly recalled his face while he said it, and I remembered knowing that what he said was true. I was scared by the evil I saw in his eyes. I knew that he would hunt me down if I tried to leave him.

Rafe was holding me so tightly that I had a hard time breathing. When I told him as much, he slightly relaxed his arms. "The night before my wedding, my mother opened the box. She told me to be quiet and to follow her. She led me to the cult's one car, and we pushed it for a long time until we were far enough away. I don't know how we managed it. That's how desperate I was to get away." For the rest of my life, I would never forget the fear in her eyes, the way she shook as she shushed me and helped me climb out of the coal bin.

Now his fingers were kneading my shoulders. "She drove me into town, where Aunt Sylvia was waiting for me. I'd never met her, but she looked just like an older version of my mom. My mother told me that Aunt Sylvia was going to take me to their family farm, and that John-Paul would never find it because my mom had always used her married name, Kim Kristofferson. There would be no connection to a Sylvia Summers or the Summers farm in Iowa. She hugged me goodbye, told me to be good, and said that she loved me. That was the last time I saw her." My voice broke at the last sentence.

"Why didn't she leave with you?"

I shrugged in response. I honestly didn't know. It had all happened so fast—as soon as my mom drove off, Sylvia put me in her rental car and drove us to the airport to exchange it for another car, which she paid cash for and later told me she'd used a fake name and ID to rent. At the airport she gave me an outfit to change into that was nothing like the old-fashioned dresses I had grown up wearing, and had me stuff all of my hair into a knit cap. She hoped that would be enough to stop anyone from following us.

But I'd always wondered why my mom didn't come with us. Was it because she didn't want to come? Was she just removing her younger competition? Had she just given up?

Or had it been something nobler? Had she stayed so that I could go? John-Paul considered us his possessions. Like we were dolls or puppets that moved around only at his whim. No one defied him. And he told whatever lie he had to in order to maintain total control. Had she sacrificed herself to give me a chance to get away from him?

Then I explained to Rafe about his lies, how he had told me so many of them about the real world that when I first moved into the farmhouse I was too scared to leave. And I was still terrified that John-Paul would find me. So Aunt Sylvia homeschooled me for three years. She was so patient, and she brought the pastor over to work with me. I immediately distrusted him because of his position. But he was nothing like John-Paul, and he was honest, loving, and kind. He had been a counselor before feeling called to his ministry. He was the one who helped me move on, who had showed me the world wasn't a scary place, and that John-Paul had been a consummate liar. It's one of the reasons I did so much volunteering at the church. I needed to give back.

When I got to high school, I was ridiculously awkward and backward, and Whitney was the one who helped me learn to socialize and act normal. She never knew what I had been through and just thought I was weird. I told him how much she meant to me and how I felt like I'd never be able to repay her.

A wave of nausea hit me as the panic set back in, and somehow Rafe must have been able to tell because he went back to saying soft words while rubbing my back. This used to happen in the coal bin, too. I would freak the freak out, and then there would be a period of calm until the fear returned.

As the anxious feelings again abated, he spoke. "But you use the last name Kelley."

"I probably should have changed my last name to Summers, but Kelley was my mother's stage name. Aunt Sylvia asked me what last name I wanted to use, and I chose it after the stories she'd told me about my mom wanting to be an actress. It made me feel connected to her, and to her hopes and dreams. And it was all I had left of my mom. That and the red hair."

He paused, thinking. "The night we met, you told me that your mother died. How do you know for sure?"

When I was younger, some part of me used to imagine that she had beat her sickness, outsmarted John-Paul again, and was coming to find me. Even though I knew it wasn't true. "One of the sister wives that my mother had been closest to sent Aunt Sylvia an email. It was my mother's last request, and she risked a lot to let us know. I'll always be grateful for that."

"So you've never even been to your mother's grave."

Hot, burning tears filled my eyes. I choked them back, not wanting to sob. I had promised myself a long time ago that I would never cry about my childhood ever again. "No, I haven't," I finally managed. "I don't even know where she's buried."

"That's terrible," he said, hugging me closer. "So it was just you and your aunt?"

"For a few years. Then she met Richard Parker at a fundraising event in Iowa City. Aunt Sylvia fell hard and fast for him. They got married two months after they first met. She'd never been married before, and I was so excited to have what felt like a real family and for her to have someone she loved. I was worried about her being alone because I was about to go off to college. Then three weeks after the wedding, he cleaned out all of their joint banking accounts, including her inheritance money, and skipped town. He left us dead broke. That's why I had to sell Marigold. A month after that, Sylvia was diagnosed with MS." The doctors had thought the extreme stress of her situation had led to her first flare-up.

I tilted my head back to look up at him. There was so much concern, affection, and tenderness in his gaze that I sighed. "The sheriff did some digging and found out that his real name was Richard Owens. He had pulled the same scam a bunch of times before." It had bankrupted us. We never had any issue taking care of the farm before, but after that everything became a struggle. Aunt Sylvia's flare-ups prevented her from trying to find a full-time job because we never knew when the next one would happen. We sold off everything we could, and I went to work. We constantly struggled.

"Did they ever catch him?"

"No. As far as the authorities know, he hasn't struck again in the United States. Their guess is that he's in some non-extradition country living off of all the money he stole."

"Hmm." It was an odd sound for him to make, and I wondered what he was thinking. "That's a lot of hardship, and yet you still stay positive."

"I'm not the only person in the world who's suffered. I do think happiness is a choice. I don't mean for people who suffer from depression or something. But for most people, it's a choice. We get to decide how we feel. And I choose to be happy."

His Adam's apple bobbed up and down. I brushed my fingers against the side of his face, and he gave me a hint of a smile. "I'm sorry you're scared and anxious right now, and I'm even more sorry for what you've been through. And this probably isn't the time, but I want to let you know that you make me happy. Happier than I thought possible. And it's been a really long time since I've felt truly happy."

His sincerity was evident. Now my heart was racing for a reason other than terror. It felt like he was saying something more, something deeper, about his feelings without actually saying it. He wasn't doing this for cameras or because someone expected him to. He really meant it. I wondered what had happened that had made him sad. I hoped he would tell me when he was ready.

"Back at ya," I said, trying to lighten the mood. "Present circumstances not included."

At that he threw his head back and laughed. The sound was contagious, and I laughed along with him.

As the laughter tapered off, his eyes were bright with merriment. He was going to kiss me again, and I very much wanted him to.

But there was something else I needed to tell him, now that he knew everything. I put my hand to his chest to stop him. "Given what I just told you, I want you to know that I can't tolerate lying. Of any degree or any kind. I know that's a little heavy-handed, but after living through two horrible men who manipulated, stole, and lied to get what they wanted, it's a deal-breaker for me. I won't go through it again. I don't think I'd ever get over it."

That light in his gaze dimmed and then died altogether. It was a warning I gave to all the guys I dated, but without the accompanying backstory. I hadn't found one yet who managed to be totally honest. I hoped Rafe could be. He turned his head right as the elevator started back up. He stood, still not making eye contact with me, and I wondered whether it was my imagination or if he was hiding something from me as he helped me to my feet.

Now I knew why he didn't say anything, because he had been lying to me on that elevator like a Lying McLiar. I sat there, opening myself up to him completely, telling him how important it was for him to be honest, and he didn't tell me the truth. In those moments I had been so vulnerable and shaken up that I think if he had come clean and just told me that he had an identical twin brother, and that they were both pretending to be the same person as a twist for the show, and that he was a prince, I probably would have forgiven him. I could have accepted it and moved on.

But he never did tell me. I found out. In the most shocking, public, and humiliating way imaginable.

I made an effort to spend more time with Aunt Sylvia. Which wasn't easy, given that she seemed to only want to talk about Rafe. Or forgiveness. Or trusting again. I was a grown woman. I didn't need my aunt trying to run interference for me.

And if someone wasn't talking about Rafe, he was there. Quietly, constantly. Taking care of whatever needed to be taken care of.

Like the next time rehearsals for the talent show rolled around. Nicole called me, saying she wasn't feeling well, and asked me to take over. Which was fine, as long as I managed to stay out of Henry's magic box.

At the rehearsals, Rafe came up behind me, studying the chaos. It suddenly felt too hot with him so close. I twisted my hair up into a bun, frustrated that I couldn't seem to manage myself when he was around. "I am going to cut this all off," I muttered, shoving a pencil through the bun to keep it in place.

"Don't!" He choked the word out, his eyes ablaze with passion. "Please don't. I love your hair."

That should not have given me the happy thrill that it did. After my heart palpitations subsided, I called for everyone's attention. But with Nicole's authority gone, the high schoolers had all decided that they were the ones in charge.

He picked up a prop onion, tossing it up in the air and then catching it. "Isn't there a saying in English, something about too many chefs ruining the soup?"

I nodded. I wondered if there was a saying in English that would make him stop driving me nuts.

"Speaking of chefs, when are you going to give me those cooking lessons?"

"You definitely need them." I'd put it on my calendar, right next to the twelfth of never. The idea of being in such close quarters with him, touching, talking, making food together . . . it made me uneasy. I shifted from one foot to the other.

"Did it ever occur to you that maybe I'm an excellent cook and the smoke alarms are just cheering me on?"

My lips twisted as I tried to keep my smile in. "I can promise you that never occurred to me. Here's your first lesson." I grabbed the onion when he threw it, showing it to him. "This is fake, but this is an onion."

He nodded seriously, taking it back. "Ah, yes. I've heard of those."

Then I had to clamp my lips together to keep from laughing. I gestured toward the teens. "I have to go take care of this."

But trying to organize the teenagers into their respective scenes was a bit like trying to organize a goat rodeo. I kept trying to tell them where to go and what to do, but everyone had a million questions.

Rafe stood up, whistling sharply with his fingers, and managed to quiet them down. I directed them to their rehearsal spots, and they finally started running their lines. I watched as he twirled the onion up, bounced it off the inside of his elbow, and caught it again. That shouldn't have impressed me, but it did. He caught me looking and winked.

I rolled my eyes. But it was more about me not being able to ignore him than him being cocky. The winking kind of reminded me of Dante. Which made me think about Lemon and Kat and the suspicions I'd had.

"If I tell you something, do you promise not to tell your brothers?"

Chapter 14

He let the onion fall to the floor. "You know that I would never tell anyone your secrets."

A feeling I didn't recognize raced through me, pumping blood into my heart. I ignored it. "Your future sisters-in-law came to see me."

"What? Why?" His reaction was genuine. So he hadn't known. Which meant he hadn't been in on it. They'd told me the truth and really had come on their own, and not because he'd asked them to.

"To apologize. Lemon and I hadn't spoken since . . ." But I trailed off, realizing that I was wandering into dangerous territory.

He knew exactly where I was headed because he finished, "Since that night. Genesis, I think maybe it's time that I explained why—"

I thanked the theater gods when Sarabeth, our soon-to-be Juliet, interrupted us, tugging on my sleeve. "Genesis, can I talk to you?"

"Sure." We walked away from Rafe, though her gaze darted back to him as we did so. "What's up?"

"We're practicing act 1, scene 5 today." She wrung her hands together while tapping her foot.

"Okay. And?"

"That's the kiss. And I've never kissed anyone before. I say, 'Saints do not move, though grant for prayers' sake.' And he says, 'Then move not, while my prayer's effect I take.' And then he kisses me." Her voice shook, and it was easy to see how worried she was.

While it sucked that her first kiss would be because of a play, at least it was with Malcolm Schroeder. That was something she could tell her grandchildren about. "Just let him take the lead and kiss you. It'll be okay."

"But I really like him."

"That does make it harder," I said sympathetically. "You don't have to kiss him in rehearsals." Problem solved.

"And have our first kiss ever be in front of a live audience?" she shrieked.

Problem not solved. I patted her awkwardly on the shoulder, not sure what I should do or say. Maybe I should text Nicole and ask her advice.

"Can you show me?" she asked.

"What? I don't think it's appropriate for me to kiss Malcolm." Not to mention that being added to the sex offender registry was not something I needed right now.

"No, I mean with Prince—I mean, Rafe. Please."

That put images in my head that made my synapses crackle. "Can't you go look it up on YouTube?" I wondered if my voice sounded as strangled as I felt.

"That's not the same." She glanced over her shoulder, and Malcolm was walking toward us. "And now there's no time. It's our turn. Please."

Again, I couldn't say no. I waved Rafe over, and while he approached, I asked Malcolm to give us a minute and promised to send Sarabeth over after.

"So the kids are doing *Romeo and Juliet*—"

"In English?" he interrupted. "Romeo and Juliet were Italian. You should have them speak Italian. I could teach them."

Then he started talking in Italian. I had no idea what he was saying, but he said it so well. He might have been saying lines from the play. He could have been reading the phone book and I still would have felt wobbly-kneed and tongue-tied. It was a good thing I never told him what him speaking foreign languages did to me.

Because he was already making it harder to do what I planned to do. "Shakespeare wrote it in English, and that's how we'll perform it."

He gave little shrug that seemed to say, *Suit yourself.*

The only way out was through. "And today they're doing the kissing scene and we need to demonstrate."

"Do we?" His words were like a low purr, and he looked much too satisfied with himself.

"Yes. But this is only for informational purposes."

He put a hand on my waist, making my blood sizzle. "Of course."

"It's not a real kiss. I'm not actually asking you to kiss me for real."

Then the other hand, pulling me in toward him. My mouth dried up. "I completely understand," he said.

He was saying the right words, but his eyes, his touch, and his teasing tone said something else.

"Okay." I turned to Sarabeth. "You guys will choreograph how you want to do the kiss, keeping in mind that this is Romeo and Juliet's first kiss, so you're aiming for something innocent, sweet, and loving." I hoped he heard my warning.

"Let him take the lead," I continued. "And do what he's doing."

This was so weird. How did I keep getting myself into situations like this?

It's because you can't say no. This time the voice in my head sounded suspiciously like Rafe's. I closed my eyes, waiting, while my lips tingled and burned.

After several beats, I opened my eyes back up. The adrenaline coursed through me, hot and heavy. "What are you doing?" I hissed. "Hurry up and get this over with."

"Anticipation makes it better," he said, his words washing over my mouth. Then he finally pressed his lips to mine, and I sagged against him as my eyelids flickered shut. He kissed me softly, tenderly, just the way that Romeo was supposed to kiss Juliet. Very PG.

Only my body was having an R-rated response to it. It was only when the wolf whistles and catcalls started that I put my hands against his shoulders and pushed him back, breaking off the kiss. "And that's how you do it," I said, so out of breath it was embarrassing.

"Oh. Wow. Uh. Th-thanks," Sarabeth said, her eyes wide, and she went off to join Malcolm.

"We might have scarred that poor girl for life," I mused out loud.

"When can we demonstrate that again?" Rafe asked, grabbing the bottom part of my earlobe with his lips. I backed off, trying to ignore the lightning that zapped the right side of my head and was traveling along my veins.

"That is not happening again," I said, flustered. "You should move on." I wanted to mean it, but I wasn't sure that I did.

"Like you did?"

I didn't know if you could call what happened between me and Tommy moving on, but I nodded.

"I tried," he said, and jealousy flared to life inside me, so ugly and twisted I wanted to inflict bodily harm on the women who had dared touch him.

"And?"

"No one was you." The jealousy quickly shifted to something bright, happy, and dangerous.

I didn't want to dwell on it. "That must have broken a lot of hearts."

"I don't plan on breaking anyone's heart ever again."

His words shivered across my spine. My emotions in that moment were careening all over the place, scary and uncontrollable. I was so moved by what he said, and I wanted to be excited, but I couldn't let him in again. I couldn't keep getting hurt. So I joked. "Too late. I think you've broken the heart of almost every woman here in town. They're all in love with you."

He made me turn and look at him, his eyes hypnotic. "There's only one heart I'm truly concerned about keeping safe."

Too much. This was too much. I had to get away from him. "I'm going outside for a second."

Where I planned to dunk my head in a snowdrift in hopes that it would cool me off.

After rehearsals ended and I'd made sure that every kid got picked up, Rafe asked me for a ride. He'd had his bodyguards drop him off at the school. Which seemed deliberate and sly.

So I turned up my favorite country station, one that played the hits from the 1990s and heavily featured my favorite singers—Garth, Reba, Travis, Shania, Faith, George. Fortunately, he picked up the signal I was broadcasting: that I wasn't interested in talking about his explanation or the kiss that had rocked my world. Again.

When we pulled up to the driveway, I asked if he would get the mail for me, since the mailbox was on his side of the truck. I could see from the color of some of the envelopes in his hand that there were a lot of final notices for bills.

After I parked the car, I took the mail from him, thanked him, and went toward the house. Laddie shot out the front door when I opened it, and I called after him. "He's not supposed to be out this late," I told Rafe. He had a tendency to wander toward the main road, and we were afraid he would get hit.

"I'll get him," Rafe said, heading after Laddie and calling for him to come back. I set the mail down on a side table and took off my coat and boots, shaking the snow off before I put them away. Rafe came in the front door, carrying a squirming Laddie. The dog leapt from his arms and ran around in circles, managing to slam into the side table and knock the lamp and all the mail to the floor.

"Laddie!" I exclaimed, but he took off for the kitchen. "I don't know what's gotten into that dog," I said, putting the lamp back while Rafe picked up the mail.

"You got a postcard," he said, handing it to me. It was a picture of tall pine trees with the words "Wish you were here" on the front. I turned it over, gasped, and promptly passed out.

When I came to, Rafe had moved me to the couch and was hovering over me, worried. "What just happened?" he asked.

"The postcard," I said, holding my shaking hand out for it. He picked it up off the ground. I had to make sure it said what I thought it said. That I hadn't just hallucinated or imagined it. I struggled to sit up, still feeling sick to my stomach.

He gave it back to me without reading it. I wasn't sure I had as much restraint as he did. I flipped the postcard to the back again. My heart sank as my pulse violently throbbed in my neck. There was my name, my address, the postmark from Washington State. And on the left side just one thing. A name.

Mary-Pauline.

A cold knot formed in my stomach, and my chest hurt as I realized what this meant. John-Paul had found me. I didn't know how it had happened, but he had found me. My lungs constricted, and I started to wheeze in and out. This couldn't be happening. It had been so long that I had thought he had given up. I should have known better.

I pulled my knees up to my chest, wrapping my arms around them. There was a rushing sound in my ears, and I couldn't concentrate. The word *How?* kept repeating itself in my mind over and over again.

"What is it? Your face has gone completely white," Rafe said, getting even more concerned. I handed him the postcard.

My lips and chin started to tremble, but I was not going to cry. I was not going to give John-Paul that kind of power over me ever again.

He read it, his eyebrows lifting and his eyes widening. He sat on the couch next to me, and I didn't protest when he hugged me, holding me close. He always knew how to make me feel safe.

But it wasn't enough. I couldn't stop shaking, couldn't stop feeling cold. It was like I was back in that box, with everything closing in around me. I could feel the wood against my fingertips, and my throat hurt as if I'd been screaming. I clenched my fists tightly.

Rafe got to his feet and started pacing. Whatever surprise or shock he'd initially felt had quickly turned to fury. "I know that I promised you I wouldn't, but now I'm going to find him and report him to the authorities."

"For what?" My voice broke. "He never technically abused me. I can't prove the coal bin thing, and nobody will testify against him. He'll say I made it up. And you can't put him in prison for anything else. He hasn't broken any laws."

"That you know of."

"Right." I reached for the crocheted afghan on the back of the couch, wrapping it around me. "I know because he was always careful."

"I want to punch something," Rafe said, his hands clenched as he kept stalking the length of the room. It reminded me of when Aunt Sylvia had taken me to the zoo in Des Moines and there had been this cheetah at the bottom of his cage. He had watched us with intent as he walked from one end of the cage to the other, over and over again. I remembered thinking that keeping all that power and rage bottled up was not a good plan.

It still wasn't. "Then punch something. But there's nothing you can do."

He stopped. "There is something I can do. I'm going to increase security. Have one of the guards move in here and follow you. I will protect you."

"It's just my name. It doesn't necessarily mean anything. It doesn't mean he will come after me." Even as I said the words, they felt hollow and untrue. I was trying to convince myself just as much as I wanted to convince him. I wanted to pretend this had never happened. That it was meaningless and I was fine.

The pacing resumed. "It doesn't mean he won't."

I was still letting John-Paul control me. That postcard was threatening to blow up my entire life. I wasn't going to live like that. Even if he was planning on coming after me, I wasn't the same little girl he'd known. I would protect myself.

I didn't need Rafe to do it.

Remembering my sessions with Pastor Dave, I started breathing in and out slowly, concentrating on the air entering and exiting my lungs. I calmed myself down. I wasn't doing myself any favors by being hysterical or panicked.

John-Paul wasn't breaking down my door to get to me. He wasn't outside lurking in the bushes. That was ridiculous. He just wanted to scare me.

And I didn't plan on giving him the satisfaction.

I'd had to fight for years to feel safe again. I wasn't going to let one postcard strip that away from me.

I wasn't going to let Rafe take it away, either.

"No extra security," I said. This postcard had just invaded my life in the worst way possible. I didn't want to have his bodyguards doing the same thing on a daily basis. "And you already promised me you wouldn't follow me and you wouldn't have Marco follow me. That extends to all bodyguards." That made him halt in his tracks.

He had an incredulous look. "You can't expect me to sit here and do nothing when that man is out there and he knows where you are."

"Actually, that's exactly what I expect. It's not your job to protect me. I can take care of myself. I have pepper spray and I've taken self-defense classes. Plus, people kind of know who I am now. Going on the show might have been the best protection for me. He'll have a hard time trying to hide me away."

Walking over, he snatched the postcard out of my hand. "Hey!" I protested.

"I'm going to have Gianni run this for prints."

"You're not listening to me," I said. I let the afghan drop on the couch as I got up to retrieve the postcard. I wanted to show it to Aunt Sylvia and then turn it over to the sheriff. Another person I'd have to tell the truth. But Sheriff Stidd was a good man. He would keep it to himself.

I took the postcard back. "I can take care of it myself. You don't need to involve your security team."

He ran his fingers through his hair, grabbing it in clumps. "I do need to!"

"Do you know how long it took for me to feel safe? How I worried every minute of every day that he would kidnap me? Or how I was always watched at the commune? I had no privacy at all. Do you want to make me feel that way now, too?"

"No, but this isn't the same."

I went into the kitchen, intent on throwing him out so he could go back to his own house. All I wanted to do was go upstairs, climb under my covers, and sleep for about twelve hours. To have some period of time where I could hide and pretend that this hadn't happened. He was hot on my heels. "Wait," he said just as I put my hand on the kitchen doorknob.

At the same exact moment I whirled around to tell him off, Laddie decided he needed to be part of this conversation and get underfoot, pitching me forward into Rafe's waiting arms. *He has awesome reflexes* was my last thought before my mind went completely and blissfully blank. It didn't feel like I had just tripped over my dog, but like I had stepped off a cliff and I was falling and falling while Rafe held me.

The anger was still there, but there was such tenderness in his expression, an overpowering affection that even I couldn't deny. "Don't you know what it would do to me if something ever happened to you?" His voice was low and heartfelt as he caressed the side of my face.

His earlier kiss still lingered on my lips. I wanted another. Any anger I'd felt quickly turned into want. That desire was driven by a frantic desperation. I wanted to forget everything else, especially that stupid postcard. I let it slip away from my fingers, not caring where it landed. There was something magical and heavy between us, something that bound me to him. Like we had been covered in shimmery pixie dust. I studied his warm, full mouth, wanting to feel it against mine. His pupils dilated and he sucked in a deep breath when he understood what I was about to do.

But before anything could happen, Aunt Sylvia called out, "I'm home!"

I quickly disentangled myself from him, even though I didn't want to leave his embrace. "In here!" I called out. The spell between us was broken. Because magic obviously had to have been involved to explain my behavior. I just couldn't admit that the real magic was what happened every time he touched me.

"Are you going to tell her?" he asked.

"Yes, I'm going to tell her," I snapped back. "But you need to leave."

"I'll go," he said. "But this conversation isn't over."

I stopped him with a touch as he opened the back door. His forearm flexed underneath my palm. He looked hopeful, but all I said was, "You gave me your word."

He nodded tersely and let the screen door slam shut.

"Was that Rafe?" Sylvia asked when she entered the kitchen. I said yes and bent down to pick up the postcard. She had a glowing smile on her face, one I hadn't seen in a very long time. "Where have you been?"

"I went on a date with Max."

"You did?" I yelped. When had this happened? How did I not know? Did Amanda know? For three blissful seconds I pushed John-Paul from my mind and focused solely on my aunt. I looked at the postcard in my hand and then shoved it into the back pocket of my jeans. I would show it to her tomorrow. I didn't want to do anything to ruin her happiness tonight.

She nodded with a girlish smile as she opened the fridge to get out a cold can of Diet Coke. It was her one vice. Mine, obviously, was hoarding chocolate bars.

"Well it's about time," I said, sitting at the kitchen table, ready to get the scoop, to banish John-Paul and his postcard from my thoughts. "He's been head over heels for you for years."

She popped the top of her soda, letting the carbonation fizzle and snap. She took a small sip. "He's asked before. I didn't think the timing was right."

"And now you do?"

"Some things have changed," she said evasively. "I should have said yes years ago. You know, he warned me about Richard and I didn't listen. I thought he was just jealous. Which he was, but that didn't make him any less right."

"I'm glad that you finally took a chance on him." I felt like she was trying to tell me something, but she wasn't being direct.

Until she said it. "I hope you're smarter than I was and don't make Rafe wait as long."

And there it was.

So I changed the subject. "We should have a spa day."

Her whole face beamed. "Yes! We haven't done that in so long!"

We'd never actually gone to a spa and it was now technically nighttime, but we did our own in-home pedicures and facials. It would be an excellent distraction. "I'll go upstairs and get my stuff."

She glanced up at the black cat clock on the wall, his tail swinging back and forth. "It's late and I'm worn out. Rain check? What we need to do is get a Christmas tree and put it up. How about tomorrow?"

We used to buy our tree and decorate the house the weekend after Thanksgiving, but we hadn't managed that in years. It had turned into something we threw together at the last minute. Probably in part because Richard had left at Christmastime, and it always seemed to make her a little sad.

"I have a meeting with the bazaar committee after school and work, but we can do it after that."

"It's a date."

"But probably not as good as the date as you just had," I teased as I helped her out of her chair and up the stairs. "You'll have to fill me in tomorrow."

She promised she would, and after making sure she was settled, I went and got ready for bed, finishing off half a Twix bar before brushing my teeth. As I slid under my covers, I told myself I was fine. The darkness felt oppressive, like a thick, heavy, suffocating blanket, so I got up and turned on a lamp on my desk. My jeans were hanging over the back of the chair, the postcard sticking out. The postmark was from Washington, so John-Paul was still there. He wasn't here. He just wanted me to know that I hadn't been able to hide from him.

Nothing would happen, I told myself sternly. I was safe.

It took a long time, but I finally managed to drift off to sleep, repeating the words in my mind over and over again.

I was safe.

Safe.

And John-Paul was not going to change that.

Chapter 15

I really was trying to be positive, but the universe seemed determined to mess with me. First, I lost my keys. I searched for about half an hour until Rafe pointed them out on the key rack. Which was weird, because I swear I'd checked there like three times.

Then I had to tell Sylvia about the postcard, and she insisted, as I thought she would, that we tell Sheriff Stidd the entire story. He sat stone-faced and listened to the whole tale. He promised to increase patrols near our home and to keep an eye out for any strangers.

Rafe insisted on coming with me to the church bazaar meeting, which was scheduled for before my shift at the diner. I told him he'd have to take his own car because, one, I didn't want to keep being in confined spaces with him considering how hard of a time I was having keeping my hands to myself, and two, I didn't want him to drive me to the diner and then have to come pick me up later. I didn't want a bodyguard, and that included him.

When we got to the church, the current committee was waiting for us—Nicole, Pastor Dave, Whitney, Mrs. Mathison, Mrs. Ramirez, and for some reason, Brooke Cooper.

I raised an eyebrow at Whitney, glancing at Brooke, but Whit just shrugged her shoulders. She didn't know why either.

We went through the agenda quickly, and when we got to the bachelor auction, Nicole told us about how well that was going. "And it would go even better if we had the most eligible bachelor included. What do you say, Rafe?"

I did not miss the way Brooke's eyes lit up. "Yes, it's for a great cause."

"I would love to help out," Rafe said. That shouldn't have bothered me. It did.

Mrs. Mathison and Mrs. Ramirez were in charge of the dinner and organizing food items for the silent auction, and they gave us an update on that front. Just as I planned to close the meeting, Brooke interjected. "Do we have enough to attract a lot of attention? Should we be adding something more kid-friendly? Like a petting zoo?"

"Since we have to hold it inside, space is an issue," I said.

"Hamsters and rabbits are small. We could just throw them all in cages together."

My guess was that Brooke had never owned a hamster or a rabbit, let alone a lot of them. They might hurt each other. Or ruin the flooring. Or worse. "We don't want to end up with a bunch of pregnant animals," I said. "They'd multiply like Tribbles."

"Like what?" she said.

"Tribbles? From *Star Trek*? Those furry little aliens? Remember?"

She looked at me blankly. "No. As you'll recall, I actually went to my prom."

I opened my mouth to say something back, but caught Pastor Dave watching me. I could refrain in a church. I just smiled sweetly instead, and she didn't seem to know how to respond to that. She glared at me and turned away.

Brooke could go Trek herself.

Even though she wasn't in charge, she called the meeting to a close and then pulled on Rafe's arm, asking to talk to him. Nicole and Whitney took seats on either side of me. "Why did she show up today?"

"Brooke's just full of surprises," Whitney said.

"I always thought she was full of something," Nicole added, and I found myself wanting to smile, which was surprising given last night's events.

"What do you think they're saying?"

Whitney sat forward and with a breathy, singsong voice said, "Oh, Rafe. I know you're in love with Genesis, but please forget about her and take me and my hair extensions and Botoxed forehead away to your castle."

Nicole chimed, in, lowering her voice to mimic Rafe's deep tones. "Thank you for the offer, Brooke. And while you have excellent Botox, I'm sorry. I can't run away with you. I'd rather shove knitting needles into my eyeballs."

Then I couldn't help but snicker, and my two friends joined in. Nicole's phone buzzed, and she turned it on and read the screen. The smile slid off her face. "Oh no. No, no, no, no . . ." she kept repeating as she scrolled through something, reading quickly.

"What is it?" Whitney asked, rubbing her hand across her swollen belly and grimacing. "Sorry. Braxton-Hicks. So annoying. You were saying?"

"I . . . last night I got a wee bit tipsy on peach schnapps and I drunk texted Duke." Duke, her ex from college. He had been her most serious boyfriend until the Thanksgiving weekend she came back early to school and found him Resident Assisting one of the freshmen in his dorm. "He just texted me back and told me to leave him alone."

"Delete his number," I said. "Delete it right now so this never happens again."

"You're right," she said, her fingers tapping away. I hoped she was getting rid of his contact information and not texting him more. "Every time I do this I get to wake up the next morning to a transcript of shame."

"In your defense, though," Whitney added, "technically you didn't drunk text him. Peach schnapps did."

"Maybe he should take it as a compliment. He was the only person you could think of when your brain wasn't working." Part of me wished Rafe had heard this. So that I could show him a real-life example of the kind of woman who would lose her shoe at midnight.

Pastor Dave approached and asked if he could speak to me. Whitney and Nicole told me goodbye. Nicole planned on going to the diner to get some dinner, while Whitney was going home. She had cut back on her hours ever since Rafe had given Christopher a job. I told them I'd see them later, and walked with the pastor back to his office.

Was this about the postcard? I wasn't ready to talk about that.

"What's going on?" I asked as we sat down at his desk. With his silver hair, lined face, and happy blue eyes, he'd always made me think of a beardless Santa Claus. He even usually smelled of peppermint candy, which I'd always associated with Santa.

"I was about to ask you the same question," he said. "It seems like something has been weighing on your mind. Is there anything you'd like to talk about?"

He was probably the only person in town who hadn't watched the show, and he wasn't one for gossip. What with it being a sin and all.

Had Aunt Sylvia put him up to this? It was like when she wanted me to go on the show. She was so determined, so fixated on that goal that I couldn't say anything to dissuade her. And now she seemed just as determined to repair my relationship with Rafe. I wouldn't put it past her to enlist a man of the cloth in her efforts. She probably figured she'd win if she could claim she had God on her side.

But Pastor Dave had been a big help to me when I was younger. Maybe he would have some good insight for me now. "What do you do when you can't trust someone because they hurt you in the past?"

"That's a really good question," he said.

Usually when somebody says "that's a really good question" you can be sure it's a lot better question than the answer you're going to get back.

But Pastor Dave was awesome at good answers. "There's a whole list I could give you, but it boils down to some simple concepts. Forgiveness and trusting in yourself."

"That's it?" I had expected something more profound.

"The best stuff is the most basic. The man that you—we are talking about that young man out there, correct?"

I hoped my face hadn't gone too bright of a red. I nodded.

"It doesn't matter what he does. You can't control him or get a guarantee out of him. The person you have to trust is yourself. Trust that you can make wise decisions." He had his hands folded together on his desk, so sincere and earnest.

"I'm not sure I know how to trust anyone anymore," I admitted.

He leaned back in his chair. "That's not true. You trust people all the time every day. Your entire life is filled up with little acts of trust. You trust the drivers around you to drive safely. You trust your customers to pay you when you bring them the bill. You trust your employer to give you a paycheck. You trust your committee members to do the things they promised to do."

That was certainly a different way of looking at it, but it didn't feel the same. "He lied to me."

"Everybody lies. Even pastors. The only person who didn't ever lie was Jesus. Nobody is perfect, and you can't ask them to be. If you ask him to earn your trust, you're asking him to never make a mistake. To never hurt you, and to never upset you. That's not realistic, even for people who don't have baggage and are blissfully in love. Like I said in the beginning, if you can forgive, and if you can trust in yourself to work through the issues, then it will all work out."

My first instinct was to say that he didn't know what he was talking about, but he'd been married to his wife for over forty years. Maybe he knew a little bit more about it than I did. "I'm not sure I do trust in myself. Or that I can work through it if he hurts me again."

"You have to realize that trust isn't about never again experiencing a negative emotion. It's about knowing that you are strong enough to deal with whatever comes your way. In my line of work, we also tend to call that faith."

He made it sound so easy. Like I could just let Rafe explain why he did what he did, and then get over it and move on. Have faith in him and faith in us that we could work through everything together.

But was that what I wanted? "I don't want to be hurt again. I'm so tired of being hurt. I just want to be . . ." I searched for the word, and it popped into my head. "Safe. I want to be safe."

"In trying to keep yourself safe, all you've accomplished is keeping yourself lonely. Let me give you this piece of advice. When you expect someone to mess up, when you put them under a microscope and wait for them to hurt you, they always will. You'll see betrayals even when there aren't any."

The pastor folded his hands together. "You're a clever, kind, strong girl. I know you can figure it out."

I gave him a fake smile, my head swimming in thoughts. Could it really be that easy? Did I want it to be that way? I said I wanted Rafe to leave me alone, but I found myself looking for him. Turning toward him whenever I heard his voice. Missing him when we weren't together. I had spent a long time denying it to myself because I thought our obstacles were insurmountable. What if they weren't?

He stood up, and I did too. He thanked me for all the work that I was doing for the new roof, but I hardly heard him because Rafe was waiting for me at the back of the church by the doors. My heart did a little skip when I saw him.

"Just remember, nothing in life is guaranteed. Well, except computers and robots. And would you rather be in a relationship with a robot or a flawed human being?"

Rafe chose that moment to smile one of his glorious smiles, and my heart said, *Flawed human being.* I mean, don't get me wrong, I loved my computer, but I wanted the flawed human being.

Heart in my throat, I smiled up at Rafe as he opened the door for me, which seemed to surprise him. I couldn't talk. Not yet. I needed to process and figure things out. He said he'd see me at the diner, and I nodded.

It was a short drive, and there were a lot of hungry people waiting when I got there, which kept my mind blank and free from thinking about everything the pastor had just said.

Until a lull hit, and it all came rushing back. I'd never been in love before, but during the show, I had thought of it as possibility. That I was falling in love with him. Maybe I already was in love and didn't know it. Maybe that's why I'd been so sad for so long and missed him so much.

Nicole was still messing with her phone and muttering under her breath. "Not going so well?" I asked.

"How did I ever think Duke was my knight in shining armor? He's just an idiot in tin foil."

I brought the water pitcher over to Rafe's table, where he had finished eating and was now working on his laptop. "What's wrong with Nicole?"

"Oh, don't mind her," I said as I filled his glass with more water. "She's having female troubles."

"What kind of female troubles?"

"The male kind." I certainly knew a lot about that. The bells on the door rang, and I looked up to see a man I didn't know. Claws of frozen terror clamped down on my heart, and I dropped the pitcher with a loud clanging sound, sending water and ice cubes everywhere. Rafe immediately came over to help me, bringing napkins. "Don't worry," he said in a soft voice so that only I could hear him. "That's one of my new employees, Shane. He's here to help teach programming."

I nodded, letting out a sigh of relief and feeling a little silly as Shane sat at Rafe's table. The two men started an intense discussion as I threw away my wet napkins and hung my rag up to dry. "Who is that?" Nicole asked.

"His name is Shane. He's new to Rafe's company."

She smiled a feline grin. "Do you think he's single? Because the odds of finding a single, hot, normal man in this town are about as likely as finding Bigfoot. Looking like that, he has to have a girlfriend. Or with my luck, a boyfriend." He was tall, broad-shouldered, and blonde. She sighed. "Like my dream Iowan farmer. If that man knows how to shuck corn, I'll be his forever."

Max called me over. He was alone today. "Did you hear about the power outage in the library at Iowa State today?"

"I didn't."

"Thirty students were stuck on the escalator for three hours."

That made me laugh, and Max chuckled along with me. "Sit down for a minute." My gaze darted toward the kitchen. "Oh, if that brother of mine gives you a hard time, you tell him to come talk to me. Sit."

I slid into the booth across from him. It was actually nice to sit. "I hear you finally took my aunt out."

"Been asking her for years. She always said no. Said she had to put you first. But that the circumstances had changed."

What circumstances? Rafe? Is that what had changed her mind? She was so sure she could marry me off that now she had time to date?

"And before you ask, it went well. Although we found one thing that we had very differing viewpoints on."

"What was that?"

"Did I ever tell you that I worked on a horse ranch in Idaho when I was a young man?" Max tore open a packet of sugar and poured it into his coffee. He swirled the spoon slowly while he talked. "The ranch specialized in taming wild horses. One of the lead wranglers told us this old story about how the first rancher caught the first wild horse. The horse would come to graze on his land, and whenever the rancher went near it, the horse would run away. So the rancher started hanging around the spot—far enough away that the horse wasn't afraid, but always around. Then he put up a fence post. At first the horse was scared and ran off. But the next day he sniffed the post and went back to grazing. The day after that the farmer added another post. And then a rail. And another post and another rail. And before you know it, a whole fence. By the end the horse was so accustomed to him and the fence that all the rancher had to do to catch him was close the gate."

He took a long sip of his coffee, while I looked over at Rafe, who was still chatting with his new employee. As if he sensed that he was being watched, he glanced over his shoulder at me. I focused on the coffee cup in Max's hand, thinking about his warning.

Max liked his jokes, but he wasn't the type to tell moral stories. Was that what Rafe had been doing this whole time? Building a fence slowly around me? Insinuating himself into every aspect of my life so that I would become accustomed to him? Making it so I could let go and forgive him?

Because, after all these conversations, that was turning into a real possibility. His plan was apparently working.

Was this what he and Aunt Sylvia had disagreed about? I excused myself, saying I had to get back to work. Max left some money on the table and stopped by Rafe's booth on the way out. I gripped my dishcloth tightly. What now?

Max's booming voice carried through the diner. "She's special, that one. Our ray of sunshine. Until you nearly put it out."

"I know, sir. That's why I'm here. To fix things."

"You don't fix this, you'll have me to answer to, understand?"

"Absolutely, sir."

Max nodded, sliding on his ball cap as he left the diner. It seemed like he was taking the potential role of uncle a little too seriously. I was torn between humiliation and a heart that melted to hear Rafe speak so respectfully to Max, who had been nothing but kindness itself to me and Aunt Sylvia ever since I'd first met him.

I moved to the farthest point of the counter away from Rafe. It was just my luck that not thirty seconds later Tommy walked in with some of his buddies. He told them he'd catch up and then came and sat right in front of me.

"Hey," he said, leaning in. "So I was thinking."

I could almost hear Whitney's voice saying, "*That would be a first.*"

"You and I should get together sometime and have some real fun. What do you say?" I had a pretty good idea of what constituted "real fun" for him. I couldn't remember what it felt like to think he was attractive.

"That's really nice, but I'm going to be super busy for a while."

"Your loss," he said, getting up to join his friends. It probably didn't even occur to him that I was nicely brushing him off. I would have loved to have been honest, but you couldn't really do that when you lived in a small town. That was the sort of thing that caused Hatfield-McCoy level feuds that would last for generations. The Coopers and Davises were already going at it. I didn't need to add in the Summers women to the mix.

Nicole kept sneaking peeks in the mirror behind the counter, watching Rafe and Shane talk. "Shane's so cute. Isn't he so cute?"

"He's so cute," I agreed. Not anywhere near as handsome as Rafe. But cute.

"They're coming over here!" she gasped.

As Rafe and Shane approached, Nicole threw her shoulders back, taking her hair out of the ponytail. She ran her fingers through it, trying to straighten it. "How do I look?"

"Perfect," I told her with a conspiratorial wink.

"Genesis, Nicole, may I introduce you to Shane Fitzgerald? He's come to work for me. Nicole, I thought you might like to give Shane a tour of the town." Nicole turned into a totally different person in front of my eyes. She was literally batting her eyelashes coyly at Shane as they shook hands. It could have set a Guinness world record for longest handshake, and he seemed just as smitten as she did.

"That won't be a very long tour," she said flirtatiously.

"I'll take what I can get," Shane responded with a grin. "Shall we?"

They walked out, with Nicole turning to mouth "OMG" at me. Then I heard her say, just before the door shut behind them, "Have you ever shucked corn?"

I hoped that wasn't some kind of euphemism.

Chapter 16

Two men whom I'd known for a long time had given me some serious and conflicting things to think about. On my way home, I picked up a tree from the Ramirez farm. It wasn't quite the tree from *A Charlie Brown Christmas*, but I had to make do with what they had left.

All the ornaments and decorations were waiting in the living room, along with my aunt. There was no way she had carried up all those boxes from the basement by herself. I didn't ask, and she didn't tell.

We got everything ready before we started decorating the tree. I made the hot chocolate and started up a fire from the logs that Rafe had cut, while Sylvia turned on a Johnny Mathis Christmas album. Even the weather cooperated, sending down little tufts of snow to blanket the yard.

Opening all of the boxes was like going through a mini time capsule. We remembered the ornaments and when and why we had bought them. I grabbed my favorite *USS Enterprise* NCC-1701 ornament, hanging it near the top. Laddie had always been a little obsessed with Christmas trees and thought everything hung on the tree should be his own personal chew toy.

Part of me felt guilty as I put up the strands of colored lights. Rafe was sitting in his little house, all alone. We probably should have invited him over. The worst part was that I wanted to.

The hardest thing about what had happened on the show wasn't just losing a boyfriend or a possible husband. In that short time, he'd become my best friend. He'd understood me and my hobbies in a way no one else ever had. When I talked about pwning some noob in a battleground, he knew what I meant. No explanation necessary.

And he was practically perfect for me. If someone had asked me to describe my ideal man, it would have been Rafe. Ridiculously smart, witty, loving, kind and thoughtful, strong and steady. He made me laugh. He liked my weirdness. We had a similar sense of humor. I had felt comfortable with him. He was the first man I had ever been my total, actual, authentic self with. I never felt like I had to hold anything back or play any games. He accepted me for me. And best of all? He made me feel safe.

To stop thinking about him, I asked Aunt Sylvia to tell me about her date with Max. She had a sparkle in her eye and a wistful tone in her voice that I hadn't heard in a very long time. She told me all about how Max had brought her daisies, her favorite. Then he had driven her to a theater in a town twenty minutes away. They were running a 1950s movie retrospective, and he knew how she loved old black-and-whites.

"I heard you two had a disagreement about something," I asked, wanting to find out whether or not my suspicions were correct.

"Not everyone agrees on everything," she said, putting me off. "Wouldn't that make the world a boring place?"

If she'd been my age, I would have asked her how the date ended, but it sort of squicked me out to think about them kissing. Or anything else. She was like my mom. You didn't want to think about your mom doing that kind of stuff. Although moms obviously must have, or else none of us would be here.

"You sound really happy," I said. I was so glad. If anyone deserved it, it was my aunt.

"I feel really happy."

There was a knock at the front door, and I half expected and wanted it to be Rafe. But it was Marco. They were going to do a sweep of the farm. Either Marco or Gianni always checked in with us first to let us know what they were doing so we wouldn't get scared. Or accidentally shoot one of them with Aunt Sylvia's shotgun. Rafe had hired extra men since the postcard had arrived, and I didn't know their names. I didn't even know if they were Monterran or not. Aunt Sylvia offered them hot chocolate, but they told us that they'd brought their own beverages with them. He smiled and wished us a merry Christmas.

After I closed the door, Aunt Sylvia handed me a bulb that had my mother's name on it and the year 1988. "This was her last ornament before she left home," she said, just as she had every other year. I put it up at the very top. I would strangle that dog if he broke this one. Well, not really. But I would possibly imagine doing it.

I plugged in the Christmas lights and turned off the living room ones. Aunt Sylvia left on a single table lamp so that we could see while we strung the popcorn she had made. This was one of my favorite traditions, because it always was so beautiful and made me feel so calm and centered.

"Can I ask you something?" I said.

"Anything, sweetheart."

We'd never really talked about the cult or what had happened there, at my request. It wasn't that I didn't want to talk about my mom. I loved hearing stories about her when she was younger. Aunt Sylvia didn't have many, as she was almost fifteen years older and had been off at college by the time my mom was three years old. My mother had been a surprise baby for my grandparents.

"Why didn't she come with us?"

I didn't have to clarify who or what I was talking about.

Aunt Sylvia put her popcorn chain down.

"Did she . . . did she not want to stay with me?" It was a question I'd always been afraid to ask. It was easier to pretend or make up my own answer than face the truth. My voice cracked, my throat hot and thick with emotion and tears.

But I had come to a point in my life where the truth had become necessary. Good or bad, I needed to know. Not just about my mom, but about Rafe, too.

"Of course she did. But she knew that if she came with you, John-Paul would never give up. It was one thing to let you go. It was another for you both to leave. She stayed behind so that you could get away. She made me promise to always keep you safe. And I've done the best that I could."

Relief, sharp and powerful, cut through me. My mother had loved me. She had made the ultimate sacrifice to keep me safe. I hugged my aunt, holding her close. "You've been the best mother I could have asked for."

"And you have been the best daughter. You have made my life complete," she said.

Now we were both crying, which ended up making both of us laugh. "Look at us," Aunt Sylvia said. "I'm glad we're the only ones here."

"Me too," I said, wiping tears from my cheeks.

She grabbed a box of tissues from the end table and offered me one. "Speaking of being alone, why don't you go ask Rafe if he'd like to string popcorn with us."

I groaned, laying my head against the back of the couch. "Why do you keep pushing this?"

"As long as we're being honest, and despite what you might think, I'm not going to live forever." She put the box back down.

"Yes, you are," I interrupted as panic bloomed inside me. "I won't let you die."

She patted my hand. "I love you, too, but I want to know that you're happy. I want you to have real love and a family, all the things I never got to have."

"You can have real love. Maybe with Max. It's never too late. And I'm your family."

"You are. But I want more for you." She pushed the needle through another piece of popcorn. Even when her hands were bothering her, she was somehow always able to do this at Christmas. "And I suppose I push Rafe because I've seen how happy he makes you."

I crossed my arms, irritated at the implication. "I can be happy on my own. I don't need a man."

"Some people are very happy on their own. But speaking as the woman who raised you, I don't think you will be. I know you. I got to see your relationship with Rafe in a way that you never will. You watch the show and all you see are the lies and the hurt. I watch it and I see the love. I see the romance. How his face lights up, even now, every time you walk in a room. I see how important you are to him. He is giving up everything just to be near you. He is disappointing his family, his nation, his staff, the charities he supports. Everything has been put aside for a chance with you. If that's not love, I don't know what is."

My heart plummeted into my stomach at her words. Because she didn't lie to me. She never would. She didn't have it in her.

Rafe had never said he loved me, but Aunt Sylvia was telling me she had witnessed it. And maybe I was so consumed by my perceived hurts and betrayals that I couldn't see it. Or wouldn't.

Maybe I'd never given him the chance to say it to me. I'd certainly never said it to him. My head started to throb, and I leaned my forehead against my hands.

What was I doing? How would I cope with any of this?

There was another knock at the door. Saved by the bell. Er, knock. I expected to see a bodyguard, but was surprised to find Amanda standing there. I turned the lights on and invited her in.

"Sorry for not calling first." She kicked the snow off of her boots and came inside. "Did you tell her yet?"

Aunt Sylvia shook her head. "Not yet. You can, if you want."

"Tell me what?"

Amanda's eyes danced with happiness. "Rafe has hired me as a full-time caretaker for your aunt. Which means I don't have to drive into the city anymore! No more two-hour commutes!"

"He what?"

"And he hired me to be on call for his new offices. I'll be able to tell people whether or not they need to go see a doctor, run some educational classes—it's going to be so great. The best part is how much more time I'll be able to spend with Austin and work at the B&B."

She opened up her bag. "So I'm just here to check on your aunt. If you wouldn't mind giving us a moment?"

I stepped into the kitchen, listening to the two women laugh and talk. *Rafe strikes again.* Pretty soon he was going to have the entire town on his payroll. I wasn't sure how I felt about that.

Whitney had worried that I was going to have an uphill battle getting the town on my side. I was more worried about the uphill battle I was about to have with myself.

Amanda popped her head in the kitchen. "I'm all done, and I'm heading out. If you ever need anything, I'm now officially on call for you and your aunt." I thanked her, and she started to leave. "Oh, by the way, even though I've thanked him a thousand times, please thank Rafe again. I can't tell you what this means for me and my family."

With that she plunged a knife into my heart and twisted. So far, since coming here, he'd spent gobs of money, taken care of me and my aunt, and solved so many problems for the little community that I considered my extended family.

So now I had to invite him over. I would be such an ungrateful wretch if I didn't. My guilt was like a large, ugly toad, squatting on me until I did the right thing. I also felt bad about him being away from home. Given that he was from such a large family, they probably had a million different traditions that he was missing out on because he had chosen to be here. I put on my coat, telling Aunt Sylvia I'd be right back. I was glad I couldn't see her face, because I could hear the smugness in her voice when she said, "Okay!"

While I trudged across the yard, I decided that there were some decisions that had to be made. I needed to get away from him for a little while. I wanted a chance to clear my head and think when he wasn't constantly around, influencing me. I had that appearance scheduled tomorrow night at a club called Element in Iowa City. That would be a good chance to think about what I wanted and whether or not I could do as Pastor Dave suggested. To figure out if I could forgive him and if I could trust myself.

You shouldn't go alone, a voice said in my head. *What about John-Paul?*

John-Paul was in Washington. Where the postmark was from. I wasn't going to stop living my life. I needed that Rafe-free time to evaluate our situation.

I knocked on his door, unprepared for his smile that nearly bowled me over. "Hi. I came to see if you'd like to come over and have some hot chocolate and help us decorate our Christmas tree."

"Yes. Let me grab a coat." I stepped inside, closing the door. He walked back toward his bedroom, which surprised me because his coat was hanging next to the front door. I was about to point that out to him, but he had already returned, picking up the coat and sliding his arms into the sleeves. "Let's go."

He opened the door for me and closed it behind us. "What's new with you?" he asked.

"Same old, same old. My guild can't find a decent healer for our Saturday night raids. I got a C on my organic chemistry lab work and I'll have to redo it. And a megalomaniac cult leader knows where I am."

That earned me a laugh, but I could only smile. Too many warring emotions struggled inside me. Right as we got to the back porch, he put his hand on my arm. "Wait. I have something for you."

I hoped it wasn't a kiss.

Okay, that was a lie. I hoped it *was* a kiss.

But it wasn't. He pulled out a small wrapped box that made my heart cease all function until I realized it was too big to be a ring box.

"Open it," he encouraged.

The silver paper ripped off easily, and I could tell that he had done it himself because there was tape everywhere. I wondered if he had ever wrapped a present before. The fact that he had personally done it softened me more than I would have admitted out loud.

I opened the box, and inside was a perfect glass slipper ornament. I held it up, and the kitchen light sparkled and danced against it. It was dazzling. "Oh," was all I managed.

"Sometimes when you lose a shoe at midnight, it's so your prince can return it to you."

My first instinct was to give it back. To tell him it was too much. I even said, "You have to take this . . ." I closed my eyes, fighting the impulse while letting my voice trail off. Because I had the sneaking suspicion this was like Swarovski crystal or something and probably cost more than my car. Rafe never did anything small.

But to reject this gift would be like rejecting him. And if there was a possibility that I would want something more at some point in the distant future, then I couldn't shut him down.

So I opened my eyes and said, "Thank you."

We got inside and I brought him into the living room, offering to hang up his coat. He gave me a look, like I'd just insulted the thousand years' worth of chivalry and honor that had been bred into him. Instead he took mine from me and hung them both up.

I went to the tree to hang up the slipper, but my aunt stopped me. "What's that?"

"This?" I held it up. "It's something Rafe gave me."

"May I see it?"

I walked over, handing her the ornament. She held it up like I had, but now we had multicolored lights to twinkle and reflect off of the surface. She leaned toward me and whispered with a satisfied smile, "This, my darling girl, is why I push."

"It's too much. I don't like him doing things like this for me."

She let the ornament dangle from her fingers, silent for a few moments. "I don't want to diminish what you've been through, but Rafe is not John-Paul. He's not trying to control your life or make you feel powerless. He's trying to show you that he loves you the only way that he can."

"He could just say it, if that's how he really felt."

"Haven't you heard that words are cheap? He's showing you instead of telling you."

And in that moment, I sort of got why she was on his side. I returned to the tree, hanging the ornament on the highest possible branch, next to my *Enterprise*. Rafe had sat next to Aunt Sylvia, and she was teaching him how to make popcorn strands. They talked and he made her laugh, like they were two old friends. I think more of the popcorn ended up in Rafe's mouth than on the string.

I sat on his other side and ignored the surprised expressions on both of their faces. Technically, he had taken my spot, and this was where all the supplies were. I concentrated on finishing up my strand. Being this close to him made my stomach somersault. And I had homework to get done.

Sylvia excused herself to get a drink. I offered to get it for her, but she said she wanted to do it on her own. I knew her independence was important to her. Apparently so did Rafe, and that had to be the reason he had hired Amanda. Rafe helped my aunt to stand, making sure she had her cane. When he sat back down, he was now much closer to me than where he had started out. His thigh pressed against mine, and his upper arm was against my shoulder. Delicious heat pulsed from him, filling my senses.

While I thought I should probably move, I didn't.

"Thank you," I said, keeping my eyes fixed on my work.

I felt his gaze on me. "You already thanked me."

"No. Amanda stopped by and told me what you did for her. And I know what you've done for half of the people in this town. You've changed all of their lives for the better. They're all important to me. Thank you."

He went strangely quiet, and I stole a glance at his face. He looked so serious. "Everyone important to you is important to me."

I gulped. *Rafe was important to me.* The realization bolted into me so fast, so furiously, that I knew it was absolutely true. He mattered. I cared. Whether or not I wanted to, I did. The delirious dizziness of my epiphany engulfed me and I wanted to talk with him, to see if we could work things out. I was in danger of folding like a bad poker hand. I didn't say anything, though.

Because I was going to have to figure out a way to start trusting myself first if I ever hoped to trust him.

Chapter 17

The last time Rafe and I had sat this close, we had been back on the show. A couple of weeks in, after all the girls had gone to bed or passed out drunk, he had me meet him in the confessional room. He had set up a TV so that we could watch a movie. The movie had been my idea; our dates had been so outlandish and had involved so many other women that I wanted a chance at normal. I just wanted to cuddle with him and watch a movie like regular people.

It was totally against the rules for us to be alone like this, but that somehow made it more exciting and romantic.

He had two options for me—an action movie or a romantic comedy. Looking back, I probably should have picked the action movie, but I wanted the rom-com. Not only because I felt like I was living in a real-life one, but because it reminded me of my aunt and home.

And toward the end, when the couple admitted their love, finally kissed for the first time, and fell into bed together, I made a weird sound from the back of my throat. I instantly went silent, praying he hadn't noticed.

Part of my reaction was because it made me so uncomfortable to be watching a scene like that with a guy I liked that much. I'm sure it would have been no problem for some other girl, but for me it was awkward squared.

It felt like a Big Deal because I'd never done anything even remotely like that. Which he knew, but still.

Despite my wish that he had hadn't heard my inelegant noise, he immediately turned to me, pausing the movie. "What?"

And he had just made it infinitely worse by pausing the characters mid-action.

So I talked about something else that bugged me instead, as my anxiety bubbled up. "They seriously just kissed for the first time thirty seconds ago and now they're jumping into bed together. Whatever happened to all the in-between stuff? The buildup? The courting? They just went from zero to sixty."

His eyes were unreadable and hooded. Like some giant hawk studying his prey. Which only served to ratchet the tension up to eleventy billion.

I continued, now that I was on a nervous babbling roll. "It's why I like movies set in different centuries. At least then there are these steps to their romance, a path they travel down before it gets to this point. Nowadays it's like there's this big buffet out and everyone just jumps in and piles their plates up and stuffs themselves without even tasting what they're eating."

He reached out, running the back of his hand slowly across my cheek. "As opposed to a six-course meal where every course is appreciated, where each dish leads to the next, and it's savored for hours."

Whoa. My heart slammed right against my lungs, while the little hairs on the back of my neck stood up. He was so not talking about food.

"A woman should be savored," he said against my lips, nibbling on them like I tasted delicious. That managed to shut my stupid, talkative brain and mouth down. We made out for a while, and I'd felt very savored afterward.

But I worried that we had wandered into a new place, one completely outside of my comfort zone.

And I felt that way now, too, like I didn't know what I was doing or what I wanted or how to get there. More uncharted territory. And I didn't know if I wanted him to boldly go where no man had gone before.

"Genesis, I need to explain—"

He broke off when my aunt came back. Aunt Sylvia wore a disappointed expression when she reentered the room with her drink. Like she was some kind of reverse chaperone and she'd hoped to catch us doing something but was let down that we weren't.

More small talk resumed, and things were going well right up until the moment when it all came crashing down around me.

Sylvia harmlessly mentioned my appearance in Iowa City the next night.

"I'll go with you," Rafe said. Which I might have been fine with if he hadn't added on the last part: "You can't go that far at night by yourself."

"Um, I go that far all the time," I said. "It's where I go to school."

"Considering the current circumstances, I think it's better if you don't ever drive into Iowa City by yourself. You need someone to protect you."

That did it. I dropped my popcorn and stood up, glaring at him. "As refreshingly sexist as that is, I can actually take care of myself. I'll be driving alone, thanks."

He jumped to his feet, eyes blazing. "I won't allow it."

I really hoped that was some kind of mistranslation on his part, because I was ready to start throwing things. Even Aunt Sylvia looked worried now. "Won't allow it?" I repeated through gritted teeth, as my melting resolve hardened right back up. "You don't get a vote. You don't get to 'allow' me to do anything. Can I just remind you that I ran away from the last man who decided what I was allowed to do?"

"This is nothing like that! I'm trying to keep you safe from that man!"

I hated that he was capable of making my emotions bounce all over the place. How he'd made me shift from maybe-this-could-work-out to thinking of ways that I might possibly make his soon-to-take-place homicide look like an accident.

But before I could scream back, Sylvia intervened. "Genesis, I know you can take care of yourself, but it would make me feel better if you'd let Rafe drive you. There's supposed to be a big storm coming in tomorrow, and I'd rest easier knowing that you weren't alone. In case something happens."

The odds of that were so low it was ridiculous. I'd been driving in Iowa winters for almost eight years. Which I might have told her, if she hadn't been so concerned. It was like she had just dumped a bucket of ice water over my head. I couldn't stay mad at her. "Fine," I said, giving in. "I will do it for Sylvia. But there are conditions."

The fire seemed to have gone out of Rafe as well. "Such as?"

"No bodyguards, and we take my car." I liked Marco and Gianni, but bodyguards were basically stalkers that you paid. I didn't want to be stalked.

"Two bodyguards, and I will drive my car. My car that was designed for inclement weather."

I glanced at Aunt Sylvia, who was becoming more despondent with each passing moment. I could negotiate and give a little. For her sake.

"Your car. You can drive. But I am not traveling with an entourage. Still no bodyguards."

He let out a sigh, rubbing the back of his neck. "Okay. No bodyguards. I'll work something out with them. But they're not going to like it."

Not my problem. If he was going to crash my event, then he could figure out a way to make it work. I also wasn't going to let him take advantage of our situation. "And no explanation conversations in the car," I added. If he thought he'd get me alone and try to make this all better after telling me I wasn't allowed to act like my own person, he had another think coming.

After several long beats he finally said, "Agreed."

Good. "I have homework," I said as my good night. I knew I was being terribly rude, but I didn't care. I needed to cool off. I tried to think of a bright side. I settled on the fact that with Rafe driving, I could probably get some studying done on the way.

When I got to the stairs, I heard Aunt Sylvia say, "It's the curse of the Summers hair. Makes all of us feisty and stubborn when we're backed into a corner."

I almost marched back downstairs. I was not feisty and stubborn! I was logical and reasonable and Rafe was the one acting like this was the twelfth century and I wasn't allowed to go outside by myself.

My inner beast needed a Reese's peanut butter cup.

At least I got what I wanted, I consoled myself, still searching for the silver lining. I'd given in to Aunt Sylvia's request, which would make her happy, and Rafe had given in to mine, which made me happy.

I had won.

But even though I might have won this particular battle, I had the feeling that I was in danger of losing the war.

Which led to us in his SUV, driving through thick and blinding snow. "We don't have to go," he said. "I think they'll understand."

"I need the money," I responded.

"I'll give you the money."

I scrunched my face up. Would he ever get it? "I need to *earn* the money. I'm not your charity case."

His hands tightened on the steering wheel. "I'm not saying you are—never mind. Forget it."

Gladly. I rested my elbow against the base of the window, looking out into the stark white landscape that was lit up by the headlights of his car. I wouldn't have admitted it to anyone, but I was glad he was driving in this and I wasn't. I might have been tempted to do just what he had suggested—turn around and go back.

But I couldn't say no to the five thousand dollars the club was paying me. This would probably be my last chance to make any more money from the show. The new season of *Marry Me* was starting up in a few weeks. I didn't know how they hoped to top identical twin princes.

Because there would soon be a new batch of contestants, nobody was going to be interested in the people from previous seasons. There wouldn't be any more big checks in my future.

The car slid a little, as the freeway hadn't been salted and cleared yet. But Rafe quickly regained control, putting us back into our lane. It was then that I realized I hadn't seen another car in a long time. What if nobody showed up?

I texted the club owner, a man named Frank. I asked if he still needed me to come, because despite my objections, maybe Rafe was right. Frank responded immediately, telling me that the snow was not bad closer to the city, and the club was already packed. They were definitely expecting me. I told him there might be a delay with the weather, and he said not to worry about it, and to just get there safely and in one piece.

"The snow gets better up ahead."

"It certainly can't get worse," he muttered, leaning forward with his arms locked into place.

"How about some music?" I said. He was in a bit of a mood, and I didn't want to be stuck trying to make conversation with him.

Without waiting for him to respond, I turned the radio on. It was set to my favorite station, which seemed odd. Weirder still—Rafe was humming along to the Garth Brooks song that was playing. I didn't know a lot about Monterra, but I was pretty sure they didn't have country music there.

"How do you know this song?"

At first he didn't say anything. And just when the silence got so oppressive I was in danger of lapsing into some nonsensical conversation to keep the quiet away, he said, "It makes me feel closer to you."

My jaw dropped as my eyebrows gathered together, right above my nose. What was I supposed to do with that?

Rafe took out his phone and handed it to me. "Please call the last number." Something in his voice made me do it. I tapped on the phone icon and went into his "Recent" tab. I selected the last call and pushed the green button to place the call. I put it on speaker for him.

The person on the other end picked up immediately. "This is Marco."

"Marco, I'm checking in. The weather's terrible," he said as he side-eyed me. "But we're fine. I'll call you again in an hour."

"Thank you, Your Highness."

The bodyguard hung up, and I handed the phone back to Rafe. "I promised to call them every hour on the hour," he explained as he put his phone back in his front jeans pocket.

I didn't know whether or not to believe that his guards had stayed away. They might have told him they would, but for all I knew they were tailing us right now like some super stealthy hound dogs.

It took longer than normal, but we finally arrived. As promised, the snow was much lighter here, but it wasn't any less cold. The SUV's GPS guided Rafe to the front of the club, where valet-sicles were waiting to take our car.

"Look at that. We made it all the way to the club and I wasn't kidnapped once," I said sarcastically, letting myself out.

A loud cheer went up from the crowd. Frank had certainly promoted this event. There was a big picture of me with my name on it, and a huge line of freezing people waiting to get inside. A wall of blistering cold wind slammed into me when I opened the door, and my teeth immediately started to chatter. I had a shawl on, but it was no match for this weather. My vanity and inability to be weather-appropriate was going to kill me.

Frank came outside, looking like a reject from a 1990s boy band. He topped off his white jeans and white hoodie with a comb-over that seemed less a hairdo and more like a wind advisory, because long strands of it were blowing everywhere.

"Genesis! So nice to finally meet you." His hand felt like ice. It somehow managed to make me even colder. "And who have you brought with you? Rafe or Dante?"

Rafe had dressed appropriately for the occasion in a black tight-knit, long-sleeved shirt and dark jeans, and he had a winter coat on. I was the idiot in danger of turning into a life-size ice cube in my ballet flats and my once-nice cocktail dress. It was the same dress I wore to all of these appearances. It was a forest green sheath that nipped in at my waist and felt like it had been made just for me. It even touched the top of my knees, which was nice since I so rarely found dresses in my size that were long enough.

But the arctic winds that blew against my legs were not at all nice, and I was ready for this conversation to move along. "This is Rafe. Can we get inside?"

Frank was way too excited, but I didn't care. I waved to everyone in the crowd, plastering on a big, faux smile. I rushed ahead of the men, hearing the words "renegotiate" as I went, but I didn't slow down.

"Should we let people take pictures?" Rafe asked.

"Those aren't people," I said over my shoulder. "They're paparazzi." They'd hounded me pretty relentlessly for the first couple of weeks after the show finished airing, but our sheriff was very good at finding ways to drive them off.

The bouncer let me right inside, and a wave of sweat- and humidity-laced heat slammed into me. They had a lot of people inside dancing and at the bar. I warmed up really quickly. Once Frank and Rafe joined me, Frank showed us to the VIP section. It was a roped-off corner with a loveseat and a low table for drinks. A waitress immediately appeared, and I wished that I could order hot chocolate. I told her I was fine, and Rafe asked for water.

Keeping my false smile firmly in place, I tried not to make eye contact with any of the people staring at us. Loud techno music shook the club, making it impossible to hear, but I could easily see everything. These club appearances always made me feel like I was a seal at Sea World. Being stared at and pointed at in my enclosure, being expected to perform and entertain the crowd.

In that regard, it was nice that Rafe was with me because he was someone else to look at besides me.

The waitress brought back his water, leaning over farther than she needed to. Rafe went for his wallet, but she said, "Everything is on the house. I'll get you whatever you want." Jealousy reared up inside me like a hissing cat. Her invitation was unmistakable, and her cleavage flashing was starting to get annoying. I was mollified when I saw that Rafe didn't look at what she wanted him to look at.

She walked off in a huff at her failed attempt, and I couldn't help it. It made me smirk, and I was definitely feeling less angry than I had been just a few minutes ago. Rafe took out his phone, typing away. He was probably contacting his security team again. Then I wondered what he had been talking about with Frank. "What were you and Frank renegotiating?" I asked, trying to make myself heard over the music.

He realized that I was talking to him, and he had to lean in and I had to yell to repeat myself, ignoring my thundering pulse at being so close.

"I said he had to double his fee because we're both here. He didn't want to, but I convinced him." His words caressed my ear, sending cascading shivers down my back. It didn't surprise me he'd gotten his way. Like Aunt Sylvia was fond of saying, Rafe could probably convince a woman in white gloves to eat a ketchup Popsicle in August.

I didn't know why he'd bothered with the fee. He didn't need the money.

A photographer approached us, and I hated the thought that one of the paparazzi had snuck inside. Yet another person exploiting my personal life to make a buck. "Frank hired me for the night. Would you mind if I got some pictures of you two?"

Oh. He was the official photographer. This was part of the deal. Frank wanted some documented evidence that we had been there. I smiled, pushing my chin forward so that I wouldn't have a double chin in all the pictures. I had learned that the hard way.

"Could you move closer together?" he asked, directing us with his hand. "Yes. Just a little bit closer. Keep moving."

We scooted until I was completely pressed against Rafe on my right side. I blamed the heat that rose in my cheeks on the warmth of the club.

"Can you put your arm around her?"

Rafe pulled his arm out from in between us and laid it across my shoulders, his warm fingers pressing against my upper arm. A strangled breath escaped, and I was glad he couldn't hear it.

"Perfect!" The photographer started clicking away, the camera's light flashing every other second. It was a struggle to keep my eyes open.

Then Rafe's thumb slowly rubbed my arm, back and forth, back and forth. I wondered if he even knew that he was doing it. It was all I could do to sit there, with him smelling like a dream and feeling strong and secure against me. I wanted to bust out of my skin. Still the pictures went on and on, with no sign of letting up.

Maybe I should contact the government and tell them about this new form of torture that I had discovered.

Finally, an eternity later, after my body had practically gone limp against Rafe, as if it wanted to stay next to him for the rest of my life, we were done. "I'll grab some candids when you guys are out dancing."

Dancing? Dancing was not part of this deal. I had no intention of dancing. It was bad enough being watched. The last time I'd danced in public to this kind of music, someone had asked me if I needed to go to the hospital, because they honestly thought I was having a seizure.

Country line dancing was a different story. I liked the patterns, the predictability of it. It wasn't just waving your limbs with reckless abandon or moving like you were trying to get pregnant right there on the dance floor.

Before I could protest, Frank was there, still blissfully happy. He yelled, "Now that you're done with photos, would you two mind dancing together?"

"I don't think so," I said, shaking my head so that he'd understand my response even if he couldn't hear me.

This was not what the club promoter wanted to hear. "Come on. I'll throw in another thousand dollars if you'll dance. Just one dance."

Then Rafe was on his feet, pulling me up by the hand. "What are you doing?" I asked.

"We're dancing."

I leaned back on my heels, stopping him from propelling me forward. "I can't!"

He studied me for a minute, like he was trying to figure out the right thing to say. "Do you trust me?"

Did he really not understand that that was our entire problem? I didn't know whether or not I could trust him.

"I won't let anything happen to you. Come on." He tugged on my hand again.

And like a lamb being led to the slaughter, I followed meekly behind him, trying my best not to remember in excruciating detail the last time we had danced together.

Chapter 18

While we were on *Marry Me,* I had taken him on a date that was about getting to know me better. I had found a nearby western bar that had dancing on Friday nights.

He was surprised when we pulled up. "I thought you didn't drink."

Rafe had been a good sport, wearing the full country getup. Cowboy boots, cowboy hat, and jeans. It made him even more scrumptious.

"I don't. But I do line dance."

He protested, but I begged and pleaded. To my delight, he gave in faster than a badly built card tower. I showed him the basics, and we stood behind the other dancers while I taught him the steps. He turned out to be a surprisingly quick study, and when I said as much, he mentioned that his mother had made him take dance classes when he was younger. Which was totally adorable.

We danced until we were both out of breath and sweating. I used my hat to fan my face. "Let's go outside," he suggested.

And even though we were in California in the summer, it was still a thousand degrees cooler outside than in the bar.

"Better?" he asked.

"Much," I said, pulling my hair up and fanning the back of my neck.

Patsy Cline's "Crazy" came on. "Listen," I said. It had always been my aunt's favorite song. It was the one she'd played during her first dance at her wedding reception. After Richard left and we discovered that he had taken all of our money, she had locked herself in her room for twenty-four hours, playing that song over and over again. The next day she came out, all steely reserves and strength, and went on with her life as if Richard had never been part of it.

She hadn't played it again since.

"Do you like this song?"

It was a song that reminded me of both good and bad times. It was haunting and beautiful. "I love it," I finally said, not wanting to explain the entire complicated history.

"Then we should dance." He offered me his left hand, and I put my right hand in it. He put my other hand on his shoulder, and his right hand went around my lower back, emptying all the breath from my chest. He pulled me in close, swaying slowly back and forth.

His gaze pierced my heart, and there was something in his expression, an emotion, that I didn't recognize.

Instead of ruining this moment by overanalyzing, I rested my head against his shoulder, closing my eyes. He put his cheek against the top of my hair, making me sigh with pleasure. I wanted this moment to last forever.

I forgot about everything. I forgot about the camera crew filming us, about the people standing in the doorway watching us, about my fears that I didn't know him very well.

Because right then only one thing mattered—I absolutely knew I had fallen in love with him. The truth slammed into me with 1.21 gigawatts of electrical power. My face felt feverish as that love filled my heart with a buoyant happiness.

I didn't know if he felt the same. I'd seen enough contestants blindsided on this show to know that he might be feeling one thing but acting like he felt another. Being with him here like this, though, seemed so true. So right. He made me feel like I belonged in his arms, in his embrace, and in his heart.

So you could imagine my shock when the techno music cut out, and "Crazy" filled the loudspeakers. I looked up to see Frank standing next to the DJ, and he gave me two thumbs up.

I was going to storm out of this club. That promoter could keep his money.

Rafe's eyes had narrowed. He immediately understood the reference and anticipated my reaction. His grip on my hand tightened. "Don't react. That's why he did it. He's trying to provoke you. Just dance with me." He sounded as upset as I felt. All of America knew we had broken up and had stayed broken up. Frank was about to give his club-goers something that no one would have thought possible.

Especially me.

I swallowed several times before finally nodding. I could do this. One dance, and then I was done with it for the night. There weren't any cameras this time. Just a roomful of people I would never see again. At least this dance wouldn't be televised.

He took my hand, raising it over my head, and twirled me around before pulling me into his arms. The crowd gathered around us seemed to enjoy that. He was holding me close, probably closer than he should have, and I followed his lead as we danced slowly. Although my head and my heart were in disagreement about how they should react to him, they both agreed that they loved how it felt to be held by him.

His hand splayed against the curve of my lower back, using pressure to let me know which way I should move next. His other hand engulfed mine, and I could feel the calluses on his palm. His broad and muscular shoulder flexed under my hand, like he was feeling the tension, too. I looked just over his shoulder, not wanting to make eye contact. I wasn't sure I could handle it. My synapses were already overloaded. I didn't need to make it worse.

A radiating warmth enveloped me, and all the other sounds, the other people, everything faded away and it was just the two of us dancing, as if we were the only ones in the club. My body shifted me forward, moving me even closer to him.

It wasn't like the first time we'd danced to this song, but all the emotions I'd had before came rushing back. I related to these words in a way that I never had before. I had been crazy for loving him, for giving him my whole heart without knowing the truth.

"You are so beautiful," he whispered against my ear, making the skin there run hot. "I don't get to tell you as often as I'd like to. But you are."

He probably didn't tell me because he knew I would argue with him about it. He knew that I grew up not wanting to be pretty or noticed. Somehow it wasn't so bad when he was the one noticing. The way he held me and looked at me made me feel beautiful.

"I love holding you," he went on as his nose nuzzled my earlobe, and that turned my knee tendons into water. "Even if it's only because we're dancing." He planted a tiny kiss in that magical spot right behind my ear, and my mouth felt parched, like I'd been marching through the Sahara and hadn't had anything to drink for a month.

Then the song ended, and everybody around us started to hoot and holler, applauding us for our dance. My heart beat so fast and so loud that the DJ could have used it for his next song. Rafe held me out to one side, and he bowed. I did a sort of curtsy, even though it was the first time I'd ever attempted one. Right then I was too dazed to do anything but let him lead me off of the dance floor. The regular music started up again, and we sat down on our little loveseat.

He had that look in his eyes. That look that said he wanted me. And given my current condition, I was in danger of giving in. His gaze dropped to my lips. Yep. No misinterpretation there.

Frank came over to introduce the VIP guests who had purchased a chance for autographs or pictures. I did my best to pull myself back together, to smile and say hello. Thankfully, I didn't have to make a lot of conversation because it was too hard to hear and make myself heard. We got a lot of, "Are you guys back together?"

And I would answer, "No."

Rafe answered, "Not yet."

That went on for a long time, and it took all my resolve to focus on the people I was supposed to be entertaining and not think about Rafe and that dance. And the magic that was always sparked when we were together. He called his bodyguards a couple more times, and the last call was interrupted by a very drunk girl who wanted to sit on his lap and take a picture.

I did not rip out her extensions one by one, even though I wanted to.

We stayed for our contractually obligated two hours, and the very second that ended, Rafe said, "Let's get out of here." He left that skeevy waitress a fifty-dollar tip on our table. For three bottles of water.

He signaled to Frank, who walked over with an envelope. He handed it to me. "Here's your money. Cash, like we agreed."

I hadn't agreed to that. I always got paid by check. I asked him a confused, "What?"

"It's all there. Your boyfriend drives a hard bargain. You two brought in a lot of business tonight. I'll call you again!"

I didn't even bother saying he wasn't my boyfriend. People generally believed what they wanted to believe, and didn't want to be bothered with the facts. I nodded, putting the envelope into the clutch I had brought with me. I held it tightly against my chest, afraid of losing that much cash.

Rafe got his coat back, and the shivering valet had our car waiting for us, all heated up. As we walked toward it, a drunk, stumbling guy slammed into Rafe on the sidewalk.

"Sorry, man." The guy slurred his words, but Rafe told him it was fine. The man shook it off and managed to start walking straight as he headed around the corner.

I gratefully got inside the waiting SUV, and a different valet shut my door. I saw Rafe tip the one who had retrieved the car, and from the look on the kid's face, it was a lot of money.

"Are you hungry?" Rafe asked as he put on his seatbelt. "I'm in the mood for seafood. Where do they have good lobster?"

"Maine," I responded, and a smile quirked the ends of his lips. "I really just want to get home, if that's okay."

I should've known that nothing is ever that easy.

"Home it is," he said, pulling out into traffic. The weirdest thing happened as we were leaving—despite security holding onlookers back, I saw someone suddenly running away from the car in the passenger side mirror. One of the bouncers chased after him.

Rafe glanced at me in the rearview mirror. The air in the car felt oppressive and awkward. I couldn't forget what he had said or how he had touched me. To distract myself, I opened up my purse and got out the envelope, which was full of one-hundred-dollar bills. There were a lot of them. Eleven thousand dollars' worth. It was so much. I held out fifty-five hundred of it to Rafe, his half of the fee. The federal government would take most of what I had left.

"Keep it."

"I can't keep it. You earned it."

He sighed. "I don't want it. So either keep it, throw it out the window, or we can take it back to Frank."

Of the three options, the first did sound the best. I could catch us up on our mortgage. This would make a huge difference in our lives. The desire to accept was overwhelming.

"Don't decide now. You can think about it for a while."

I should probably do something more noble with it. Like help repair the church roof. I'd get a tax deduction and possibly buy myself a spot in heaven.

But I had to put my family first. I closed my purse again and hoped God and Pastor Dave would understand. Rafe turned the radio on again, to my relief. I wasn't ready to talk about what had just happened.

We weren't far outside the city when the wall of snow slammed into us again, obscuring our view. I'd hoped the storm would have let up by now, but it hadn't.

My phone buzzed, and there was a text from Whitney.

How are things going? Are you back in love yet?

I started to text a reply when my phone went dead. I tried turning it back on, but the little battery picture popped up, showing I had no juice. I probably should have charged it before we left, but I was mad and distracted. No big deal. I slid it back in my purse.

We were nearly back to the town when Rafe murmured, "*Uffa!*"

He had told me once that the word meant uh-oh. I remembered it because it sounded funny. I could see a light flashing on his dash. "What is it?"

"Flat back tire. On both sides," he said incredulously. He turned on his blinkers and pulled over onto the shoulder. "I'll be right back." He left the car running and went out to investigate. The headlights were shining on a busted mile marker sign that I recognized.

He got back in the car, snow glistening in his hair and on his coat. He held his bare hands in front of the vents. "No mistake. Both of the back tires are flat. Someone caused a slow leak."

That must have been what I saw back at the club. The man who had been crouched next to the SUV. Why did people do stuff like this? "How did it take them so long to go flat?"

"They were really good tires," he said, reaching into his pockets.

"Now what?"

"It is too dangerous for us to be driving in these conditions on two flat tires, and I only have one spare. I was going to call Marco, but I can't find my phone." He kept checking his pockets while I looked around on the seat and on the floor.

"My phone is dead. Do you have a charger in here? We could plug it in," I offered.

"No," he said, sounding more frustrated with each passing moment.

"When do you last remember having your phone?"

He blinked a couple of times. "I texted Marco right after I got my coat. I distinctly remember sliding it into my front pocket." He put his hand on his chest over the spot where it had been.

I gasped as I remembered the events that had occurred as we were leaving the club. "That drunk guy! He totally Keyser Söze-d us! He was pretending to be drunk to mug you, and then he just walked away!"

"He was hardly a criminal mastermind. He wasn't even a very good thief. He completely missed my wallet."

So going to Iowa City had led to a nexus of crap—it left us stranded in the middle of a snowstorm, without a phone to call for help, and it had made me even more confused on where things stood with Rafe.

All in all, not a good night.

He rested his forehead on one of his hands. I knew that gesture. He was severely stressed. My hand reached out of its own volition, squeezing his shoulder. "It's just a phone. You can replace it."

"It's not that. The phone itself doesn't matter. It's what's on the phone that's the problem."

That hadn't even occurred to me. If someone ever stole my phone, it would be no big deal. But I wasn't royalty. I didn't have my family's privacy to protect the same way that he did. He probably had pictures and videos on there that he would not like to share with the entire world.

"That sucks."

He straightened up, and I ordered my hand back to my lap. "It's password protected. Unless he knows exactly what he's doing, he shouldn't be able to get access. Hopefully he had no idea who I was. My security team should be able to find it and get it back."

"How?"

"There's a tracker on my phone. Behind the battery," he said absentmindedly.

I couldn't help myself. I pulled out my phone, taking off the back panel and lifting out the battery.

"What are you doing?"

"I wanted to make sure you hadn't put a tracker on my phone." I reassembled the device and slid it back into my clutch. Because I wouldn't have put it past him.

It made me suspicious that he didn't look insulted. "Did you consider tracking my phone?"

Several beats passed before he said, "After the postcard. Yes."

"Okay, promise me you won't do that. No trackers." It felt creepy. I didn't want someone always knowing where I was.

His jaw clenched, but he said, "I promise you I won't put a tracker on your phone."

Good.

"Okay," he started, thinking out loud. "Best-case scenario, in the next hour or so my men will come looking for me. The problem is when they activate the tracker, it will lead them into Iowa City. The weather's so bad they may not see our car on the opposite side of the road."

"And we won't have enough gas to keep the car going for that long," I added as I pointed at the gauge. The needle was down past empty.

"What?" he said, following my gaze. He slammed both of his hands against the wheel, making me jump. He uttered what Mr. Spock referred to as "colorful metaphors."

"*Che brutto!* That was so stupid of me! I can't believe we're going to run out of gas!"

It wasn't typical for him to slip into Italian. He must really be upset.

Then, as if on command and as if to prove that the universe really was conspiring against me, the engine sputtered and died.

He turned the key in the ignition, trying to start it up again. No response. He hit the wheel again, then the anger seemed to empty out and he leaned forward. "I'm sorry. I was just so focused on . . . other things."

"You were concentrating on the road and the storm," I said. "It happens."

"I should have checked the gas before we left. I wanted to keep you safe, and all I did was put you in more danger." He sounded so dejected.

We couldn't stay here and hope his bodyguards would find us. It would take them a long time to drive into the city because of the storm, and even longer to figure out what had happened to us and find Rafe's car. I had experienced enough of these kinds of snowstorms to know that people had frozen to death in them when they were stranded. Or didn't have heat.

I knew where we could find heat and shelter. It would just really suck to get there. But what other choice did we have?

If I was going to die, it was not going to be in some SUV, waiting for help. Even if I had to march into the freezing night in my cocktail dress and flats.

I wouldn't go down without a fight.

Chapter 19

"Max has a cabin up here, near the lake," I told him. "The road to get there is half a mile north, and then it's another mile out to the cabin. He keeps it stocked, so we'll be able to stay there and keep warm until they find us."

"Are you sure?"

"Very sure. Amanda had a lot of parties up here in high school, and we used that broken mile marker to know when to turn off. You can see it easily when there's no snow."

He sighed. "Then that's what we'll have to do. Is there a landline there?"

"No. He wanted it to be off the grid." I hoped I still had all of my toes when this was over.

"We can't go like this. Stay here."

He zipped up his coat and got out of the car again. This time when he opened his door and the frigid air blew in, it made me scared. This was serious. Life-and-death stuff. He popped up the trunk, and the wind pushed against my hair, icing my exposed skin. I tugged my shawl tighter around my shoulders, but it didn't do me much good.

A red glow reflected in my mirror. I turned around, hopeful that it was a police car, but I quickly realized that it was from the flares Rafe had set around the car. He slammed the rear hatch shut and jogged around to his door. He threw a bag and some blankets to me. For the second time that night, he shook the snow from his hair, and he had to blow on his hands, rubbing them together because there was no more heat coming in. He pushed the button to turn on his hazard flashers. The snow fell even thicker and faster, and it reflected the pulsating lights and the red glow of the flares.

"That's my workout bag. I keep it in the car in case I feel like going for a run. There's a pair of sweats for you to put on. You give me the hoodie, and I'll give you my coat."

"I can't—" I started to protest.

"For once, don't argue. There's a pair of socks and shoes in there, as well. You'll have to put them on. They'll be too big, but it's better than what you have on."

Nodding meekly, I climbed into the backseat. The windows had started to fog up. I had the jarring memory of the sheriff knocking on our car windows when we were teenagers and threatening to call our parents because we were parking and making out. I would have given anything for the sheriff to show up right then.

As I unzipped the bag I watched Rafe in the mirror, wondering if he might sneak a peek. Ever the gentleman, he didn't. I pulled up the sweats, tugging the string at the waist as tightly as I could and knotting it in place. I passed the hoodie up to him, and he took off his coat, giving it to me.

I was so anxious and scared that I didn't even pay attention to the masculine scent that seemed imbued in every fiber, or how warm his body had made the coat inside.

Okay, maybe I paid a little attention.

His running shoes were like big clown shoes on my feet, so I tied them as tightly as I could. I'd probably still get snow inside them, but they were much better than the flats I was wearing. I wanted to inappropriately giggle at the thought that Rafe was like a grown-up Boy Scout with his blankets and extra clothes and flares. I didn't have any of that stuff in my truck, and I knew better. He had grown up in a place where it snowed constantly, so I probably shouldn't have been surprised.

While I got changed, he pulled something out of the glove compartment. I saw that it was a pen and some paper. He was leaving a note. He asked me to repeat the directions, and he wrote them down. He put the note on his seat and then climbed into the back with me, bringing the blankets.

He sat close, pulling me against him. I didn't protest or try to move. Logically, I knew we could conserve body heat this way. Emotionally, I wanted to be held.

"The flares will last for about fifteen minutes. Let's stay here and see if anyone comes along. If not, well, we'll get a chance to get good and warmed up before we head out."

That almost made it worse. It would be terrible and shocking to go from this heat and coziness out into the frigid cold. Sort of like knowing what it was like to fall in love with Rafe and then realizing I couldn't be with him.

He rubbed my upper arm even though I wasn't cold yet. It was a reassuring touch, but I wasn't very reassured.

I could feel the edge of the cold in the air around us, as the car got slightly colder with each passing minute. Pretty soon it would be as cold in here as it was out there. The snow seemed to get heavier and thicker, enclosing the car in a white tomb. The silence was eerie. The world had become too still.

My claustrophobia started to creep in as the snow piled up against the windshield. *We will be fine,* I had to keep telling myself. *Rafe will keep me safe.*

He would. I knew he would.

"Maybe I was wrong about that whole no bodyguard thing," I said, as an apology. Just in case.

"You're only admitting you were wrong because you think we're going to die." He was teasing, and that made me feel slightly better.

Right up until my subconscious mind decided to terrify me. "The stuff that happened in the city—do you think it was deliberate? Did John-Paul do this?" I tried to remember the man who'd run into Rafe and the one I'd seen next to the car, but I hadn't paid them much attention.

He sat quietly next to me, not answering right away. "Nothing's impossible, but it seems unlikely. If his plan was to stop us or slow us down, then where is he?"

He sounded rational and reasonable, but he didn't know John-Paul the way that I did. I could believe that he would orchestrate something like this. It put me even more on edge.

The car's clock showed that our time was up. The fifteen minutes had passed too quickly. "Time to go," he said. He reached into the pocket of his coat, brushing my side as he pulled out a pair of gloves. "I'm going to wear these. Keep your hands in the pockets or inside the sleeves."

He wrapped a blanket around my head, telling me to keep my face as covered as I could as he knotted it in place. He zipped up his hoodie and took my shawl, wrapping it around his head and covering his nose and mouth. He took one blanket for his body and gave me the other.

"It's like we're going out into the ice world of Hoth," I said, earning me a combination grimace and smile from him. "Hey, do you know what the internal temperature of a tauntaun is?"

"What?" He fastened his blanket in place.

"Luke-warm."

He gave me a real smile. "That was a little 'Forced.'"

Not a single one of my friends would have understood my joke, let alone been able to respond in kind. "How about this one? Where do Sith lords shop? At Darth Mall. Where all the prices are cut in half."

"We can't stay here," he said gently, picking up on my nervousness and my obvious delay tactics. Leaning across me, he opened the door. "Let's go."

The wind and snow slammed into us, cutting across my exposed skin like sharpened little knives. I jumped out, and Rafe was right behind me. He figured out which way the wind was blowing and then stood in front of me at that angle, trying to give me as much protection as he could.

My nose started to run, and the wind blew up the edges of the blanket around me. I had my hands in the coat's sleeves, but in order to keep the blanket seams closed together, I had to keep slipping my fingers out. And they quickly turned into frozen hot dogs, feeling too stiff to move.

We were walking quickly, knowing the movement would help keep us warm. I started to lose track of time, and I didn't know how long we'd been walking when we finally found the road to the cabin. Turning west, Rafe shifted his position to just behind me, again blocking the wind with his broad frame. My own personal Han Solo keeping me safe from the storm.

I tried to keep my breathing shallow as the cold lined my throat, my airway, and the inner lining of my lungs. It hurt to breathe. Whenever I did breathe too deeply, I would cough.

The glacial wind made my eyes water, making it difficult to see. I put my head down, concentrating on taking one step at a time. I could feel the cold on my scalp, even through the blanket. I seriously missed the long, quilted, puffy coat I'd left at home, which would have protected me.

Icicles stabbed at my blood cells. I couldn't remember the last time I had been this cold. We had been walking for forever, and I briefly worried that we might have gone the wrong way. With all this blinding whiteness, it would be very easy to get lost. I hoped we didn't end up out on the lake. It might not have had time to freeze over yet.

The snow and the storm was unending, and as I'd predicted, snow was getting into my shoes, making my socks wet. My teeth chattered in response, but all I could do was push forward. We couldn't go back.

The cold was starting to feel like a burn, singeing me all over. I knew that was very bad. I increased my pace and wondered how it was possible to be both frozen and sweating at the same time.

I saw a big lump on the landscape, covered in snow. I went over and reached out, using my sleeve to brush the snow away. It was the old rusted truck Max kept on blocks near his cabin.

"We're almost there," I said with relief, instantly regretting the words as the cold rushed into my mouth, making my teeth sting.

Finally, after what felt like an actual eternity, the cabin came into view. "Is there a key somewhere?" Rafe asked.

"It won't be locked."

We stepped onto the porch at the same time with Rafe muttering under his breath about people who didn't take security seriously. Just as I'd predicted, the knob turned.

He ushered me in, closing the door tightly. "Are there light switches?"

"No electricity," I told him. "Off the grid, remember?"

I heard the sound of something being knocked over and Rafe saying some words he probably shouldn't have said in mixed company.

I let my blanket drop and unwrapped the other one from around my head. I put my hands out in front of me and walked until I hit the couch. Running my hand along the back, I headed for the kitchen, managing not to stumble over anything.

"I found the fireplace," Rafe said. "With my toes."

I ran my hand over the countertops and stopped at the sink. There. "And I found a Coleman lantern!" Max typically used kerosene lamps at his place, but I was worried that given the personal beef the universe seemed to have with me, I'd end up burning the whole cabin down. This one was an LED light that ran on batteries. I turned the knob, and light filled the cabin.

Taking the lantern from me, Rafe increased the light output and walked over to the bedroom area. He took off his hoodie, throwing it on the bed. He opened the armoire and found some dry clothes there. "We need to change."

Then he pulled off his shirt. The image of his wet hair and bare chest sparked a memory inside me.

The memory of the night I found out he was a liar.

Toward the end of the reality show, when there was only me, Lemon, and Evil Abigail left, we were supposed to be invited to have an overnight date in the Romance Room.

But the show had changed it up. Instead of it being a sure thing, we had been told by the host that we might or might not receive invitations. Then they separated us into different bedrooms so that none of us would know who had been asked and who had not. I didn't even have my things. A production assistant brought me some out-of-date magazines, but I couldn't read them.

All I cared about was whether or not I got an invitation. Would he invite me? Would I go? I mean, there was a certain understanding about what happened in those rooms. Did I want all of America assuming that we'd slept together? Did I want the show to use it as a promotional tool? I could already hear the announcer's voice: "Tune in tonight to find out whether or not Genesis is still a virgin!"

But as time went on, I realized that there was no invitation. Which either meant that he didn't intend to invite me or he had asked another girl to go with him.

Something was happening downstairs. It was muted, but I heard voices. One of the girls must have been asked. A girl who was not me. I lay down on the bed, putting my arm over my eyes. My chest ached, and the room seemed to spin in circles.

Did he not feel the same way about me? Whenever we were together, it felt right. Like we were, I don't know, destined or something.

He never said he loved you.

That made me sit straight up. And I had never told him that I loved him!

One reason I hadn't was that I didn't want to scare him off. Half the women on this show had probably already sworn their undying devotion to him. And the other reason was that it took me a long time to figure out that what I felt was love.

Maybe he was feeling that same way that I was. Maybe he was wondering where I stood. Maybe he thought Lemon or Abigail liked him more.

I had seen girls at the end get sent home because they refused to open up and tell the suitor how they really felt.

I would not be one of those girls.

Rummaging around in the desk, I quickly found pink stationery and a pen. It was easier to write than I might have imagined. The words flowed out of me as I told him that I loved him. That I could see a life with him. That even if he was a prince, we would find a way to make it work. Maybe we could spend half the year in Monterra and half the year in Iowa.

I told him I couldn't imagine my life without him in it. That he made me the happiest I had ever been. That he was everything I was looking for, and that I loved him in spite of, and not because of, his title. I wrote that I hoped he felt the same.

Sliding the letter inside an envelope, I made a plan to sneak up to his room. I was not a rule breaker, but this was important. I cracked the door open and peeked my head out. The hallway was empty.

At the landing to the third staircase, I paused again, listening. The only sound was my nervous heartbeat. I didn't know what the punishment for this transgression would be on this show, but I was worried it might entail getting sent home.

Still silent. I climbed over the stupid rope they kept there, like it was an actual deflector shield that would make the stairs inaccessible. Creeping up the steps carefully, I continued to listen for sounds. Something that would let me know I'd been discovered. I didn't hear anything.

Carefully opening his door, I snuck inside and gently closed it shut. This room was enormous. It took up the entire top floor, and the view from his windows was amazing. I was sure that during the daytime you could see all the way to the ocean. Part of me wanted to explore, thinking that if I investigated a little I might learn more about him. But the other part wanted me to leave my letter and get out before I got caught.

I had just put it on his pillow when a door opened up. But it wasn't the door I had used.

It was the door from the bathroom.

And a bare-chested, wet-haired Rafe walked into the room, towel-drying his hair.

"Holy Shatner," I whispered. And despite my protests when we watched that movie together, I suddenly completely understood why couples jumped from A to Z. Waves of lust pulsed through me, stealing my breath and making it hard to stay steady. I leaned out to hold on to the bedpost.

"Genesis?"

I gulped in response, unable to speak. He was beyond beautiful. Total perfection. I'd seen him in the pool before, but this was different. I didn't know why. The intimacy of the setting? The fact that I was standing next to his bed? That I was doing something I wasn't supposed to? That we were alone, and not surrounded by twenty other people?

"What are you doing here?" He tossed the towel into a basket.

I regained the gift of speech and shook my head, like I could clear it of the lust-induced haze. "I was going to leave you a note."

It sounded so pathetic. What had seemed like an excellent idea just two minutes ago now seemed stupid and embarrassing.

A smile shadowed his lips. "A note?"

"I thought you were gone. I thought you were with someone else." I tried to keep the hurt out of my voice, but from the way his smile faded, I knew he'd caught it.

"I'm not gone. I'm not with anyone else." Each slow step brought him closer and closer, and it made my pulse increase in intensity until I worried my veins might actually explode.

"I can see that," I said. What I didn't say was how relieved I felt, like something washed through me, carrying away all my fears, insecurities, and worries.

There was only me and this incredibly gorgeous half-naked man whom I loved desperately. "I heard noises downstairs."

"The crew can get loud." He walked toward me slowly, leisurely, like the way a wolf would stalk a very stupid sheep who had left her pen and waltzed into his lair.

"I thought you would invite me. I've been waiting all night."

"I hadn't planned on giving you an invitation."

And just like that, all the fears, insecurities, and worries came back, bringing along some brand-new ones I'd never considered.

His ghost smile returned, as if he could read me like an open book and knew how I was internally struggling with his words. And as if he knew about the other struggle I was currently experiencing to keep my eyes away from his torso. "I know what your standards are. I didn't want anyone else to judge you. And I didn't want to ask you and have you think that I expected something to happen."

That something made my insides quiver. "Yes." I swallowed back the intense longing. "Because that would be, um . . ." What was that word again? Oh, right. "Bad." Definitely bad. Very, very bad.

"What does your note say?"

I couldn't let him see it now. "Nothing." He was here. He wasn't with anyone else. He was with me, which made my heart sing. But my desperate confession of my feelings suddenly felt beyond lame, and I couldn't let him read it.

"It can't say nothing if you broke the rules and came up here to leave it for me."

Then he was so close we were almost touching. One deep exhale would have had me pressed against him. My blood thickened and heated, which apparently rendered me stupid, because I put the note behind my back. Like he was two years old and would suddenly forget about it if he couldn't see it.

I would have been better off if I'd just eaten the stupid thing.

He got a mischievous glint in his eye. Uh-oh.

I should have turned around and run, but I didn't.

Because part of me fiercely wanted what happened next.

Chapter 20

"Is your letter addressed to me?"

"Yes." What did that have to do with anything? Did he not know that I was distracted by the sprinkling of dark hair across the top of his chest, wondering if it was coarse or soft? That I was busy watching the clever way his muscles flexed in his shoulders and abdomen every time he shifted? Or how I wanted to stare into his intense, beautiful eyes? Or what a firm, fantastic mouth he had? How I just wanted to watch it move, remembering what it had felt like on my shivering, goosebumpy skin?

"Then it belongs to me." He reached both of his arms around me, grabbing for the note. I twisted and turned to keep it away from him. He laughed as I managed to just keep it out of his hands, which in turn made me laugh.

Right up until the moment when it stopped being funny. When awareness struck us both, our hearts pounding against each other as I stood flush to him, our quick breaths intermingling because our faces were too close.

The laughter died in my throat a moment before he kissed me. His lips brushed mine so lightly, feather-softly, like a shadow. A promising beginning, but it was over before it had even started. His face looked like he hadn't even intended to do that much.

It wasn't enough.

"We're almost to the end." I watched his mouth form words, mesmerized. Heat and fire burned in his eyes, which made my heart beat too fast, and my entire body throbbed in time with it. "And there's something I need to say."

It could have been the formula to cure cancer. Didn't care. Couldn't have heard it even if I wanted to. I only wanted to be kissed. A lot.

So I did what any rational, reasonable woman would do in similar circumstances. I threw myself at him.

He was caught off guard only for a second before he thoroughly, deeply kissed me back. The mint from his toothpaste tingled against my mouth, making me sigh.

I knotted my fingers in his hair, pulling him to me, feeling him shudder against me as I ran my fingertips across his scalp.

And like the rom-com characters I had condemned, I understood how a kiss might lead to much more, as we were pawing at each other, trying to get closer. There was a frantic passion that obliterated thought, that made me run my eager fingers over all his exposed bumps and edges and revel in the way his warm skin felt under my fingertips. It was like a summer storm had started building up inside me, with thunder reverberating through my body and lightning electrifying his every touch.

Our kisses started out tender and gentle and quickly escalated. Probably faster than they should have. But there was no long warming up period here. It was just all savage, hungry desperation and longing that blasted us into Warp 8.

Like we were the subjects of a *National Geographic* special about the mating habits of the virginal redhead and the hot-blooded prince.

It all made me a bit delirious as everything inside me heated up and swirled into clouds of desire, causing me to forget who I was and what I'd said I wanted. I felt his bed against the back of my knees. We both sat at the same time. Whether by design or accident I didn't know, and I didn't care.

I wanted him, wanted more of this, and all my other principles ceased to exist. I cried out in protest when he suddenly stopped. My lips felt fabulously raw, my jaw wondrously sore.

"Genesis, wait." His words were breathy and disconcerting. Mouths had much better uses than speaking.

And I didn't want to waste his or mine on talking. I put my hands on the back of his neck, pulling him against me, reveling in the feeling of his hot, passionate lips responding. Several minutes passed before he stopped again. He actually moved back, like he didn't trust himself to stay close to me. "There's something I have to tell you first."

"I don't care," I told him, as I closed the gap, kissing that pulsing point in the hollow of his neck. With a growl he dragged me up to meet his lips, giving me more of the delicious and intoxicating feelings only he had ever managed to invoke.

Molten lava traveled along my nervous system, burning everything in its path. Like I'd swallowed a bucket of burning coals. I had stopped breathing at some point, but while he devoured me like this, it didn't matter.

His hands on me and his mouth on mine were the only things that mattered.

I wanted to feast on him. Turned out I had a real problem with gluttony. Until his hands started inching toward some seriously dangerous territory.

Should you be doing this? some little worried voice asked, restoring some of my sanity.

I moved his hand away, and he left it where I'd moved it. He started to lean back, and I instinctively stopped him. That was too much. I wouldn't lie down with him. I had to keep some boundaries, and I knew if I did what he wanted, we wouldn't stop. And even though I didn't want this to end, even though it felt like everything was building to some inevitable conclusion that I didn't want to frustrate, I had to stop him. Stop this from going further. Even if he might be the right man, this wasn't the right time.

Just a few more minutes of this ecstasy and I would stop.

I would.

"Genesis," he said in a low voice against my lips, short-circuiting my higher reasoning. And then everything else faded away into oblivion, leaving only fire and want in its wake.

Then I heard a sound that seemed very far away. It was like a voice coming from the bottom of a well, echoing and indecipherable. It sounded like, "Dante, I wanted to tell you . . ."

We abruptly stopped kissing. My eyes tried to focus. Lemon was here. Why was Lemon in Rafe's room?

It took me a moment to understand what was happening.

She threw a vase at Rafe, just missing him. I gasped. She'd kept saying she didn't have feelings for him. Why was she reacting this way? Why would she care what we were doing?

They started to argue. She called him names, and he tried to figure out what she wanted. I was in total shock. Then she got angry at me, which upset me. I thought of how it must have looked to her. If she was in love with him too, it must have devastated her. It would have destroyed me. Which made me angry and disappointed at myself and at Rafe. Why did this happen with us? Why did I always respond to his touch and his kisses like that? I saw the camera crew behind her, recording everything. I raised a hand to my flushed cheek. Had they seen anything? Filmed anything that had happened between me and Rafe? It didn't even matter. All of America would jump to the same conclusion Lemon had when they saw me in his room, on his bed, and him without a shirt.

Lemon finally stormed out, and Rafe roughly ran his fingers through his hair. "This is the worst possible—" he said, stopping when he saw me, as if he'd forgotten I was in the room. I did not like how that felt at all.

"I have to fix this. Stay here, please. I will explain everything to you." His tone was all desperation and pleading.

Before I could respond, he chased after another woman.

There was only so much humiliation I could stand in one night. Holding my head high, I walked past the crew without even a glance, heading back to my room. From his actions, it was obvious he liked Lemon more. Normally I might have cried, but I was still in shock at what had just occurred. I wondered if I could leave the show. There was no point in staying here now.

At some point Taylor, the field producer, came by to talk to me. I only caught every other word that she said. Like I was underwater and everything was distorted by shimmering, moving waves.

"Can I leave?"

"The show?" Taylor looked totally panicked, her voice high and anxious. "No. You can't leave the show. You'll be in violation of your contract and there will be monetary fines if you do that."

I found out later that Lemon had walked out, going back home, but she had the money to pay whatever the penalty was.

I didn't.

The ache in my heart was incredible, unlike anything I'd ever experienced before. I had been head over heels in love, and he wanted someone else. And I was stuck in my room like some kind of prisoner, refusing to speak to any of the producers who filed in and out, asking me with fake concern if I wanted to talk about what had just happened.

My whole body was numb. Where there had been fire, now there was only ice.

And regret.

Then emptiness set in. I'd been used. He had used me. Taken advantage of me and of my naïveté. Like I was some stupid country bumpkin who was about to become the punch line in the monologues of late-night talk show hosts.

Taylor came back in at some point. She sat on the bed across from me talking. I mostly tuned her out. I knew she wanted a reaction. Then something she said caught my ear.

"Identical twins?" I repeated.

She nodded. "Yes. Dante and Rafe are identical twins. You have been spending time with Rafe, and Lemon has spent all of her time with Dante. We didn't want any of you to know that there were two men and not just one."

"But why? Why would you do that?"

She cocked her head to the side, the way Laddie did when he was listening to me. "Why else? Ratings."

She'd torn my heart out of my chest for ratings. To make rich producers and show owners even richer. She'd made me a laughingstock and stomped all over my broken heart to entertain.

"So Lemon was angry because she thought you were kissing Dante, but it's totally fine because you were kissing Rafe."

"How does that matter?" I ask. What she told me made things worse. Despite my fears that Rafe wanted Lemon, which might still be an issue, the bigger problem was that he had lied.

Lied, and lied, and then lied some more. He wasn't who he said he was. Yes, he'd told me his real name, but he had insinuated that it was a nickname and made me feel special that I was the only one who got to use it.

I got into my bed, pulling the covers up over my head like I used to when I was little and I had pretended my blanket was a force field that could protect me from nightmares or ghosts or cult leaders.

Taylor kept talking, and tears started to roll down the side of my nose, falling onto the sheet. Eventually she gave up, leaving me alone in a darkened room.

I couldn't sleep. I wanted to. I wanted to black out and forget this had happened. He lied. Even after I told him how important it was for him to always be honest. The only sound was my harsh, angry breathing.

A knock at my door. It was Rafe. Even if I couldn't see him, I knew who it was.

The door slowly opened. "Genesis?"

"Go. Away."

He came in, closed the door, and sat on the other bed.

After several silent minutes, he said, "I would have come sooner, but Dante and I had some things we had to work out with the executive producer. And I wanted us to be able to talk alone."

Without a camera crew to document every excruciating moment. "I know English isn't your first language, but what you're doing is the opposite of going away. Leave me alone."

He sighed, but I didn't move. I lay there, completely covered up.

"I found your note."

That sent a jolt of sadness through me. I didn't want him to read it. I didn't want him to know how I felt about him. Or, how I used to feel about him.

"Did you mean what you said?" His voice had a rough, jagged quality to it.

I sat up as indignation made my stomach burn. I was torches-and-pitchforks-storming-the-castle mad. There was enough moonlight for me to see him. He was wearing glasses. Something he'd never done before. "You lied to me. You didn't tell me from the beginning that you were a prince, so that was a lie. You didn't tell me you had an identical twin brother. You pretended to be him, and you made me believe that you had feelings . . ." I trailed off as my throat squeezed, not willing to go there. "Was this some kind of game? A joke?"

"Never. What I feel for you is very real. And I had to lie. I owe Dante. When I was younger and dumber—"

I held up my hand. "I don't want to hear your excuses. I don't know how you could have lied to me after I opened up to you about John-Paul. And Richard. About how important it was to me that the man I loved be totally honest with me. And this entire time, every minute of every day, you've lied. Everything about us was a lie. Every time you kissed me and touched me. Lies."

"The only thing I've lied about was that Dante and I were the same person. Everything else was me. I was always myself with you."

"But very careful not to share too many personal details," I pointed out, as my heart clenched in agony. "You've always kept me at arm's length because you knew what you were doing was wrong. And you knew how much it would upset me."

My voice wobbled, and I knew I was going to cry. Not just falling tears, but deep, painful, chest-wrenching sobs. "Get out. I don't want to see you or talk to you ever again."

"But I need to explain."

"No!" I screamed. "Get out!" I slammed my fists against the bed. "Out! Now!"

He looked heartbroken, but I didn't care. My icy, furious heart had no room for sympathy or compassion.

But he went.

And I spent the rest of the night crying until I had no more tears left.

Even now, just the memory of that night still managed to bring tears to my eyes. I turned around, not willing to let him see.

I heard the bathroom door close as I rubbed at my eyes. He must have gone in to change. For the benefit of my virgin eyes, I supposed. I went over to the armoire, digging through the clothes. Amanda had left some things there, things she probably hadn't worn since high school. Taking off my wet shoes and socks, I pulled off Rafe's sweats and put on a pair of hers. They came mid-calf on me and were tight, but they were dry.

Her shirts were out of the question. Every single one was too tight and too short for me to put on and wear around Rafe.

I settled on the smallest T-shirt of Max's I could find. It was green and had the outline of the state of Iowa on it, and said, "Kiss me, I'm Iowish."

The zipper on my dress caught. Oh no. I tugged at it, but my fingers still felt cold and didn't work quite right. I wanted to get changed before he walked back in the room and saw parts of me I had no intention of showing him. I twisted at a weird angle, trying to hurry.

"Problems?"

My heart slammed into my throat as I straightened up. When had he opened the door? He leaned against the doorway, wearing pants that were too big and too short, and a red-and-black plaid flannel shirt that made me giggle.

"What?"

"Your shirt looks like you're about to go hunting wabbits."

That reference he didn't seem to get. He pointed at the shirt I'd laid out on the bed. "Probably better than a blatant invitation."

Oh. I hadn't thought of that. My cheeks colored.

"Turn around. I'll help you."

I did as he asked and turned, lifting my hair up to give him easier access. He messed with the zipper until it slid easily, smoothly, with his knuckles running over my exposed skin as he did so. My pulse was beating frantically. I stepped away, holding my dress against my chest. It was too much.

"Thanks," I said before running into the bathroom like a coward. A big window at the top of the shower gave me enough light to see.

After I got changed and hung up my dress on the shower rod to dry alongside his clothes, I searched for a blow dryer until I realized how truly dumb that was, given that we had no electricity.

He had left a pair of dry socks for me on the bed. He was crouched over the fireplace. "What are you doing?" I asked.

"Making a fire."

"How do you know how to make a fire?" I asked as I went into the kitchen, looking to see if there was anything to eat. Rafe had mentioned after we left the club that he was hungry, and I'd made him drive home. If I had just gone to a restaurant with him, we would have discovered the flat tires while still in civilization and would never have ended up here. Since I was the reason we were in this situation, the least I could do was feed him.

Despite my expectation that the cabin would be fully stocked, the fridge only had condiments and a dozen eggs that were so far past their expiration date that I worried they might fight back if I tried to cook them. The cabinets were no better. They had been totally cleaned out except for some cans of dog food for Max's pet. I did find an unopened box of Cheez-Its, but they'd been there so long that the crackers had disintegrated into a kilo of Cheez-It powder.

"I've been watching a lot of YouTube videos since I got here," Rafe explained, and I turned my attention back to him and his fire-building efforts.

"Do you want me to help?"

He gave me a look of displeasure. "You're implying that I lack the basic abilities of an average caveman. I can make a fire. You do realize that you're slandering my masculinity, don't you?"

I bit the inside of my cheek so that I wouldn't laugh.

There was a noise outside that couldn't be from the wind. It sounded like a door slamming shut on a car. My throat closed in as my heart beat desperately against my ribcage, like it wanted to break free. "Did you hear that?" I whispered.

Rafe took one look at my expression and went over to the door, yanking it open. The cold air rushed inside, but I didn't move. He went out onto the covered porch, holding the lantern up. There were no further scary sounds. Just the wind.

"I don't hear anything," he said as he came back in.

"I swear I heard something," I murmured. I was freezing, so I pulled the quilt off of the bed and wrapped myself up, sitting on the couch. Had I imagined it? What if right now John-Paul was closing in on us? We were totally helpless out here. Stranded.

Straining my ears, I kept listening as Rafe went back to making the fire. After several minutes passed and I didn't hear anything else, I started to calm down. It must have been my overactive imagination.

Eight matches later, he managed to get the fire going past the kindling stage and caught the actual logs. He surveyed it with satisfaction before coming to sit in the chair next to the couch. We watched the fire for a while, the way it danced and burned over the logs.

"We need to talk. And we're going to talk. I'm going to explain why I did what I did."

Chapter 21

"That was one of my conditions," I said, alarmed. "No explanation conversations."

"You said no talking about it in the car. We're not in the car."

Darn him and his infernal and correct logic.

Smoke started to hang heavy in the room, making my eyes water and my lungs ache. "Did you open the flue?" I asked, running over to the fireplace. It wasn't enough that we'd nearly frozen to death? Now we had to suffocate? So much for his "I know how to make a fire."

I opened the flue with the knob, and the smoke started to dissipate. I also opened a window in the kitchen, but the wind blew too hard and too much snow came in for me to leave it open for long.

"What's a flue?" he asked as I shut the window. Poor Rafe. He probably had flue-opening servants, too.

"Something you make sure is open when you build a fire so everybody around you doesn't die from asphyxiation."

"Where's a smoke alarm when you need one?" he teased, and I saw that he had moved over to the couch. He patted a spot next to him and I sat down, holding the quilt around me like a shield.

I couldn't delay the inevitable forever. I had to let him explain. Even if it hurt, even if it didn't excuse what he did, I needed to know.

"First, I'm sorry about tonight and everything that's happened. It's my fault."

Not what I had expected. "It wasn't your fault."

"Wasn't it?"

He didn't control the weather, and the mugging and tire puncturing could have just as easily happened to me without him there. It might have had nothing to do with him. It was my fault for being in Iowa City. That had been my decision. Of the two of us, I was probably more to blame. But it had all been an accident.

Or one giant cosmic joke.

I refused to believe that it had been orchestrated.

"Did you stop to think that things might have been worse if you hadn't been here? What if I'd been alone in Old Bess in my dress and trapped in this storm?" I shouldn't have been so insistent on having things my way. We probably wouldn't be stuck in this cabin. I took one hand out of the blanket shield and stroked his forearm. Solely to comfort him. It had nothing to do with how much I liked the way his skin felt.

He put his other hand on top of mine, and I had to pull back my rogue appendage. I needed all my wits about me for whatever he was about to say.

"Regardless, I am sorry. Not only for tonight," he said, as he looked up at the ceiling and let out a deep breath. "But for everything. For the way that I hurt you. For the deception."

I didn't say anything. I would let him talk.

He rubbed the inside of one of his palms with his thumb, and his eyes got a far-off look. "I met Veronique Renault when I was twelve and at boarding school. I had just discovered girls, and she was beautiful and an heiress. I fancied myself in love with her. So much so that I didn't date anyone else. All through boarding school, we were boyfriend and girlfriend. Which didn't mean much at first, but had more meaning as time went on."

He coughed, clearing his throat. The smoke was nearly gone. "When I was eighteen, I decided I wanted to marry her. I proposed, and she happily accepted. Dante tried to talk me out of it. He had heard rumors about her, and he thought I could do better. My parents were livid. There was no way they were going to let their teenage son marry. It caused a rift in my family."

The pain in his voice was evident. "We made plans to elope when I graduated. We got an apartment together in Paris, and I enrolled at the university. A year later, Veronique was murdered."

Of all the things I had imagined him saying, that was the absolute last. I gasped, my hand flying to my mouth. "I'm so sorry."

"The authorities initially suspected me. I couldn't blame them. They always suspect the boyfriend. Or the fiancé, to be more accurate. The paparazzi were relentless. I had lost my love, and they thought I had done it. I had no privacy, no time to grieve. I didn't want to go home to Monterra, where I could have been left alone, because part of me blamed my family. I thought that if they'd just accepted us, maybe it wouldn't have happened. I know now that wasn't true, but I wasn't in the right frame of mind. I even blamed myself. Given who I was, the resources I had, I should have been able to keep her safe."

He rubbed the back of his neck. "Everyone else was right. The rumors were true. Veronique had a revolving string of lovers and cheated on me every chance she got. One of those men murdered her out of jealousy. It didn't matter that they caught him. Then the tabloids said my parents had paid someone to take the fall and that I was actually guilty. No matter where I went, no matter what I did, there were cameras and accusations. I had to deal with my loss while I also dealt with the discovery that I had never really known her. One of her friends admitted to me that Veronique had never loved me and had only stayed with me because she wanted to be a princess more than anything. My relationship had been fictional, and I had been betrayed."

"It wasn't fictional," I said, unable to stay quiet. My heart ached for him and the pain that he had felt. I couldn't help it. "Your feelings were real." Even if that skanky, cheating French slut's feelings were not.

He let out a deep sigh. "Have you ever felt like you owed someone everything?"

That was a change from what we had been talking about. "Yes," I replied, because I did. It was how I felt about Aunt Sylvia.

"Dante saw what was happening. He took it upon himself to save me. He started going out with a different actress or model or noblewoman every night of the week. He called the paparazzi himself, telling them where he would be and who he would be with. I transferred to MIT in the States, while my brother put on a circus act to draw the spotlight away from me. For the past four years, he has protected me by feeding the tabloids with his supposed conquests. None of the relationships were real. They were only for the publicity. But he earned himself an undeserved reputation as a heartbreaker and a playboy, just for my benefit."

Lemon and I'd had a conversation one night where we talked about our pasts. She explained to me that she'd never had a boyfriend who hadn't cheated on her. I could see now why she'd held back where Dante was concerned. And why it must have destroyed her to see me and Rafe together, if she'd thought he was his brother. It would have been confirmation of her worst fears. He must have told her the truth and she forgave him.

Which I understood, because the truth was having the same kind of effect on me.

He leaned forward, resting his elbows on his knees. "There are no words to say how much I owe my brother. He allowed me to heal. He gave me the privacy and anonymity that I needed. He let me come to terms with what had happened. So when he asked me to do this show, to pretend that we were the same person, I immediately said yes. Dante had never asked me for anything, and after all that he had done for me, I couldn't say no."

I would have done the same thing for Aunt Sylvia. I *had* done the same thing for her. She wanted me to go on the show, and despite my reservations, I did. For her. I couldn't tell her no, either.

He shifted his position again, turning his body toward me, his voice clear and strong. "Dante had fallen in love with Lemon, and he would have done anything to make her happy. She had a publicity firm that she was trying to get off the ground. Dante convinced our family to hire her. He volunteered to be on the show to help. And he begged me to do whatever I could to make the show a success to benefit her career."

I pulled my blanket tighter around me. Despite the weather outside, the ice wall enclosing my heart had shattered into a million pieces. And like the Grinch's, because it was no longer bound, my heart grew three sizes.

"It was just something I had to get through. I didn't imagine I would meet anyone that I liked. I didn't want to. I hadn't had a real relationship since Veronique died. I thought that I might never be happy again. I thought I would never be able to trust a woman again." His eyes flicked up to mine. "Until I met you."

My breath caught. If someone had asked me to describe each emotion I felt in that moment, I wouldn't have been able to. I was moved by what he had said. Excited. Sad for what he had gone through. Angry at him for not telling me sooner. Angry at myself for not letting him tell me. Forgiving. And a million other things. But they were all tangled up, and I couldn't figure out which ones were the strongest or which ones I should listen to.

"I can't describe what happened the night we met. There you were tangled up in your evening gown, dangling on that fence, and you were laughing. It made my heart feel light. I didn't know what to think about you. But from that first moment, as clear as I knew anything else,

I knew we were meant to be together. I knew I would fall in love with you. Somehow, I just knew you were the one for me. I didn't want that to happen. I fought it. But I couldn't stay away from you."

He had his arm along the couch cushions, and by pure instinct, I reached out to take his hand. He interlaced our fingers. "I started seeking you out. I thought about you constantly. I kissed you, even when I shouldn't have. The more I fell for you, the more I wanted to tell you, but I couldn't. I'd made a promise to Dante, and I always keep my word. But it made me sick that I was lying to you. Especially after Cozumel."

"Why didn't you tell me the truth in the elevator? When I told you everything, why weren't you just honest with me then?"

His fingers tightened around mine. "Because it wasn't just my secret. It involved Dante, and I had to talk to him first. When we got back, I talked to him. I talked and talked. And he begged me not to tell you. He was afraid of what you might do, that you would tell the others and ruin the show. And he was worried that if something went wrong, Matthew Burdette, the show's owner, would ruin Lemon's business."

"I wouldn't have told anyone. I would have kept it between us."

"I know," he said, his thumb stroking my hand, setting off little whirlpools of fire. "But Dante doesn't know you like I do. Now I would choose differently. If I could go back and do it over, I would have told you the first night we met."

"Since Doctor Who isn't real, there's no TARDIS to let you go back and change it."

"And it is the biggest regret of my life."

Mine too.

"That night in my room on the show," he went on, and my skin heated. It was a night I didn't think I'd ever forget. "I wanted to tell you then. I tried. Three different times. It's no excuse, but I wanted you to know the truth before things . . . progressed."

And I had told him I didn't care. I couldn't exactly accuse him and get angry with him when he had tried to tell me and I hadn't let him. Should I apologize? Say something?

But I didn't have a chance to speak. "I know how selfish I've been. I probably should have left you alone and let you move on with your life. But I couldn't. I missed you so much that it was like somebody had torn out my heart and carried it across the ocean. I tried to live my life. But all I wanted was to talk to you. See you. Hold you. And even if you never want to be with me again, I had to at least try to make things up to you. To at least be your friend. Because I don't want to live the rest of my life without you in it."

What could you say to something like that? My heart had jumped up into my ears. Despite what I'd thought, he hadn't come here to manipulate me or force his way into my life. He wasn't trying to win anyone over or get me into a relationship. He just wanted to be near me.

He tugged on my hand, pulling me even closer. I put my legs on top of his lap. But he didn't hold me. Because he still wanted to look at me. He reached out, holding my face and tenderly stroking my cheeks.

"I love you."

What the Spock? "You love me?" I asked in a teeny voice. It probably should have been obvious, but sometimes I was slow on the uptake. And it was one thing to guess at his feelings, but it was totally different to hear him say the words.

A spectacular smile lit up his whole face, the kind that threatened to set the snow surrounding us on fire. There was a smokiness in his voice that had nothing to do with the flue. "I'm not like my brother. I can't quote poetry. I can only tell you how I feel. And I feel like I have always loved you and have spent my whole life waiting to find you. Even when I didn't want to love you, because it hurt, I still did. It's not something I could control. I couldn't stop loving you any more than I could stop breathing—it's become so much a part of me."

He might not have been able to recite poems, but he had a poetic soul. A thousand thoughts screamed inside my head. That I should say it back. Wondering if I did still love him, too. Recognizing the enormity of this moment and what it meant to me that he said he loved me. Finally understanding why he did what he did, and finding that I could forgive him for it.

And knowing that I could trust in myself, and in him, and that we could move past this.

Together.

He ran one of his rough thumbs over my lower lip and my bones liquefied.

"I tried to leave you alone. I figured if you wanted to see me, you would contact me. I stayed away for as long as I could, until I couldn't spend another moment away from you. So I moved here to be near you. But it's time for me to stop being selfish. Tell me to leave, and I will."

The thought of him going, the very thing I had said I wanted all along, terrified me. His voice fell lower, and he was practically whispering the words. "But if you think there's any chance at all that someday you might forgive me, then let me stay and earn back your trust and your love."

My skin shimmered with heat from the nearness of his lips to mine. I wanted to totally surrender, completely give in. To agree to whatever he said, forget whatever I had to forget.

But that was while I was under the influence. Because, a second later, there was a loud banging at the cabin door. Rafe reluctantly got up to open it, and when he moved away my sanity returned. Outside stood a very anxious Marco, and they began a rapid conversation in Italian.

I got up to collect our things and return the quilt to the bed. Gianni had parked the SUV practically on the front porch, so we wouldn't be out in the cold for long. With Marco still talking, Rafe poured a pitcher of water on the fire he'd worked so hard to light, and white billowing smoke went straight up the chimney. It was as if my hurt and worries had evaporated with it.

Pondering his offer, I ran through a list of all the reasons he should go. But none of them held much weight anymore. I thought of all the practical reasons he should stay. Sylvia and I needed his rent. The town needed his business—so many families were now dependent on him.

But that's not what moved me. That's not what tugged on my heartstrings.

We settled into the back of his bodyguards' black SUV. The two men up front were listening to what sounded like a soccer game, but it was in Italian. Rafe had his head tilted, as if he was trying to catch the game, too.

"Rafe," I whispered.

He immediately gave me his full attention. "Yes?"

This was huge. Monumental. Scary and risky, but it was what I wanted. I would have to take that leap and have faith.

So I just said it.

"There's a chance."

Chapter 22

Things had changed. Maybe not the way Rafe had hoped or wanted, but it was going to be a process. I couldn't just get over it. We had to navigate how to go down a new path together.

I was surprised that he hadn't tried to kiss me. But he was a man of his word, and I had to ask first. Despite wanting to, I didn't. The adult part of me wanted to figure things out without his drugging kisses influencing me.

The hormonal teenager side of me thought the adult part was an idiot.

But there were hungry, lingering looks, and a lot more touching and holding. I'd asked him to keep that sort of stuff between us, but we lived in a small town. And the thing about living in a small town—even when you don't know what you're doing, everybody else does.

They all knew right away that things had changed. And they teased me relentlessly. Even Max had altered his jokes to include things that pertained to Rafe. Like how he played polo. "Did you hear Iowa State had to disband their water polo team? All the horses drowned."

Aunt Sylvia couldn't have been happier. And whether those glowing smiles were due to her nearly nightly dates with Max, or what was happening between me and Rafe, I didn't know.

A week later, while Aunt Sylvia was out playing gin with her girlfriends, I was running a raid with my guild. The guild master, a guy I only knew as Kamro, sent me a whisper in-game. He said he'd found a shaman healer named Hatchet with a super high item level.

And Hatchet knew what he was doing. I didn't have to spend half the time using cooldowns to keep myself alive. After we'd one-shotted the first boss, everybody was celebrating. I typed in the guild chat:

Great job, new healer! That was crazy easy!

Hatchet responded.

Thanks, Eclipse. You know what they say. You can't fight the moonlight.

"What?" I yelled, slamming my hands on my desk. What did Rafe think he was doing? I thought we were done with the deceptions. I was going to . . . I didn't know what I was going to do. Something bad. Possibly physical.

Why didn't he just tell me before? He had to have known I would figure it out when he used my mom's phrase. A long time ago I had told him my user name and that I played on the Doomhammer server. If I had known then he had a memory like a steel trap, I would have been more careful about what I shared. I ran downstairs, through the kitchen, and across the yard to throw open the door to Rafe's house.

He sat on the couch with his computer on his lap. "I'm no expert on American law, but I believe you aren't allowed to just walk into someone's house without permission. Isn't that called breaking and entering?"

Rafe was being playful, but I was annoyed. "I didn't break anything. I just entered. And I'm allowed because it's my house."

"Not according to the lease."

Could he not see that I wasn't in the mood for teasing? "Why did you do that?"

"Please specify the context."

"Why didn't you tell me it was you?"

He looked confused. He shut his laptop. "In the game? I did. Just now. I used our phrase."

It wasn't our phrase. It was something my mom said that I told him about. Even if it gave me happy chills to have our own little saying.

"I had no idea who you were. Why didn't you just whisper me or something?"

He put the laptop on the couch next to him. "Because gamers are incredibly savvy, and I don't think the game is totally secure. And I didn't tell you before because I wanted to surprise you. You said you needed a healer; I have a healer."

I put my fingers against my temples. "That's not the point. I don't like surprises. You can't keep things from me. I can't keep trying to trust you and then get let down, even if it's just a lie of omission."

"You're trying to trust me?" He got up and walked over to me. There was so much hope infused in his words that it buoyed my own spirits.

"Yes, I'm trying. So stop doing stuff to mess it up."

He put his hands on my shoulders and let them run down the length of my arms until he was holding both of my hands. "If you wanted to see me, all you had to do was ask."

Rafe was still missing the point, even if he knew exactly how to make me a love zombie, with no control over my own limbs, fixating on only one thing. It wasn't about wanting to see him. Although, honestly, that was an issue. I wanted and wanted where he was concerned, but I denied myself. For the good of our possible relationship.

"And in the interest of full disclosure, and since you don't like surprises, in a few minutes I'm supposed to find a reason to lure you into town for your surprise birthday party."

"What? It's not my birthday for another two days."

"Hence, the surprise part."

"They felt like I didn't have enough surprises in my life lately?" For most of my life, surprises had never appealed to me because I liked knowing what would happen when I walked around the corner. Fear of being found had played a big part in that. I wanted each day to be like the last. For nothing scary or different to happen. I had chucked all that out the window when I went on a reality television show, which ended up being nothing but surprises, and that had reinforced to me how much I disliked them.

But it was sweet that people had made the effort. I had to be thankful for that. Rafe went for his keys. "Come on. You can practice your surprised face in the car. Did you want to grab a coat?"

"I don't need it," I said, following him out. "But I'm going to bring it anyway. Just in case." Despite our almost-blizzard last week, it had recently warmed up. Which was nice for when I was outside, but the bad thing about Iowa weather was that it would snow, then it would warm up and melt the snow, and then it would freeze again. Which caused black ice on the roads and slipping hazards on every sidewalk.

"What is it with your weather? In Monterra when it's winter, it's winter."

We went into my house and through the kitchen, where I got my coat. "We have four seasons here. Winter, *Game of Thrones* winter, road construction, and insanely hot. It's the only place where you can get sunburn and frostbite in the same week. All of our weather forecasts on the news are basically made up."

Laddie started to bark. It was a happy bark, which meant we had company and someone new to rub his belly. "Your security?" I asked.

He shook his head. "Gianni's waiting in town."

And they would tell us when they patrolled.

My heart started to pound hard. With everything I'd been through with Rafe, I'd forgotten the postcard.

Maybe I shouldn't have.

"Do you think . . ." I stopped talking when he put a finger up to his lips. He turned off the kitchen lights. He took my best cutting knife from the block. I pulled my keys out of my front pocket, putting one finger on the button to activate the pepper spray.

He took me by his free hand, and we crept into the front room. Rafe turned off the lights in there, too. The tree lights still blinked. I saw that an unsupervised Laddie had managed to pull off every popcorn string from the Christmas tree without disturbing a single ornament.

He padded over to us with a wagging tail, eager to be part of the team. "Why can't you be a regular guard dog?" I whispered. He licked my face in response before going off to the kitchen.

Rafe stood by the front widow, behind a curtain. "There is definitely someone out there. More than one person. I'm texting my men."

I dragged air in and out. It would take his team too long to reach us. But we could barricade ourselves in here. If John-Paul was actually out there, he wouldn't find easy prey.

A loud knock on the door made us both jump. "Stay there," he told me. For once, I didn't argue.

He threw the door open, the knife behind his back. If he had to stab someone . . . that made my stomach turn. I couldn't let him do that. Even for me.

A distinctive and unforgettable voice said, "Hey there, Prince Rafael. I was *not* expecting to find you here. Is Genesis home?"

Rafe stepped back to show me Taylor Hodges standing on my front porch. Maybe I should rethink my no stabbing policy.

She came in without being invited, dropping her coat on the couch. "Is it okay if my crew comes in with me?"

"It is not okay. It's not okay for you to come in, either." She was the cause of so much pain. Not only for me and Rafe, but for Lemon and Dante as well.

But she sat down in a chair like I hadn't even spoken. "Is something wrong with your electricity? Do your lights not work?"

Rafe flicked them back on, asking me with his eyes if I was okay. I nodded as he closed the front door and pulled the curtains shut, preventing the crew from getting any footage.

"You haven't been answering my texts or phone calls," she said, her finger wagging at me.

I folded my arms. "That's because I don't want to talk to you. Or see you. Or have anything to do with you."

She laughed, leaning over. I backed up. "Come on now, we're friends. And I'm here with an opportunity for you! I know you need money. The producers have decided that you would be a perfect fit for *Enchanted Eden*."

Enchanted Eden was the sister show to *Marry Me*. Losing contestants were invited to some exotic location with other contestants from other seasons in hopes that they would fall in love. They had a few success stories, but I was not even a little bit interested. I would never go on reality television ever again.

"No thanks. And if that's it, good night." I opened the door. Laddie came into the room, eyed Taylor, yawned, and left. Even my dog, who loved everybody, could see through her BS.

She didn't move other than to point her left shoulder toward us. "So, what's the deets here? Are the two of you back together? Is there something we should know? All of America is rooting for you to reunite!"

I heard a car driving over snow. The security team. They could pick her up and carry her out. She couldn't have weighed very much. Evil made you skinny, apparently.

"Are you filming this?" Rafe asked.

She paused. "Always."

At that, Rafe went out to the porch. "These people are all trespassing on private property and have taken photographs without permission." He turned back to Taylor. "Any agreements that we signed with you have long since lapsed."

His men sprang into action, confiscating the cameras and deleting whatever footage they had. The cameramen protested, but not one of them resisted. Marco came inside and demanded the spy camera that Taylor had pinned on the left side of her chest by hiding it in a brooch. She slapped it into his hand, glaring at us. Maybe it wasn't so bad to have bodyguards around, after all.

"If you persist in bothering Ms. Kelley and His Royal Highness," Marco said, "we will file legal documents and generally make your life miserable."

Taylor shoved her arms back into her coat, muttering under her breath about ungrateful and unappreciative people as she went. Rafe offered me his arm. "Off to your celebration?"

I put my hand on his arm. As we drove off, I saw Taylor and her crew being herded into their car. I enjoyed it far more than I should have. I even waved to her.

My earlier freak-out had been over nothing. No John-Paul. No cult members. Just a sociopathic field producer and her scummy camera guys.

I pulled down the visor and opened the mirror to practice my surprised face. I got a real one when the SUV hit black ice. The back of the car started to fishtail, but Rafe quickly corrected and straightened us back out. It happened so fast I barely had time to be scared. "That was impressive."

He waggled his fingers at me. "It's all the gaming. I have catlike reflexes and excellent manual dexterity."

I knew just how dexterous he could be, which made heat color my cheeks.

"That's not always true," he added. "I might have clipped a deer two days ago. I got out and looked, but I couldn't find one."

Glad that he didn't see and correctly interpret my reaction to thoughts of what he could do with his hands, I cleared my throat. "Everybody I know here has clipped a deer. More than once. And depending on how they get hit, they can run off."

We pulled into the diner parking lot. "We're here," he said. "Show me your face again."

I tried for my best I-had-no-idea!

"That's the one. Let's go."

The diner's lights were all off, which would have been my first clue since it wasn't anywhere near closing time.

We walked in, and the room erupted into a loud chorus of "Surprise!"

I didn't have to fake anything, as seeing half the town there really did shock me. I hugged Aunt Sylvia first, and then I went through a long line of people who all wanted to hug me and wish me a happy birthday. If we had a fire marshal, he would have closed the place down.

Meredith threw her arms around my legs, grinning up at me. "Were you surprised, Jen-sis?"

"Very!" I told her, ruffling her hair.

Beau growled at Rafe, baring his teeth.

"What did I ever do to that boy to make him not like me?" Rafe whispered, his hot breath warming my skin.

"He probably senses that you're a deer killer."

"*Alleged* deer killer," he corrected. He crouched down. "Look at those sharp teeth. Like a dinosaur."

"I not a dinosaur," Beau responded angrily. "I a boy!"

He stomped off to join Gracie, who sat under one of the tables unwrapping my birthday gifts one by one. She looked so cute while doing it I couldn't even be mad.

Several of Rafe's new employees wanted to chat with him, and Whitney seized her chance to get me alone. I had called her every night for the last week, but face-to-face gossip was always the best.

I updated her on the Taylor situation, and she told me about how Gracie had taken a tub of butter from the fridge and covered the entire kitchen floor in the time it took Whitney to go to the bathroom.

"But enough about the kids. What about your prince? Are you engaged yet? A diamond ring would be an excellent birthday present." She actually grabbed my left hand to inspect it, as if I wouldn't have told her first thing if he had proposed. "Everybody's talking about how you two are obviously going to get married."

"They are?" I said in surprise.

"Well, it's mostly just me saying it, but everybody nods whenever I bring it up."

I laughed. "It's way too soon for that. I haven't even told him that I love him yet."

"Do you? Love him?" She sat down on a barstool. "Why am I even asking that? Of course you do. Why haven't you told him?"

I sat next to her. "It's kind of dumb."

"Oh sweetie, you're in love. Dumb is a prerequisite."

"I want to be sure. I'm like ninety percent sure, but I want to get all the way to a hundred before I dive back into anything. I don't want to get hurt again. And he's being really patient with me."

Rafe had coaxed Gracie out from under the table and was putting the presents back, trying to fix them as best he could. It was sweet.

"Look at you smiling at him. I don't know how to tell you this, Genesis, but you're already at a hundred percent."

I wanted to tell her she was wrong, but found that I couldn't.

"So if he didn't get you a diamond, what did he give you?"

Other than keeping me out of Taylor's clutches and giving me an easy raid on *Warcraft*? "Nothing yet."

Whitney finally realized what Gracie had been doing and went over to help clean up the mess her daughter had made.

Rafe's gift would probably be something extravagant that I would have to make him take back. A new car? Beach house? My own space shuttle? A private island?

Rafe came up behind me, putting his hand on the small of my back. "What are you thinking about?"

"About what kind of present you got me."

"Who says I got you a present?" he teased.

He'd been doing nothing but giving me gifts since he rolled into town. There was no way he hadn't gotten me one. So I just gave him a pointed look, which made him chuckle.

"You're right. I did get you something. But since you told me you hate surprises, I'm trying to decide whether I should tell you what it is or wait. Technically, every gift here is a surprise."

"Not every gift. Gracie's opened half of them."

"True." He pressed his lips together. "But I think I'd prefer to see your face. A present is a loophole in the no-surprises rule."

Whit came back and said she needed to get home to put her kids in bed, so she had some of the guests bring the cake out. It was the biggest sheet cake I had ever seen, covered in teal roses. My favorite color. I hoped the twenty-four candles wouldn't accidentally set off the sprinkler system. Everybody sang "Happy Birthday" to me, and Rafe seemed to sing it the loudest.

"Make a wish!" Sylvia told me when they were finished, as some of the kids sang about me looking like a monkey and smelling like one too. I grinned, mentally picking out the candle I'd make my wish on. I closed my eyes.

I wish I could figure out a way to work things out with Rafe.
And save the farm. And make Aunt Sylvia better.

That was three wishes, but I was the only one who knew. I opened my eyes and blew out all the candles and everybody clapped. Aunt

Sylvia had Whitney start cutting up the cake, and Amanda helped to pass it out, giving me the first piece.

I reached over to the cake and plucked out the candle I'd made my wishes on. I sucked the whipped frosting off the edge. I caught Rafe looking at me, and the hooded expression in his eyes made me cough the icing back up. I had to turn away, sticking the candle in my front pocket.

"What are you doing?" he asked.

"It's a tradition. My mom and aunt did it as girls and now I do it. I keep the candle I made a wish on so that my wish can come true."

One side of his mouth quirked up. "So somewhere you have a box full of wish candles?"

I nodded.

"Do you think your wish will come true this year?"

His gaze fixed on my mouth. I wondered if I had frosting on me. I ran my hand across my lips, making sure. "I think it might."

Then he smiled for real. "I think it might, too."

I opened gifts from the people who had to leave first. There were gift cards and homemade cards and lotions and candles and a pile of candy bars big enough that I could have opened my own candy store.

"Don't eat too much of that candy," Whitney warned on her way out the door. "The older you get, the harder it is to lose weight because by then your body and your fat have become super good friends."

She always made me laugh.

The families with small children started to file out, and I thanked everyone for coming. Rafe and his guards took it upon themselves to load all of my presents and cards in the back of his car.

But there was no gift from him. I hadn't opened every card, because people had generally lost interest in watching me open presents and were talking to one another. Maybe his card was in there somewhere? I didn't get much of a chance to look, because they were too efficient at getting everything packed up.

Rafe told me we needed to go. He still needed to give me his present. I felt bad about leaving my own party, but I had to admit, I was curious. What did he want to give me that he couldn't give me in front of everyone else?

When we got back to the farmhouse, he held up a blindfold.

"What do you think you're going to do with that?"

"Trust me," he said as he put it on me.

"Okay, but if this ends up someplace weird, you're in trouble."

He helped me out of the car, and as soon as I stumbled over some snow, he swooped me up into his arms. I put my arms around him, enjoying not only that he was strong enough to carry someone as tall as me and that it didn't seem to faze him, but also getting to be close to him like this. I laid my head on his shoulder. As birthday gifts went, so far it was a pretty good one.

He set me down. "Ready?"

"Yes." Nervousness bounced along my veins, cranking up my excitement.

He took off my blindfold.

In front of me, in her stall, stood Marigold.

I blinked a couple of times, not sure of what I was seeing. It was my horse. My wonderful, beautiful, lazy horse. She came to the front of the stall as I walked over, her ears forward and alert, her eyes bright and wide as she nickered at me.

When my hand went flat against the side of her soft coat, I started to cry. Marigold nudged me with her nose, and I wrapped my arms around her neck, sobbing against it.

After my tears had slowed, I turned to him. "How did you . . . where did you . . . I don't understand . . ."

Rafe wore the world's biggest grin. "You're not going to make me send her back, are you?"

I tightened my arms around her. "I can't afford to keep her."

"That won't be an issue. It's already taken care of."

This time, I wouldn't argue with him. I wouldn't fight or tell him to return her. I didn't care that it was too extravagant or too expensive. I would accept his gift and not complain. I loved her too much for that.

Marigold tugged her head away, heading over to her feeding trough. She'd had enough reuniting for one night.

So I went over to Rafe and hugged him tightly instead. "Thank you. Thank you, thank you, thank you."

"You're welcome," he murmured into the top of my hair as his arms held me close. I loved this. Loved the way it felt when he held me. Even in the past when I had been upset with him, I still craved his touch. That had to mean something.

Maybe Whitney was right. Maybe I was already at a hundred percent.

Chapter 23

I was sorely tempted to tell Rafe he could kiss me. But I didn't want to kiss him just because he'd bought me a horse. When I kissed him, and by now I knew that would happen again, and soon, it would be because I wanted to more than anything else. And there would be no extenuating circumstances.

We walked hand in hand back to his car, where we started to unload my presents. A card slipped out of the pile I had been carrying, and I stopped to pick it up.

When I got into the kitchen, I opened the envelope. But there wasn't a birthday card inside. It was a folded up piece of paper.

I unfolded it and gasped, and it felt like hot liquid silver filled my mouth. Rafe was immediately by my side. "What is it?"

With a shaky hand, I gave him the paper. It was a black-and-white picture of me on campus, on my way to class. "I'll see you soon, Mary-Pauline," was written across the top. I couldn't tell if it was a recent photo or not. For all I knew he had taken the picture years ago. Rafe took one look at it and got on the phone. First he called his team to come over, and then he called the sheriff.

The picture was blurry, but there was no mistaking that it was me. "He's messing with me," I told Rafe.

"Why would he do that?" he said. He had just finished his calls and hung up his phone.

"It's hard to explain, but that was one of the ways he kept control over everyone. He kept us off balance all the time. We never knew what he would do next."

My knees didn't work, and I fell hard onto one of the kitchen chairs. "The worst part of this is that he didn't mail it. It was with my other presents. Which means either he or someone who follows him came here to Frog Hollow"—here my voice started to tremble—"and left that with my other presents."

The thought that John-Paul could have been standing next to me, close enough to touch me, made me nauseous. Bile burned in my stomach as I thought of what he could have done to Aunt Sylvia. Or Whitney. Or Nicole.

Or Rafe.

He crouched down next to me. "I swear to you, on my life, I'm not going to let anything happen to you."

Then he held me until the sheriff, his bodyguards, and Max and Aunt Sylvia all arrived at the same time.

Rafe told his men to hire even more security. This being the most exciting thing that had happened to the sheriff's department in the last ten years, the sheriff promised again to increase their patrols and keep a closer eye on who was coming and going. They promised to contact everyone at the party to see if anybody had any footage on their phone that they could look at.

I stayed up that whole night, unable to sleep. I just sat in the front room, and Rafe stayed with me. He held me the entire night. We didn't speak. We didn't need to.

I couldn't bear the thought of going to the diner. To where he had been the night before. So Rafe got Laura to cover my shift. "I have to go to the church bazaar tonight," I told him. "I'm in charge."

He agreed, but only if we had a bunch of bodyguards with us. I didn't argue. But as the sun rose higher in the sky, I started to feel silly. As I sat encircled in Rafe's protective arms, I decided that John-Paul would have to be the world's biggest idiot to try to get at me while I was literally surrounded by men who would love to have an excuse to shoot him. And he might have been a lot of things, but he wasn't an idiot.

Rafe reluctantly left me to shower and change.

A worn-out and worried Aunt Sylvia took his place on the couch. "Are you glad to have Marigold back?"

I was glad that she didn't want to talk about John-Paul. "I am. But I feel bad that he gives me those kinds of presents. Like I'm some poor girl he has to take care of."

My aunt huffed. "That's ridiculous. Especially since his money is inherited. Would you like him less if he was poor?"

"Of course not!"

"Right. You're being a reverse snob and feeling bad about something that isn't his fault. And even if he works hard and earns more, so what? He shouldn't have it? And he shouldn't spend it on someone he loves?"

She was right. The money might make me uncomfortable, but I would probably have to figure out a way to cope with it.

I hoped she didn't see my secret smile. Aunt Sylvia only guessed that Rafe loved me. She didn't know that he had told me as much. No one did. Not even Whitney. It was between him and me and I intended to keep it that way. At least for a little while.

We all went together to the church bazaar. I felt bad about making them come early with me, but I had a lot of things to set up. Only it didn't take anywhere near as long as I thought it would because the security team volunteered to help and everything got done super fast.

I enjoyed getting everything ready. I made sure the booths were set up correctly, that the silent auction was ready to accept bids, and that the food for dinner was hot and ready.

Nicole arrived, all dolled up in a little black dress for her MC-ing duties. She hugged me when she saw me. "Sorry I didn't get to talk to you at your birthday last night, but you were a little busy."

"Back at you," I said. "And how are things going with Mr. Shane?"

"Um, completely perfect. Which is worrisome. Like three of the horsemen of the apocalypse are already here and I'm waiting for the fourth one to show up and destroy everything."

"Or you have nothing to worry about because you're amazing and Shane appreciates it."

She was holding a plate of cookies in one hand. "He said he'd bid on my cookies. I've been trying to feed him more because you know the way to a man's heart is through his stomach. Either you're a good cook and he'll marry you to keep getting fed, or you're a bad cook who will give him food poisoning, making him delirious, and then you can lock it down."

I put my arm around her shoulders and squeezed. "Things will work out the way they're supposed to work out."

She shook her head. "Maybe. But enough about me. What's up with you and Rafe? Way to get back on that goat!"

"I think you mean back on that horse."

"Back on that horse, under your prince, whatever," she said with a wave of her hand. "Now I'm going to go put these on the auction table, and then I'm going to stuff food in my mouth until the feelings stop."

It was time for the bazaar to start. All of Frog Hollow showed up to support the church getting a new roof, and to enjoy the socializing. I ran around the entire night, making sure that everything ran smoothly. I didn't even get to eat dinner. There were games to supervise and an auction to oversee and activities to get going. I was so glad to be busy. It made it almost impossible for me to think about John-Paul.

Max was in a bluegrass band that met in the city, and he had convinced his bandmates to come out for the evening and play for free. They were up on the stage, and we even had people dancing to their music. Every time I made a pass around the room, I collected money from the various booths. It was so gratifying to see everybody so happy and having so much fun.

Rafe kept an eye on me the whole evening. Whenever I would look up or stop for a moment to catch my breath, he was there. Making me feel safe. And loved.

Nicole volunteered to help me count the money. "I need to know how much this auction has to earn."

We were both disappointed when we realized we had only collected a little over ten thousand dollars. "I would have to auction everyone off for at least a thousand dollars apiece," she said sadly. There was no way that would happen.

And it wasn't like we could buy a third of a roof.

"Just trust in me," she said. "I have faith we'll do it."

I had used up what little trust I had left on Rafe. I could probably give her some paranoia or anxiety. I still had loads of those.

When Nicole started the auction up, her first eligible bachelor was Tommy. "If you win Tommy, you will win a night in Iowa City at the restaurant of your choosing! Do I hear ten dollars?"

"Ten dollars!" someone yelled out.

"Going to bid?" Rafe asked, as he came to stand next to me.

I had told him the details about my single date with Tommy, the one he'd crashed. After I'd finished, Rafe had laughed for like five minutes. Which annoyed me because it was not that funny. "Ha-ha."

Tommy sold for seventy-five dollars, which seemed awfully high to me. Nicole gave me a panicked look.

Fortunately, she had been smart enough to recruit an entire team of firefighters to come out and participate from a neighboring town. The women in the crowd got to their feet, cheering and holding up their dollar bills like we were at some strip club instead of the house of the Lord.

The firefighters had planned dates ranging from cooking chili to going salsa dancing. Nicole racked up a bunch of money by playing the women off of one another.

"It's not going to be enough," I muttered.

"What's not going to be enough?" Rafe asked.

"We've only raised about ten thousand so far. I don't know how we're going to raise another twenty thousand dollars."

Brooke Cooper walked over to us, interrupting our conversation. "Hello, Rafael," she cooed.

"Ms. Cooper. Nice to see you again."

She narrowed her eyes, not liking his response. Or lack thereof. So she turned her attention to me. "Genesis, I was hoping to talk to you tonight."

Uh-oh. This would not be good.

"I wanted to make sure you'd be able to head up the blood drive again. You did such a great job on it last year." She was being nice to me solely for Rafe's benefit. She'd never spoken so sweetly to me in her entire life. In fact, even though she was talking to me, she only had eyes for Rafe.

"I . . ." I was going to say yes. It was like a reflex. Somebody asked me for help and I said yes.

I glanced at Rafe next to me, and a power I didn't know I had swelled up inside me. "No."

"Thanks, that's . . . what? Did you say no?" She might have looked stunned if the Botox had allowed her forehead to move.

"I said no. I can't. I'm too busy right now. You'll need to find someone else."

"Oh. Fine. Whatever." And with a flick of her blonde hair, she was gone.

He put his arm around my waist, pulling me into his side. His pressed a soft kiss against my ear, his breath warm and tingly. "Well done. I don't enjoy you saying no to me, but I've discovered I love it when you say it to other people."

I elbowed him. "Stop it."

"She doesn't seem very nice," he observed.

"Well, what she lacks in niceness and compassion, she makes up for in expensive shoes. Plus, she was married to Tommy. We have to give her a pass for that reason alone."

He gave me a half smile and glanced at his watch. "Almost my turn. Are you going to bid on me?"

Now it was my turn to act nonchalant. I lazily shrugged one shoulder. "We'll see."

He grabbed my hand and pressed a warm kiss onto my palm before going backstage. I found Aunt Sylvia and Max and sat next to them at their table. Aunt Sylvia handed me her bidding number. "I have a feeling you'll be needing this soon," she said with a wink.

Shane came out on stage. Nicole announced, "This is Shane Fitzgerald. His date will be a horse and sleigh ride out to Frog Hollow Lake, where there will be a romantic dinner and heater waiting. Let's start this bid at a hundred dollars."

She started it high on purpose. She didn't want there to be any competition. But someone raised a number. Nicole counter-bid.

"You can't bid!" someone protested.

"Yes I can!" Nicole retorted. "Three hundred dollars!"

The bidding got all the way up to five hundred, and then Nicole smacked her podium. "One thousand dollars!"

The room went silent, and she asked sweetly, "Are there any other bids? Going once, going twice, sold to me!"

And then Shane walked across the stage to Nicole and grabbed her. He leaned her backward and kissed her in front of the entire audience. Everyone went nuts, whistling and clapping for them.

Nicole's face was bright red when he finally released her, but she was deliriously happy. "Okay! Our final bid for this evening. Here we have

His Royal Highness, Prince Rafael, and his date is . . . to be determined?" She put her hand over the microphone and said something to him. He responded.

"Okay, so Rafe says that his date will accompany him on his private plane to his oldest brother's wedding in his home country of Monterra, where you will be his personal guest and stay in his palace. Do I hear a hundred dollars?"

"Five hundred dollars!" Brooke called out.

I couldn't let her get him. I still had some of that club opening money left. I raised my number.

"We have six hundred. Do I hear seven?"

"A thousand!" Brooke said.

She was not going to touch Rafe. "Two thousand dollars!" I yelled, jumping to my feet. Brooke looked at me, as if trying to ascertain how serious I was.

"Three thousand!"

I didn't have that much left. I sank back down in my chair. Max offered to lend me some money, but I held up my hand. I couldn't go any more into debt. Not even for Rafe.

"Do I hear four thousand?" Nicole asked, but she knew she wouldn't get a response. No one but the Coopers had that kind of money here. I swallowed back the lump in my throat. Brooke would get to go to the wedding. The one I had imagined going to, where I had imagined I'd get to see Lemon and Kat and his whole family again. The church needed the money. I had to think about things besides what I wanted.

"It's okay," I told my aunt, my eyes bright with unshed tears. "It would have meant that I would miss getting to spend Christmas Eve and Christmas with you."

"Which would have been fine. We could have spent one holiday apart. That's normally what happens when children grow up."

"Four thousand? Anyone? Anyone at all? Four thousand?"

"Announce me as the winner!" Brooke insisted loudly from the crowd.

Rafe walked over to Nicole. "If I bid on myself, can I choose my date?"

"Absolutely," Nicole said, her eyes lighting up. "Do you bid four thousand?"

"How much more do you need to hit your goal?" he asked.

Nicole studied her notepad where she had written down the winning bids. She quickly calculated. "About seventeen thousand."

"Then I bid seventeen thousand dollars."

The room went so quiet, you could hear the snow falling outside. "I have seventeen thousand dollars! Do I hear eighteen thousand? No? Didn't think so. Going once, going twice, sold to Prince Rafael, and we have a new church roof!"

Everyone got to their feet, cheering and clapping for Rafe and yet another amazing thing that he'd done to support the town that I loved.

"And just who, I wonder, will you choose as your date?" Nicole asked.

His gaze settled on me, and he held out one hand. "Genesis Kelley, will you come with me to Monterra?"

I raised my eyebrows at Aunt Sylvia, who nodded so hard she looked like a bobblehead toy.

"Are you sure you're okay with this?" I asked.

"You'd better say yes before Brooke kidnaps him and keeps him locked up in her basement!" she responded.

"I will!" I yelled to him, and the town's cheering got even louder.

The church had its roof, Nicole had Shane, and I had a date with my prince.

Chapter 24

Aunt Sylvia made plans to spend Christmas with Max, Amanda, and her son, Austin, and I was on Rafe's jet, holding his hand and talking to him as we flew halfway across the world.

We were nearly to Monterra. He pointed out the mountain ranges near his home. It was sunny outside, but everything was covered in a blanket of white. He excused himself to use the restroom before we had to put on our seatbelts, and I got up to get my purse and send Aunt Sylvia a text to let her know that I was nearly there.

But when I pulled on the straps, my purse caught on Rafe's bag, and it emptied the contents all over the floor. I bent down to put his things back. I glanced at his passport, smiling at the picture of him.

His wallet. I glanced up at the bathroom door. I couldn't help it. I wondered what he had in it. Pictures? Was there one of me?

"I should put it back," I whispered.

I didn't.

He had black and platinum credit cards in his wallet. A bunch of cash in different national currencies. No pictures.

But there was something behind the cash. Something pink.

It was my letter. The one I had written him on the show. I pulled it out to make sure. He had folded it neatly, and he carried it around with him everywhere he went. The whole time he'd been in Iowa, he'd had it with him.

If there had been any doubt about his sincerity, this took it all away. He loved me. He really, really loved me.

My heart leapt in happy excitement. I heard the sink running, and I put the note back where I had found it, shoving his bag back into the overhead compartment just as he came out.

He was so amazing. So handsome, so smart, so kind and generous.

Why was I waiting? What was I waiting for? I loved him. Totally, completely loved him. I never stopped. Just like he'd never stopped loving me.

Resistance really was futile.

"Hi!" I beamed at him, breathless but elated.

"Hi," he responded, giving me a strange look. "Everything okay?"

"Everything is fan-freaking-tastic." I couldn't help it. I giggled. I loved Rafe. I loved him.

But as I started to tell him, the flight attendant came out to tell us that we were beginning our descent and asked us to put on our seatbelts.

I could tell him later. We had four full days in Monterra before we had to head home.

The palace was in total chaos. When we entered the front hall, there were relatives and wedding guests everywhere, and members of the palace staff were trying to direct everyone to their rooms and get their luggage situation straightened out. Despite the people running around like an army of confused ants, the front hall was stunning. Like a winter wonderland. It had been impressive on my first visit, but now, decorated for the holidays and the wedding, it was just magical. There was greenery and red ribbons and gold accents everywhere I looked. Red and gold were the colors on his family's crest, as well as the colors of the country's flag, and with this royal wedding the royal family seemed determined to display those colors proudly.

"Follow me," Rafe said. He took me up a staircase that had been blocked off because it led to his family's personal suites.

"I had them put you in the guest room next to Lemon's," he said. It was the same room I had used when I first met his family during filming the show. When he opened the door to put down my luggage, his seven-year-old sister Serafina was lying on my bed.

"Genesis!" she said, bounding across the room to me. I picked her up and hugged her. She was the friendliest little girl I had ever met. I knew Lemon and Kat both adored her.

"What are you doing up here?" Rafe asked. "Shouldn't you be downstairs helping *Mamma* with the guests?

"Prince Matteo is here." She said it the same way someone else might say, "The Grim Reaper is here."

"Who is Prince Matteo?" I mouthed the words to Rafe, but Serafina caught me.

"He is *un cretino, uno sciocco, uno scemo, proprio un idiota!*"

I figured the lapse into vehement Italian wasn't good. "Basically a punk?"

"*Si.* He is horrible," she seethed. "I hate him."

"His mother is best friends with our mother, so you should probably go down there and be nice," Rafe said.

Serafina fell dramatically backward against my bed. "I can't be nice to him!"

He took his phone out of his pocket. "Just pretend. And I'll let you use my phone."

She stood straight up, a diabolical gleam in her eye. "Maybe I can be nice." She took the phone, tapping away as she went out into the hallway.

"Did you just bribe your little sister to get me alone?"

He put his arms around my waist, tugging me close. "I might have."

I giggled as he pressed a kiss against my forehead.

"What's all this? My poor innocent eyes!" Rafe's twin brother, Dante, entered the room, hand in hand with Lemon. We pulled apart as the two brothers greeted each other. Lemon hugged me. "I'm so glad you were able to make it."

"And it only cost Rafe seventeen thousand dollars."

"You'll have to tell me that story later," Lemon said with a conspiratorial grin. "Kat would have come by, but as you can imagine she's really busy."

I totally got it. Given the horde downstairs, I didn't know how they were planning on pulling this all off.

"You know, you're ruining all of Mother's plans. She had a line of women she planned on introducing you to, since you're now her only son who's not engaged." Dante jumped and landed on the bed. This family really did just make themselves at home wherever they were.

"You can't be serious," Lemon retorted. "She has to know how Rafe feels . . ." Her words died as she looked between us. I hadn't had a real conversation with her since she came to visit me. She didn't know how things had changed, and she was being careful.

Dante got a wounded expression and put a hand over his heart. "I try not to be serious, but sometimes it just slips out!" Lemon laughed.

I couldn't believe that I had ever thought Dante and Rafe were the same person. They were nearly polar opposites. Where Dante was all kinetic energy bundled up with constant flirting, Rafe was a mountain in a storm—sheltering, unmoving, reliable.

And they had chosen women who balanced them out. Lemon made Dante more responsible and serious, and he reminded her to slow down and enjoy life. Which was the opposite of Rafe and me. I helped him to be happy, and he made me feel safe and loved.

There was a knock at my door. A short, formal-looking man stood there, and he bowed slightly to me. "Signorina Genesis, I am Giacomo. I understand that you might need a dress for this evening and tomorrow's festivities?"

That had to be Rafe's doing. He knew I didn't own anything fancy enough to attend a royal wedding.

"Whatever you need, ask Giacomo. He's like a fairy godfather," Lemon told me.

"Let's go," Dante said, as he stood up and grabbed Lemon's hand. "I think there are some things I still want to show you in the castle."

She grinned. "I know exactly the kind of thing you want to show me."

"You wound me again with your insinuations!" he said. "You're lucky I love you so much."

He kissed her gently. It was an odd experience to see someone with Rafe's face kissing someone else.

They told us they'd see us at the rehearsal dinner that evening. After they left, Rafe said, "I'm going to go see my parents while Giacomo helps you sort everything out." He kissed my hand and said goodbye.

I felt a little uneasy at being left alone, but I remembered that Lemon had told me I was in good hands.

"Why don't you show me what you brought with you, and then we'll go downstairs and select whatever you're lacking?" Giacomo pulled out a tablet, ready to go through my stuff. I was sure this very stylish man would find my clothes lacked a lot.

"What do you mean?" I asked. Did the palace have a store inside of it?

"There are several different Monterran designers who have come to the palace, and they have brought evening gowns, shoes, and accessories, in case a guest's luggage was lost or someone had an accident with their dress. Or"—he leaned in as if sharing a great secret—"if they want to borrow something to upgrade their jewelry."

I nodded, and the mention of jewelry made me remember the last time I was at the palace, when the show had sent me to meet Rafe's family. He had taken me shopping in town among the little gingerbread shops, which were edged in white lattice. It was like walking into a fairy tale.

I had admired a diamond necklace in a jewelry store, and he was ready to go in and buy it for me. I told him not to, because it cost too much money. "But you would look beautiful with it on!"

I cringed, and he hadn't missed it. "Why do you do that whenever I say you're beautiful?"

Making sure we were far enough away, I turned off my mike pack and he did the same. "John-Paul always told me I was pretty. That's why he wanted me. So for a long time I stayed away from anything that might make anyone think I was pretty and just focused on other stuff. When I got older I wanted to be thought of that way, but it was too late. I didn't know how to do my hair or makeup, and it made me feel too stupid to ask. Then you stop believing it's even possible and you think that no one will ever want you."

I had turned my head away from him during my confession. He put his fingers on my chin, making me look at him. "I don't think you're pretty."

That made little stabbing knives tear at my heart at his confirmation.

"You're unbelievably beautiful. And I want you."

Then he had kissed me in the middle of the city's main square, not caring who saw or if the show filmed it, proving to me that his words were true.

It was one of my favorite memories with Rafe.

He thought I was unbelievably beautiful. I had to remember that. I smiled at Giacomo. "Let's go grab something stunning."

Giacomo did not disappoint. He found me a royal-blue cocktail dress for the rehearsal dinner and a beautiful full-length emerald gown for the wedding. He even sent up a makeup artist to get me ready for the dinner, which I did not have a problem with considering the kind of people who would be in the dining room. Actual royalty from all over the world. Heads of state.

Rafe.

He came and knocked on my door, looking amazing in a custom-tailored tuxedo. Seeing Rafe in a tux was a little like looking directly into the sun. Painfully, blindingly bright, and now I had little spots at the periphery of my vision.

"I'm trying to think of how to tell you just how beautiful you are," he admitted. "I don't think I know enough English for that."

A million butterflies burst to life inside my stomach, making my whole body feel lighter. Like I could float away. I grinned at him.

He held out his hand. "It would be my great privilege to escort you down to dinner."

"And it would be my great privilege to go with you."

"Would you two just get a room already? We literally have hundreds of them," Dante said as he breezed past us to knock on Lemon's door.

"Ignore him," Rafe whispered. "He's just jealous that I look so much better in a tuxedo than he does."

"I heard that! And you do not!"

I giggled as we went downstairs. Two servants pulled open the large double doors to the dining room. I had been in this room before, but it had seemed much smaller then. Now there were several long dining tables set up to accommodate all the guests who had been invited. I didn't know how they had determined who made the cut and who didn't, but I was dazzled by the elegant gowns and sparkling jewelry.

We were seated at the main table with Rafe's family. His two other sisters, Chiara and Violetta, nodded to me as Rafe held out my chair. I smiled at them as I sat down and he helped me scoot the chair back in. He sat across from me. Lemon was seated next to me, with Dante next to Rafe. Everyone stood as Nico and Kat entered the room. They were a stunning couple, both tall and dark-haired. And they looked at each other with such love, such adoration, that I wanted to sigh. They sat in the center of the table, next to King Dominic and Queen Aria.

Everyone sat when they did. The servants began bringing out the first course. Rafe elbowed his brother and said, "Those are my feet."

Dante shoved him back, laughing. "Get them out of my way! I'm trying to flirt with my fiancée!"

"Just so you know," Lemon said as she leaned to one side, allowing the server to put a bowl of soup in front of her, "this does not get better. They're always like this. Like two pigs set loose in a cornfield."

I liked it. It made me happy to see Rafe this way. At ease. Surrounded by his family. And she was right. They bantered away the rest of the evening, keeping Lemon and me laughing.

During the second course, the woman on my right, who had a thick Italian accent, introduced herself as the queen's sister. After I told her my name, she said, "You'll have to forgive me, but you have the most beautiful red hair."

Lemon leaned past me to say, "And it's natural, if you can believe that."

"I remember reading an article that said looking at the color red increases your heart rate and respiration," Rafe's aunt said.

"I can attest to that," Rafe butted in, making me blush. She said something to him in Italian, and he responded. I couldn't exactly ask them what they said. Not if I wanted to stay one color.

The rest of dinner seemed to fly by. I tried to imagine my life always being like this. So elegant and glamorous. I felt out of place.

But when Rafe smiled at me, that feeling went away.

"My family's going to celebrate Christmas early," he said, leading me from the room. "Since the wedding is tomorrow."

"Oh." That would be awkward. "I can't celebrate Christmas with your family." Talk about an imposition! They weren't planning on me coming out here.

"You can," he insisted.

"I don't have any gifts for anyone."

"That doesn't matter."

"It will matter if I get gifts and don't have any to give back." I couldn't explain to him what that would do to my pride. But he seemed to instinctively understand.

"That won't be a problem," he reassured me. He took out his phone, typed in something, and put it back in his pocket.

"Aren't we going to get changed first?"

"Christmas is more fun in formal wear." He took me into his family's private rooms, right into a large, comfortable family room dominated by a massive Christmas tree. There was a roaring fire going. "Look at that," I pointed out. "No smoke."

He gave me a wry smile, seating me on one of the couches. The rest of the family joined us not long after that—the king in his wheelchair with his queen walking alongside him, the princesses following, and Nico, Kat, Lemon, and Dante all arriving together a minute later.

Serafina sat next to me. "I'm asking *La Befana* for a sister this Christmas."

I was pretty sure there wasn't one of those under the tree. "Is your mother going to have a baby?"

"Ew. No. She's old. Rafe's going to marry you."

How could a simple statement both thrill and terrify me? "He's not," I told her. I didn't want her to get her hopes up. We were nowhere near that yet.

"He is."

"I wouldn't bet against her," Kat said as she walked past, slowing down long enough to speak to me. "She's two for two on that front."

"I used to only have two sisters, but now I have five."

"Almost four," I corrected her.

"Five," she said stubbornly, eyeing me.

They all settled in and started exchanging gifts, mostly novelty and prank items that made everybody laugh. Lemon handed Kat a clothing box. When Kat got it open, she pulled out a risqué piece of lingerie that had her blushing, Nico smiling, and Lemon cackling with delight.

As promised, there were no gifts for me, which made me feel more relaxed. There weren't as many presents in total as I had expected, and Rafe explained that the majority of their gift-giving took place later, in early January.

"Well, my parents are going to be here early in the morning, so we're going to say good night to y'all." Lemon kissed the king and queen on both cheeks, and Dante did the same. Everybody seemed to empty out of the room quickly after that.

Rafe offered to put a sleeping Serafina in bed, but Nico insisted he be the one to do it. "Because if I walk my soon-to-be-bride to her bedroom door, she won't be able to wear white tomorrow."

Kat put her hands on her hips in mock anger and said, "I'll have you know I'm perfectly capable of controlling—"

He interrupted her with an "Until tomorrow, *cuore mio*," and a kiss so passionate and intense that I studied the wallpaper behind them instead of looking. As if remembering that we were there, a breathless Kat made him stop, and they left the room in separate directions, even though they were both reluctant to do so.

Which left me and Rafe alone. I'd always imagined myself too young to get married, but I wanted what Nico and Kat had. I liked the idea of making a permanent commitment. Standing up in front of everyone I knew and telling them that I loved Rafe and would spend the rest of my life with him.

That was not where my head should have been. I kicked off my shoes, rubbing my feet. "I feel bad about missing the talent show."

"Nicole will film the whole thing for you. She even said she would be Henry's assistant."

Just the memory of the box made me shudder. We were quiet for a moment before I asked, "They had presents for me, didn't they?"

He stifled a yawn. "Yes."

"And you had someone remove them?"

"I did. I'll have someone ship them back home to us."

Besides being touched by the idea that he would go out of his way to make sure that I was comfortable, my heart flittered at him calling Iowa home.

Home is where the people you love are.

I saw that once on a sign, and it had stuck with me. Home *was* where the people you loved were. I slipped my hand into his.

He put his arm around me, pulling me against him. He closed his eyes and leaned his head against the back of the couch.

I couldn't believe how much I loved him. How much everything had changed. "Hey. I got you something for Christmas."

He opened one eye and focused it on me. "You did?"

Getting up on my knees, I put my hands against his chest for balance. Now he had both eyes open, watching me. I very slowly, very deliberately leaned forward, pressing my lips against his.

Amusement tugged at the corner of his eyes. "Was that your way of asking me to kiss you? Because that wasn't asking."

"Are you saying you don't want to kiss me?"

His hands slid around me, pulling me into his lap. "Maybe I don't."

"Liar," I said, tugging at his undone bow tie.

He smiled, and then he kissed me for a very enjoyable and very long time.

When we had to come up for air, he leaned his forehead against mine. "That was the best Christmas present ever."

I totally agreed.

Chapter 25

The entire castle was in another uproar the following morning. I got myself dressed just as two frazzled looking women knocked on my door, telling me that they had come to do my hair and makeup. They spoke some English, so I found out that they'd been up since four in the morning helping everyone get ready. They were extremely fast and efficient, and they finished up right as Rafe arrived to escort me to the wedding. "You look beautiful," he said, holding me at arm's length while he took me in, head to foot.

"You make me feel beautiful," I told him. He kissed me gently, softly. Like a whispered promise.

He had to be to the church early, so he led me with him into a waiting limo. We didn't talk as the limo drove toward the center of town. Snow glittered all around us, but the roads had been totally cleared. The closer we got, the more people we saw lined up behind barricades, waving to us. Rafe rolled down his window, smiling and waving back.

Could I do this? Could I really be part of his life? Could I be a princess and a veterinarian at the same time? Could I be happy here?

Then he turned his smile to me and I thought, yes, absolutely. I could be very, very happy in Monterra.

Rafe put me in a seat near the front of the church. He reached inside his pocket. "For while you're waiting."

It was a Snickers bar. It wasn't exactly breakfast food, but I loved that he knew me well enough to know what I wanted. I ate my candy bar as other people began to file in and were seated by ushers. I realized he had put me on his family's side of the church, and in a spot where we could easily see each other as he performed his groomsman duties. He stood talking to a man who looked vaguely like the prince of England, near where Nico and Dante were speaking to each other. Although I couldn't hear what was being said, it looked like Dante was teasing Nico, but nothing could remove the huge grin on Nico's face. He didn't look at all nervous or worried. He looked thrilled and excited.

The music started, and everyone stood. I got up a half second later, as I hadn't known that was expected of me. I hadn't ever been to an actual royal wedding before.

Rafe's sisters entered the church in adorable red ball gowns. Serafina had a basket and seemed to be taking her flower girl duties very seriously. She threw big fistfuls of flowers in a pattern only she seemed to understand. Chiara and Violetta followed behind her, with Lemon bringing up the rear. They each carried bouquets of red and white flowers.

A choir started to sing, and it was Kat's turn to enter the church. I heard sighs and murmurs around me as everyone fixed their gaze on her. She held on to the king's wheelchair, letting him escort her down the aisle. Her dress sparkled like snow, and she was so happy she glowed. She had a red velvet bow around her waist, and she wore a tiara filled with red hearts. She was stunning.

I could tell she was trying to be dignified and move slowly, but she had to keep adjusting her pace because she wanted to get up to the front quicker, to where her soon-to-be husband was waiting for her.

When she finally got to the altar, everyone sat down. Nico and Kat spoke briefly and quietly to each other, the love and exhilaration of the moment evident on their faces.

As I sat through a ceremony that was sometimes in English but mostly in other languages, I watched Rafe. Would that be us? Did I want that to be us?

I did. I wanted to marry him. I wanted all of this with him. I wanted a life, a family, a forever with him. It didn't matter that he was from here and I was from Iowa. That he was a prince and I was a college student. We would find a way to work it out.

After a bunch of standing and kneeling, they were finally pronounced husband and wife. The entire church erupted into applause and cheering as they marched down the aisle together, waving to everyone. The noise from the crowd outside the church was even louder when they opened the doors, and there were bells ringing and sounds of celebration. Rafe escorted Violetta down the aisle, and he waited outside for me.

I threw myself into his arms, kissing him hard. "What was that for?" he asked.

"For being you."

The reception was loud and teeming with people. I couldn't remember the last time I'd had that much fun. Despite generally hating dancing, I decided I didn't care what anyone else thought about my moves and spent the night with Rafe and his family out on the dance floor.

I was shocked when Rafe had the DJ put on a country song, and asked me to teach everyone the steps to a line dance. I did it, and I couldn't help but laugh as I watched all of his family, including the new bride and groom, trying to do the Tush Push.

But Nico and Kat didn't stick around for long. They said their goodbyes and left quickly, their eyes full of longing, anticipation, and joy.

Sariah Wilson

Rafe's arm went around my waist. That could be us.

The rest of the time in Monterra seemed to fly by. That might have been because I spent a lot of it making out with Rafe. As always, Rafe's family was so kind and generous with me that I found myself not wanting to leave.

After Kat left for her honeymoon, Lemon had teased me relentlessly about being under Rafe's thrall. I told her I wasn't.

"So you're saying you're not in love with him? That you're not kissing on him every chance you get?"

What could I say to that that would be true without admitting anything?

"See how you're not responding? Total thrall."

Obviously, I wanted to get back to Aunt Sylvia and Whitney and my horse and my dog, but there was something special about being in Monterra, too. I didn't want to leave. There were people I loved here, as well.

When our time was finished and we flew back to Iowa, we held hands as Rafe drove back to the farmhouse from the airport. It was dark out, and the full moon illuminated the snow beneath it. "I'm excited to get home, but I am not excited to see Brooke. She's going to be even madder at me now that I won't run the blood drive."

He kissed the back of my hand. "What brought out your inner rebel?"

"You did." I put my head against the seat, watching his profile. "You're also the one who made me consider why I always say yes. I think it goes back to when I went to live with Aunt Sylvia. John-Paul had spent my entire childhood telling me how wicked I was. Obedience was the first thing he ever drilled into me. So when Aunt Sylvia rescued me, I wanted to make her happy. I wanted to be the perfect child. Some part of me was afraid that if I didn't do everything she said, she'd send me back. I know she wouldn't have, but little kids aren't always rational. And I think it stuck."

262

"What did?"

"I really do like helping people. I like making people happy. But what stuck was the obedience thing. Feeling like I had to be good and say yes every time someone asked for help, even if I didn't want to or didn't have the time."

He glanced at me. "Let's continue the streak. What is something you've always wanted to do but haven't because you wanted to be good?"

His bare chest flashed into my mind, and I was grateful his eyes were on the road so he wouldn't notice how my cheeks burned. "It's going to sound stupid. But I always wanted to climb the water tower."

"Let's do it then." I gave him directions, and his SUV had no problem handling the snow-covered dirt road out to the tower. He called his guards and told them not to follow us, and that he would see them back in town.

Climbing the water tower was something the seniors always did on ditch day. I was the dork who stayed in class, studying, while all my classmates were off enjoying themselves.

We got out, and I showed him the hole in the chain-link fence that we could climb through. "Is this legal?" he asked.

"Probably not," I said as I started to climb. The rungs were a little slippery, but my rubber-soled boots did a good job of clinging to the metal.

When we were halfway up, Rafe called up to me, "This wasn't quite what I had in mind when I pictured this."

"Are you afraid of heights?"

"No, just very aware of my own mortality and that unlike my character in *World of Warcraft*, I can't fall a hundred feet and survive."

But once we got to the top, it was totally worth it. We could see the entire county, the Christmas lights that twinkled on the houses, the empty cornfields blanketed with sparkling snow. "It's not a turret in a castle, but the view is breathtaking."

He kissed the spot on my neck that I loved, and heat blossomed under my skin, rushing to meet his lips.

"One of the things I love most about living here is that I never have to look up to see the sky. Everything is so open."

"That's how I feel about the mountains in Monterra."

Was that going to be a problem? He was a prince. He couldn't stay in Iowa for forever. He had a life and a family that he had to get back to. Just like I had a life and a family here.

We would make it work. We had to. He kissed me again. "I love you."

This was it. My chance to tell him. To let him know that I was on the same page. "I . . ."

My throat locked up. I couldn't speak. I loved him. I wanted to tell him. Why couldn't I? Was I just not ready?

"I'm not telling you so that you'll say it back. I say it to you because it's how I'm feeling and I don't want to keep that from you."

I felt a prickling sensation at the back of my neck. Like we were being watched. Normally I would have dismissed it as his security, but they weren't here. Or at least they weren't supposed to be.

A figure emerged from the tree line and held up a bullhorn. "Get down from the water tower, Genesis."

It was Sheriff Stidd.

"Busted," I said. Rafe started down the ladder first.

"Are we going to be in trouble? I have lawyers on speed-dial."

"Well, considering that you just saved the church and this is literally my only offense, I'm guessing we'll be just fine."

I was right. The sheriff yelled at us for a few minutes about being reckless and irresponsible, and it was all I could do not to break into pealing laughter. I actually clamped my lips shut. But as soon as we were back in the SUV, we both laughed.

"I really love you," he said after his laughter died down.

"Yeah, yeah. You said that already."

"Did I say this?" He leaned in to brush a soft kiss against my lips. "Or this?" The next kiss was firmer, longer. "What about this?" That kiss nearly made my socks explode.

The sheriff banged on Rafe's window. "And no parking!"

Rafe nodded, and we laughed again as he headed back out toward the main road.

My phone rang, and I saw that it was Whitney. "Hey! What's up?"

"You're back in town, right? Do you have your key to the diner? I left my wallet in the kitchen, and I drove all the way back to get it before I realized I left my work key at home. Total pregnancy brain. Can you help?"

"You know I always have my keys." I felt them in my front pocket. "I'm actually fairly close." Rafe was massaging the back of my neck, which made my head loll all over the place. It was not easy to form words. "I'll be there in a few."

I explained the situation to him, and he headed straight for the diner. Whitney stood out front with a tired Gracie. I knew Christopher was in Iowa City for a training seminar. Meredith and Beau were asleep in the car. That was the nice thing about our town. She could have even left the car running and we wouldn't have had to worry.

"I'll go in and get it for you," I said. "You go get in the car and rest."

We walked back to her car. Well, Gracie and I walked while Whitney waddled. "How did your trip go? Did you finally realize that you like him?"

Rafe sat in the SUV waiting for me. "I like him more than I like candy and *Star Trek* combined."

"Wow," Whit said as she climbed in the front and I buckled Gracie into her car seat. "That's huge."

"I know." I kissed the top of Gracie's soft hair, and she sucked her thumb, resting her head against the side of her seat. "Where is your wallet?"

"It's um, behind the, uh, ow, ow, ow, ow!"

She grabbed the steering wheel so tight her knuckles turned a bright white. "Are you okay?"

"Either somebody poured a Sprite all over my front seat while I was outside, or else my water just broke."

"Oh. That's not good. What do I do? Do I call an ambulance?" I turned, panicking. "Rafe! We need help!"

He sprinted to my side before Whitney could speak again. Like the Flash.

"No, an ambulance will take too long. Man, this really hurts. Why did I want to do this again?"

She obviously couldn't drive. And Christopher's seminar was in Iowa City, so he was already near the hospital. It would take too long for him to get back here.

"Marco's got first aid training. Let me text him."

"Or I could call Amanda."

"Marco's closer," Rafe said.

A minute later, Marco pulled up. "I thought you sent them home," I said.

"They don't always listen."

Rafe explained the situation to his bodyguard, while Whitney moaned again in pain, leaning against the wheel. Gracie started to cry. "It's okay, Gracie, Mommy's okay."

"I'll drive you to the hospital," I told her. "You and Marco can sit in the backseat and he can help you."

"No!" she said. "Somebody's got to take care of the kids. They only know you. It has to be you. Gracie will freak out otherwise. You have to take them over to my mother's house. Please."

"I'll drive her," Rafe said. "And I'll have Marco find Christopher when we get to Iowa City. It's my fault he's there. You take the kids to Whitney's mother's house, and then go straight back to the farmhouse. Stay there until I get back."

She was going to need her wallet for the hospital. Her insurance card, driver's license. That kind of stuff. Right?

I told them I'd be right back and ran inside to look for her wallet. I used my phone as a flashlight and finally found the wallet in one of the refrigerators. I put my phone down and filled up a to-go bag with some snacks for her. I didn't know what she'd need. I only knew that horses liked to eat when they were in labor. People couldn't be much different, could they?

They'd moved Whitney into Rafe's SUV, and I handed him the bag and her wallet. "Be careful," I told him, kissing him quickly.

"You too."

They drove off. Taking off my coat, I laid it on the front seat of Whitney's car. I was going to have to sterilize everything I was wearing. "It's okay, Gracie. I'm taking you guys to Grandma's house."

She cried intermittently and only stopped because she had fallen asleep. Whitney was right. If Rafe had driven them, she would have been hysterical. She got that way when she was tired.

It only took me about ten minutes to get to Whitney's mom's house. I carried Gracie up to the front door, and when they answered I explained what had happened. Her mom took Gracie from me, and her dad and I carried in Meredith and Beau. They thanked me for bringing the kids over and invited me in.

I told them I needed to get home, and congratulated them on adding another grandchild to their family. By the time I got back to the farmhouse, it was really late. Aunt Sylvia was already asleep.

Laddie was excited to see me, at least. He jumped up on me, and I ruffled his fur. "Did you miss me, boy? Did you?"

I wondered if there was an update. My phone wasn't in my pocket. Had I left it in my purse? My purse that was still in Rafe's car? I checked my coat pockets before throwing it in the washing machine, along with my jeans and socks. I put my shoes aside to wash later.

When was the last time I had the phone? Whitney had called me. I went to the diner and I had taken it inside with me.

Where I had left it on the counter. I wanted to thwack myself in the forehead. Apparently Whitney's pregnancy brain was contagious.

Rafe wanted me to stay put. But how would I know what was happening? How would I know if Whitney was okay? If the baby was okay? If they'd made it safely to Iowa City? If they'd contacted Christopher?

I needed my phone.

We didn't have a landline. That would mean I'd have to go upstairs, wake up Aunt Sylvia, and call Rafe. She needed her rest, and Rafe would probably tell me they were fine and to stay home.

Running upstairs, I quickly put on some pants and clean shoes and socks, and grabbed an old coat. "Come on, Laddie! Want to go for a ride?"

He scampered out of the kitchen, as I had just spoken his favorite words. This way I wouldn't be alone, and he would let me know if something was wrong. I opened Old Bess's door, and he jumped in. Not that Laddie would be any help. If somebody tried to take me, he'd be like, "You're here to kidnap Genesis? Can you kidnap me, too?"

Laddie ran back and forth along the backseat, barking as we went, clearly thrilled to be out driving with me. His tail wagged so hard I was afraid he might break it off. I had tried to restrain him once, but he had chewed through the harness. And he hated if I used the kennel. I knew it wasn't safe, but it made him so happy.

As we pulled up to the diner, I rolled down the window. "Stay," I told him. He sat in my seat, panting. I unlocked the diner door, letting myself in. My phone was right where I had left it, on the counter. I turned it on, but there weren't any texts or messages. No news yet.

Coming back out, I locked the door again and shoved my keys into my front pocket. I considered calling Rafe, but I didn't want to distract him while he was rushing my best friend to the hospital.

There was a strange sound that at first I couldn't place. It came from my truck. It was Laddie.

Laddie was growling.

I had never heard Laddie growl before.

He leapt out the truck's window, dashing to stand right in front of me. Off to my left, three shadowy figures approached me. "Hello?" I called out. "Who's there?" The growling got louder, and then Laddie started to bark furiously.

My heart pounded. This wasn't like him. The shadows turned into men I didn't recognize.

Until the one in front stepped under a streetlamp. "Hello, Mary-Pauline."

Chapter 26

Frozen in shock, I couldn't move.

"Time to go home, Mary-Pauline." His voice was like a thousand tarantulas crawling all over my skin.

Laddie sprang forward, trying to bite one of the men. At the same time, I ran for my truck, hoping I could get inside before they could reach me.

I wasn't fast enough. John-Paul grabbed me by the hair, yanking me backward to the ground. I cried out in pain, just as Laddie wrapped his teeth around one of the men's ankles. The third man hit Laddie with a bat, making him whimper, but he didn't let go of the ankle.

"Stop!" I screamed. "Leave him alone!"

My phone. I pulled it out of my pocket and pressed the Emergency Call button. I managed to enter the digits and push the green button before John-Paul saw what I was doing. He kicked my hand, and the phone went flying.

"Help!" I yelled as loud as I could. "Somebody help me!"

I hoped the call had gone through and the 911 operator could hear me. "I'm in Frog Hollow, Iowa. My name is Genesis Kelley—"

He dragged me by the hair, my roots screaming in agony, over to my phone and used his boot to destroy it. He stomped it on it several times while I clawed at his hand, desperate to make him let go. "You think you can be with someone else? You think you can leave me for that boy? Tell me you don't love him. Tell me you don't love Rafe."

He was insane. This was insane. And how did he know how about Rafe? How long had he been watching me?

The third man kept hitting Laddie. They were going to kill him. Adrenaline surged inside me, and I kicked John-Paul in the kneecap, making him double over. He let go of my hair, and I ran over to Laddie. I couldn't let them kill my dog. I kept yelling for help, while I pulled Laddie off, telling him to run.

That stupid, stubborn dog wouldn't leave me. He was breathing hard, clearly in extreme pain, but he attacked the two men again, this time keeping just out of range of the bat.

Tears kept burning and blinding my eyes. That made me remember my keys. I reached into my pocket with trembling fingers, trying to get my pepper spray out, but John-Paul had come up behind me, encircling my neck with his arms. He pressed against my windpipe, making it difficult for me to breathe. I punched his forearms, but from this angle I couldn't put much power behind it.

Angling my head, I bit down as hard as I could. John-Paul yelled and punched me in the ear. Stars exploded behind my eyes, making me dizzy. I ran forward, trying to get away, no longer able to think, acting on pure instinct.

"Help! I need help!"

He grabbed my ponytail like a handle, throwing me against the ground, and I skidded along the asphalt, tearing up the skin of my hands and face. I started scooting backward, but before I could get far, he pulled me upright and again positioned himself behind me in a chokehold.

My head swam and my vision clouded, but something about this felt familiar. That class I had taken at school! I slammed my heel into the inside of his foot, elbowing his ribs at the same time, just as my self-defense instructor had taught me. But before I could do more to break his hold, he shoved a damp cloth against my face. There was a sweet, chemical smell, and then the world went black.

I awoke in a dark place, unable to see or move. It took me a second to realize what had happened. John-Paul and his men had knocked me out, and they had bound my hands, my ankles, and my mouth. I had use of my arms, but they had tethered my ankles to something, so I couldn't move my legs very far.

There was a bumping sensation. I was moving. I was in a car. John-Paul's car. In the trunk.

The claustrophobia kicked in so fast and so hard I couldn't focus. The tie around my mouth smelled like sweat, and it made me gag.

Sharp pain radiated through my chest, like I was having a heart attack. I was going to die. I banged against the top of the trunk, trying to scratch my way out. There was soft padding all along the walls, something they had installed. They had been planning this for a long time. I screamed over and over again, but the sound was muffled.

I had a horrific full-blown panic attack that lasted an eternity, sweat soaking my hair and my clothes, my heart pounding so hard I expected it to rupture. There wasn't enough air in the trunk. I couldn't breathe. All of the oxygen was disappearing.

It got so bad that I fainted.

When I came to, the attack had subsided. I knew I had a short amount of time until it started up again. I remembered watching a show about what to do if you got thrown into a trunk. You were supposed to kick the taillights out and stick your hands through them.

But you had to use your feet to do that. I couldn't move my feet. I tried doing it with my hands, but the taillight didn't move, and all that happened was I bloodied up my knuckles.

I wanted to get the gag off of my mouth, but no matter what I did, how I pulled or tugged, it wouldn't come loose. They had made it too tight.

Think! How do I get out of this?

I turned on my side, wondering if I could swing my feet out that direction, but it was no use. I felt something digging into my hip.

My keys.

I rolled onto my back and very carefully angled my arm so that I could use my fingers to pull my keys out. If nothing else, I had a weapon now for when they opened the trunk, and in the meantime, I could try to use it to get myself free.

After repeated attempts to use a key edge to cut the zip tie around my wrists, I finally figured out a way to position the keys against my stomach and run the tie against the jagged teeth. As my eyes adjusted, I became aware of light appearing at the seams of the trunk, and I realized it was daytime. I didn't know how long I'd been unconscious. A dry sob twisted my breath, but I kept going.

Did Rafe know I was gone? How many hours had it been? Had he tried to call me? Did he know something was wrong?

I'd never even told him that I loved him. I should have told him. I wished I had told him. Now he might never know.

Was Laddie dead? Was Aunt Sylvia worried? They would know this wasn't like me. Had anyone notified the sheriff? Did they know which direction John-Paul had gone? Did they know what kind of car to look for?

This trunk was a million times worse than Henry's magic box had ever been. At least then I'd had the hope of getting out. I wouldn't get out of this. Ever. Even when they opened the trunk I would be confined in a different way.

Although, I thought with a morbid laugh, I probably wouldn't fit in the coal bin anymore.

The car came to a stop, and my whole body went rigid. We couldn't possibly be all the way back to Washington yet. But who knew what they planned on doing to me? I flipped my key ring around, making sure I could point the pepper spray at them. I lay there, unmoving and tense, waiting.

I realized they were getting gas. I started pounding against the trunk, kicking my feet as best I could, and screaming. The padding prevented me from making any sound. I couldn't let anyone know what was happening to me. I listened to the ding-ding as cars drove into the station, the sound of people talking and laughing. I screamed and screamed as tears poured down my cheeks, but the gag made it so that no one could hear me.

It was like I wasn't even there.

"No one can hear you," John-Paul said through the trunk, banging hard on it a couple of times, which made me jump.

Even as we drove away, I kept trying to make noise, to do something to let somebody, anybody, know what was happening.

The panic started to swell, and I tried my best to stay calm. I told myself the walls of the trunk were not moving and wouldn't crush me. It was all in my head.

My body didn't care that I wasn't in any danger of being squished. All the sweating, nausea, heart palpitations, headaches, and tears started right back up. I went back to trying to cut the zip tie around my wrist, but I was having a hard time concentrating and holding still.

Time had become meaningless, but I was aware of the car slowing down, and my heart thumped painfully in response. Were we there? Was this it?

I again tried to position my keys and use my pepper spray as a weapon, but I was shaking so hard that when they threw the trunk open, the light flooded in and my keys slipped from my fingers. I rolled, trying to grab at them, but the men yanked me out of the trunk. I landed on the ground, hard. I tried to control my breathing and get my bearings, but panic kept me from being in control.

"You can't go back home dressed like this," John-Paul said. He stood in front of me, blocking out the sun so that all I could see was his outline. He threw something at me. It was a dress. Like the ones we used to wear.

"You have to get changed." He pulled me up by my wrists and pulled out a large knife. I tried to scream and get away from him, but he used the knife to slit the tie at my wrists and, before I could react, the one around my ankles. My hands and feet ached as the blood rushed into them, causing prickling sensations.

He didn't remove the gag.

I saw two men with him and recognized one of them as the man who had mugged Rafe. "You were at the club," I tried to say. I didn't know if they could understand me.

"No one's interested in anything you have to say," John-Paul replied, as he pushed me toward some bushes. "Get changed. And don't even think about running. Because we will catch you, and then I'll have to punish you."

All that time in the trunk had messed with my ability to think or to plan. Instead I went behind the bushes and hurried to take off my clothes and put the dress on. I knew the kind of punishments he was capable of.

"Do you know how long I've been watching your sinful life? How easy it was to find you after you paraded yourself around on television for the whole world to see?"

I had been so stupid to go on that show. So careless. I had thought myself untouchable. My temporary rebellion had stripped me of my loved ones. And my freedom.

"As if I didn't raise you better. I sent you messages. To let you know that I was watching you. I gave you a chance to repent. But instead you flaunted that man in my face. I was going to teach you a lesson the night you went into the city with him. But we weren't able to follow you because Simon got our car towed. Just know that that night, you were supposed to have been mine."

The night I decided to give Rafe another chance. A night that had been special and meaningful to me was now tainted by John-Paul.

"And then there was your self-indulgent party, where you made yourself the center of attention. Do you know how easy it was for me to sneak in? To leave you that picture? I was there. In that room with you. And you didn't even know it."

I hadn't even sensed him. I had been so caught up in Rafe and my friends that he had stood in the diner with me and I had been completely unaware. I dropped my head into my hands. I had finished dressing a while ago, but I really didn't want to get back in that trunk.

John-Paul crashed through the bushes, pointing his knife at me. "Your salvation is my responsibility, and it is up to me to make sure you obey and live a sinless life."

"Please don't put me in the trunk," I tried to say, as he put the zip ties back around my ankles and wrists. One of the men came over to help him pick me up, and although I struggled and fought, arching away from them, they threw me back in the trunk, slamming the lid shut.

I cried and endured panic attack after panic attack. I felt like I was drowning. Like someone had dropped me into a washing machine, turned it on high, and I was stuck in a dark pool of agitating water, being thrown back and forth, never able to find my way out or catch my breath. For hours and hours.

In the midst of that, someone slammed on the brakes, throwing me forward. My head hit something hard, making me go dizzy. I thought I heard yelling and doors slamming, and then somebody messing with the trunk. Sunlight blinded me, and I held my hands up to shade my eyes.

All the voices around me sounded so far away. One voice kept trying to get my attention, calling me by name. I couldn't understand what it was saying.

There were flashing lights on cars behind us. My fingers and toes felt completely numb, my whole body shaking. People were tugging at me, trying to get the restraints off.

I was lifted out of the trunk, and I passed out.

"She's gone into shock," I heard someone say as I came to, all the sounds still muffled, my vision blurry and hazy.

A face came into my sight line. "Genesis, please. Say something."

It was Rafe. How could it be Rafe? Was I dreaming? Was I still in that trunk and imagining being rescued? I blinked, trying to focus. It looked like we were in an ambulance. And I was on a gurney.

"Rafe?" My voice sounded like a kitten's mewl, with no strength at all behind it. What was wrong with me? Why couldn't I talk?

He hugged me, and it sounded like he had been crying. "He is never going to hurt you again. I promise you. Never again." His words echoed around me, bouncing off my ears. I squinted and put my hands up to prevent sound from coming in. He was so loud.

"How . . . how . . . Am I still in the trunk?" It hurt to talk. It hurt my chest, my head, and my mouth was so dry. What kind of dream was this? Everything was so fuzzy and removed.

I heard the words "tracker" and "key." My mind attempted to put it all together. "There's a tracker on my keys?" I tried to feel for my keys in my pocket. I needed them to cut my bindings. But my fingers weren't cooperating.

For some reason, a tracker on my keys felt extraordinarily bad. Wrong. Like a broken promise.

"You're just like him. Like John-Paul. You want to own me." I flinched. I didn't mean those words. I didn't even want to say them. But they came out. As if someone else was in charge of my mouth.

It was like an out-of-body experience. I was watching the dream, removed from it, but unable to control what was happening. My stomach doubled up in pain, and I groaned, trying to curl myself into a ball. I heard yelling and beeping.

Then I was in the coal bin, with John-Paul standing outside of it, yelling at me while he slammed on the wood. "Tell me you don't love him! You don't love Rafe!"

All I wanted was to escape. I would have said anything. "I don't love Rafe! I don't love him! Let me out!"

The coal bin swirled away, and I was back in the bright ambulance. Rafe's face looked so pale. Poor imaginary man. I wished the dream was better. I also wished this pounding in my head would go away. I swung my hands, connecting with a hard surface, and I beat against it, still trying to get out.

"Just go away," I told my throbbing headache. "I want you to go away. How many times do I have to tell you to go away?"

Blessed darkness engulfed me then, taking away my dreams and pain in one fell swoop.

I woke up in a hospital bed with the worst headache of my entire life. My eyes felt swollen, and it was hard to open them.

"Rafe," I said weakly. My mouth and throat were so parched, my tongue puffy. My lips were cracked and dried.

My nose throbbed, and I reached up to feel a bandage across it. I tried to sit up, but it made my head spin, and I lay back down. My room was empty.

I'd never been in a hospital before. How could I get someone to help me? I tried calling out, but my voice was raspy and soft.

Time passed strangely, surreally, with lights and shadows moving across the wall as I slipped in and out of consciousness.

Finally a nurse in light blue scrubs came in to check on me. "Where's Rafe?" I asked. She jumped, like it surprised her that I was awake. She ran out of the room, but she brought back a doctor with her who flashed a light in my eyes and started asking me questions.

I answered them as best I could and again asked for Rafe. They didn't respond.

Aunt Sylvia and Max came rushing into the room, with Aunt Sylvia crying and saying my name over and over again. She went to hug me, but Max stopped her. He put his arm around her and held her while she cried.

"Is Laddie okay?" I asked them in my raspy voice, bracing myself for the worst as the doctor continued to examine me.

"He's with Dr. Pavich," Max said. "He had several broken ribs, some internal bleeding, but he's a tough dog. He's on the mend and doing better."

Relief engulfed me. I was so afraid that he had died. The doctor gave Max a dirty look, and he immediately stopped talking, chagrined.

Before I could ask about anything else, the doctor started speaking to me. There were a bunch of medical terms I didn't understand and some words I did get, like *acute stress reaction, dehydration, panic attack, broken nose, and concussion.*

He told me that I would need to stay for a few more days because they wanted to monitor me to make sure that my condition didn't worsen, and to determine whether or not there were more extensive internal injuries.

I nodded. I asked for water, and the nurse told me that for now I could have ice chips. She said she would get me some.

Then I was alone with Max and Aunt Sylvia. She took my bandaged hand and squeezed softly. "I want to hug you, but I don't want to hurt you," she said.

"Where's Rafe?"

Max and Aunt Sylvia exchanged glances. "We're not supposed to tell you anything that might upset you," Max said.

"What would upset me?" My heart thudded slowly. "You guys are scaring me. Where is he?"

Aunt Sylvia gave me a sad smile. "Rafe is gone."

Chapter 27

"Gone? What do you mean *gone*? Where is he?" I asked. I again tried to sit up, and the pain knocked me back flat.

"You told him you didn't love him and that you wanted him to go away. After he made sure you would completely recover, he left," Aunt Sylvia said, as gently as possible.

"We're not supposed to tell her anything that might stress her out," Max reminded her, as if I wasn't even in the room.

"She deserves to know the truth," she retorted.

"I didn't say that to him. I wouldn't say that to him." Whispers of a memory played around my conscious mind, like strands or fragments of a dream I couldn't piece together. Rafe was there. I said something to him. But that wasn't real. I had imagined it. Hadn't I? What did I say? Could I have actually said those things?

And he left me? I thought he would never leave. He promised he would protect me and keep me safe, and then he took off? I was kidnapped and beaten up by a psychopath, and he was gone?

"You were angry about the tracker." Max had gotten Aunt Sylvia a chair and had moved it close to my bed so she could still hold my hand.

"Tracker?" That seemed familiar.

"After you got the postcard, Rafe had his team install a tracker on your collie key chain." It was a leather figure of a shepherd collie, like Laddie. He could have easily put something inside of it, and I never would have noticed. I remembered that morning when my keys had gone missing, and how Rafe had been the one to find them. He must have done it then.

"Why didn't he tell me?"

"He thought it would make you mad."

It did make me mad. He had promised not to put a tracker on me.

He promised not to put it on your phone.

So he used a technicality to lie? Okay. He didn't put it on my phone, but he was still tracking me.

Which made it so that he could save your life.

True, which I was obviously grateful for, but part of me still felt betrayed.

"How long has it been since . . . everything happened?"

"Two days," Max told me. "They've had to keep you sedated because you were having night terrors that were worsening your injury."

Fantastic. Rafe had been gone for two days, and I was now a mental basket case.

Suddenly my eyes felt heavy, like I couldn't keep them open. I heard Aunt Sylvia say that they would be back soon, and then I fell into a dreamless sleep.

I woke up screaming, still inside the trunk, not able to get out. Nurses and a doctor ran in to check on me and tried to reassure me, telling me I'd had a nightmare. The doctor said that it was normal given the trauma I had experienced, and he recommended that I see a psychologist when I was released. He left a referral card on my bedside table.

It was pitch black outside, which meant it was probably the middle of the night. There was no way I was going back to sleep.

I still couldn't believe Rafe was gone. I mean, I would get over the tracker thing. Was he worried that I wouldn't?

And if I'd said those things to him, that I didn't love him and I wanted him to leave, I was obviously out of my mind. I didn't mean them. Didn't he know that I didn't mean them?

I had always thought that he understood me so well. How could he not know what his leaving would do to me?

Didn't he know how much I needed him?

"Knock, knock," a soft voice said at my door. "I heard you were awake."

"Whitney?"

She came into my room wearing a hospital gown and a bathrobe, pushing a small, wheeled, see-through bin that had her baby inside. "Auntie Genesis, meet Marco Rafael."

The baby was wrapped up in a blanket like a burrito, his little head covered with a blue knit cap. "He's so small!"

"That's what happens when they come early," she told me, putting him right next to my bed so I could see him. "Fortunately, he was strong enough and far enough along that he didn't even have to go in the NICU." I reached out to touch the skin on his cheek with my fingertips, the only parts of my hand that weren't bandaged up. His skin was the softest thing I had ever felt.

"He's so beautiful," I breathed, looking up at Whitney.

"I know." She smiled, sitting down in the chair that Aunt Sylvia had occupied earlier.

"Why did you choose that name?"

"We didn't quite make it to the hospital, although Rafe did his best. Marco delivered this little guy in the backseat of Rafe's SUV. I don't recommend childbirth without an epidural, by the way. Anyway, I was so hopped up on pain that I demanded he be named Marco Rafael after the two of them, and Christopher was so relieved we were okay that he was fine with it. So Marco it is." She put her hand on top of little Marco's chest.

I started to cry.

"What is it?"

"Rafe's gone. He left me. Everybody leaves me," I said, in between sobs.

She handed me the tissue box next to my bed. I couldn't blow my nose, but I could wipe away the tears and the snot.

"He blames himself, you know."

I tried to put the tissues in the trash can, but missed. "What? Why?"

"Both Rafe and Marco blame themselves. Marco had promised to watch over you, and Rafe said he'd never let anything happen to you. You should have seen them after they brought you in. They were both a mess."

"What happened?" The last thing I remembered was being put in the trunk. Everything after that was a total blur.

And if we had lived anywhere else, Whitney wouldn't have known, but by now every single person in our town had probably told and retold this story and had started adding embellishments to it. "After they dropped me off at the hospital, they got a phone call from the sheriff. Your 911 call got through, but they couldn't hear anything. They managed to triangulate the location of your cell phone, and they found Laddie and your broken phone and your truck. Rafe and Marco raced out of here, but your kidnappers had a couple of hours' head start."

Little Marco yawned, drawing her attention for a minute, and she smiled a serene, motherly smile. "Anyway, they completely broke every imaginable traffic law, calling the rest of the security team to come with them. Police tried to pull them over for speeding, but they didn't stop. They called the local stations to tell them what they were doing, and somehow those police officers let them keep going. They caught up to your kidnappers halfway through Missouri, which adds crossing state lines to the charges. Marco got ahead of them and swerved, forcing them to stop. The other bodyguards used their guns to force the kidnappers out of the car while every highway patrolman and sheriff's department from here to Missouri pulled up behind them. Sheriff Stidd says Rafe was the one who got you out of the trunk and put you in an ambulance. They initially stopped at a hospital in Missouri, where they figured out your injuries weren't life-threatening, and he insisted you be brought here, close to home so your family could visit you. He rode with you all the way here. He stayed to make sure you would be fine, and then he left. He cleared out of your guesthouse, and his guards checked out of the B&B. They're just gone."

"What about Royal Productions?" Had I just unemployed the entire town with whatever I said during my delirium? "Did he shut that down too?"

"No. Amanda says he paid two years' worth of rent on the B&B because of the short notice, the lease on the building is paid through five years, and he has managers in place at work to run things. He didn't close anything down. He's just not here."

"And John-Paul is locked up? They have him?" I wondered if she noticed how shaky my voice was.

"Whoever that man is who took you, he's not getting out of prison for a very, very long time. Kidnapping is a Class A felony in both Iowa and Missouri, and both states plan to prosecute. The FBI is also getting involved, from what it sounds like, and they are investigating his background."

I nodded at the news and somehow managed to start crying again. I'd have thought my dehydration diagnosis would have prevented it.

"Are you going to tell me why somebody would kidnap you?" She asked the question gently, probably expecting me not to tell her.

After swearing her to secrecy, I told her the entire messy, sordid story. She had a pitying, shocked look on her face, but it felt good to share it with her. As it did every time I told the story, my soul got lighter. As if I was giving away part of the burden to my friend. I expected her pity, but instead she said, "I am so proud of you. You are such a strong woman. I am honored to call you my friend."

As my eyes teared up, Baby Marco started to actually cry. "It's feeding time," she said. "I'm going home in the morning, but we'll come back and visit you."

"Don't," I told her. "I'll be home soon. I'll come see you then."

"Thank you for trusting me. I'm so sorry for everything you've been through, but know that I am always here for you." She put one hand on my shoulder and squeezed gently, and then she told me to get better before going back to her own room.

It wasn't Rafe's fault. It was my fault. He had told me to stay home, but after our vacation in Monterra, John-Paul had seemed so far away. So meaningless and unimportant. I'd never thought he would show up and do what he did. I should have stayed at the farmhouse. I shouldn't have put myself or Laddie in danger.

Maybe he left because I'd been so stupid.

I wished I could call him. But I didn't have a phone.

Not that it mattered. I wouldn't have even known what to say to him.

I stayed in the hospital for another three days. The longer I stayed in the bed, the madder I got.

Mad about John-Paul hurting me and kidnapping me, mad about what he had done to Laddie, mad about the nightmares that plagued my sleep.

But I was mostly mad at Rafe for abandoning me. How could he say he loved me and then fly off like nothing had ever happened between us? You didn't treat someone you loved that way. You stayed by their side when they were in the hospital. You gave them support and helped them.

My nose started to heal, the pain in my head went away, my wounds scabbed over, and my bruises started to fade.

The pain that Rafe had shoved into my heart did not go away. It only multiplied.

When I finally checked out and discovered that Rafe had paid for all of my hospital bills, I wasn't grateful. It just made me angrier.

I went home and continued to heal. Life returned to normal, except now I felt like I was walking around with a sucking chest wound, unable to breathe. I went back to school, ignoring the stares and whispers on campus. Apparently my kidnapping had been all over the news, and my red hair and height made me instantly recognizable. When I worked my shifts at the diner, the townspeople were again handling me with kid gloves, like I might break if somebody said the wrong thing.

Even Max had stopped telling me jokes.

Whitney was the only person willing to speak honestly to me. When I went to visit her and the baby, she said, "You're totally pining for him."

"I am not," I said dismissively.

"You are. Pining like a whole forest of pine trees."

I held the baby against me, smelling the delicious baby smell on the back of his neck. "I'm not pining. He's the one who left me. I'm not pining." I didn't know which one of us I was trying to convince more.

"Mm-hmm," she said, not believing me.

"Maybe I'm pining a little," I admitted a minute later. "I don't want to see him. Or talk to him. But I set up a Google alert with his name. Does that make me weird?"

"Oh, sweetie. It's on the list." She set aside her laundry to sit next to me. "You should call him."

That wasn't going to happen.

To get through it, I told myself I didn't need Rafe. He obviously didn't need or want me. He could walk away without a second glance. He never called. He didn't email or text me. There were so many times I considered reaching out myself, but pride got in the way.

When I spoke to Pastor Dave about it, he talked about something called transference—that I might have taken all my negative and hostile feelings about John-Paul, a scary person who hurt me and whom I didn't want to think about, and transferred them to Rafe, a safe person whom I loved and did want to think about. That it was easier and safer for me to be mad at Rafe than John-Paul. I told him I had plenty of anger for them both.

Not to mention the anger I had at myself. I hated that every time the phone rang, I hoped it would be him. That every time there was a notification that someone from the guild had logged on to *World of Warcraft*, I longed to see the name Hatchet. That when I got a notification of an email or a Facebook post, I hoped he would be the one who had done it.

I hated that everywhere I turned in my own home, in my town, there was a memory of him. I couldn't get away from him even if I wanted to.

And now, when there was a knock at the door, I was mad about how my heart did a funny flip-flop. When I opened it, I didn't really expect to see Rafe, but I still had that letdown feeling to see Max standing there.

"Come on in," I told him. "Aunt Sylvia's not here."

"I know," he said as he took off his faded ball cap. He had that tan line around his head that most of the men in this town had because they wore hats all the time. "I came to see you. I wanted to talk to you about something."

"Sit," I said. I asked if I could get him anything, but he told me was fine.

He played with the brim of his hat. He seemed nervous. I'd never known Max to be nervous about anything. "I came here to ask for your blessing to marry your aunt."

I smiled for the first time in a long time. "That's awesome! But you don't need my blessing. You two can make your own choices."

"I'm old-fashioned that way, and you're the only family she has left."

"Okay. You have my total blessing." Despite my excitement, I had to ask, "But what about her—"

"Her MS?" He cut me off. "The vows I'm going to take say sickness and health. We'll work through it. Nothing's guaranteed. I could go out tomorrow and get hit by a bus and need to be taken care of for the rest of my life. None of us know what's coming, and no, she's not perfect. But neither am I. We'll be imperfect together, and that's good enough for me."

We chatted for a while longer, and he left much happier and more relaxed than when he arrived. I went out to the barn to brush Marigold. Another constant reminder of Rafe. I thought about what Max had said and the conversation I'd had with the pastor so long ago. About how I had expected Rafe to be perfect and had set him up to fail.

Was that what was happening now? That because Rafe didn't perfectly act the way I expected him to, I was angry with him? Had I made it so he couldn't win, no matter what he did?

Did I want the perfect robot or the imperfect human?

A couple of days later, I was sitting next to Aunt Sylvia, Max, Amanda, and Austin in church. The pastor was giving a sermon about forgiveness and trust that seemed to be pointed directly at me. In my purse I had Lemon's invitation to her engagement party. It was less than a week away.

Rafe would be there. Would he dance with someone else? Had he already moved on? My heart constricted at the thought.

When we got home, I expected Max and his family to join us for dinner, but Aunt Sylvia sent them home.

"Sit down." She pointed at the kitchen table. "You and I are going to have a conversation."

"A conversation about what?" I asked, suddenly uneasy. I sat, and still-recovering Laddie padded over, laying his head in my lap.

"*The* conversation."

Chapter 28

"You didn't ask for my opinion, but I'm old, which means I get to give it to you anyway," Aunt Sylvia said as she sat across from me at the table, opening her Diet Coke. "First, I wanted to let you know that I got a phone call from the sheriff. They found Richard."

She took a drink while she let the shock of that set in. "What? How?"

"He was in Dubai, and they brought him back to the US. He said he was at a party on a private plane and woke up bound and gagged on the front steps of a police station in New York."

I couldn't believe how calmly she was telling me this. "Did they find any money?"

She set her can down. "The money's gone. But he's caught. Now we have both of the men who screwed up our lives behind bars."

Rafe had done this. He was the only one I'd ever told about Richard, and the only one with the resources to track him down and get him back into this country. I was overcome with an incredible sadness. Not that Richard had been caught—I was thrilled about that. But that Rafe was gone.

And I knew where she was headed with this. "Speaking of money, we're going to need to list the guesthouse again. We need the money," I said.

"No, we don't."

"What do you mean?"

She sighed, playing with the tab on the soda. "Rafe paid for two years of rent on the guesthouse. And he paid off the mortgage on the farmhouse and the back taxes. Everything is taken care of."

Anger came rushing back. "What? You can't accept it. We don't need his charity."

"We actually do need his charity. We've been barely keeping our heads above water for years, and I took the help from the wonderful young man who offered because of his feelings for you."

"I'm not taking it!"

"Well, then it's a good thing he offered it to me and not to you, because I'm not too proud to accept it. You got your horse and I got my house. And the last time I checked, charity was the pure love of Christ. What kind of Christian would I be if I denied someone else the chance to show us that kind of love?"

Love was the reason for it. Maybe not the religious kind, but definitely love. I wanted to say he had a guilty conscience or had done it just to be kind. But deep down, I knew that wasn't the reason.

He'd run away, but there was no denying that he still loved me.

Hope took hold of my heart and refused to let go. I stroked Laddie's head as a distraction.

"And I know that the way that you deal with things is to hide. I can't blame you after all you've been through. But it's time to stop hiding. It's time to woman up and go after the man you love."

My chin trembled. "He left me."

"Yes, just like your mother. Like I told you in the hospital, he left because you told him you didn't love him and wanted him to go. And he loved you enough to do it."

Back in Max's cabin, Rafe had said he would leave if I wanted him to. If I told him there was no chance. I still didn't remember what had happened in the ambulance. There was this wisp of familiarity about it, but nothing I could catch and pin down. Did I really tell him I didn't love him and that there was no chance for us? That I wanted him to go?

Maybe it was better this way, for us to be apart. "He put a tracking device on me." It was a weak argument, and we both knew it.

"And thank heavens he did. Who knows what that man would have done to you if Rafe hadn't found you when he did? What if I was the one in danger? Or Whitney? Or Rafe? Wouldn't you have done anything to keep us safe?"

That was true. And he was overly protective after what had happened with Veronique. The woman he loved had died on his watch. It wasn't his fault, but he was the kind of man who would always blame himself and spend the rest of his life trying to make up for it by keeping his loved ones safe.

Including me. Especially me.

"Loving him hurts," I admitted. Laddie must have heard my sadness, because he licked my hand in sympathy.

"Loving someone doesn't hurt. MS hurts. Lies hurt. Regrets hurt. But love doesn't. Love is the one thing that makes all those other things better."

She was right. My heart ached because he was gone, not because I loved him. "I didn't want him to leave."

"You had a funny way of showing it."

I tried another tactic. "And I don't want to leave you."

"Genesis, you're not leaving me. You're living your life. Do you think that I want you to give up on love and happiness to be my nursemaid? I don't. I have Max, and Rafe hired Amanda to take care of me. My only job as your parent was to turn you into an independent adult. So start being one."

I leaned back in my chair, and Laddie went over to get some food from his bowl. His movements were slower than they used to be. I could tell he still hurt, too. "I'm happy here. The people I love are here."

"You haven't been happy since before the kidnapping. Not all the people you love are here. And Frog Hollow's not going anywhere. I'll visit you, you'll visit me." She took another drink. She made it all seem so rational and logical.

I threw out my last excuse. "I can't be a princess. I'm just some farm girl from Iowa."

"James T. Kirk was from Iowa, and he became an admiral in Starfleet. There's no reason you can't be a princess."

"I can't believe you remember that," I said, laughing.

"Not everything you say goes in one ear and out the other," she said with a smile.

I'd been so worried about Rafe hurting me that I hadn't stopped to consider what would happen if I hurt him. I'd only been focused on how everything affected me. "I've been kind of a selfish jerk."

She leaned over and laid her hand on my arm. "You were beaten up and kidnapped. You get a selfish jerk pass."

The nightmares had begun to taper off. Pastor Dave had mentioned something about facing my absolute worst fear and surviving it. He was right. That fear was gone. And when I did have those dreams, they always ended the same way. Just before I would wake up, Rafe was there, rescuing me. I went from feeling terrified to feeling safe and secure. That was how he made me feel, just by being himself. And as someone who had waited her whole life to feel truly safe, that realization was pretty wonderful.

And when I woke up one morning a few days later, the anger was completely gone. It was like someone had flipped a switch. I felt like my old self again. I wanted to be happy. I didn't want to be mad. I understood that I had clung to the anger for so long because what was left behind was an unbearable heartache. I missed him more than anything. I wanted to say something that would make him smile. To feel his arms around me, comforting me. To have the passion of his lips against mine.

I wanted to love him.

Even if he had moved on, even if he didn't want to see me, I at least had to tell him the truth of how I felt. I owed him that. I didn't care about the money or about missing school or work or anything else—I just had to get to him. Had this been how he'd felt when he first came to Iowa?

Excited and highly motivated, I ran downstairs and found Aunt Sylvia sitting in the kitchen, reading the newspaper. "I have to go to Monterra! I'm going to tell Rafe I love him."

Her eyes got big. "I'll make some calls."

"Not to Rafe! I want to surprise him. How am I going to afford a plane ticket?"

I'd worry about that later. First I had to pack.

Lemon's engagement party invitation was stuck into my mirror frame. It was tomorrow night. Monterra was seven hours ahead of us, but if I got a flight today, even with layovers, I could definitely get in by tomorrow. I grabbed my suitcase out of the closet. It was still packed with everything from my last trip to Monterra. Somebody must have brought it in from Rafe's car and left it in my room. But it was perfect. Those dresses and shoes from the wedding were still in it. I would have something to wear. I took out the dirty clothes and packed clean ones.

Whitney called me. After I said hi, she responded, "How much do you need? We can give you two hundred dollars."

"What? Hold on. I have another call." I transferred between the calls. It was Nicole.

"I was just talking to Shane and we think we can give you five hundred dollars. Will that be enough to help with your ticket?"

Aunt Sylvia had made her calls. That was fast. I told them it would definitely help. Now that everything was paid off, I knew I could get at least a thousand dollars out of the bank. That would almost cover it, along with what Whitney and Nicole were offering.

"Amanda's going to pitch in a hundred!" Aunt Sylvia called up the stairs.

"Okay!" I told Whitney and Nicole to meet me at the diner, and they said they would.

Aunt Sylvia and I stopped off at an ATM, but I was only able to take out a few hundred dollars. I tried not to freak out about how to come up with the rest while we drove to the diner. My mouth dropped at what I saw—it was like my birthday party all over again. The parking lot was packed. People were handing me wads of cash, pressing it into my hand, shoving it in my pocket, each giving whatever they could afford. It made my eyes tear up and my throat feel tight, seeing how much they loved and supported me. "You go get your handsome prince!" Mrs. Mathison yelled, which made me laugh. I thanked everyone, hugged them all, and said I would let them know how it went.

"What do you mean?" Whitney asked. "We're going with you to the airport!"

So I drove to the Quad City International Airport with most of Frog Hollow in a caravan behind me, honking along the way. They didn't come inside with me, though. Max said he'd drive my truck home with Aunt Sylvia. She kissed me on the cheek, hugging me close and said, "I'm so proud of you."

With the money the town had given me, I was able to book a direct flight to Milan. Of course, the flight didn't leave for four hours, which left me stranded in an airport with boundless energy, giddy hope, and nowhere to go. I did a lot of pacing.

When it was finally time, the flight took forever to board and then to take off. But once we were in the air I realized I didn't have a way to get from the Milan airport to the palace.

But I knew someone who did.

I called Lemon, and she answered immediately. "If this is another reporter, I'm going to wring your neck like Sunday's chicken dinner. No more questions about the engagement party!"

"This is Genesis! Wait, I'll show you." I tapped on the button to turn it into a FaceTime call. She did the same.

"I didn't recognize your number!" I had replaced the phone John-Paul destroyed, and I hadn't given her my new contact info.

"I'm sorry, I should have given it to you. I've been a little self-centered lately."

"No surprise there, given what happened to you." She turned over her shoulder and called, "Kat! Genesis is calling." She turned back. "Where are you? Are you on a plane?"

Kat appeared over her shoulder. "Hey, Genesis. What are you doing? Where are you?"

"I'm coming to tell Rafe that I love him."

They both squealed with delight, making Lemon's phone bounce. Kat said, "I'm so glad you're coming. Rafe is like, destroyed."

"Miserable," Lemon added.

"Such a mess."

"Dante had to force him to shower today."

"Don't tell him!" I warned them, and they both nodded. "I want it to be a surprise. But I'm calling because I need a ride from the airport."

"We will totally take care of that," Kat said.

"You should have called us before you bought a ticket. We could have sent the plane," Lemon added.

They could have. In my hurry to get to him, it hadn't even occurred to me. "Too late now. So Princess Kat, how does it feel to be a married lady?"

"It's frakking amazing," she said with a vivid and knowing smile. "I highly recommend it."

Depending on how all this went, maybe someday I would find out.

We chatted for a bit longer, and they caught me up on what had been going on in Monterra. We finalized plans for my ride after I told them my flight number and what time I should be arriving. I had to hang up when I started getting pointed looks from other passengers. We were a little loud.

Hours and hours and hours later, I finally arrived in Milan. I went through customs and got to the front entrance, where I found Giacomo waiting for me. "Signorina Genesis, this way please." He led me out to a black town car, where two women waited inside. He made introductions, and I immediately forgot their European-sounding names. He told me that one was a makeup artist and the other a hairstylist, and they were going to work their magic before we arrived at the palace.

"And we will stop here in the city to find you a new dress."

"I brought two dresses with me," I told him as the women conversed in Italian about the state of my airplane-dried-out hair.

"From the wedding?" When I said yes, he shook his head. "That won't do. He can't see you in the same dress twice, can he?"

I didn't know anywhere else in the world where that would be true, but I trusted Giacomo. Besides, it would be the dress I wore when I told Rafe I loved him.

We stopped at a store that had a locked door and a security guard out front. Giacomo found the perfect dress—it was a one-shouldered teal gown that cinched in at the waist, went all the way to the floor, and made me feel like a Grecian goddess.

It didn't even have a price tag—that's how expensive it was. I didn't care. All I cared about was getting to Rafe.

When we finally arrived at the palace, with me feeling about the best I had ever had in my whole life, I found Lemon and Kat waiting for me. They were dressed up too, and they squealed and hugged me when they saw me. We were all careful not to mess up each other's hair or makeup.

But now that I was actually here, standing in the front hall, anxiety, jet lag, and exhaustion took over. "I don't know what I'm supposed to do or say," I confessed. I was tempted to sit down and put my head between my knees until the dizzy feeling went away. I didn't know why I'd thought this would be a good idea.

"You will figure it out. Just say what's in your heart. He's in the main ballroom. Dante and I haven't made our entrance yet, so I can't go with you."

"And Nico's still upstairs getting ready." Kat rolled her eyes. "I swear, he always takes longer than I do to get pretty. But you go in there and get your man!"

I nodded, pretending at a confidence I did not feel. It would be fine. I would totally seduce him with my awkwardness and get him to love me again.

The servants opened the door to the ballroom for me, and I immediately found Rafe. He was looking out a window while people around him laughed, danced, and ate. He had a drink in his hand, but he just stood there, holding it. He was unbelievably handsome, but he seemed so sad that my heart ached for him.

Mustering all of the courage I had, I walked over. And with all those hours of planning and preparation, I laid the best opening line ever on him.

"Hi."

He blinked at me a couple of times, as if he didn't know what he was seeing. "Genesis? What are you doing? How are you here?"

I opened my mouth, but the words stuck. I glanced over my shoulder, wondering if people were watching us.

He grabbed my wrist and pulled me from the ballroom, setting down his drink along the way. I felt a thrill at the sensation of his strong hand on me. We went into a drawing room, and I only had a second to admire the old, expensive paintings on the wall and the antique furniture before he whirled me around to face him.

"What are you doing here?"

It was not quite the reception I had expected. So I decided to take Lemon's advice and just tell him how I felt. "Someone tore my heart out and carried it across the ocean."

I saw him swallow several times. I took a step forward. He stepped back.

"But it's okay. I don't want it back. You can keep it. It was always yours, anyways."

He shook his head. "You don't have to say those things to me. You're not obligated to. You don't have to say them because you feel guilty or you think you owe me. You don't."

"Is that what you think?" That was so far from how I felt that it stunned me. "That's not why I'm here. I came here to tell you no."

"No?" he repeated.

"You were always encouraging me to say no. So, no, I won't accept you leaving me. No, I won't be apart from you. No, you can't go on without knowing how I feel about you."

I put my hand out and let it fall when he didn't make a move to take it.

"Aunt Sylvia told me what you told her. About the things I said in the ambulance. I don't remember saying them. I never would have said any of that stuff to you if I'd been in my right mind. Because it was the opposite of how I feel. If I could slingshot a starship around the sun, go back in time, and undo it, I would."

"You know that's theoretically impossible." Finally, a glimmer of hope.

"I know. And I wish you'd given me a chance to explain instead of leaving. Because that made me discover I kind of have serious abandonment issues."

"I thought you wanted me to go. That you couldn't or didn't love me. And I loved you enough to respect your wishes, even though it killed me. And I was ashamed. Ashamed that I couldn't keep you safe." His voice had a jagged edge to it, the pain evident, twisting my insides.

When I stepped forward again, this time he didn't move back. "Nothing that happened was your fault. I'm so sorry that you felt like you had to go. It was the very last thing I wanted. Because . . ." This was it. No hesitation this time. I wanted to say it. "I love you. You make me crazy sometimes, but I love you. I love your smile, I love your mind, I love that you get all my jokes, I love how you take care of me, I love your good heart, I love—"

He didn't let me finish. He crushed me against him, pulling me into the warmest, strongest, most loving kiss imaginable. It was better than I had remembered.

". . . you," I said breathily when he let me up for air. "I love you."

Closing his eyes, he put his forehead against mine. "*Ti adoro. Ti amo*, Genesis. I love you so much. I never thought I'd hear you say those words to me."

"I'm going to spend the rest of my life saying them to you." Being like this, here in his arms, it was all I ever wanted. It made me feel complete. Whole.

I was where I belonged.

"I will never leave you again," he promised in a low voice that made shivers dance over my bare skin. "And I know you don't like surprises, so I'm telling you up front. I'm going to ask you to marry me."

Delirious, happy zings shot around inside me. That sounded like a good plan to me.

Until he got down on one knee and my stomach plummeted into my ankles. "You mean now?"

"Yes, now. I did warn you first." He reached inside his coat pocket and pulled out a ring box.

"Have you just been walking around with a ring box?" I asked as I pressed my hands against my flushed face, realizing that wasn't possible. "Did Lemon and Kat tell you I was coming?"

"This is the ring I picked out for you on the show. I carried it in my pocket when I missed you, which was all the time." I thought of all the time we'd spent together. He'd had this with him the whole time? "And don't be upset, but when you were taken, Marco put a watch on your passport just in case that monster tried to take you out of the country. So he got an alert when you got on a plane to Milan, and he told me. I didn't know what you would say or why you were coming, but for the first time in a long time, I had hope."

This was how my life would be. It would be more public than I'd prefer. Sometimes I would be watched. Sometimes I might feel trapped. But the trade-off was that I got Rafe, and he was worth anything else I had to go through. "I'm not mad," I told him. "But I will have to go back to Iowa on Monday. I have class."

"We can spend part of the year here, part in Iowa. We can create a room for your aunt and her husband in the palace, if you'd like. Whatever you want."

I'd never felt as loved as I did in that moment.

He started to open the box, and then stopped. "Wait. I'm not sure you have follow-through. You never did do what you said you would."

What in the world was he talking about? "Which was?"

"You never taught me to cook," he said, his eyes sparkling.

"I suppose I do still owe you cooking lessons." I put my hands on the sides of his face. "Especially since you taught me to love."

"In that case . . ." He opened the ring box, and there was an enormous marquise-cut diamond that threatened to blind me.

"Was that your way of asking me to marry you? Because that wasn't asking."

He immediately caught my reference to the moment when I'd kissed him on Christmas Eve. "Are you saying you don't want to marry me?"

"Maybe I don't."

"Liar." He grinned. "Genesis Kelley, will you do me the honor of becoming my princess?"

"Princess Genesis." I shook my head at the reminder.

"It only rhymes in English. We can make sure you're addressed as *La Principessa* Genesis."

"If you promise not to make me a walking Dr. Seuss character, then yes, I suppose I can marry you."

He slid the ring onto my finger and finally stood up, kissing me again and turning my knees to jelly. "I'm glad to see you still have a way with words."

"Yes, I'm quite the orator," he said, holding me close. "So . . . it turns out that I'm the right man. Any idea when the right time will be?"

Probably not as soon as he hoped for. "I'm willing to entertain oral arguments."

Then he launched into the most persuasive, compelling, mind-blowing argument ever.

Things had started to get a little interesting when we heard someone say, "Ha!"

The sound had come from the open doorway. We broke apart to see Serafina. "I told you! Five sisters! But ew, kissing."

His sister ran off, cracking up both me and my Prince Wonderful. He kissed me again. "Kat warned you about betting against Serafina."

She had. And where before it had just been me and Aunt Sylvia, now I would jump full speed ahead to five sisters, two brothers, parents-in-law, an assortment of animals, an uncle, a quasi-stepsister, homes in two countries, and the best husband I could have ever hoped for.

NOTE FROM THE AUTHOR

I just can't thank you enough for choosing to read this book and coming along for Rafe and Genesis's wild ride. It is because of readers like you that I get to keep playing in my Monterra sandbox!

If you want to be kept up to date on all the happenings in Monterra (including those princesses who need to grow up and find their own soul mates), please sign up for my mailing list on my website: www.sariahwilson.com.

It's an e-book jungle out there, and authors need all the help they can get. Reviews will help other readers discover and experience that royal Monterran *amore*. I would love it (and be so, so grateful) if you could leave a review of this book on sites like Amazon and Goodreads, should you feel so inclined. Thank you!

Do you want the Monterran stories to continue? Do you wish I'd done something different and want to write your own version? Be sure to check out "The Royals of Monterra" Kindle World on Amazon. You can read stories about the royals by other authors, and you can even submit your own story!

https://kindleworlds.amazon.com/world/Monterra

ACKNOWLEDGMENTS

First, I must thank each and every reader who has come with me on this journey, who demanded to know what happened to all the princes and left reviews, encouraging me. I am so thankful for all of you!

Thanks to Chris Werner for taking my drama, obstinacy, and competitiveness all in stride, for encouraging me and letting me know how to change things and keeping me on track, and for going out on a limb for me. Thank you to the entire Montlake team, and especially Susan, Kim, Marlene, and Jessica (the awesome sender of flowers!), for everything that you do. I may not be aware of all of it, but I am grateful. Thanks to my developmental editor, Melody Guy, for letting me know all the times I went off the rails (in the absolute nicest way possible) and what did work. And for making me laugh when she changed her mind. Thank you to Sharon Turner Mulvihill for her suggestions and Montreux Rotholtz for completely getting my inner nerd and helping me correct my Iowan mistakes (and for all the excellent copyediting). Achievement earned by fellow gamer Jessica Fogleman for excellent proofreading. Thank you to Damon Freeman of Damonza for my absolutely beautiful cover.

Thanks to Sean Fitzgerald, Joshua Abells, Thom Kephart, and Kindle Worlds for making "The Royals of Monterra" a Kindle World, allowing other authors to write their own stories set in this world. Thanks to M. R. Pritchard, Rebecca Connolly, Jina Bacarr, Marie Long, Carly Carson, Rachel Branton, Caroline Mickelson, Annette Lyon,

Carolyn Rae, Debra Erfert, Jennifer D. Bokal, and Cindy Hogan for writing their own Monterran stories.

I also have to thank Lisa Ladle for always quickly and instantly translating whatever I want to say into Italian.

Thank you to Brilliance Audio for creating an audio version of this book, and to Lauren Ezzo for her narration.

To my four children, who continue to grow like weeds, all my love and gratitude that you let me keep writing books.

And thank you to my husband, Kevin, who I don't think has ever read a single one of my acknowledgements to him, but supports me and loves me in every other way possible.

ABOUT THE AUTHOR

 Sariah Wilson has never jumped out of an airplane, never climbed Mount Everest, and is not a former CIA operative. She has, however, been madly, passionately in love with her soul mate and is a fervent believer in happily-ever-afters—which is why she writes romance. *Royal Games* is her seventh happily-ever-after novel. She grew up in Southern California, graduated from Brigham Young University (go Cougars!) with a semi-useless degree in history, and is the oldest of nine (yes, nine) children. She currently lives with the aforementioned soul mate and their four children in Utah, along with three tiger barb fish, a cat named Tiger, and a recently departed hamster that is buried in the backyard (and has nothing at all to do with tigers).

Her website is www.sariahwilson.com.